wicked

HALSTON U | PART TWO

minds

R.A. SMYTH

I may have escaped their house but there is no running from Grayson, Royce, and Logan.

Not when Royce knows my most precious secret, Logan refuses to let me go, and Grayson hates to see me remotely happy.

As if I don't have enough to deal with already, between worrying about my daughter and dodging my sleazy boss, not to mention keeping up my grades, now I have to worry about what Royce might do with my secret while attempting to get over Logan and avoid Grayson at all costs.

Except Halston is a small campus, and at least one of them keeps showing up in my life. It makes forgetting they exist impossible.

However, when shit hits the fan, they're the ones I end up turning to. The only ones I can trust.

Who knew my life would only get more complicated second semester?

HALSTON U PLAYLIST

Doom Days – Bastille
Grenade – Bruno Mars
Standing in the Dark – Nickelback
Change – Kodi Lee
Brave – Danger Twins
Apologize – Timbaland, One Republic
Adrenaline –CRMNL
A Storm Is Coming – Tommee Profitt, Liv Ash
Bad Things – The Phantoms
Breathe In Bleed Out – Jared Lee
Wildfire – Rayelle
Ruins – Olivia May
Hollow – Jordan Powers
...And many more

TRIGGER WARNINGS

- History of sexual abuse
- History of self harm and contemplation of suicide
- Sexual assault
- On page self harm
- PTSD
- Dubcon
- Blood Play
- Knife Play
- Degradation
- Violence

*****Spoiler Trigger*****
Sexual assault resulting in pregnancy (past event; does not occur on page)

BERTRAM

PROLOGUE

"Breakthrough Academy, how can I help you?"

"Good afternoon. My name is Bertram Van Doren. My stepdaughter, Riley, is a new student of yours and I wanted to know how she was settling in."

"Oh, Mr. Van Doren, what a pleasure. Riley has adjusted to life here quite well. There have been no issues so far."

"I'm glad to hear that. I want to send her a care package. Something to help her feel more at home."

"Of course. Students are not allowed personal items in their rooms—we find regiment and uniformity help to keep everyone in line. However, you are welcome to write her letters, and we do, of course, have Parents' Weekend twice a year, which you and your wife are welcome to attend. The first one of the academic year will be next weekend."

"Unfortunately we will be unable to attend," I state brusquely. Now that I have what I called for, I'm done with this conversation.

"Oh, that is such a shame. I know Riley was hoping to see Aurora."

I pause. "Aurora?"

"Her, uh, daughter? God, I hope I remembered her name correctly."

Daughter?

"Oh, Aurora, yes. Yes, of course." The cover falls seamlessly from my lips. "Apologies, I was unaware that you knew of her. Thank you so much for your help. I'll be sure to write to Riley shortly. Goodbye."

I hang up before she can respond, staring at the payphone as the receptionist's words drill into my skull.

Daughter.

"Aurora." I say the name slowly, grinning slyly.

Well, isn't this an interesting turn of events.

RILEY

CHAPTER ONE

My hands are shaking so badly that I struggle to get my key in the door. When I finally do, I stumble through it, taking in the sight of my apartment for the first time since Logan picked me up after work, drugged me, and proceeded to chain me to a stripper pole, all in the name of Grayson getting his revenge.

I fall to the floor, barely feeling the knock my knees take as everything crashes down around me.

The fear I felt when I woke up in that house.

The shock of discovering Grayson attended Halston.

That he'd known I was here.

That Logan and Royce were his friends.

It explained so much about why Logan had pulled away. Why Royce kept showing up at the club.

And now Royce knows my greatest secret.

He knows about Aurora.

I cave inward.

There wasn't any other way. I don't regret letting him find out; I just wish he didn't have to.

Because now the power to destroy me is in his hands.

My fingers are chilled to the bone as I hug myself, my breathing catching on a sob as the rough edges of panic prick at the edges of my mind.

There is absolutely nothing I can do, and *that* is what is so terrifying. The fact that I have no control over what Royce does with this knowledge.

If he tells Logan.

If he tells Grayson.

I shudder at the thought. Which reminds me, I haven't locked my door—in case Royce skips straight home to tell them and Grayson comes storming over here to choke me out again. Not that a flimsy lock would keep him out for long, but still. I reach up and flip it, the click of the bolt sliding into place only offering me a modicum of relief as I sag against the door.

Eyes falling closed, I bring my knees up as my head drops back.

It's your secret to tell.

I think they should know the truth.

The laugh that leaves me is mirthless.

In the span of one sentence, Royce went from giving me hope that he might keep this to himself to making me think he'll tell the others—especially if I don't.

He promised to keep both Grayson and Logan away, but now that I think back on it, he never promised not to tell them about Aurora.

Although I had left his car with the sense that he wouldn't.

Do I believe him? Can I trust him? Do I have a choice?

I huddle against the door, struggling to breathe past the weight pressing down on my chest. Squeezing my eyes shut, I force myself to suck in a shaky breath, filling my lungs and holding it for the count of three before slowly blowing it out. I need to ground myself. Need to put a stop to this spiral before it escalates. Freaking out won't do me any good. It won't help Aurora.

I need to be strong.

I need to accept that there is nothing I can do to change this situation. Royce will do whatever he does. The best thing I can do now is prepare myself.

There is still a shakiness in my limbs as I push to my feet and lift my chin, standing tall in the face of what could be my ruination.

What will be will be, and there is only one place I can go to work through this fear and construct the armor I'm going to need for the battle ahead. To prepare myself to go toe-to-toe with three sinful devils.

The dance studio.

It takes hours. I spend all afternoon in the dance studio, the pounding rhythm of the music a cathartic release to the terror gripping me. With every spin, I shed the weight of that despair, and with every leap, I reclaimed my inner strength, using the powerful beat of the music to hammer it into determined resolve.

By the time I leave the dance studio, I'm brimming with fiery perseverance and ungodly rage. My feet slap against the sidewalk as I march back to my apartment. Except, it's not the street before me that I see, it's Logan's fucking face when he sneered at me in the bathroom that day. Grayson's haughty smirk when he told me to get on my knees for Royce. Royce's indifference when he loomed over me on the sofa that first morning.

I stomp up the stairs to my apartment with all the fury of a woman scorned.

How dare Logan simply take Grayson at his word. After *months* of chasing after me. Hadn't I earned the fucking right to defend myself? To express my side before he fell into line at Grayson's side?

Don't even get me fucking started on Grayson. His *audacity*. The fucking arrogance. I'm boiling with fury over how he thought he had any right to kidnap and hold me hostage. He might be hurting, but it is no excuse for his actions.

Reaching my apartment, I let the door slam behind me as I go straight to the bathroom, turning the water in the shower to scalding before stripping out of my clothes.

Just like dancing purged me of my fear, the shower does a good job of dulling my wrath to a simmering anger. By the time I step out, steam fogs up the bathroom mirror, and wrapping a towel around myself, I step up to it. I deliberately kept the lights off in the dance studio so I wouldn't have to see the marks I know litter my skin from last night, but I can't ignore the damage for much longer.

Taking a fortifying breath, I swipe a hand across the mirror.

I suck in a breath as my gaze zeroes in on my neck, already purple and blue from Grayson's bite, before slowly dipping lower over the little nicks across my chest, the harsh red lines from Grayson's blade.

Closing my eyes, images from last night flick through my mind. Of Grayson's rigid stance as he stood in the kitchen, exuding hatred like sweat from his pores while the air crackled with the sheer intensity of his wrath.

Wrath directly aimed at *me*.

I don't know what set him off, what specifically sparked this outpouring of emotion beyond his typical antipathy, but whatever it was, I could *feel* every ounce of his strife in a way I hadn't before. It was all-consuming. More than one person can bear. I don't know how it didn't cripple him.

I'd wanted to help. Wanted to offer him some much-needed relief. I'd thought perhaps he could release it much like he had that day in the field. He'd been in a similar state then—enraged and rabid, and while he'd still been angry afterward, the beast had been sated.

Except yesterday wasn't like last time.

And I didn't pick up on the tells until it was too late.

Releasing a shuttering exhale, a shiver rushes down my spine as I recall the feel of the cold blade pressed against my skin.

I'd noticed his devolving before then, but that was the moment when my own anger spiked. The moment when my insecurities came barreling to the forefront, and I was reduced to the whimpering child of my past.

Weak.

Pathetic.

Defenseless.

I wasn't afraid. Not exactly. Grayson may have changed, his actions volatile—but he wasn't... *isn't* his father. However, I was... *I am*, terrified... of reverting back to that little girl, pressed up against her bed, wishing to be saved... to be seen... to be heard.

A fresh wave of fury blazes through my veins. At Grayson. At myself.

I am *not* that child anymore.

I won't be ever again.

I refuse to be someone who will roll over and allow Grayson to take his anger out on.

I'm no one's punching bag, and perhaps it's time Grayson realized that.

Eyes blazing, I snap them open to see the reminder of

Grayson's rage painted on my skin. The canvas of torment strikes me as ironic, given that his father never left a physical mark. Although, I often wished he had because at least then it would have reflected the stain, the darkness each of his touches left on my soul.

My fingertips graze the mark on my neck, and pressing down, I wince as pain races along my nerves. I'd rather wear Grayson's necklace of bruises, unbidden, unbound, and on display for the world to see.

Perhaps that's why I find myself inexplicably drawn to these three unrepentant men. Each of them carries their own demons. Their darkness doesn't hide behind false veneers. They let it out, unafraid to show the world the violence that lies beneath.

What you see is what you get—good or bad. There are no pretenses. If you don't like what you see, then feel free to fuck right off.

I've borne the same mentality. I might keep the broken fragments tucked away, out of sight, but I'm not afraid to show the world that I've been changed by trauma. It's not a weight I *want* to carry, but I do. Moreso, I accept it. It's part of who I am. An integral piece that has formed the person I am today and has gotten me to this point in my life.

Turning away, I pull in a calming breath as I retrieve clothes from my closet that are all my own. After so long spent in only underwear or Logan's clothing, it feels like another layer of protection to be wearing my own things.

A layer of protection against them.

More of a distance between reality and those lost days in their house.

By the time I towel-dry my hair and collapse onto the couch, my anger has fizzled out, and all I am is exhausted.

I look around my small, sparsely-furnished apartment, and despite wishing so many times that I was back here, I don't feel any of the peace I expected to. There's none of the comforts I desperately need. It just feels... cold. Silent. Empty.

Missing Royce's quiet presence and Logan's boisterous laugh.

As I sit here, I can't stop the memories from playing on a timeless loop: Logan's teasing, Royce's droll remarks, and the hint of a smile that would occasionally play on his lips. Hell, even Grayson's cutting remarks—although I could live without those.

It leaves an ache in my chest that I have no right feeling.

A longing that scares me.

In a bid to ignore that feeling, I grab the remote and flick on the TV. A Christmas movie is playing and I wriggle deeper into the couch cushions to watch, except it's not the same.

Logan isn't shouting at the TV, and Royce isn't grumbling about how cliche every scene is. I don't feel their warmth on either side of me—the relaxing comfort of their presence.

Frustrated, I blow out a breath as I turn the television off. Frowning as I do another scan of my apartment, trying to understand what exactly this feeling is. This disconnect.

My books still sit on the shelf, the latest one I was reading tossed haphazardly on the table. The furniture is the same, and even when I breathe in, the scents are familiar. Yet I feel as though I'm looking through the space with the eyes of a stranger.

Untethered.

That's how I feel—Untethered.

So much has changed in the past few weeks. Actually, since I started at Halston.

I've changed.

They've changed me.

This apartment is no longer my safe hideaway from the world. It's no longer the source of comfort I relied on.

A laugh erupts from my throat, growing more hysterical, more desperate, by the second. It's a wild sound that is foreign to my ears, bouncing off the walls as I clutch my head, tears welling in my eyes. A knot forms in the pit of my stomach, and I struggle to fill my lungs. The laughter bubbles into frantic sobs as I realize what—or rather *who*—has become that source of comfort.

"I'm so fucked up," I croak to myself, wiping at my tears. To miss them—to *crave* them—after everything they've done.

After Logan's heartbreak.

Royce's indifference.

Grayson's... well, Grayson can go die in a ditch. I'm still so fucking angry with him.

At a loss for what else to do, I grab my phone and pull up my chat with Tara, hoping to distract myself from the utter shit-show that is my life.

ME

> Hope you're having a good Christmas. If you're free tomorrow, want to have a girl's night in? I need to vent.

Within seconds, my phone vibrates with her response.

TARA

> Vent? Please tell me you finally fucked the hockey hottie.

Or was it Ruthless?

OMG, please tell me it was both!

ME

I did not fuck both of them!!

TARA

But you did take one of their dicks for a ride...

Oh my god!

ME

No! Nobody got ridden!

TARA

You're ruining my Christmas vibe with thoughts
of your cobwebbed vagina.

ME

Then stop thinking about it!

TARA

I'll be over at 5.

ME:

Today? You don't need to come today, it's
Christmas!

TARA

Xander is heading in then to open The Depot.
Christmas night is one of his busiest days...
something about being around family brings
out everyone's aggression and need to drink.

Have you eaten? I'll grab us Chinese.

ME

Chinese sounds good. I'll see you then.

TARA

I'll bring hard liquor!

I chuckle as I relax back on the sofa, feeling more at ease knowing I'll be able to talk all of this through with her in a few hours.

I keep myself busy waiting for Tara by thoroughly cleaning my apartment. You can't miss boys you *shouldn't* when you're pulling gunk from your shower drain and trying not to gag.

When the buzzer for my apartment sounds, I nearly jump out of my skin, whirling to stare bug-eyed at the offending device as my heart tries to leap from my chest.

What if it's Grayson, come to drag me back there? What if it's Logan coming to... I don't even know what.

My gaze darts to the clock on my oven, and logically, I know it's Tara, but what if...

Slowly moving over to the buzzer, my throat is dry as I reach out to push the intercom button, refusing to say anything.

"Yo, bitch, let me up! I have all the goodies!"

The air in my lungs whooshes out, my body sagging forward as I huff out a strained laugh while pressing the button to let her into the building.

However, my reaction makes me realize just how stressed I am that Grayson or Logan might show up.

Before I can dwell on it, Tara is at my door, greeting me with a wide grin.

"Girl, this better be good," she says, giving me a one-arm embrace. "You owe me for leaving me hanging all of Christmas without so much as a text to let me know you were alive. With all that time off, you better have been getting some mighty fine orgasms!"

She makes herself at home, dropping the bag of takeout onto the countertop.

"Eh, yeah, not quite," I respond grimly, gesturing to the liquor bottle in her hand. "Why don't you open that, and I'll tell you everything."

We eat our food while she plies me with alcohol—probably sensing how badly I need it—and when I'm full and sitting back on the sofa, I dive headfirst into the shitshow that is my life.

I've given this some consideration while I was elbow-deep in my sink, and I've decided to tell her everything. So, after giving her a heads-up that this was going to be rough, I start at the very beginning.

I tell her about my mom marrying Bertram. About going to live with Grayson. I tell her about the crush I had on him as a teenager. Those early happy days in that house. Then I confide in her how it all changed. The days that grew steadily darker until they ended in a positive pregnancy test.

I show her pictures of Aurora and explain why I'm at Halston.

And then, I explain to her what happened after I left Lux that first night of winter break. Of the past eleven days spent inside their house.

I pour out all my fury, my heartache, my confusion, and because she's an amazing friend, she listens to it all. We coo over baby photos, and she holds me while I cry. Then, before she heads home, she leaves me with words that remain in my head for the rest of the night...

If those boys want your forgiveness, Riley, then they better get on their knees and grovel.

GRAYSON

"We fucked up. You. Me... Logan. We *really* fucked up."

I stare at my best friend, slumped in the living room armchair and looking as defeated as he did the day he was cut from the football team. Shit has been falling apart for days between the three of us.

All because of *her*.

Intuitively, I know this is her doing, too, and it takes me a moment of staring at Royce to put the pieces together.

Royce is a brick fucking wall. Nothing gets to him because he doesn't allow himself to give enough of a crap about anything to *let* it get to him.

Except, somehow, Riley has wriggled her way in.

She has gotten to him.

Practically vibrating with anger, my voice is threaded with steel as I step into the room. "What did you do?"

He doesn't respond, and my ears strain to listen for any sounds elsewhere in the house. Nothing. Only silence greets me. Logan is likely still at his parents', but any time I'm not around, Riley has made herself at home. If Royce was here, she wouldn't be holed up in her room—like she's *supposed* to be.

"What did you do, Royce?" I bark louder.

The asshole doesn't even twitch.

"Where is Riley?"

I'm already turning to storm down the hall in search of her when he states in a deadened tone, "She's gone. I took her home." Slowly, my head swivels to face him, teeth grinding. His eyes lift to mine. Glacial. Deadly. "She should never have been here."

"You took her *home?*" Where his anger is ice cold, mine is boiling hot, coursing through my veins like lava and leaving a scorched path in its wake. My hands shake as I fist them at my sides. My restraint a twig on the verge of snapping. "You had no fucking right!" I yell, pointing a reproachful finger at him.

He jumps out of the chair, feet planted wide and muscles straining as he stares me down. "No, Grayson. *You* had no right. *We* had no right." He shakes his head, his face set into a hard mask. "I was so wrapped up in my shit and wanting vengeance for what was done to *me* that I took it out on the wrong girl." Eyes piercing mine, "*We* took it out on the wrong person."

I scoff, unable to believe what I'm hearing from Royce, of all people. "She manipulated you. I don't know how, but she's filled your head with nonsense. That bitch is nothing but a conniving liar. A master manipulator. A narcissist—"

"Stop." His deep bellow slices through the air, drawing battle lines between us.

The urge to track Riley down and strangle her is overwhelming, but I have to know, "What the hell did she do to bring you to her side?" It's the one thing I can't work out. Logan, I can understand. He's led by his heart and readily handed it over to her, willing to be yanked along on that leash, but Royce... "You're not Logan. You're too cynical to believe the best in people, so what the hell did she do?"

I'd almost wonder if she blackmailed him into it, or something nefarious like that. But, no, Royce wouldn't allow another person—especially a woman, to put him in a compromising position again. Not to mention, he wouldn't be sitting here looking so torn up over everything we'd done during the break if she'd coerced him into letting her go.

Somehow the she-devil has managed to get the man usually incapable of giving a damn to honestly give a shit about her. It's the only thing that makes sense, but *how*?

Lips pursed, Royce stares at me. I can see the wheels turning behind his eyes, and for a brief moment, I think he's going to clue me in. Explain it to me.

However, in the next second, his features shutter and he cuts his gaze away. I know whatever he was contemplating saying, he's decided to keep to himself. Fine. Whatever. Not like I actually care how she achieved it.

"This is fucking bullshit!" I yell at him, flipping the coffee table in my anger. *That goddamn fucking bitch!* Royce doesn't so much as blink at my outrage. He simply stands and watches as I heave in burning breaths and glare at him like I've never seen him before. "You're *my* friend!"

"I'm still your friend," he retorts far too calmly.

I scoff in disdain, a sneer curling my lips. "You know what, fuck this."

Turning on my heel, I march back out of the room, intent on tracking down the woman truly to blame for all of this. I won't let her get away with this again. I *will not* let her destroy my family for a second time.

The creak of the floorboards is my only warning before two hundred pounds of pure muscle knocks me off my feet. The air is pushed out of my lungs as I hit the floor, rasping out an angry, "What the fuck, man?!"

"You're not going to do anything more to her," Royce snarls in my ear, sounding truly furious for the first time. His hand fists the back of my shirt and pins me to the floor. "From now on, you're going to stay away from her."

Either he was able to read my intentions from my expression, or I must have said aloud what I planned to do. Either way, it's sent him into a feral rage, the likes of which I've never been on the receiving end.

"What are you?" I sneer. "Her protector?"

"Yeah," he hisses back just as vehemently. "Her protector from *you*."

I bark out a cruel laugh even as I buck against his crushing weight. "So this is what we've become? She tells you some sob story that tugs at your heartstrings, and four years of friendship is just washed down the drain?"

His grip on the back of my shirt becomes bruising as he presses down with more force until I'm half convinced he's going to crush my ribcage just to keep me away from her. *What has our friendship become that I even have to be concerned that that's his line of thinking?*

Leaning in until his lips hover at my ear, he whispers, "You're forgetting I don't have a heart. Which means I'll have no problem removing yours from your chest if you go anywhere near her."

"Merry—What the hell is going on here?"

I manage to lift my head enough to find Logan gaping at us from the doorway. His initially cheerful tone—so at odds with the tense situation sparking in the living room—has turned to confusion as he takes us in.

I shuck Royce off my back, glaring at him as I get to my feet and brush down my slacks and shirt.

"Where's Riley?"

Of course, that's Logan's primary concern. Couldn't even wait to hear what transpired between us before enquiring about her.

Scoffing, I can't fucking look at either of them.

"I took her home," Royce states bluntly.

"You did what?" Logan cries. "Why?"

"Because she doesn't fucking belong here," Royce practically yells at him, clearly exasperated.

Logan gapes at him for a moment, before his eyes go wide. "You know. You believe her."

"Jesus fucking Christ," I mutter under my breath. Louder, I say, "This is too fucking pathetic to listen to," before striding toward the door.

"You better sort your fucking shit out, or we're going to have issues," Royce calls after me. *Yeah, as if we don't already have a steaming pile of problems.*

Ignoring him, I head upstairs and lock myself in my room for the rest of the night.

LOGAN

CHAPTER THREE

"You know," I repeat after Grayson storms upstairs. I probably should have checked if he was okay first, but I'm so fucking exhausted from all this bullshit. The time away at my parents' today made me realize just how done I am with it all.

I'd rushed back for the conversation we were all supposed to sit down and have, intent on ensuring Riley told Royce and Grayson the truth, and on guaranteeing Grayson fucking listened to every word she said. Even if I had to hog-tie him to a chair and duct tape his mouth.

Instead, I find my two best friends fighting on the floor like idiots and Riley fucking gone—a matter I intend to address once I've confirmed that *is* the reason he took her home, and not because Riley actually managed to worm her way into his steel-capped heart (which I know for a fact, she was totally achieving, even if Royce would deny it until he's blue in the face).

"Know what?" Royce responds cagily, eyes narrowed and posture rigid.

I blink at him for a moment, but he's a blank fucking wall.

"For fuck's sake," I grumble with a roll of my eyes. "You know she's telling the truth. That Grayson's dad"—I lower my voice, although I don't really know why—"*raped* her."

At my admission, his shoulders come down, and with a bob of his throat, he nods.

"That's why you sent her home," I deduce when he says nothing.

"Yeah. That and the fact she should never have been here in the first place." His expression turns hostile when he says. "*You* should have taken her home the second you believed her instead of keeping her around for your own selfish needs."

"Hold on a minute," I snap back at him as I approach him, appreciating the benefit of my two extra inches of height as I glare down into his face. "I agree with you that I should never have brought her here, but she also doesn't belong *there*." I point out the living room window in the direction of her apartment across town. "Especially not during the holidays."

"You think she'd rather endure Grayson's wrath than be alone in her apartment?" Royce volleys with a scoff.

"No. I think she'd rather have heat and electricity and food in her fucking belly than freeze and starve to death in her shitty little apartment."

"What are you talking about?" he demands, all traces of sneering wiped away.

I throw my hands up in exasperation. "She's a scholarship student, you fuckwit. She eats all of her meals in the dining hall —which is *closed* over the holidays—and I'm guessing she has fuck all in her cupboards or fridge. Nor will she be able to buy anything, even if she does have spare change lying around, what with it being Christmas Day."

Deep lines mar his forehead as his lips pull down in a frown. His mouth opens, but he shuts it before any words can pass.

"Yeah, didn't think of that, did you?"

"Shut up, asshole," he snarls, but there's no heat behind it. Turning away, he runs a hand through his hair. "There was… a lot to process at the time. I didn't think."

Releasing a sigh, I let him off the hook. "I get it, man. It's not an easy pill to swallow." Reaching out, I clap a hand on his shoulder. "Honestly, I'm glad you know. Can't say I was looking forward to having to convince both of you that Riley was telling the truth."

He huffs out a laugh, but I can tell his mind is elsewhere.

"Look, don't worry about Riley. She's a survivor—clearly. She knew the dining hall would be closed, so I'm sure she had some sort of plan in place—even if it was to live off microwave noodles for the entirety of the break."

Thankfully, Royce isn't looking at me as I grimace at the thought of three straight weeks of noodles. *Yeah, no, I'll not be letting her live off that for a single day, never mind the full two weeks left of winter break.*

I'm already planning to drive around town until I find whatever fast food joint is open and deliver it to her like a modern-day hero, when Royce rounds on me, catching my half smile as I imagine a freshly showered Riley answering the door in nothing but a towel with her pale skin damp and heated. *Oh, the ways in which she'll thank me.*

"No," Royce states firmly, pointing a finger in my face. "There won't be any of that."

I scoff, swatting at his hand. "You don't even know what I was thinking."

"That you were going to show up on her doorstep like a knight in Wrangler jeans, with enough food to feed a third-world country," he counters with a knowing arch of his eyebrow.

I gape at him incredulously. "I was not!"

Damn, the asshole can read me too well.

"You're not to go anywhere near her, Logan."

"Excuse me?" I bite, squaring my shoulders.

"You heard me. You're to stay away from her. It's what she wants."

"And I'm just supposed to take *your* word for it?"

"Don't you think we've done enough to her?" he volleys, and I find myself at a loss for words because, god fucking dammit, he's right.

Still... I can't just stay away from her.

"Well, I can at least call her and make sure she's okay." I take out my phone to do exactly that. However, it's knocked from my hand before I can find her contact information. "Hey!" I bark, glowering at the asshole as he scrolls through *my* phone. "What are you doing?"

The dickhead doesn't respond, tossing it back to me a moment later. "Are you fucking serious?" I snarl as I scroll through my contacts. "You deleted her number? How fucking old are you?"

Turning on my heel, I march toward the front door where I left my car keys, but before I can grab them, a shove from behind has me propelling into the wood with an *oomph*.

"You're starting to piss me off!" I bellow as Royce shoves past me, snatching my keys from the hall table and flipping the lock on the front door before facing me with a triumphant grin.

Crossing my arms over my chest, I stare him down. "What's your plan now, huh? Gonna lock me in here for the rest of winter break? And what about when school starts up again? Gonna buy a collar and leash to make sure I never leave your side?"

He rolls his eyes at my dramatics. "I'm hoping the fact that Riley *asked* for space—from *all of us*, will be enough to keep you from storming over there and inserting yourself in her life."

My muscles go stiff. "She said that?"

He nods, his eyes softening with sympathy and perhaps a touch of his own pain. "She did. It's the least she deserves, don't you think?"

I swallow roughly, guilt swarming me at everything we've put her through recently, and while she may have been starting to feel at ease here, with Grayson always looming nearby, she could never fully relax. Not the same way she'll be able to in her own space.

"She really said she didn't want to see me?" I can't help the whine that enters my voice. It's just... she was in my bed last night and now she doesn't want to see me.

Royce sighs, his expression a mixture of pity and basically *grow a pair*.

"Well, you did kidnap her."

I grimace. *I did do that, didn't I?*

"For how long?"

He shakes his head. "I dunno. I promised her two weeks."

"Two weeks?!" I screech in horror. "That's... fuck." I wipe my hand down my face. "Two weeks. Okay, I can totally deal with that. That's fine. No time, really. Will fly in." Lifting my head to stare at Royce, my eyes go wide. "What if she wants nothing to do with us after the two weeks?"

He's silent, not that he could say anything to make me feel better.

Fucking hell. Worst. Christmas. Ever.

And the plans I had for the rest of the break... Everything was supposed to be different after the conversation we would all have tonight. Grayson was finally going to open his eyes, and we'd all be on the same page, and then I could take her ice skating and to my favorite waffle place, and everything was supposed to be great.

Closing my eyes, I breathe deeply. "You promise she's safe? That she wasn't upset or angry or..."

"She's safe," he assures. "She was tired and needed time alone, but otherwise, she was fine."

I nod, my throat too tight to speak as I turn away. I get it. Truly, I do. I just... fucking hate it.

I trudge up the stairs to my room so I can wallow alone. Collapsing onto my bed, the tightness in my chest grows taut as I'm swamped in the scent of my Shortcake. Like the genuinely pathetic being that I am, I roll onto my stomach and bury my face in her pillow, inhaling deeply until all of my senses are flooded with strawberries.

Only when I'm bathed in all things Riley, do I roll over and dig my phone out of my pocket. Going to my messages, I curse out a breath when I realize Royce also deleted my chat with Riley. *So much for that idea.* Giving myself no more than a moment to wallow, I then search for the local grocery store and schedule a delivery for the first available slot.

Just because I can't see her, doesn't mean I can't take care of her.

ROYCE

CHAPTER FOUR

"*Grayson's dad lied.*"

Those words have haunted my every waking moment, filling the silence that has become unbearably loud inside my head. They flood my thoughts as I try to go to sleep at night and blare like an alarm the instant I wake each morning.

Even now, as I stare across the street at the door to her building with my shoulder propped against the wall, legs crossed at the ankle, and arms folded over my chest, I'm consumed with thoughts of her. Of that day.

I'm in turmoil. Guilt swallowing me alive at the acknowledgement that we've been tormenting an innocent woman. *Oh, the irony.* It makes me physically ill to realize what I did to her and what was done to me. Too blinded by my past, my distrust, I cast the same stone that was thrown so ruthlessly at me.

It makes it even more pertinent that I make it up to her. So she's not left with the same scars I bear. God knows she's already got enough of her own for one lifetime.

...A daughter.

I still can't quite believe it.

. . .

"Are you going to tell them?" Riley asks in a weary yet on-edge voice, and I pull my focus from the worn door of her rundown building, trying to remember how the hell I ended up here. The last thing I remember is pulling out of the lot at the park.

How I got here doesn't matter. For once, my subconscious recognized the right thing to do and followed through. This is where she should be. Not locked inside our house. Even if, by the end, she was no longer confined to her room. Roaming the house as though she had as much right to be there as we did—sleeping in Logan's bed and curling up between the two of us while we watched TV.

I run my gaze over the perplexing woman beside me. She's staring out the window, but sensing my eyes on her, she turns to face me, her expression pulled tight in anticipation of my answer.

Am I going to tell them? It's a damn good question.

For a moment, I understand the predicament Logan has been in —torn between his loyalty to us and his feelings for her.

The answer should be yes. Easy. My loyalties should lie with the men who've been like brothers to me. The only family who's ever given a damn about me—who has chosen me. Chosen my side. Believed my truth.

And yet, it's not that easy. Not that black and white. Because, while I agree that Grayson has a right to know, it's not my secret to tell, and I can understand Riley's hesitancy to make herself vulnerable like that. To peel back that layer of protection she has encased around her daughter.

There's a reason she's kept her daughter a secret all these years. Why she never went to the cops or demanded a DNA sample.

A mother's love.

A mother's protection.

While my own mother is as maternal as a rottweiler trained to go for the jugular, Riley is made of different stuff. Better fabric. With *this new insight, I can see that everything she has done has been for her daughter.*

Halston.

Lux.

Enduring us.

All of it has been to protect that little girl.

"It's your secret to tell," I finally respond, eyes scouring her face. "And I know you have no reason to trust them—any of us—with it, but I think they should know the truth. Grayson in particular."

Riley snorts. "Grayson would rather choke to death on his father's lies than accept the truth. My daughter isn't a bargaining chip or a pawn. I won't use her to make Grayson believe me over his father. I refused to use her back then, and I won't do it now."

I'm not entirely sure what she means by that, but now isn't the time to pry. Sighing, I run my hand through my hair. "That's fair. I can try talking to Gray." I grimace at the notion, already suspecting how that conversation will end. "But you should tell Logan. He's already on your side. Pretty much has been this entire time."

"Other than that one time when he drugged me, brought me to your house and chained me to a stripper pole," Riley snarks, filled with pent-up fire. "Oh, and the other time when he accused me of trying to ruin him with a false rape accusation."

My face contorts, and I wisely keep my mouth shut. I know damn well why Logan jumped to that assumption, and I equally under-stand why Riley would be bitter toward us—Logan in particular. Regardless, her daughter is Gray's half-sister, which, holy fuck, I hadn't quite connected those dots until right now. Grayson has a little sister. And he fucked her mom. Jesus, talk about complicated family dynamics.

Anyway, that's not the point.

Grayson is a total ass, but he's loyal and very family oriented. His Gran means everything to him. If he has a sister, he'll want to know about her. Be there for her. Help her if she needs it, which I'm not sure she does. Logan mentioned how Riley's mom was a bitch to her, demanding money, yet her daughter lives with her, and based on the urgency with which she came to me this morning, I can't help but think there's more to the situation than meets the eye. A theory that solidifies as I scan Riley's face, noting the weariness tugging at her features. She looks exhausted, and I know these last few days haven't been easy on her, except I sense it's more than that.

Her exhaustion is the kind that comes from years of being beaten down. Years of struggling to survive. Of barely holding it together. Is there more going on than I'm aware of? Other pressures on her shoulders? I have so many questions.

The sudden realization hits me, metaphorically knocking me off my feet. I want to know everything there is to know about Riley James. Whatever this is, it is no longer purely physical. I'm not entirely sure if it ever was simply that. This chemistry between us has always been potent. Drawing me in. I wanted to keep her at a distance. I needed to. And Grayson's belief helped me to ensure that, but now...

Now, there's no denying that my obsession isn't solely with her body but also with her mind. Her personality. Her soul. Her history. Her past and her future. Her life. Her daughter. Her fears and concerns. Her hopes and dreams.

Every little nuance that makes Riley Riley.

I want to know it all.

Own it as my own.

The realization shakes me to my core and needing to put some distance between us and be alone with my thoughts, I clear my throat and focus back on her face. "What do you want to happen now?" I ask, figuring it is about time she had an actual say in what happens.

Her eyes search mine before her shoulders deflate, and looking away, she stares out the front windshield as she shakes her head. "Honestly, I don't know. I need time to process." Looking back at me, she squares her shoulders as if preparing for a fight. "I need time alone."

We both know exactly what she's saying—she needs time without Logan banging on her door and Grayson tormenting her.

"I'll make certain that happens. The others will leave you in peace for the rest of the break," I promise. A peace offering. A tentative olive branch.

"And after that?" she queries tentatively.

"That's up to you, James. You know Logan won't stay away for long, and Grayson won't give up his vendetta. You're the only one with the power to make him stop. It's up to you whether you wield it or not."

Her eyes dart between mine. "And what about you?"

"You don't need to worry about me. I'll leave you alone."

"That's it?" she questions, unable to believe it's that easy. "I get out of this car, and you drive off, and what... We start the new semester pretending none of this happened?"

"If that's what you want, then yes."

Her heavy sigh belies just how uncertain she is. How conflicted.

"You don't need to solve it all today," I assure her, gesturing toward her building. "Go inside. There's plenty of time until the new semester begins. I'll make sure the others don't bother you."

"And you won't bother me either?" Something in her voice makes me think she's not entirely decided whether she wants me to leave her alone or not... or maybe I'm just reading too much into it. God knows I don't want to leave her.

"I'll be around," I say instead. When she still looks undecided, I tack on, "I'll have your back, but you don't want me around you, Ry. Trust me, I'm too damaged, and you've already got enough to contend with."

. . .

Sighing, I blink back into my surroundings as the woman herself steps out of her building and walks down the street toward the dance studio.

It's the first time she's left the apartment today, although I was here when a delivery van pulled up earlier, offloading a food delivery so large that it left no doubt in my mind Logan had purchased it for her.

Perhaps it should have annoyed me that he had, but all I felt was relief knowing she wouldn't have to worry about what she was going to eat for the remainder of winter break. I was embarrassed that I hadn't even thought about that until Logan brought it up.

I've never had to worry about money. Even now, the black sheep of the King family, I still have my trust fund to live off. It never crossed my mind that she couldn't afford something as simple as food, electricity, and heating.

Seems Logan took care of that too. After seeing the food truck pull up, I looked up the landlord for her building and put in a call, wanting to do something to alleviate some of the burden she carries. Color me surprised when I was told her rent and bills had been paid for the rest of the academic year.

That's fine. If Logan wants to look after her financially, then I'll stick to my job of lurking in the shadows, watching her back, and ensuring no one messes with her—including my two best friends.

I trail her with my eyes as she saunters down the street before disappearing into the dance studio. Only when the street is empty do I slip out of the hidden doorway I was in and move to a better spot where I can peer through the large, fronted window while remaining out of sight.

I made Riley a promise to keep Logan and Grayson away.

I promised her time and space.

And that's precisely what I'm going to give her.

However, I'm not purely here to keep them away and fulfill my promise. I'm here because *I* can't stay away.

Later that night, I collapse onto my bed and close my eyes. Immediately, pictures of her bubble to the forefront of my mind. The way she looked on stage tonight. The artful sway of her hips. How she moved in time to the sultry music.

It was pure, agonizing torture. And yet, I wouldn't have been anywhere else. I told her she wouldn't be left alone with that skeevy boss of hers, and I meant it. If that sly fuck was happy for me to fork over a few dollar bills to be left alone with her, then fuck knows what else he's capable of. It was plain as day that Riley was uncomfortable. That she didn't want to dance for me. And I'm sure she put up a fight with her boss—probably before he threatened to fire her.

I know how much that job means to her—especially now.

So, I sit at a table in the back, features obscured by the low lighting, and watch her. A silent sentinel protecting his queen.

Of course, she knew I was there the second she walked into the room. She's as attuned to my presence as I am to hers. Still, we acted as though the other didn't exist. She a dancer; me a spectator.

The promise I made to her that day in my car didn't solely apply to Grayson and Logan. It was to keep *everyone* away. Anyone who would dare hurt her.

Grayson. Her boss. Whoever thinks she can be taken advantage of because she's sweet, kind, and caring.

Fuck no.

She's been through enough.

We've put her through enough.

Call it penance or remorse or an inability to stay away from her.

She's under my skin, in my veins, stamped on my brain. I told her I'd leave her alone, and I have, though I'm not sure I could stay away even if I tried. I'm the last thing she needs. The worst thing for her. I'm carrying just as much baggage as she is. The only difference is, she's processed hers. That's not to say she doesn't struggle, but she's faced it... whereas I'm still running. Still burying it in distractions.

Riley and I... our traumas recognize each other, but where she fought and conquered her demons, I allowed mine to swallow me whole. To carve out my insides and turn me into a hollow, mechanical shell.

So, I'll hide out of sight and obsess from afar. I'll keep my distance, like I said, like I *should*. I'll fight every overwhelming urge to put myself in her orbit. To hear her sultry voice. To bask in the warmth of her smile. To feel the smoothness of her skin beneath mine.

Meanwhile, I'll commit everything about her to memory so I can lift it out in the quiet solitude of my room and examine; turn it over until I know her better than I know myself.

It's to images of her coy smile and sparkling skin beneath the stage lights, combined with the fierce fire I saw burning in her eyes earlier today in the dance studio, that I push my hand beneath the waistband of my jeans and palm my growing erection.

It's been five years since I was inside a woman. Since I felt that slick heat spasming around my shaft. The gush of wetness triggering my own explosion of pleasure.

I've barely missed it. Made do with my fist and blowjobs from whatever girl was pawing over me at some post-game celebration. With utter hatred burning through my veins, it was easy to maintain. To suppress the yearning. To distance myself from that desire.

I'd almost convinced myself I didn't miss it.

And then, like an unexpected spark in the darkness, she walked into my life. Literally crashed right into it, igniting a long-dormant ember within me and tugging at the edges of my restraint until all I can see is her.

I didn't want to become obsessed, except when she cut me down with her sharp words that night at The Depot, I had no choice.

Every moment since has been a battle. Clash after clash in a war I'm slowly losing. Every brush of her skin, every inhale of her strawberry shampoo, a battering ram to my palpable urge, leaving me torn between the instinct to lean in and savor the intoxicating taste of her desire and remaining firmly behind the walls of ice that has shielded me for so long.

Those walls around me have been melting without provocation—*she* has melted them with every unguarded smile. With every lingering look, I feel like I'm someone worthy of her time and attention. Someone worth getting to know. Deserving of the time it would take to get through my defenses.

The only thing that has kept me at bay was telling myself she was exactly like Melissa. That she'd ruin me just as badly, if not worse. Even if, deep in my gut, I started to doubt that.

Now, that argument has been shattered. Obliterated into pieces, and only my own thin sliver of restraint stands in the way of driving myself so deep inside of her that there would be no question left in her mind that she belongs to me.

My sigh is more of a groan as I squeeze my engorged cock. Hurriedly undoing the button, I yank my jeans and boxers down enough to pull out my dick, hissing as I feel every single one of those five years of celibacy. The heavy ache of my need grates with the wrongness of it all. Yet, I can't bring myself to feel bad as I remember how fucking fantastic it felt to have Riley's lips wrapped around my cock, my shaft buried deep in her throat.

Precum beads at my tip as I stroke myself to the memory of her on her knees, eyes shining with tears as she stared up at me, lust brimming in those endless hazel hues. I recall how it felt, hopped up on lust and driven by how fucking tempting she'd been on stage. I'd been obsessed. Consumed. Bewitched. My blood had been alight with the need to have her, and nothing would quench the craving. She'd been nervous, so small and fragile looking as I'd stroked my thumb over her cheek, but she'd wanted it as much as I did.

My breathing deepens as I inch closer, fisting myself with fervor while I pretend it's her mouth instead.

The intensity had been building between us for weeks. Since Thanksgiving, when she'd come all over my fingers like a goddamn goddess. Before then, even. The delicate dance of push and pull has been escalating with every night spent in that club—the world a far-off concept hazy in the glare of her magnetism.

Remembering the sway of her hips, how she'd lean in so only a whisper of air remained between us, driving me right to the edge of my restraint, that tingling need at the base of my spine becomes a pulsating pressure, my hand jerking feverishly as my breath catches.

Yanking up my top in the nick of time, hot cum splashes onto my abs, and I moan in pleasure, mellow and wrung out as my head falls back against the pillow. Still, my urge for her presses against my skin, an ever-present longing to be near her. To touch. To have. To devour.

In a bid to stop myself from chasing after her—the exact opposite of what I'm *supposed* to be doing—I clean myself up and move to my desk, dropping into the chair and flicking on the desk lamp.

I stare down at the sketch pad open in front of me to a picture of Riley. It's become a habit—drawing her. I have at least ten sketches of her face, each one with a different expression: The jubilant glee from that day in the play park, the defiant glare at us from her first night here, her sultry eyes and pouty lips when she's staring at me from across the room at Lux.

I'm acutely aware of the delicate balance I'm treading and just how tempted I am to say fuck it. The problem is, Riley is more than just a desire. She's become a mirror reflecting the facets of my own suffering and pain, forcing me to confront what I'm not yet ready to face. And by opening myself up to her, I'm acknowledging everything I've been running from. The second I allow myself to become entirely consumed by her, there will be no more hiding behind bruised knuckles and split skin. No shirking in the darkness. I'll have to finally step into the light, and as someone who prospers in the shadows, I don't know how to survive any other way.

RILEY

CHAPTER FIVE

I roll my eyes at her dramatics. I've left the apartment... I go to the dance studio. Look, it's been an emotional few weeks. I needed a week to sit at home and just be.

However, I'm now sick of being inside, alone with my thoughts and memories. After having spent all day trying and failing to get through to my mom so I could wish Rora a Happy New Year, I decided that a night out might do me good.

So long as there's no risk of running into one of the guys.

Decision made: I go in search of a suitable outfit for tonight and get ready, and I'm just sliding on my lipstick when I hear the blast of a horn from outside, followed a moment later by a text from Tara letting me know she's here.

Giving myself a final once-over in the mirror, I decide I look pretty good in a slinky black dress and black glittery heels, with my hair lightly curled and makeup heavier than usual.

Grabbing my purse, I tuck my phone inside and lock the door behind me before heading down the stairs. When I reach the street, I smile at Tara as she bounces out of the back of the cab.

"Ready to ring in the new year?" she squeals excitedly, not waiting for a response before ushering me inside. She's probably concerned I'll change my mind, but I won't. I'm all for letting off a bit of steam tonight.

The taxi is large enough to fit six people in the back, and all but one seat is already taken by other girls who work at Lux.

I'm greeted with hellos and more excited chatter as I climb inside, settling into the middle spot as Tara squeezes in beside me.

I relax back in my seat, letting the wave of conversation wash over me as the taxi pulls away from the curb. Streetlights pass us by until we leave Halston behind, the dark road awning before us as we head toward Springview.

Seeped in darkness, I pull my view from the window to take in the excited faces of my coworkers. Tara, with her vivacious spirit, can't contain her enthusiasm, already bopping to an unheard rhythm. On my left is the new girl who started just before Christmas—Kelsey—her eyes wide with anticipation.

The cab hums with a contagious energy as the six of us embark on our New Year's Eve adventure, and I can't help but feel a mixture of excitement and trepidation. Tara, draped in sequins and carrying the enthusiasm of a firework, chats animatedly with the others about the wonders of some new club we're going to in Springview. Apparently, it's the *it* place to go for a memorable night out.

"Riley, you're gonna love it! The vibe there is insane," she gushes, nudging me with her shoulder. Her infectious energy could make anyone forget their reservations, even a homebody like me.

I grin at my closest friend, knowing she wouldn't steer us wrong, before glancing at Kelsey, who seems slightly overwhelmed by the lively banter. Leaning closer to her, I give her a friendly smile. "We're going to have a great night," I assure her, relaxing when she smiles back and bobs her head.

Eventually, the glow of city lights flickers outside the window as we enter Springview, and a few minutes later, the cab rolls to a stop in front of the new club. Its entrance pulsates with vibrant colors and the muffled beat of music escaping into the night. Tara practically leaps from the cab, the others on her heels as their laughter melds with the distant cheers of the city, and I can't help but grin, soaking up the buzzing atmosphere of a promising night out.

Giving Kelsey a final reassuring glance, I step out onto the sidewalk. The cold December air nips at my exposed skin, awakening a sense of exhilaration as I stare up at the pink neon sign that spells out *Rogue* in cursive writing, before shifting my focus to the line of people queuing outside.

We join the back of the line, chatting animatedly as we slowly inch closer to the doors, and I'm only half frozen to death by the time we pay the entrance fee and step inside, the thumping bass engulfing us instantly.

The vibrant atmosphere envelops our senses, the dance floor pulsing with bodies in motion and the air thick with celebration. I can't help but grin, and spotting it, Tara squeezes my arm, her broad grin plastered to her face. "Oh yeah, this place is epic!"

All of us are dancers at heart, so we immediately gravitate toward the dance floor. We are swallowed up by the heart of the crowd, and soon, we're all dancing as one, a kaleidoscope of laughter and joy under the neon lights.

Even Kelsey has shed her initial reservations and is grinning like a loon as we sway our hips and pump our arms in time to the rhythm.

"I need a drink," I yell into Tara's ear sometime later. My skin is dampened with sweat, my dress sticking to my back from the heat of so many bodies packed into one space, but I feel lighter than I have in forever. I hadn't appreciated how much I truly needed this—a carefree night out with people I trust.

Nodding, Tara indicates that she'll come too, and we tell the others before pushing our way through the crowd toward the bar. When we reach it, we order two bottles of water, and with an acknowledging nod, the bartender goes to grab them.

"See, isn't this fun," Tara teases playfully. "Look, you're actually smiling. I think that's the first time all week I've seen a genuine smile on your face."

Tara has been an amazing friend since she came over on Christmas Day. She's constantly checking in on me and has helped me get through the mountain of food someone—Logan, I'm guessing?—had delivered.

I've pulled my phone out several times to message him, but ultimately, I decided not to. Distance. That's what I'm giving myself. It's what I'm owed... and, shockingly, what the three of them have given me.

A seed of warmth glows inside me at knowing Royce is responsible for that. Whatever he's done to keep them away, it's working, and I'm grateful. I've needed that space to clear my head. Not that having a clearer mind has helped me sift through my complicated feelings for each of them... but tonight isn't the night to dwell on any of that.

Instead, I pull Tara in for a hug, so grateful to have this awesome girl in my corner.

"That's right," a leering voice calls in our direction, followed by a wolf whistle. "Get it on!"

Pulling back from Tara, my face scrunches in disgust as I turn to look at the two men who have sidled up beside us. They're both preppy-looking, wearing expensive shirts and pants and sporting arrogant smirks as they unashamedly roll their eyes over us. "Why don't you kiss her, gorgeous," the one nearest the bar says, waggling his eyebrows like a douchebag.

"We don't kiss for other guys' amusement," Tara snaps in an ice-cold tone.

"No need to bite my face off, darlin'. We're just looking for a good time."

With a hungry look in his eyes, his buddy tacks on, "And the two of you look like you know how to have a good time." He does another leering sweep of our bodies that only serves to piss me off.

"Oh, we do," I say sweetly, "But we're not interested in having a *good time* with either of you."

"Cold, sweetheart. Cold," the one closest to me sidles even closer, clearly having zero understanding of personal boundaries. His breath stinks of bitter alcohol, and even though he's not unattractive looking, his personality is a *huge* turn-off.

"Why don't you let me heat you up? Melt some of that ice, yeah?"

It's a struggle not to roll my eyes at his cheesy lines. Seriously, does that ever work for him?

"Since you didn't seem to understand us the first time," Tara chimes in, brimming with hostile aggression and giving off very obvious *don't fuck with me* vibes, "we said no. We're not interested." With a condescending flit of her fingers, she finishes, "Now, why don't you go be annoying little gnats somewhere else."

"Hey," the buddy snaps, instantly riled. "There's no need to be a bitch."

"There was no need for you to be a sexist pig," Tara tosses back. "But you were, and for the record, I am a bitch. Trust-fund kids like you wouldn't stand a chance in hell in keeping up with us, so cut your losses while you're behind and go find easier targets."

Not appearing as though he's going to take them out, I inwardly sigh as both men square their shoulders and prepare to argue back. However, before either of them can construct a comeback, a different voice enters the conversation, this one deep and authoritative. "You heard the ladies."

I turn in time to see a tall, broad-shouldered man with dark hair shaved on the sides and short on top, wearing what looks to be a tailor-made suit of onyx black that only enhances his aura, has materialized behind us. His thick beard exaggerates his ruthless, hard edge, and there's a meanness about him. A savage brutality that unnerves me.

With a lift of his chin, two men appear out of nowhere and grab the guys who'd been hassling us by the upper arms. As they drag them through the crowd, their protests are quickly drowned out by the thumping bass.

I stare up at the mystery man with wide eyes, ready to

thank him for interfering, when Tara beats me to it. "What the *fuck* are you doing here?"

Ehhh, what?!

I whirl on her with a gasp, shocked to find her outright hostile glare drilling into the stranger. It makes the expression she gave the guys before look like it belonged on a kitten.

The stranger gives Tara a slow once-over. However, it doesn't look seedy or gross like it did with the guys. This man seems absolutely *ravenous*. Like he hasn't had a lick of water in years and has stumbled across the most tempting waterfall.

When his gaze returns to her face, his eyes spark, and his plump lips lift on one side. "Nice to see you again, Tink."

Tink? Wait, do Tara and this guy know one another?

"Don't. Call. Me. That," Tara hisses between clenched teeth.

... Well, I guess that answers that.

"And answer my question."

The man's smirk splits into a full-blown smile as he holds his hands out at the side. "This is my club."

Tara splutters. "Bullshit. You don't own a club."

"I don't think you're in a position to know what I do and do not own," he teases. However, it's the wrong thing to say as it only infuriates Tara further.

"And whose fault is that?!" Hurt underlines her anger, and the smile instantly drops from his face, his shoulders deflating somewhat.

Spotting the injury she inflicted, Tara goes in for the kill. "I didn't need your help with those idiots, and I don't need it now, *Dax*." Holy fuck, Dax? As in her old flame, *Dax?* Daaaaamn, no wonder Tara is *pissed*. "We're out to celebrate, and if I'd known *you'd* be here, we'd have gone elsewhere. So do me a favor and pretend I don't exist. God knows you've done an excellent job of it all these years."

Ouch. I wince in sympathy for the man as Tara pulls on my

arm, practically dragging me through the crowd and away from the stranger.

Before he completely disappears from view, I look back at him. His stare bores into Tara with an intensity that reminds me a lot of how Royce looks at me.

Tara may have told Dax to forget she exists, but something tells me that now he's caught a glimpse, he won't be able to go back to forgetting her so easily.

"That was Dax?" I hiss when we're on the far side of the room.

Her lips are pinched tight when she turns to look at me, giving a sharp nod.

"Did you really not know this was his club?"

"Fuck no. I'd never have suggested coming here if I had. He's supposed to be a fighter, for fuck's sake. What the hell is he doing running a trendy club?" She groans in exasperation. I don't think I've ever seen her appear so flustered, with her cheeks red and eyes glassy.

"Are you okay?" I ask, worried about seeing her so put out.

She blows out a long breath. "I'm fine. Just... taken by surprise. I haven't seen Dax in... It's been years since I last saw him. Here, now, tonight... I wasn't expecting it, that's all."

Sensing she needs comforting, I wrap my arms around her. She sinks into my embrace, her arms going around my waist as she buries her face in the crook of my neck.

"Why couldn't he have been bald and fat?" she whines after a moment, making me laugh. "He was hot with a capital H." She groans, her bottom lip pushing out in a pout. "As if my imagination didn't already make him my dream man, then he has to go and outdo even my wildest fantasies. What a douchecanoe."

"Total douchecanoe," I agree, even though I'm barely restraining my laughter.

When Tara's gaze meets mine, I can't hold it back any

longer and we both burst out laughing. "Ughhh," she groans. "Out of all the clubs…"

Squeezing her hand, I say, "Hey, forget about him. It's girls' night. We're out to have a good time and bring in the new year, right."

A slow grin brightens Tara's face, and with a fist pump, she declares, "Hell yeah, we are!"

We rejoin our friends, and when a staff member approaches our group and says we've been invited to make use of the VIP area, Tara simply shrugs her shoulders and accepts the glass of Champagne she's offered before we follow the guy behind the roped-off area.

With a private dance floor and unlimited free drinks, all of us are laughing and living it up, and as the clock strikes midnight, we huddle in for a group embrace, sharing in the promise of an adventurous year ahead.

***

I roll back my shoulders, releasing some of the tension from a night spent on stage as I push out the staff exit and into the cold January night. Walking up the side of the building, the floodlight shines overhead when I reach the front and look out over the parking lot.

My gaze pauses on a noticeable black truck parked dead center in the lot. A very *familiar* truck.

Royce.

Of course, I already knew he was here. As if I could disregard the feel of his eyes caressing my skin while I was on the stage. He hasn't missed a shift since I started back after everything happened, and when I step outside at the end of the night, he's always there, waiting to trail me home. Always watching but never overstepping. Keeping his promise to protect me but never encroaching on the space I asked for.

I never acknowledge him. Never look his way in the club, and I ignore his monstrous truck hovering out front, but tonight I glance toward the road—my usual route home—before making a split-second decision. Rather than heading for the dark street, I march straight to the black truck and yank open the door. I lean into the cab, staring at the dark-haired boy whose eyes I've felt on me all night.

"Don't take this to mean that I've forgiven you, but if you're going to follow me home, then I may as well take advantage of your heated seats," I state with sass, climbing in and pulling the door closed behind me before I can change my mind.

His hands rest against the wheel as his eyes rake over me, a thousand pinpricks striking my awareness and causing me to shiver. "Noted," he returns, lips twitching in what may or may not be the beginnings of a small smile. Only before it can gain momentum, he shifts the truck into gear and pulls out of the lot, heading toward my apartment.

The air inside the cab is thick with silence, but it's not uncomfortable. If anything, it feels... like us. Going so far as to bring a nostalgic smile to my lips as I remember the night I sat while he drew me, days spent on the sofa watching Christmas movies, and the occasional couple of hours we had together when I read while he sketched. I've missed the comfort I found in his silence. How easy it was to just *be* when I was alone with him.

Admittedly, amongst the stress and chaos of my eleven days inside their house, I found little pockets of peace in the quiet moments with Royce. That same sense of peace washes over me now as I sink into the leather seat and watch the world pass out my window.

"Have you been doing okay?" he asks tentatively when we're halfway home. "You don't need anything?"

His offering takes me by surprise. "After receiving a food delivery large enough to feed the entire Halston student body, there is absolutely nothing I could want."

Royce snorts. "Don't look my way, it wasn't me."

"Oh, I know. I'm thinking it was a certain blond-haired hockey player."

Royce chuckles. "He wanted to ensure you were taken care of and to make sure you'd know he was thinking of you."

"They've stayed away," I hedge.

"They have."

Biting on my lower lip, I offer, "Thank you."

"You don't need to thank me, Riley."

We lapse into silence for the rest of the journey home, yet I don't immediately move to get out when he pulls up at the curb outside my building.

I'm not sure why I linger; I just know that the silence inside this truck isn't the same as the oppressive silence waiting for me in my apartment. Don't get me wrong, my apartment has been a sanctuary for me this last week, but it's also been a prison. The quiet awaiting me up there isn't the same as the one I'm sitting in now. It's solitary. Barren. It's missing Logan's teasing and Royce's quiet brooding. It's missing my daughter's squealing laughter and off-pitch singing.

It's missing any vivaciousness of life.

Honestly, it's lonely in a way I hadn't noticed before.

"I, uh, have something to show you," Royce says uncertainly, before reaching into the backseat to retrieve a sketchpad.

He flicks through it until he finds what he's looking for, then hesitates.

"Is it my sketch?" I question when he appears stuck as to what to do.

"Huh? Oh, no. I'm still working on that. It's uh... Just, here." He practically shoves the sketchpad into my hands, and I gasp at the drawing of a woman dancing, her arms extended above her head, toes pointed toward the ground.

"Is this me?" I question with awe, unable to look up from the drawing as I trace the dancer's figure with my fingers. The sharp lines, the way they've somehow captured exactly how the dancer was feeling... it's indescribable. Poignant and ethereal.

"It is," he confesses in a rough voice.

I can practically feel the emotions jumping off the page as though I'm back there in the studio, even though I don't know when he drew this or what reason had driven me to the studio that day.

"It's beautiful, Royce."

Gently taking the sketchpad back from me, he carefully tears out the page. "I want you to have it."

"Oh, I can't—"

"Take it," he insists. "You should have it."

I glance down at the drawing before looking up at him. "Why?"

Glancing away, he rubs at the back of his neck, clearly uncomfortable. "Because I want you to see what I do when I look at you. The strength and poise you wear so elegantly. The determination that burns from within like an eternal flame. You're a fighter—a survivor. The next time you doubt yourself, look at this drawing. Remember who you are. What you're capable of. Everything you've overcome."

A ball of emotion has wedged itself in the back of my throat, making it impossible to respond. All I can do is give him a jerky nod. My gaze is still focused on the drawing as I try to see for myself everything he just pointed out.

Eventually, I clear my throat, gathering myself and

cautiously taking the drawing in my hand, careful not to crease the page as I move to get out of the truck.

With my fingers wrapped around the door handle, I look over at Royce. "I'm working again tomorrow night—which I'm guessing you already know." He gives an acknowledging nod. "Perhaps I'll avail of your stalking to hitch a ride home," I half-tease.

A smile touches his lips. "Sleep well, Riley."

"Good night, Royce."

As I step out of the car, I feel as if a hesitant, fragile truce has formed between us. Perhaps the building blocks to something new... if I can ever find it in myself to forgive him for the role he's played to date.

Out of the three of them, Royce would be the easiest to forgive, but as I step into my building, waving goodbye to Royce before he pulls onto the road and disappears, I know I'm not there yet. Not even close.

ROYCE

CHAPTER SIX

I wait until Riley is safely inside her building before pulling away and making the short journey home, unable to fight my smile. *She got in my car.* After that first night when I saw her walking home alone, I'd been making my presence known. I'd forgotten entirely that Logan had been picking her up after her shifts... and without him, she was left to walk alone in the dark.

So, I made it obvious that I was sitting outside her work, giving her the option of accepting a ride if she wanted to take it. Until now, she'd ignored my presence.

Except, tonight, she got into my car!

And now I'm smiling like a goof.

Oh, god no. Not like a goof, like fucking Logan. What has my life become?

That realization is enough to wipe the smile from my face, but it can't eradicate the lightness in my chest. The warmth that crept in from her proximity. From the fact she trusted me enough to get her home safely. The fact she stalled getting out of my car as if she wanted to stay a moment longer. Which is why I made the spur-of-the-moment decision to give her one of my drawings. An offer of... I'm not quite sure what. I'm not good at opening up to people, at talking to them, but for Riley, I want to try.

I *should* be encouraging her to stay far away from me. I'm not suitable for someone like Riley, but months of stalking her from the shadows have taught me that I *can't* stay away from her. I might not be ready to fall entirely into her light, but if she wants to bask me in her presence, there's no way in hell I could refuse.

I'm still carrying that fuzzy lightness as I step into the house, nearly colliding with Logan in the hallway.

He gives me a once over, frowning. "Were you at The Depot?" I'm not surprised by his question. Typically, at this hour, that's exactly where I would've been. Although the fact I'm not sporting any new bruises or split knuckles is probably what has him appearing confused.

I shake my head. "Not tonight."

"Then where..." His eyes widen, snapping to my face. "You're still stalking her... which means Riley was working tonight."

"She was."

"How is she? Is she doing okay? Does she need anything?" His expression turns serious. "Did you make sure she got home okay? I can't stand the thought of her walking home alone at this time of night. I'd even considered sneaking out to follow her home, except, well, I don't know her schedule. Plus, I never heard from her after the food delivery, so I'm guessing she doesn't want to see me."

He somehow manages to cycle through a dozen emotions in that one ramble, ending on a put-out pout. I throw the guy a bone cause he's been moping around the house since Christmas Day, constantly saying things like *"I wonder what she's up to today," or "Do you think she has any plans for New Year's Eve? I wish she was spending it with us."*

So far, I haven't given him a hint that I've been keeping an eye on her. That I know the answers to his hypothetical questions because I knew once I did, he wouldn't leave me alone. But we're only three days away from the start of the semester, so I figure I can handle his relentless hassling until then. Then he'll be able to see for himself how she's been, and Riley can decide whether she's ready to talk to him or not.

"She's doing fine. She's okay. She got your food delivery—which I think you went a little OTT on, by the way."

"I didn't know what she liked to eat, so I felt it was better to be safe and buy a bit of everything," he says unapologetically.

Restraining the desire to roll my eyes, I answer his final question, "And yes, I've been making sure she makes it home okay after her shift."

"Good," he responds, nodding thoughtfully. "I hate that she walks home." Yeah, he's not the only one. "How do you think she'd respond if I bought her a car?"

"No," I tell him enigmatically. "Absolutely not."

Mostly because *I've* been considering buying her a car. She needs one—for work, for going to see her daughter and taking her out places, for emergencies. A car is independence... and a hell of a lot safer than walking in the dark or taking public transport late at night.

The only reason I haven't yet is because I *know* Riley wouldn't take it well. I'm supposed to be keeping my distance, and buying her a car doesn't exactly scream *I'm giving you your space.*

Or maybe it does since she wouldn't feel obliged to accept rides from one of us...

I realize I'd zoned Logan out as I spiraled into my own thoughts, and when I focus back into the conversation, his hands are moving energetically as he tries to sell me on why buying Riley a car is a good idea.

"Logan," I interject. "Stop. Do not buy her a car. You've already bought her food."

"But I need to do more," he whines.

"No, you don't. You *need* to give her her space, and buying her a car is just going to push her further away."

"But—"

"No, Logan. I'm telling you, if you want any chance of having anything with her again, you'll give her the space she asked for, and that includes not suffocating her with expensive gifts—*like a car*. She needs space right now, in every way. She's hurting because *we* hurt her. She needs time to heal herself."

I feel bad as Logan's expression crumbles. "She's hurting," he says in a broken rasp. "You could tell?" His face is pinched, his eyes shining with self-disgust.

"She just looks a little lost," I tell him, blowing out a breath. "We haven't made life easy on her."

"Me, especially," he says in a dejected tone.

I remain silent because, well, he's not wrong. He equally shouldn't carry the entirety of the blame. We all participated, and Grayson should shoulder a fair amount of the responsibility. However, Logan possibly hurt her the most.

He's used to fixing things by throwing money at them or brandishing one of his charming smiles, although neither will work with Riley. If he wants her forgiveness, he'll have to respect her boundaries instead of barreling full steam ahead and throwing whatever he can at the problem until it's fixed.

"I'm heading to bed," he says with a heavy sigh.

"Alright, man. See ya in the morning."

With a half-assed wave of his hand, he climbs the stairs, and I wait until I hear his bedroom door close before heading up to my room. I fall asleep to dreams of Riley dancing on stage solely for me.

I'm standing in the kitchen the next morning, cooking breakfast, when Grayson walks in. Logan left early this morning, looking like shit after presumably barely sleeping all night. When he's not moping around the house, he's spent as much time as possible at the rink, trying to forget about a certain redhead. Or perhaps trying to prevent himself from going to see her.

Casting a glance over Gray, I can't say he looks any better than Logan did. "You look like shit."

"Thanks," he grunts sarcastically, before pouring himself a cup of coffee from the pot.

Just like Logan, he's been mostly MIA since Christmas Day, holing himself up in his office at work. Whenever he's home, there's a noticeable tension in the air that was never there before.

Before Riley careened into our lives.

Before we had the stupid idea to kidnap her.

Before I realized how badly we fucked up.

Now, it's impossible to miss. Our friendship is fractured, and until Grayson gets over his little vendetta, I don't see how we can repair it.

"Off to the office today?" I ask, even though it's obvious being that he's dressed for work in a tailored Armani suit.

My only response is another grunt, and giving him my back, I plate up the bacon and eggs I made for myself. He scowls as I sit down at the island with my plate for one, not having offered him any. Usually, I'd cook breakfast for the three of us, but not anymore.

Behaving like an angry bear, he pulls open cupboard doors until he finds a cereal box, bowl, and spoon, fixing himself breakfast.

"How long are we going to ignore the elephant in the room, Grayson?" I ask with a sigh.

"Until the two of you come to your senses."

I shake my head. "If both of us are telling you you're wrong, then can't you at least consider the fact that you're actually wrong this time?"

He scoffs. "Maybe if I didn't know what she was capable of."

"What about what your dad's capable of?" I argue back, earning an icy glare from him. "He stole from his own company. *He* did that. Isn't it possible he's also crossed other moral and legal lines?"

"Theft is a far cry from *rape*, Royce. Just because he committed one crime doesn't mean he committed the other."

I blow out my breath, realizing I'm not getting anywhere. "I get that," I appease. "However, I need you to just open your mind to the possibility. To hear us out. Hear *her* out."

I realize I've said the wrong thing when his entire posture stiffens. "And allow her to brainwash me the same way she has you? No fucking thanks. I thought she wanted nothing to do with either of you, so why are you still fighting her corner?"

"Because we all have to amicably co-exist on campus for the next six months, and I want to know that you're going to leave her in peace," I bark back at him, except it's more than that. He has a half-sister out there that he knows nothing about. He can agree to leave Riley alone, to not bother her for the rest of the school year, but the two of them need to resolve this once and for all. If not for themselves, then for that little girl. Because I know if Grayson would just stop being an unbelievable pigheaded twat he'd step up and be the best brother in the world for that kid. Just like he's the best friend anyone could ask for. *Again, when he's not being an insufferable pigheaded twat.*

And even if Riley wants nothing to do with us ever again, at least she'd have support in the form of Grayson. She wouldn't be so alone in everything she's going through, and he'd ensure she got whatever part of the Van Doren wealth she was entitled to.

"You want me to cross my heart and swear to stay away from the lying bitch," Grayson mocks, getting my hackles up. "Then fine, I'll stay away from her. She's done enough damage to last a lifetime." He drops his empty cereal bowl into the sink with a clatter. "Maybe when we're finally done with this university, and she's out of our lives, the two of you will pull your heads out of your asses in time to save our friendship."

With that, he stalks out of the kitchen, which is probably for the best since he was one more insult away from winning himself a black eye. If anyone is responsible for the demise of our friendship, it's him and his bullheadedness.

GRAYSON

CHAPTER SEVEN

Leaning back in my office chair, I fist the Barbie-pink scrunchie in my hand as I stare out the floor-to-ceiling window that provides me with a bird's-eye view over downtown Springview.

Except it isn't the city I see before me.

It's a red-haired girl with gleaming hazel eyes and the ability to haunt my every waking and sleeping moment. The only woman who fills my veins with hatred and makes my dick fucking weep for her. The only one who could possibly come between me and my best friends.

The fact that I've spent more time in my office than at home —where I should be over the holidays—says everything about just how perfectly she placed herself between us. Created a wedge so damn big that we're practically standing on separate continents.

The three of us have barely spoken since Christmas Day, moving around one another like ghosts. This morning's confrontation with Royce is the first actual conversation we've had—and look how it went down. A fresh wave of anger boils through my veins.

I should never have brought that bitch into our home. It did more harm than good. I just wanted some good old-fashioned revenge, and instead, she's tossed a grenade into my friendship with Royce and Logan.

All of this is because of her.

She is the one responsible for our ruination.

Still, as I stare down at the pink scrunchie twisted around my fingers, I can't help but wonder how she managed to get to Royce.

Of all people...

He can see through people's bullshit better than most.

It was on the tip of my tongue to ask him this morning, but I could see the sky-high walls erected around him, braced for impact, along with the hostility in his stare, and I decided *fuck that.* If he wants to see me as the enemy instead of her, fine. I'd be the fucking enemy. Nothing I say or do is going to change his mind. She's got him wrapped around her finger too tightly.

How can he not see through her manipulations? See the snake hiding beneath her pretty exterior?

But then, once upon a time, I couldn't see her for who she really was either...

The teenage girl I used to know never came across as malicious. She was sweet and shy, blushing anytime she caught me staring at her and quickly ducking her head. At the time, I found it endearing. Cute, even. I relished in making her cheeks burn.

Now, that sweet and shy teenager has grown into a firecracker of a woman. One who blazes defiance and hisses snarky comebacks like they're weapons.

Still... Royce should have seen through it, and I can't make heads or tails out of the fact he hasn't. Out of the fact he's now fucking *defending* her.

He'd looked sick to his stomach when I walked in that night, finding him sitting in the dark like some cheesy villain in a Brated movie, and his voice fucking *cracked* as he told me how badly we'd fucked up.

It just doesn't make any sense.

Nothing is making sense anymore.

Not my best friends.

Not my dad.

And definitely not the fact my dick gets rock-hard in Riley's presence. Or when I think of her.

Ignoring that tidbit, my mind drifts to Gran's wide eyes and the way she trembled, thinking I was my dad when I visited her on Christmas Eve.

"Do you think I don't know what you're doing to my daughter? You've already taken her from me, what more can you possibly want? Haven't you hurt my family enough?"

What the hell did she mean by that? When I visited her yesterday, she was back to her *usual* self, which means, for most of our visit she thought I was either my grandfather or the seventeen-year-old version of myself who went to live with her after Dad's incarceration.

I didn't want to bring it up and upset her or stress her out, so I left it, but the words have replayed constantly, along with the fear I saw in her eyes when she thought I was my father.

I've never seen that before. She's always disliked him. Very rarely spoke of him in my presence, but she's never spoken ill of him to me. Never expressed concern or fear.

So, her reaction just doesn't make any sense to me.

But then, like I said, nothing makes sense to me anymore.

The world has become a strange and confusing place, and the only relief I get is when I'm burying myself in my work. I've got a Dad who I'm beginning to wonder if I truly know at all, best friends who hate my guts, and a woman I hate who I can't stop thinking about. Envisioning. Dreaming of.

My life is truly and utterly fucked up.

I absently stretch the scrunchie around my fingers, recalling the day I stole it from her room. She'd only been living with us for a few weeks, and already I'd become obsessed with my new step-sister.

She was shiny and radiant and the complete opposite of what our house had been like before her presence. Before, it had been stilted and cold, but she breathed life into the building and brought about a warmth I'd long forgotten existed. My mother had died when I was eight, and along with her life, all happiness had been sucked out of our house. Out of my life.

It became stark and chilling, my father clueless as to how to deal with a grieving child. So he left me to figure it out for myself, really only interacting with me when it came to my grades and school.

Of course, he'd been struggling with his own grief at the time. Struggling to adapt to being a single parent. My mother had always been the comforting one. She was patient, nurturing, and sympathetic, whereas my father was more regimented. He had certain expectations and expected them to be met. That didn't mean he didn't care. I'd see the gleam of pride in his eyes when I'd come first in my year at school or win a trophy in an extracurricular.

In her absence, he was incapable of filling her shoes... and eventually, I learned to adapt to that. To accept it. To appreciate my new normal.

Except now... Now, I'm wracking my brain trying to recall a single interaction between my parents. Trying to remember how they looked at one another, how he spoke to her.

"Do you think I don't know what you're doing to my daughter?"

"You've already taken her from me, what more can you possibly want?

"Haven't you hurt my family enough?"

Gran's words echo deafeningly in my head as I scream internally for answers. For understanding.

She's buried a seed of doubt in my chest, and with each passing day, it's planting roots, growing sprouts.

Now, I don't know who or what to believe.

I'm interrupted by a knock on my office door, and I barely have time to hide the scrunchie in my hand before David strides in as though he owns the place.

"What?" I snap irritably. The dickhead has his head so far up my dad's ass that all he can taste is his shit, so I have absolutely no patience for him, especially today.

"Your dad's lawyers have been trying to reach you. You've been ignoring their calls."

And what, they reached out to Dad, who got his errand boy to come berate me into taking their call? I don't bother to hide the rolling of my eyes.

"I've been busy," I drawl. It's not a total lie, even if I've mostly been busy thinking about a certain forbidden snake-woman. "I'll get back to them when I get back to them."

David huffs haughtily. "It's almost as though you don't want your father to be released."

I arch a warning eyebrow, a casual reminder of exactly who he's speaking to. He may be my father's little bitch, but he works *for me*.

"You would be wise to remember your place, *David*," I warn in a glacial tone that's cold enough to make him straighten where he stands in front of my desk. "And *never* question my desire to see my father a free man. The only person who desires it more is my father."

That's not a lie either, even if I am apprehensive about what changes will come about upon my father's release. Still, that's not a problem for today. First, he has to be granted parole.

"Right," David says tightly, "Well, the lawyers are awaiting your call *today*."

I glower at him as he exits my office, waiting until my door is closed and his footsteps have disappeared down the hall before I relax back into my chair, unclenching my hand as I begin to twist the scrunchie around my fingers once more.

Before I call my father's lawyers, I need to pay a visit to my Gran and put these suspicions to bed once and for all.

"Hey, Gran," I greet as I step into her room, spotting her sitting in her usual armchair, knitting like she typically is when I come to visit.

"Grayson, sweetie, how was school today?"

"It was fine, Gran," I respond, knowing better than to correct her. Bending down, I kiss her paper-thin cheek.

"Not long now until you can be off to college, and no one there will care who you are." She gives my palm a reassuring pat, and I merely smile.

I mean, she wasn't wrong, but I'm fairly certain the only reason no one gives a shit about who I am at Halston is because I'm enrolled under McKinstry—Gran's maiden name—instead of Van Doren. So nobody other than Logan and Royce, and well, Riley, knows who I actually am. And I like it that way. After being bullied and isolated during my senior year of high school, I was more than happy to become a nameless, faceless person in a sea of other rich, entitled assholes.

"Gran," I hedge, lowering into the seat beside her and angling so I can see her face. "Can I ask you something... about Dad?"

Her face scrunches, as it always did when I was a teenager

and brought up my father. I always put it down to her dislike of him. The fact that they never got along, but the questions swimming around in my head since she showed me a glimpse into her inner fear directed at my father has me second-guessing. The not knowing is driving me crazy.

This and Riley have stolen every one of my thoughts, my sleep, and any moment of peace I could have hoped to obtain over the Christmas period.

When she remains silent, I ask, "Why don't you two get along?" My tone is pitched, light, and curious as I skirt delicately around the subject to not upset her.

Eyes glued to the television playing some daytime soap drama, she waves away my question. "You don't need to concern yourself with that, Grayson, dear. We're just two stubborn individuals with differing opinions."

Licking my dry lips, I take a moment to gather the questions on the tip of my tongue before allowing them to spill. "He never... did anything to you?... To Mom?"

If I wasn't seeing it with my own eyes, I wouldn't believe it—the way Gran blanches, her face leaching of color as all emotion drains from it. Her breathing hitches, and when I drop my gaze, I notice her hands tightly gripping her knitting needles as though they're the only thing grounding her.

Slowly, her head turns toward mine, and the anguish staring back at me tears me apart. "Freddy," she croaks, sounding broken. Devastated. "I don't know what to do. He's killing our baby girl, and she won't listen to me. I wish you were here. She needs you. Our grandson needs you."

My heart slams against my chest, beating a chaotic rhythm as I stare unblinkingly at my grandmother, working to piece together her cryptic words. Not wanting to startle her, I lean in slowly, my hand sliding over hers in what I hope is a reassuring manner. "What is he doing to her?" I ask, my voice trembling despite the effort I put in to try and steady it.

For the first time in my life, I watch as my stoic, always put-together grandmother breaks. Her face crumples, her eyes gleam with tears before they overflow, and her shoulders shake with quiet sobs. "He broke our girl. He shattered her heart, and now he's taking her soul. She's wasting away before my eyes, and I'm helpless to stop it."

Dread slices through me, leaving behind a sticky residue that stings my nostrils and sludges like tar through my veins. My throat is thick—with shock or vomit, I'm not quite sure. Rooted in my chair, I'm at a loss for words as my Gran sobs beside me. All I can do is hold her hand in an empty attempt at comfort as I sit in what she has said, turning over every word in an effort to understand the meaning behind them.

"Freddy," Gran eventually says, my grandfather's name a whispered prayer on her tongue. "It's been so long since I've seen you. Won't you dance with me?"

I have so many more questions. I'm more lost now than I was when I walked in, but my Gran is looking at me like I hung the moon, and she gets so few moments with my grandfather that I can't wrench this one away from her.

"You never have to ask," I rasp, throat choked with emotion as I help her to her feet and hold her in my arms as we dance in silence in her small room.

She's sound asleep in her armchair an hour later when I leave her room, stopping at the reception desk to sign out.

"How was she with you today?" the nurse behind the desk asks.

"She was good. At one point, she got a little emotional—thought I was my grandfather," I admit because sometimes emotions like that can linger. Although Gran was in better form when I left, she might be more prone to melancholy or even aggressive outbursts for the rest of the day. "Does she... Has she ever mentioned anything about my father, her son-in-law, to anyone here?"

The nurse's lips purse as she thinks. "Not that I am aware. Did she say something tonight?"

I shake my head, not willing to divulge. "I'm not sure. It didn't really make much sense."

She nods knowingly. "As you are aware, with her disease, she is prone to moments of confusion and misinterpretation. Paranoia and emotional outbursts can become more recurrent as her Alzheimer's progresses."

I wipe a weary hand down my face. Right. For all I know, everything Gran said could be in her head. Perhaps she had seen something on the television earlier or overheard a staff member or resident talking, and her brain had created a falsehood to make sense of her reality.

Or perhaps I'm grasping at straws in a bid for what she hinted at not to be true.

"I know," I grit out, the words sharper than I intend. "Thank you. Have a good day." My head is a mess as I walk outside, lost in my thoughts. I'm exhausted, confused, and doubting myself and everyone around me. Which is truth, and which is lies? It's impossible to distinguish one from the other. Who's the liar, Riley or my dad? It grates that I don't have an immediate answer to that. That I don't instantly dive to my father's defense the way I always have. The way I *should*.

The problem is, nothing is making sense anymore.

Honestly, I'm beginning to wonder if it ever did.

Have I been walking around with rose-tinted glasses, only seeing what I wanted to?

I shake my head. Surely not. I'm not that oblivious.

Like the nurse said, perhaps this is Gran's disease progressing. It would make sense that she'd focus on my father since she's never liked him.

However, that only leads back to the age-old question of *why* doesn't she like him? What did he do? What happened? Is their animosity truly over VDH... or does it run deeper? Darker?

"Fuck," I groan aloud, frustration welling within as I smack my hand against the leather steering wheel.

Truth. Lies.

How the fuck am I meant to differentiate the two? Who am I supposed to believe?

The sound of my phone ringing disrupts the silence in the car, cutting off my rambling thoughts, and I glance toward the screen in the center console. *Incoming call from Springview Federal Correctional Center.*

I scoff aloud, declining the call without a second thought. I am in no mood to deal with my father's bullshit today. No doubt he is calling to yell at me for not having called his lawyers back yet. His parole hearing is coming up soon, and it's basically all we've talked about recently. I know if I answer his call now, I'll say something I shouldn't. I can already picture the entire conversation. Whatever I say will piss him off. He'll question my loyalty and be mortally offended that I'm doubting him. He'll make *me* doubt myself more than I already am. He'll also want to know why now—what has me questioning everything *now*, and for some reason, I'm reluctant to tell him about Riley's disruptive re-emergence in my life.

Inhaling deeply, I rest the back of my head against the headrest and close my eyes. Auburn hair and hazel eyes float to the surface of my mind before I wrench them open, glaring across the nursing home's parking lot.

Still, I feel them all around me. My small sports car crowded with so many ghosts.

Riley's sweet voice mixes with Gran's fearful tone and Dad's indignation from the day he was arrested, twisting my stomach and hurting my head until I can't tell up from down. I've been shoved so deep underwater that I've lost all sense of direction. I can't see the sunlight and have no way to determine which way is up to the surface and which will only drag me deeper into the murky depths below.

LOGAN

CHAPTER EIGHT

My blades glide across the ice, the puck under my complete control as I beeline for the net. Lining up the shot, I effortlessly knock it in.

Of course, it helps that there's no goalie to put up a fight.

Nico—the traitor bailed on me half an hour ago, but I wasn't ready to call it quits yet. I've basically been living at the rink since Christmas Day.

Since I got home and discovered she was gone.

Even now, so many emotions well up that I can't identify them. They're just this hobbled mishmash of conflicting feelings.

Anger. Guilt. Concern. Relief. Heartache.

I still can't believe that fucker deleted her number from my phone. I should have memorized it. However, even as I think that, I know I'd be facing the same challenge of dying to see her while also wanting to respect the space she's asked for.

I'm trying, dammit, but not being able to see her is killing me. To see with my own eyes that she's doing okay.

I hate this whole situation. Hate that she even wants space from me. That I forced her into needing to distance herself.

And if I'm being completely honest with myself, I'm angry for not doing what Royce did. He did what I should have done the second Riley poured her heart out to me—he took her *home*. Where she belongs. Where she is safe from Grayson, and ultimately from us too.

It's what I should have done. I was being selfish, keeping her around. I wanted to keep her near, to be the one taking care of her. I was afraid that if I let her go, she'd run and never look back, and I couldn't bear that thought.

The thought of being without her.

Because, through all of this, I've only fallen harder for Riley. I've fallen for her quiet strength. Her bold resilience. She's sweet and tough, pliable yet unyielding.

Even the fact she's putting her foot down and standing up to us gives me a boner. It's messed up.

She's a paradox of contradictions.

And I'm pretty sure I'm in love with her.

That I have been since the first time she leveled me with her smile. Or when she looked at me with pride after I got a B on that first test. Or blushed when I surprised her with a pumpkin spice latte. Or showed up at my game. Or made herself come while I watched.

Hell, there are a hundred different moments in which I fell in love with Riley James.

And I'm fucking terrified that she doesn't feel the same.

Especially after everything we put her through.

Fucking hell. I drugged and kidnapped her, and looking back on it now, I cringe, my self-disgust pushing me faster across the ice until the world becomes a blur.

I cut the ice up, lost to my thoughts and oblivious to anything around me until my name is bellowed. Snapping my head up, I find Coach watching me, and based on his expression, he's been calling my name for some time now. "Practice ended two hours ago."

"Just wanted to get a little extra in." I gesture toward the net I've been slapping pucks into like they're balls being shot from a cannon.

On the ice is the only time I can successfully fight the urge to go to her. It's the only time I can push thoughts of her aside and focus on the game. Which is ironic, considering she's been influencing my game since I first set eyes on her.

Some stupid part of me thinks that if I can improve my game and earn that NHL contract, maybe I'll be worthy of her. If I can make it, guarantee that salary, and offer her a life she's deserving of..., maybe she'll give *us* a second chance.

I just want to make up for turning my back on her, even though I know she doesn't give a shit about my money. Nevertheless, I don't know how else to say I'm sorry. To show her that I'll have her back from here on out.

"Well, there's someone here who wants to meet with you."

For the first time, I properly take in my coach, noticing the tiny smile on his lips. I perk up, skating over to him. "Who?"

"Guess you better get your ass in the shower and come find out."

I'm already bounding toward the locker rooms when he calls out, "Meet us in the conference room."

Twenty minutes later, freshly showered and my hair still damp, I walk into the conference room where Coach is sitting with a tall, broad-shouldered man with cropped brown hair and perfectly straight, white teeth.

The man gets to his feet, holding out his hand as he approaches. "Ah, you must be Logan, I'm—"

"Neil Hanoman. Manager for the Pacific Penguins."

He gives me that perfect smile of his as I shake his hand,

glancing at Coach before returning my attention to the manager of the motherfucking Penguins.

"It's an honor to meet you, Sir."

"Please, call me Neil, and the pleasure is all mine, Logan. I've been watching you on the ice this season, and, well, you've impressed me. Not an easy feat to achieve."

"Thank you, Sir. I mean, Neil."

He beckons to an empty chair, reclaiming his own but keeping his attention on me. "I came out today to have a chat with your coach here, and he's had nothing but good things to say about you."

"He's the real star. Without his support and guidance, I wouldn't be half the player I am today. The odd cuff around the head helps, too."

Both men laugh. "I'm glad to hear it," Neil says before growing serious. "The truth is, Logan, I think you'd make an excellent addition to the Penguins roster. You're a shark on the ice, but your moves are smart, calculated, and you have no issues passing to your teammates if they have an opening. Teamwork is what this game is all about."

"I agree."

"Good." He gives a sharp nod before getting to his feet. "Well, I wasn't expecting to meet you today, although it has been a pleasure." With a final handshake, he says, "You can expect to hear from us soon, Logan, and I hope I'll see you in the fall wearing Black and White."

"Y-yes, Sir. T-thank you."

With a chuckle, he shakes Coach's hand, leaving me dumb-struck as he walks out the door.

"Did I hit my head during practice and hallucinate that Neil fucking Hanoman basically offered me a place on his team?" I ask aloud, staring at the now-closed door.

Coach simply claps me on the shoulder. "Nope. That's just how it feels when your dreams finally come true, Son."

If that's the case, then it feels really fucking great.

Except, as I absently leave the stadium and climb into my car, I realize there's one problem.

Accepting a place on the Penguins team would mean I'd have to move to the West Coast once I've graduated. I'd be thousands of miles from Halston.

From Riley.

And if this week away from her has taught me anything, it's that I wouldn't survive being that far away from her.

Everything I've worked for, dreamt of, has just come true. And yet, I feel more conflicted than ever.

Despite my concerns, I'm pumped as I walk into the house, puffed up with pride after my chat with Neil fucking Hanoman, and excited to tell the guys my good news. Even if his offer does bring about its own set of problems I hadn't considered until today, it's still a fucking NHL offer, and since I can't celebrate with my girl, I wanna celebrate with my guys.

"Yo, fuckers, you home?" I call out as the door closes behind me. "We're celebrating!"

I've hardly spoken a word to Grayson all week. Barely even seen him, but I don't give a fuck about the tension between us right now. Regardless of the other shit going on, I know he'll be happy for me, just like I'd be happy for him.

I find the asshole himself sitting in the kitchen, appearing about as glum as a rainstorm with a bottle of half-drunk whiskey in front of him. He looks up when I walk in, his expression unchanging.

"Who died?" I freeze in my tracks. "Oh, shit, your Gran didn't actually die, did she?"

His huff of a laugh is humorless. "No, you're good. She's still alive."

Oh, thank fuck. I seriously thought I put my foot in it there. Which certainly isn't uncommon, but talk about awkward.

"So what's got you drinking whiskey in the middle of the day?"

He shakes his head, stare intent on the countertop, but doesn't answer me.

"Gray," I nudge. "Something is bothering you, what is it?"

"I—" Lifting his head to look at me, he swipes a hand through his unusually messy hair. "I don't even know. Everything's so fucked up."

Brows furrowed, I take him in. His ruffled clothing and the dark rings under his eyes. He looks like shit. "Look, I know we haven't seen eye-to-eye much recently, but no matter what, I'm here for you. Both me and Royce are."

I'm not sure what it is I've said, but his shoulders straighten, his entire body going taut, as something dark flashes across his face too quickly for me to decipher.

"It's nothing you need to concern yourself with," he says in a tight tone that clearly states *end of discussion*. "What was it you were yelling about when you got in?"

Lips pinched, I feel like a bit of a douche for telling him my good news when he's clearly conflicted over something. "Oh, uh... I think I just got offered a spot with the Penguins next year."

Foul mood forgotten, his eyebrows lift as he gapes at me before a grin spreads across his tired face. "That's fantastic, man. Congrats. No one deserves it more."

The little tendril of tension I hadn't even realized I was holding on to unfurls at his genuine happiness for me. I mean, I knew he would be, but fuck, maybe I was a little worried he wouldn't. Things haven't been good around here recently.

Getting out of his seat, he comes over to give me a bro hug. "Thanks, man." My smile comes easier now. "Is Royce around? Maybe the three of us could hang—like old times."

"He's not, but I can kick your ass at virtual hockey until he gets home."

"You only win 'cause I let you," I scoff, before grabbing a beer from the fridge and offering him one. He shakes his head, retrieving his bottle of whiskey before we head into the living room, where Royce finds us when he gets home.

"About fucking time you got home," Grayson gripes. "Logan was about to cry if I beat his ass again."

"Shut the fuck up, asshole." I chuck a cushion at his head for good measure as Royce's gaze bounces back and forth between us. Yeah, after our week of barely talking, I'm sure the scene before him looks about as wild as seeing a dolphin in the desert.

"We're celebrating," Grayson says jovially, words slurring slightly. Yeah, he's definitely drunk. I drop my gaze to the bottle of whiskey at his feet, finding it empty. Oh yeah, totally hammered. "We're in the presence of true greatness, Royce."

"What the fuck is he talking about?" Royce interjects, brows lowered over his cold eyes in confusion.

"Logan's officially an NHL player," Gray declares with a raise of his empty bottle.

"Well, it's not official yet," I explain.

"No shit, seriously?" Royce says, his stance relaxing as he moves further into the room to claim an empty chair.

"Yeah. Neil Hanoman himself came to talk to Coach today. Told me an offer would be coming my way."

"Fucking hell, dude, that's amazing."

"Thanks, man." I return Royce's smile, and the three of us fall into easy banter for the rest of the night, an unspoken truce called between us. Of course, it helps that Gray is drunk off his ass.

"Does he seem okay to you?" I murmur quietly to Royce later that evening. Gray is half asleep on the sofa. He's been slurring his speech and talking utter shit for the last hour.

Royce scoffs quietly. "Are any of us okay?"

"Fair point, he just... I dunno. He looked troubled when I came home earlier."

Royce shrugs. "Perhaps he's finally realizing what an ass he's been."

My lips twist. "Maybe."

"So, the Penguins, huh?" he asks, side-eyeing me. "That's a long way from here."

I huff out a breath. "Yeah. I realized that the second I left the stadium."

"Are you gonna take it?" he asks bluntly.

Sagging into the couch cushions, I admit, "I dunno." Picking absently at the label of my empty beer, I hold his gaze. "What would you do?"

He shakes his head. "I can't answer that for you. Only you can figure out what you want more and what you're willing to sacrifice."

Ugh, yeah, that's what I thought.

My brows furrow as I try to imagine my life without Riley in it... not having her at my games. Not seeing how her face blushes when I bring her coffee or how she lights up when she discusses a topic she's enthusiastic about.

Could I live without any of that? Without her?

Sensing my heavy thoughts, Royce nudges my shoulder. "Help me get him up to bed."

Between us, we get Gray's arms thrown over our shoulders, and it takes some careful maneuvering as we climb the stairs to make sure all of us don't go careening backward. What a sad fucking story that would be if I finally made it big, only to snap my spine trying to get this drunk asshole to his bed.

"Jesus Christ," I pant when we finally reach his bedroom on the third floor. "For a lean dude, he weighs a fucking ton."

Royce just grunts his agreement as we unceremoniously dump the asshole on his bed.

As we stare down at him, I confess, "I've missed nights like tonight."

"Same," Royce admits wearily. "But until he pulls his head out of his ass…"

"I know. I just wish he'd hurry up about it." I step away from the bed, pausing when Gray mumbles something. "What did he say?"

"No clue," Royce responds with a shake of his head.

"Don't know who to believe," Gray murmurs half incoherently. "So many lies."

I give Royce a questioning eyebrow, but he just shrugs his shoulders. He is no more knowledgeable than I am on what the hell Gray is mumbling about.

"Hopefully, that means he's working through his issues," he whispers as we step outside of the room, leaving Gray to sleep off his hangover.

"We can only hope."

We say goodnight before I slip into my bedroom, stripping down before climbing into bed. Staring at the ceiling with my arm bent behind my head, I can't help but acknowledge how much better tonight would have been if Riley had been here, too.

God, what would it be like to even have her and Gray in the same room without the hostile glares and snippy comments?

The weird thing is, I *can* picture it. The four of us together… if she would only talk to him and he would actually *listen.*

However, before any of that can be resolved, I need to work

out my own issues with Riley. I've my own making-up to do, and with school starting back tomorrow, Riley has officially run out of *me time*. She's had the two weeks of space she asked for. Starting tomorrow, I'm going to work on making her mine—permanently.

ITEM 1 OF 2
**LOGAN
PUMPKIN SP

RILEY

CHAPTER NINE

My first day back at Halston, and I'm a jittery mess—and that's without any caffeine in my system.

The messed up thing is it's got nothing to do with school itself. I'm excited for my classes this semester. It's the people. Specifically, the three men who have infiltrated and completely upended my life.

Royce has been able to ensure I got the space I asked for these past two weeks, but now all bets are off. He can't keep them away from me indefinitely, nor is it his job to. I've had my time to wallow in self-pity and figure out what I'm going to do—not that I've actually worked that out yet. Now, it's time for me to face the three demons head-on.

Lifting my chin, I focus purely on feeling confident as I grab my belongings before leaving my apartment. As I'm walking down the stairs, I check my phone, not surprised in the least to see no missed calls or voicemails from my mom. My heart sinks, regardless. I've called her several times since Christmas Day, and not once has she answered. I should be used to this by now, but I just want to talk to my daughter. Is that so much to ask for?

Less than three weeks, I tell myself. In less than three weeks, I'll see her again. Get to hold her in my arms. Hear her laugh and drink in her smile. I can get through till then.

Any confidence I mustered before leaving my apartment gets knocked aside the second I step onto the street.

"Logan?" My voice comes out far too breathless as I stop in my tracks.

I am so damn glad I prepared myself for seeing him again by watching his game on TV the other night. Even that didn't do him justice. Logan truly has the ability to take my breath away. Which fucking sucks, considering I'm trying my hardest to get over him.

Still, with my night off on Friday, I'd told myself I was watching the game purely because I'd developed an interest in the sport. Of course, part of my interest stems from the fact Logan was playing. It's not like I ever sit down to watch other college teams face off against one another.

Even as a tiny figure on the screen, buried beneath his hockey gear and face hidden behind his helmet, he'd still rendered me speechless. It's like my brain downplays how hot he is, then I see him on the TV or face to face, and it slams into me anew that this man is sex personified. I hate it. It's disgustingly unfair on us mere mortals simply trying to go about our day without melting into a puddle of hormones.

It hadn't escaped my notice how his eyes had raked over the crowd as though searching for someone before the game began. Again, I told myself he was probably looking for Royce or Grayson, but I didn't miss the flash of disappointment in his eyes before he focused on the game.

Despite that, he still played phenomenally. Even the sportscaster said so, and right before he came off the ice at the end of the night, he turned around, seeking out the camera closest to him and staring into it as though... as though he was staring directly into *me*.

"What are you doing here?"

My question is more of a croak; my nerves are already frayed, and he hasn't even spoken yet.

He's leaning against the side of his car, looking gorgeous as ever in jeans that mold to his thighs and a rich, maroon-colored hoodie. There's a jacket sitting on the hood and a coffee cup in his hand as his eyes slowly rake over me, as if cataloging each and every aspect he might have forgotten about me in our time apart.

"Riley." It makes me feel marginally better that his voice is raspy. Licking his lips, he pushes off the car but makes no move to come any closer. "You look gorgeous."

Yeah, I'm wearing jeans that do *not* hug my thighs or ass the way his do, and a coat so thick and puffy that I resemble a penguin.

"What are you doing here?" I repeat, satisfied when my voice comes out steady, this time with a hint of steel in it.

"Wanted to offer you a ride to campus." He holds out his hand, offering me the coffee cup. "And bring you coffee."

"Is that a pumpkin spice latte?" The question spills from my lips before I can bite it back, and Logan grins as though he's won something. It infuriates me that he thinks I'll cave and forgive him so easily.

"You know it is."

Channeling the woman in Royce's drawing—the version of myself that he sees—I take a measured step toward Logan, accepting the coffee from his outstretched hand. The scent of cinnamon and nutmeg makes my mouth water, and I have to swallow my groan of appreciation. Ducking my head, I inhale deeply. "Thank you for the coffee," I tell Logan after I've had my moment. "As for the ride, no, thank you. I'd rather walk."

With that, I turn on my heel and stride away from him, the biggest grin stretching across my face.

"Wait, what? Shortcake! Are you serious?" Logan calls after me.

My only response is to lift my hand and waggle my fingers goodbye.

Damn fucking straight, I'm serious.

It's about time Logan Astor discovered that bewitching smile of his won't win him everything in life.

After all, the best things in life aren't free, and if Logan wants my forgiveness, he will have to *earn it.*

———

After my run-in with Logan, I'm on edge, expecting to find Royce or Grayson lurking behind every corner as I traverse campus. Which is ridiculous. Out of the three of them, Logan was the one most likely to track me down. Since Grayson didn't come to drag me back to his place over winter break, he's hardly going to show up now and cause a scene on campus.

Still, as unprepared as I am for seeing Logan, I'm sweating bullets at the thought of running into Grayson. That is one confrontation I am *so* not ready for. I swear I can still feel the ache of him inside me from our last battle, and I may or may not have woken up more than once since then with the memory of how good he felt inside me and my thighs damp with need.

I know I'm a disgrace to all womankind.

Still, just because I have lewd fantasies about the jackhole doesn't mean I'm going to act on them. It's not my fault my subconscious focuses solely on the sweet boy I used to know. The one who no longer exists.

As if conjured by my thoughts, I catch sight of Grayson as I'm walking across the green toward my next class. He spots me at the same time, the two of us stopping in our tracks to stare as the world continues around us.

Seeing him only twists me up further. That clash between past and present is even more volatile. Classes have barely even started, and he already looks haggard. No longer the put-together man who tied me to a stripper pole and taunted me. His expression is blank as he takes me in, face pinched tight before storm clouds roll in. *Oh great. I'm guessing he hasn't moved on from the past yet, then.*

Scoffing under my breath, I shake my head and pull my attention from him as I continue along my route, and when I look over to where he was standing before I leave the green behind, he's gone.

By the time lunch rolls around, I have had a day. The straps of my backpack dig into my shoulders from the amount of booklets and textbooks I've had to lug around, and I already have three essays and a group presentation to prepare for. They weren't kidding when they said things ramped up in the second semester.

And to top off my craptastic day, I have a meeting with my advisor after lunch.

I'm in desperate need of coffee—even if it is the crappy kind —by the time I step into the dining hall, and the last thing I need is to come face-to-face with Logan—again. However, whatever god is responsible for doling out luck clearly hates me because they never give me the good kind.

Knowing he won't leave me alone until I talk to him, I march straight for the table he's sitting at, with an overflowing tray of what most definitely is not dining hall food sitting in front of him. The room is pretty much empty since only scholar-ship students ever come in here. Good. Less of an audience to witness while I rip into the school's golden boy.

"Before you say anything," Logan blurts, holding up both hands in a placating gesture. "I only came to bring you lunch."

He gestures toward the tray and my gaze drops, taking in the various types of food on it. "What is all that?"

"Stuff from the food court. I wasn't sure what you'd want, so I got a little bit of everything. Or, as much of it as would fit on the tray."

"The dining hall serves perfectly good food."

His face twists in blatant disagreement. "It serves something that passes for *food,* but it is not *good food.* If you believe that it is, then that only means I'll have to prove to you how wrong you are." With another gesture at the tray that, admittedly, looks and smells delicious, he says, "By supplying you with *proper* food."

I mean, it would be stupid to turn down good food, right? Yes. Totally. And the last thing I am is stupid.

Besides, I do have something I actually need to discuss with him.

Without a word, I pull out a seat and sit opposite him, dragging the tray closer as I decide what to try first. All of it looks amazing, and although I won't admit it aloud, it's *nothing* like the cafeteria-style food they offer in the dining hall.

Thankfully, seeming content to eat his food while I do my best not to devour mine like a woman starved, I wait until I'm finished before I broach the topic. "I gather you're the one who thinks I eat ten thousand calories a day." At his confused expression, I clarify, "The food deliveries, that was you, yes?"

"Oh, uh, yeah."

"And can I also assume that you're the benevolent Samaritan who has paid my rent and bills for the rest of the academic year?"

Yeah, that one came as a shock to me, too, when I had to

contact my landlord last week to ask why my rent money for the month had been returned to me.

Seems he's copped on to the fact I'm not exactly happy at the fact he's trying to financially fix my life for me as this time his sheepish gaze remains on the tabletop as he murmurs his admission.

Leaning across the table, I pitch my voice low even though there's no one sitting nearby. "I don't need or want your money or pity, or whatever this is."

"What? No. That's not... That's not at all what I was..." Growing in exasperation, he tries again, "I know money's tight, and I just wanted to help. I felt it was the least I could do after... everything. It has absolutely nothing to do with pity. Hell, Riley, the last thing I feel for you is pity." He shakes his head as if baffled. "How can I pity you when I'm in fucking *awe* of you? Of everything you've survived, you've achieved? It's got nothing to do with controlling your life or buying your forgiveness, either. I genuinely just wanted to do something nice for you. That's it. No strings attached. You can choose to never talk to me again, and it... well, it'll kill me inside, but it won't change a thing. Your rent and bills are covered for the rest of the year. Think of it as one less thing to worry about so you can focus on your studies."

Well, damn. I'm left speechless in the wake of his confession. Even when I go to speak, I find my throat dry. Logan's anguish is written all over his face and in his dejected posture. I genuinely believe he just wants to help in the only way he knows how.

"Thank you." The words break as they come out. "I... I don't know what to say, that's... it's incredibly generous. Too generous, but I imagine if I continue to argue with you over it, I won't get anywhere."

"You won't," he states baldly.

"*However.*" He winces, any hope that had started to bloom at my acceptance of his generosity, dying a quick and painful death. "It doesn't change anything. It doesn't change the fact that you hurt me, Logan. Not once, but *twice*. *Twice*, I let you in, and you proved me wrong. What sort of idiot would that make me if I gave you a third opportunity to break my heart? To destroy my trust?" Each word I deliver is a sharpened knife to his chest, inflicting him with a flinch.

"It probably doesn't mean anything," he says in a small, haggard voice, "but I swear I'll never abuse your trust again. You *can* count on me, Riley. Whatever our issues in the past, that was all me, and I'm so fucking sorry for what I put you through. All I can say is that I was a complete idiot, but I'll do whatever it takes to make it up to you. To prove that I can be better. That I can be someone deserving of you."

My throat is thick with emotion, my chest constricted with grief, and my stomach twisted in anguish. "You're right," I croak, hating myself even though I have to say these next words aloud—for both of our sakes. "It doesn't mean anything. Your *words* mean nothing, Logan."

He nods decisively, pushing up from his seat and leaning across the table until his lips are at the shell of my ear. "Then I'll just have to *show* you how serious I am. About you. About us. Especially, because there *will* be an us again, Riley. I refuse to accept a reality where there isn't, and just so you know, there isn't a thing on this planet that I've gone after and not gotten. You're tempting a famished husky with raw meat, and rest assured, I'll snatch it from right under your nose."

His expression is full of steely resolve before he stands to his full height and walks away, leaving me reeling in the remnants of our lunch.

The next morning, Logan is once again waiting outside my apartment building with a coffee in hand. However, this time he doesn't offer me a ride. He simply wishes me good morning, hands me my coffee, and tells me I look beautiful before getting in his car. I'm left momentarily stunned as I watch him drive off, before beginning the walk to campus.

I guess this is his version of giving me space, while also reminding me of what he said yesterday.

Since I'm alone, I call my mom while sipping my coffee. Not surprised but definitely frustrated when she doesn't answer. I continue trying her for the entire walk to campus and before I walk into my first class of the day, then I send her a text telling her to call me.

When I enter the dining hall at lunchtime, Logan's already there, and when our eyes meet, he gestures to a tray over-flowing with food set one table over from his. "Space," he reminds me when I give him a quizzical look.

"Your version of it, anyway."

His lips twist in a wry smirk. "I don't remember saying I would stay away from you. Frankly, that would be counterintu-itive to my plan to win you over."

"Mmm," is my only response as I head toward the empty table, doing my best to ignore the hulking hockey god silently following my every move.

"Won't your fans be missing you?" I ask, halfway through eating my food.

He waves a dismissive hand. "They'll survive. I'd far rather be here."

I scan his face for any signs of sarcasm or a hint of a lie, except he's completely genuine. Not missing what I imagine to be a buzzing lunch with his team and the clique of fans who constantly surround him.

"How does bringing me coffee in the morning and sitting a table away at lunch prove to me that you are serious?"

"I'm showing you that I'm here. That you can rely on me to show up every day and just sit with you while still giving you the space you asked for," he explains logically. "Because I *am* here for you, Riley. I know I've let you down in the past, but never again."

I don't have anything to say to that, so I finish off the last bits of my lunch before getting to my feet. "Alright, I guess I'll see you in the morning then."

"I can't wait, Shortcake."

A shiver rolls through me at the use of his nickname. Still, I don't let it show as I walk away. Logan's going to do what Logan's going to do, and only time will tell if this time is different than before. If it is... then I guess I'll have a decision to make. And if it's not... then better I find out before I hand him over the remaining pieces of my heart.

LOGAN

CHAPTER TEN

Stepping onto the ice, I sigh, that sense of release I always feel when I step out dropping over me. It's like a physical separation of the soul. Everything except my body, the puck, and the net get left behind.

The sharp scent of freshly resurfaced ice fills my lungs, the familiar sounds of skates slicing through the rink echoing in my ears as my teammates warm up on the ice in preparation for today's practice.

Coach directs us through warm-up drills, my breath hanging in the air like mist as I execute swift crossovers, my blades biting into the ice. With each powerful stride, that familiar rush of adrenaline heats my veins, and my head clears in a way no drug could ever achieve.

"There was some fumbling with the puck in last week's game, so we're doing puck-handling drills today, and just so you all know, the missus is visiting her sister in Ridgeway so I can stay here all day until every single one of you can navigate the cones blindfolded," Coach barks. "Astor, Barnes, Rickman. You're up first. Don't let me down."

"No, Sir, Coach," I chant, skating toward where cones have

been laid out, stretching from one side of the rink to the other. "Last one to the far side buys drinks tonight," Jacob Barnes calls, lining up beside me.

"I'll take that action," I respond. "No way either of you are going to be able to see through the ice spray in my dust."

"You know, cockiness is not a sexy quality," Thomas Rickman teases.

"Yet I'm the only one with a girlfriend," I throw back at him. Okay, so girlfriend might be a bit of a stretch, but it's an inevitability. A girlfriend is exactly what Riley is to me—even if she's not entirely on board with it yet. As far as I'm concerned, I'm taken. I'm hers, and soon she'll realize that, too. Besides, I don't want any of these fuckers thinking they have a shot with her.

"That girl you were all googly-eyed over? I haven't seen her at our last few games. You sure she's still your girl?"

"Shut up, asshole. She works nights on the weekends, so she can't always make it."

"Uh-huh, whatever you say, buddy."

I send a glower Thomas' way. "She's the one. I'm not ever letting her go."

"The one?" Jacob questions. "Dude, you're about to enter the NHL. It's going to be pussy heaven. Why would you tie yourself down right before walking into the promised land?"

Before I can explain it to these two knuckleheads, Coach blows the whistle, and like a bat out of hell, I take off down the ice. My gloved hands move with precision as I guide the puck effortlessly between the cones.

I'm the first across the rink, Rickman bringing up the rear after accidentally sending his puck wide.

"Looks like drinks are on you," I say with a smirk when he finally makes it over.

"You're the Captain. Aren't you supposed to say something uplifting or some shit," he grouses.

"Sure. Do fucking better next time. You presented a prime opening for our opponent to swoop in and steal possession of the puck."

"Excellent pep-talk, man. Word of advice, though. When you bum out of the pros, don't go into coaching. Don't think it's your thing."

I bark out a laugh, the three of us skating back to the boards as the next row of guys line up.

When we're done, Coach splits us up, sending the forwards to one end of the ice for an intense round of shooting drills, while the defensemen do their thing at the other net, before we all come together for a scrimmage to finish off the session.

"Alright, that will do for today," Coach calls out when we're all drenched in sweat and my legs feel like a lead weight. Unlike the smooth surface I skated onto several hours ago, the rink is now cut to pieces, a testament to the effort every single one of my teammates put in today. "Go shower and see the physical therapists if you need to."

"Yo, Astor, you still coming out with us?" Rickman asks after I've hurried through a shower before I can duck out of the locker room.

I pause in the doorway.

"Come on, man. You can't bail on us again," Gavin chimes in, making me internally groan. I have been blowing them recently, and for no good reason. Purely so I could sit at home and *pine* over Riley like a lovesick idiot.

"Fine," I relent. "Meet you at the Huddle in thirty? I need talk to Coach first."

Gavin points a finger in my direction. "You better be I'll even buy you a beer." Laughing, I promise him I w before heading out the door in search of Coach.

"Logan," he greets, when I knock on his office door. "To what do I owe the pleasure."

"You know, I can never tell if you're being genuine or sarcastic when you say that."

Coach merely smiles, giving nothing away. *Nope, I still have no idea.*

"Stop wasting my time, what do you want?"

I hesitate before hedging, "I wanted to talk to you about the Penguins contract." A draft copy was sent over the other day, along with an agreement that I wouldn't have to sign until after the season was over, meaning if we make it to the Frozen Four, I'll be able to play.

"Did you get your agent to look at it?"

"Yeah, he's going over it now."

"Then what's the problem?"

Sighing, I lower myself into the chair opposite Coach's desk. "How stupid of a decision would it be to turn them down?"

Coach gives nothing away as he stares me down, causing me to fidget. "It'd be up there. Probably one of the stupidest decisions I've come across in my entire career."

I grimace, but yeah, I'd assumed as much.

Leaning forward, elbows resting on his desk, Coach asks, "What's this about, Son? Is it last-minute jitters? This is what you've been working toward these last four years—An NHL career. The Penguins are one of the best teams in the league."

"I know." I scrub a hand along the back of my head. "I just think maybe I should try to stay closer to here."

Eyes narrowing in confusion, Coach remarks, "Wouldn't have pegged you for the homesick type."

I shake my head, sighing again, because *fuck me*, how can I finally be getting everything I want only to discover that having the career of my dreams means leaving the *woman* of my dreams.

I've been thinking about this a lot since Sunday when Royce asked me which one I'd sacrifice—the Penguins or Riley. Honestly, the answer was an easy one. One that has only solidified with every coffee I've brought Riley and lunch I've eaten with her this week.

However, while I'd give up the Penguins, I'm hoping I don't have to sacrifice an entire NHL hockey career, hence why I wanted to talk to Coach today.

"Is this about a girl?" Coach astutely deduces.

"Not just *a* girl," I tell him. "*The* girl."

I watch Coach out of the corner of my eye, wanting to see his reaction, but admittedly terrified he's going to tell me I'm the biggest idiot he's ever met.

His expression is carefully blank, but there's an understanding in his eyes as he stares at me. "The one, huh?"

I nod.

Blowing out a breath, he leans back in his swivel chair. "Well, that's a tough one. What does she have to say about everything?"

My nose scrunches. "She, uh, doesn't know yet." It would probably freak her out if she did since she's barely even talking to me right now. Best to win her over first, make her realize I'm here for the long haul before dropping this on her.

Coach stares at me before shaking his head. "Jesus, Logan. Just when I thought you weren't a complete airhead."

"Harsh."

"Not when you go doing stupid shit like that. You wanna build a future with this girl? Well, you can't do that when you keep the important things from her."

Exhaling, I rub at the back of my neck. "Aren't you supposed to be telling me pussy comes and goes and that I'd have to be braindead to pass up an opportunity like this?"

"Don't be crass," Coach snaps, making me smirk. "If that's

what you want me to tell you, then that's what I'll do, but if you want some real-world advice, then shut your mouth for two seconds before you say something that makes me lose even more respect for you."

I mime shutting my mouth, earning an eye roll.

"I've watched you these last four years pouring absolutely everything you have into this sport. You're always the first one at practice and the last to leave. You push yourself harder than any other player I've known, and I know how much an NHL career means to you."

Ah, here it comes. The whole, don't give your dreams up for some girl.

"Having said that, hockey isn't everything." *Wait, what?* "You never know when an injury could take you out of the game, and even if you're one of the fortunate ones to have a long and healthy career, hockey cannot replace the absence of friends and family, or even a partner who is at your side.

"An NHL career is time-consuming. For half the year, you fly all over the country, and on top of that, you have endorsement deals, advertising, and the public to contend with. You know how challenging that can be. However, if you ask me, all of that makes it even more important to have a supportive and understanding partner in your corner. A woman you can come home to after a week of being on the road. Someone who can handle the hardship of this lifestyle. If you think you've found that in this girl, then Logan, you'd be a complete fucking fool not to do everything within your power to make it work."

I gape at Coach. I'm not sure he's ever said anything so profound in all the years I've known him. Ninety percent of the time, he's reaming us out, and the other ten, he's telling us to shut up or to leave him alone.

"I have a contact in the Springview Timberwolves. They're not the Penguins, but they're a solid team. I'll reach out. If they know the Penguins are in talks with you, it might be enough to pique their interest."

"Y-you will?" I ask, eyes wide. This was not at all how I imagined this conversation going. "I mean, thank you. Yeah. Yes, I'd really appreciate that."

He nods before arching a brow in expectation. It takes me a second to get my brain into gear and realize he's telling me to fuck off.

"Thank you, Coach," I stutter as I head for the door. "Uh, Coach?" I hedge, pausing in the doorway. "If you don't mind me asking..."

He smiles softly, regrets buried in the lines of his face. "I made the same mistake once—picked an NHL career over the girl I loved. Then, less than a year into my dream job, I tore my ACL, and despite surgery and extensive therapy, I never regained the speed and agility needed to play the sport at that level."

"You lost the girl and the career."

He nods. "I did. Those were dark days."

Sensing that I've lost him to his memories, I go to leave but again stop. "What happened with the girl?"

It takes a moment before he comes back into the room, his eyes lifting to mine, and a smile filled with love and affection brightens his face. "We crossed paths a year later, and after a lot of groveling, she finally took me back. I put a ring on her finger as soon as she'd allow, and we married several months later. Popped out a bunch of kids who now have kids of their own, and every day I tell her how much she means to me."

"Sounds like you got the dream anyway," I muse.

Coach nods. "Sometimes the dream isn't always what we think it is. If we're lucky, it's better than we ever hoped for."

Feeling better after my chat with Coach, I step into the Huddle looking forward to catching up with my teammates for a few hours. This is our typical hangout after Thursday's practice session, where we can shoot the shit and talk ourselves up before the weekend's games.

The Huddle is Halston U's campus resident sports bar, where players from all sports come to chill and decompress after a brutal practice to celebrate a win or forget a loss. It's a quintessential sports bar tucked on the edge of campus. The interior is all exposed bricks; you can hardly see behind the memorabilia from the university's various sports triumphs adorning the walls. Dim, warm lighting casts a cozy glow over the wooden tables, leather barstools, and booths.

My stomach grumbles as the aroma of sizzling bar snacks hits me. I swear nothing smells better after you've burned your body weight in energy. Spotting the team taking up four tables that have been dragged together in the center of the room, I head toward them.

"You actually came!" Gavin teases as I take a seat beside him at the end of the table.

"I haven't missed that many nights out."

"Yeah, but you never used to miss any."

"Drinks are on you and Rickman all night. I wasn't about to miss that."

The asshole laughs as he reaches for a tray in the middle of the table with beers sitting on it. "Don't say I never gave you anything," he teases as he passes me the cold drink.

"Dude, did you just quote *One Tree Hill* to me? You sad motherfucker."

He barks out a laugh. "You're the one who recognized the quote. I'd say *you're* the sad motherfucker."

"Yo, Captain's here," someone further down the table shouts. "We need a speech from the newest Penguin player."

I groan. I swear the entire team knew before I'd even stepped out of the conference room after talking to Neil Hanoman. I never told a soul, but they were all over me the next day, demanding to know what went down.

"Nothing is set in stone," I tell the table. No way am I about to tell these assholes that I'm turning the offer down. They'd think I'd lost my mind. Honestly, six months ago, I'd have thought the same. I never would have believed a girl was worth throwing away a dream I've spent most of my life working toward. But then I met Riley, and she's worth *everything*.

However, the fact the entire team knows about the offer makes me feel like shit for eating lunch with Riley all week and not saying a word to her about it. The only thing that stayed my tongue was that I know exactly how she'll react. She'll be happy for me. Tell me to go. That my dreams matter more than she does. Which is complete and utter bullshit, obviously, and exactly why I didn't say anything.

Not until I convince her that *we* are everything.

"Speech. Speech." Before I know it, everyone is banging their fists against the table and demanding a speech. And these fuckers wonder why I don't wanna come out with them.

"Alright, boys," I say, standing and raising my glass. "Here's to the Frozen Four! We're not just going to make it there, we're winning it all!" Cheers go up from the table, glasses banging on the table, feet stomping, and I wait for the noise to cease before continuing. "In all seriousness, we have an amazing team this year. The best fucking goalie in collegiate hockey"—I point to Nico, our resident goalie who doesn't so much as smile at my acknowledgment—"a star forward line, and some sensitive defensemen whose egos will be bruised if I don't mention them, but really all they need to do is skate around and look pretty for the crowd cause there ain't no fucking way we're letting a puck get through to them."

"Oi, how many times have I saved your ass when you were too busy staring at your reflection in the ice to notice the puck going straight past you?" Gavin shouts.

I point a finger at him. "That was one time! And I had something in my teeth. It was driving me nuts." Raising my voice over the cacophony of noise, I yell, "What are we?"

"Huskies!" The team responds, and I'm pretty sure I hear some of the other patrons join in, too.

"What do we do?"

"Win!"

"How do we do it?"

"Together!"

"Damn fucking straight! Now let me hear it!" As a team, we throw back our heads, the entire bar erupting into howls.

Collapsing into my chair, Gavin claps my shoulders, grinning broadly. "This is our year, man."

My smile is equally broad and relaxed. "Fucking right it is." We're both seniors. This is our final year playing collegiate hockey. We'll never get this time back. Even if we both go on to play professionally, it won't be the same. It won't be this team. *My* team.

So, with that in mind, I sit back in my chair and just enjoy being with my team.

I stop after two beers, but others in the team continue drinking, our table growing rowdier as the night wears on. We also seem to have grown in size, too. A few guys I recognize from the football team came in a while ago and pulled up chairs to our table, and the typical puck bunnies and cleat chasers have ventured closer, a few even climbing into some of the guys' laps.

Typically, I'd have messaged Royce and Grayson to come hang with us too, if Royce wasn't already out here with his team, except that's no longer the norm. As much as I enjoy being with the guys, I also miss having my friends here.

"Yo, man." Todd, the captain of the football team, drops into Gavin's vacant chair beside me.

"How's things?" I ask, lifting my chin in greeting.

"You still living with Royce?"

Eyeing him, I cautiously admit that I am.

"How's he doing? I ran into him a while ago on campus, but he rushed away. Now, he's been impossible to find this year. I never see him around and he's stopped answering my calls or returning my texts."

Sighing, I relax back into my chair. "It's been rough on him. He didn't take his ejection from the team well, but I think he's turned a corner recently." All because of a certain redhead.

"That's good. Thanks, man. I've been worried about him."

"Same. He's getting there just... don't give up on him, Todd. He might not be open to reciprocating right now, but I'm sure he appreciates knowing that you're there."

He gives me a friendly smile and a nod before wandering back to his teammates as Gavin reappears from the bathroom.

"I think I'm gonna—"

"Hey there, Logan." A feminine voice cuts me off, and I turn to find a girl I vaguely recognize. I wanna say her name is Kaitlin or Kami. Something like that that begins with a K instead of a C. "Hi Karly," I hedge, hoping I'm right.

Her smile drops a little. "It's Karoline."

Right, now I remember. Even more ridiculous than I imagined. "Sorry."

Instantly forgiven, her coy expression returns. "It's not a problem."

Of course, because a guy calling you by the wrong name is such a turn-on. Kill me now.

"You've been playing amazing this year. Do you mind if I join you?"

"Oh, I was just heading out."

Her lower lip pushes out in a pout that I'm relatively certain she intends to look cute, except it has zero effect on me. *She* has zero effect on me. How can she, when I have Riley? No other girl on campus could hold a candle to her, and especially not a fake like *Karoline*. One of the people who only smiles and acknowledges me because of my popularity and the dollar signs they see surrounding me.

"Come on, stay a little longer." She places her hand on my arm. "We can get to know each other."

My responding smile is tight. "Nah, I'm going."

She pivots impressively well. "Even better, we can get to know one another back at yours." Her insinuation is clear, even as her inability to pick up on my rejection is aggravating.

Angry now, I pull her hand off my arm. "Not happening. I have a girlfriend."

Damn, now that's the second time tonight I've gone and called her that. Riley would probably murder me for it, but I fucking love calling her mine.

"Oh, well, hey, relationships aren't forever, right? Call me when you're bored of her. I promise I'll show you a far better time."

Fucking bitch.

Hands fisted at my sides, my teeth grind as I lean in, letting her see the raging inferno in my eyes. "Maybe *your* relationships don't last, but mine will, and if you demean my girl in any way again, you and I are going to have problems."

Gasping as though I've thoroughly offended her when she's the one who wouldn't take no for an answer, she clasps a hand to her chest.

"Fine, but I won't be making this offer again. I hope you regret missing out on this."

Turning on her heel, she storms out the exit.

"Jesus," I sigh, shaking my head as I look toward Gavin. The dickhead is laughing into his pint glass. "Some of the students in this place are so full of themselves."

"It's the price you bear when you come from money," he retorts.

"Yes, it looks like such a hardship for you." Asshole has nearly as much money as I do.

"You're seriously choosing the scholarship student over that girl?" one of the freshman rookies interjects, appearing baffled.

"What the fuck did you say?" I growl, worked up now and in need of an outlet.

He holds up his hands. "Wow, hey. I was just asking. Doesn't make any sense to me. Have you seen the new scholarship girl? Does she even have tits under those clothes?" He barks out a laugh, not realizing he's about to lose the ability to speak ever again if he doesn't shut the fuck up. "Maybe she's secretly a boy."

In a flash, I'm in front of him, sending his chair flying as I fist the front of his shirt and yank him to his feet. "Say another fucking word about Riley, and it'll be your last."

"Wow, hold up. I'm sorry. I didn't mean it. I just don't get it."

"You don't need to fucking get it, you just need to keep your nose out of my business."

I wait until he nods before shoving him backward. He trips over his fallen chair and hits the ground, and I glare at the now-silent table. "Anyone else got something to say about Riley?"

My question is met with murmured no's and shaken heads. "Trent, you fucking idiot, learn to keep your mouth shut, or the only action your ass is going to see for the next three years is the bench," Gavin snaps, glaring at the douchebag who is officially on my shit list. Asshole better keep both eyes open at our next practice, that's all I'm saying.

Giving Gavin a nod in thanks, I send a final glare around the table before walking out of the bar.

Walking across campus, rage still pounds through my system as I pull my phone out to text Riley. Except I no longer have her fucking number. I could stop by her apartment, but something tells me that might undo all the hard work I've put in this week trying to get her to open up to me again.

Instead, I fire off a message to Royce.

ME

I fucking hate you.

ROYCE

kissing face emoji

Some of the anger dissipates as I burst out laughing, and I respond with a middle finger emoji before pocketing my phone and climbing into my car.

RILEY

CHAPTER ELEVEN

The rest of the week goes by relatively uneventfully. I've spotted Royce a few times on campus, the two of us exchanging nothing more than a brief nod or acknowledging smile before going our separate ways. Logan has shown up every morning and lunch as though it's become his life's mission to ensure I'm caffeinated and fed. Despite my telling him on Monday that I don't need his charity, food deliveries have continued to arrive every few days with organic fruit and vegetables and the expensive kind of pure orange juice that I usually gloss over when I'm at the grocery store. I wouldn't ever admit it to Logan, but I groaned *loudly* when I took that first sip. It was *a-mazing!* There will be no going back to the cheap stuff now.

As for Grayson, well, if I didn't know any better, I'd say he's avoiding me. On a campus this size, it's impossible *not* to cross paths with him, and yet I haven't seen hide nor hair of him since Monday. The only reason we mustn't have come across each other last semester is because he actively went out of his way to avoid me... which is why I'm starting to believe he's using the same tactic this term. The question is why. Why does he feel like he needs to avoid me? If anything, I'd have expected him to be doing everything he could to torture me.

The fact he's stayed away has a little bubble of hope growing in my stomach. Hope that he may be starting to question everything. That he may be starting to believe what I've been telling him.

Of course, it's just as likely—more so, probably—that he's avoiding me so he doesn't strangle the life out of me and end up joining his dad in a prison cell.

Yeah, that seems much more conceivable.

All thoughts of Grayson fall by the wayside as I step into the dining hall on Friday and find Logan sitting at what has become my regular table. He's remained a table over all week, although he has moved a seat closer to mine every day, and today, it looks like he's taken the leap to actually sit with me.

He's also been talking more during our lunches. Asking me questions about my classes this semester and my life in general. Sometimes, I've had to evade because the answers involved telling him about Aurora, and any time that's happened, it's left me feeling guilty. Not necessarily guilty for not telling him. I know I don't owe him that. More that I know he'd *want* to know. He'd be excited. I still remember how he talked about his nieces and nephews, the way he lit up. He loves kids, and I'm pretty sure if he knew of Rora's existence, he'd have a hundred and one questions about her.

I stall in the doorway, picturing it... them together. Laughing as they discuss their favorite Paw Patrol episodes and argue over which color is the best. He'd be good at making my little girl smile, something I fear she doesn't do nearly as often as she should.

Thinking of her only reminds me that I still haven't spoken to Aurora since Christmas Day. Frustration bubbles up within me, and I have to push it away as I approach Logan, not wanting him to ask questions I'm not ready to answer.

"Figured we could eat lunch at the same table rather than talking across the room," Logan says with an easy smile.

I arch a brow at him, making it obvious I know exactly what he's doing. His responding smile is unrepentant.

Not seeing any point in arguing with him, I sit down and take in today's variety of options. Every day is something different, and I have to admit I'm enjoying the mixture and variety. Beats the same old dining hall food every day.

"How come you always eat alone?" Logan asks as I'm sampling the BBQ ribs.

"Ehh, because there's only one scholarship student every year."

"What about the scholarship students in other years?"

I shrug, having never actually met the other students. I guess, usually, I'd be in a dorm with at least one of them, and we'd have had a better chance of meeting and getting to know one another, but living off campus, I haven't had that same opportunity.

"Well, what about the other students in our year? Aren't you friends with any of them?"

I can't stop the skeptical look that crosses my face. "Have you met most of the student body here? You're the only one who is happy to hang out in the dining hall."

"There are other places to hang out," Logan argues.

"Not when you're broke, there aren't. Some students are polite and say hi in classes, but I don't hang out with any of them outside of class."

Creases form along his forehead as he takes in this information.

"Royce said the school isn't covering your accommodation fees because you're living off campus, even though you're only living there because they're redoing the dorms this year. He bribed a lady in the office," he tacks on at my puzzled look. "Is that why you're working at Lux?"

It's another one of those questions that veers particularly close to acknowledging Aurora. "It's one of the reasons," I say vaguely.

"That's bullshit. The school is ripping the dick out of that."

I shrug but don't disagree. "It is what it is."

"Maybe so, but if you'd been in the dorms, you'd have had more time and opportunities to get to know the other students. You could have hung out in the communal kitchen or the theatre room. It was always a really friendly place to chill when I was a freshman."

"There was a theatre room in the dorms?" I ask, surprised. Although, I'm not sure why. Of course, somewhere like Halston would have the likes of a theatre room in its dorms. Most kids are probably accustomed to having cinema rooms in their parents' houses.

"Oh yeah. It's where everyone congregates to chat and catch up. Big comfy armchairs and a widescreen TV constantly playing but turned on mute. Usually, one of the guys would hook up a gaming console. It was great fun."

I smile wistfully. "Sounds like it."

At my tone, his frown returns.

"Between classes and work, I barely have time for friends anyway, so it's no great loss," I tell him, not entirely sure if I'm trying to reassure him or remind myself. Either way, he doesn't seem to buy it, and we lapse into a heavy silence as we finish our lunch.

When we're done, he clears our trays away before following me outside, where other students are milling around in line at the coffee cart or heading to or from the food court. "Let me buy you—"

"Logan!"

A high-pitched shrill cuts him off, and I internally groan as Whitney strides toward us, two of her sidekicks in tow.

"Uhh, hey," Logan greets, that professional smile of his sliding into place. He clearly has no idea who she is, which makes me feel a little better.

"Where have you been hiding all week? The food court has been awfully quiet without you."

"Just been hanging with my girl here," Logan says casually, with a hint of what sounds like pride in his voice as he says *my girl*. I'm certainly not about to correct him on the fact that I am most definitely *not* his girl, regardless of what he might think or believe. Not when Whitney's gaze slides to mine, and she startles as though only now noticing I'm standing right here. *Bitch.*

Eyes shifting to the building behind us, she gasps. "In the dining hall? Logan, that is so beneath you. You shouldn't have to lower yourself just to hang out with the poor kids. Not when the food court has *everything* you could ever want."

Oh my god, the way she intoned that, she made it very fucking obvious that *she's* on the exclusive food court's menu—specially for Logan Astor. *Barf.*

Whitney's smile is laced with sugar when she turns it on me. "No offense, sweetie, but your kind just doesn't belong with the likes of Logan Astor."

"No offense taken," I say just as sweetly.

"Actually," Logan interjects, tone cold as ice. "Offense has very much been taken. Where the hell do you get off talking to Riley like that? To *anyone* like that. You're not better than her, and *I'm* sure as fuck not better than her. Or anyone. Having everything handed to you in life doesn't make you superior. Riley has had to work her ass off for *everything* she's achieved. Unlike *some,* she clearly understands the meaning of hard work. The gratification that comes with putting your all into something and seeing the result pay off. Which, from where I'm standing, makes her perfect for me. If anyone doesn't belong *with the likes of me*, it's you."

Wide-eyed, Whitney gapes at Logan before regaining her composure, although her cheeks are still blazing with embarrassment. With a painfully tight smile and a glare that screams murder, she storms off, her hands flapping in front of her as she no doubt rants to her sidekicks.

"Is that the kind of shit you've been dealing with this year?" Logan asks when they're out of earshot, sounding just as furious as he did before.

"Eh, more or less. It got worse, especially from Whitney, when you and I started hanging out, but I don't let it get to me. Girls like that aren't the sorts of people I want to know or spend my time with anyway."

"You still shouldn't have to put up with that shit. I can't believe I didn't know that you were."

"Well, she's hardly going to do it in front of you. She probably only said that since she assumed you'd agree with her."

He harrumphs. "And it's not like you would have said anything." I roll my eyes at his indignation. I'd point out the fact that I don't need him fighting my battles for me, but I fear it would be wasted breath. "What's her name again?"

I chuckle, letting loose a grin. "Whitney."

"Right, well, *Whitney* won't be bothering you again. I'll make sure the rest of the team knows she's on our shit list."

"You have a shit list?"

With a shrug, he explains, "There's always someone trying to make money off of us. Guys looking to start a fight so their buddies can record it and fuck up our chances of making it pro. Girls who want us for our money yet think it's acceptable to bang other guys because we're on the road so much."

"That's messed up."

"It is," he agrees. "Whitney and her friends are officially on that list now, which means she's as good as shunned. None of the guys will touch her. She'll be banned from all social events. No more Halston hockey for her."

"That sounds... excessive," I say as I chew on my lip.

Logan snorts. "She messed with what's mine. She's lucky I don't completely destroy her."

"Now you've gone and said twice that I'm yours so I feel the need to point out the fact that I'm not."

He only grins wickedly at me. "That's where we beg to differ," he says, stepping into me so all I can see is him. "But you'll soon see that you *are mine*. You never stopped." Reaching up, he tucks a strand of hair behind my ear, lingering as though he can't bring himself to pull away. "I've waited my whole life for you. I fucked up, and I have my dues to pay; I get that. I'll happily pay them, seeing as the alternative... losing you altogether is not an option. So maybe you're right. Maybe you're not mine, but I am most certainly yours."

"Logan." I'm honestly not entirely sure what I was going to say. My heart feels as though it's trapped in a vice. He places a finger over my lips, that slight bit of contact sending a zing along them that leaves them tingling. It only serves to remind me how safe I always felt with him. How gentle and caring he was. Despite his size and stature, Logan always touched me as though I needed to be handled with care.

"Don't say anything. I know where you stand, and I understand it. I just had to say my piece, especially since I get the distinct impression you don't fully believe me yet."

He's right, I don't. Or didn't?

"Okay," I say instead. With a final sweep of his gaze over my face, he steps back, and cold rushes in, the distance between us leaving a frigid ache in my bones. "I should go."

"No, don't. Please. Maybe we can walk and talk for a bit? I

was about to suggest grabbing a coffee before we were interrupted. If you have time before your next class, we could go for a walk while we drink or just sit and talk." His lips quirk up on one side. "Like old times."

I find it impossible to say no to that face, so I end up agreeing, and we line up at the coffee cart, getting our drinks before strolling along one of the numerous campus paths.

As we walk, I notice, unlike before, where Logan would have talked about himself, hockey, and the team, he peppers *me* with questions instead. The conversation is more balanced as we exchange anecdotes about our lives back and forth.

I don't even notice the time passing until we circle back to the coffee cart, and I actually feel a little sad that we're parting.

"Thank you," he says as we come to a stop back where we started. He's standing so close, the front of my coat brushes his, but I don't move away. If anything, the more time I spend in his presence, the more I crave him. I remember how good it felt to have his arm around me, his warmth seeping into my skin.

God, I miss that. I don't want to. I don't want to miss anything about Logan Astor, except that doesn't negate the fact that I miss everything. I miss *him*.

He heaves out a shuddering breath that draws my attention. "It's just... fuck, Riley, I feel like I'm going out of my mind."

My mouth drops open in surprise at his admission. At the torment scored into his face. It's not like he hasn't seen or talked to me all week. "Why?" I ask curiously.

"Why?" he repeats like it's the most absurd question. "Because I've barely spoken to you in weeks." His expression turns pained as his gaze drops over me, and he unconsciously leans closer. "Because I can't touch you. Because every time we're together, all I can think about is kissing you, and knowing you don't want that is eating me alive inside. I just... I know I can't do anything to change the past, but *god,* do I wish Grayson had never seen you in that club. That we were still back when everything was fucking perfect between us. When you trusted me, and I could see it in your eyes that you were falling for me just as fast and as hard as I've been falling for you."

Oh, how I wish we could go back to that time too. When everything between Logan and me was so easy. So perfect. When I believed I could count on him and thought he was the most faultless man ever.

Except no one is perfect, and we can't go back in time. It wouldn't do us any good even if we could.

"I can't stand this distance between us," he continues. "I'll do anything to make things right between us, Riley. Anything." He sounds so pained, so anguished that it shreds up my insides. I hate this distance between us, too. I don't *want* to be on the outs with Logan, but keeping him at arm's length is for my own good. My own safety. I *have* to keep him as far away from what remains of my masticated heart, or he'll devour the scraps that remain.

"*Anything,* Riley." Reaching up, he squeezes the tops of my arms in an almost desperate plea. "Tell me what I have to do."

"I can't," I tell him heavily. "There is no one thing you can do to make this better, Logan. It's not something you can fix just like that. It takes time to heal these sorts of wounds... I need *time* to know if I can ever trust you again."

His head drops between his shoulders, his large hands moving over my shoulders until they cradle the back of my head. "Okay," he says after he's taken a moment to gather himself. "It's okay. I understand. I get it, I do. I'm not trying to pressure you. I just... God, I miss you so fucking much, Short-cake." We're cheek to cheek, his admission a shattered whisper in my ear as his arms hold me snuggly against him.

Tears burn the backs of my eyes, and my traitorous heart begs for me to throw in the towel and tell him he's forgiven because keeping him at arm's length is so goddamn hard. Agonizingly so.

As if sensing I need this moment of intimacy as badly as he does, his arms band tightly around me, crushing me against him, and I welcome it as I bury my face in his chest and allow myself to pretend everything is okay between us.

"I'm so sorry," he murmurs against my ear. "I'm sorry that I hurt you. Sorry that I'm *still* hurting you. Sorry that I couldn't see what was right in front of me. I want everything with you, Shortcake. Every. Fucking. Thing. My life without you is not an option. I know it's hard right now, and you're scared to trust me. One day, however, you *will* trust me so wholeheartedly it'll be like we're one person." He pulls back only enough to look me in the eyes, searing me with the fierceness of his promise. "We just have to get through this first, just... don't give up on me, okay? Do that one thing for me. Don't shut your heart off from loving me. Protect it, keep it safe, but don't shut it off. Can you do that for me?"

The world ceases to exist as I gaze into those chestnut hues, brimming with anguish and regret but shining with intensity, nonetheless.

"Isn't this cozy." The voice scratches through the moment like the scrape of a needle along a record, and I reluctantly look away from Logan to take in Grayson's sneering expression. "I see she's still leading you by the balls," he says to Logan, ignoring my presence altogether.

"Grayson," Logan growls in warning as he moves to stand beside me, our shoulders brushing. "Don't start."

"Don't start what? I'm not starting anything."

"Done avoiding me, I see," I interject before their argument can escalate. Far better to divert Grayson's anger to me than have him take out his bad mood on Logan and risk further damage to their friendship.

"Avoiding you?" he sneers. "Not sure why you'd think I'd go out of my way to do that."

"Avoidance seems to be your specialty."

"Why you—"

Grayson takes a menacing step forward at the same time Logan shifts, putting himself between us so I have to peer around his broad shoulder to see Grayson's thunderous expression.

"Watch it!" Logan snaps. "Don't think I've forgotten what happened on Christmas Eve. You're not to go anywhere near her!"

Scoffing, Grayson shakes his head. "Of course, you're defending her. Should have known the other night was just a fluke. Guess we're back to being on opposite sides of the battle lines."

"There doesn't need to be a battle at all," Logan counters.

"Tough shit. This war was started four years ago—long before you decided to grab a weapon and enter the fight."

Throwing up his hands, Logan sighs in exasperation. "I have no weapon. There is no war. There's only you and Riley and a fuckton of history that you *both* need to talk through."

Scoffing in derision, Grayson gestures toward Logan. "There you go again, taking her side."

"I'm not taking any fucking side," Logan snaps before straightening. "Actually, you know what? Yeah, I am taking her side, since you're being completely unreasonable." He sighs, shaking his head as though he's bone tired. "I love you like a brother, Grayson, but this has gotten out of control. Until you're ready to talk and listen, I don't know how to help you."

Grayson stares at Logan as though he's never seen him before, his teeth grinding and pain flashing behind his irises. "Good thing I don't need your help then," is all he says before storming away.

"Okay," I say after the silence has dragged out too long. Logan jerks his head from where Grayson disappeared to glance at me. "I won't shut my heart off from you."

Closing his eyes, he inhales deeply before opening them again, a weak smile coming to his lips. "Thank fuck for that, at least."

GRAYSON

CHAPTER TWELVE

The handle squeaks as I open the door to Gran's room. I'm exhausted after my first week back at Halston. Balancing my senior class schedule with running Van Doren Holdings is always challenging, although the true cause of my weariness is the tension simmering between me and the guys. The heaviness in the air every time I step into the house. The awkwardness that underpins every conversation.

That and my conversation with Gran last week have been weighing on my mind. I've tried to dismiss it as the ramblings of a sick woman, but how can I? How can I simply ignore the fear that was in her eyes? What she said about my dad possibly hurting—*killing*—my mom?

Perhaps it is just the Alzheimer's playing with her mind, but what if it isn't?

It's that, right there, that keeps me awake at night. That distracts me during meetings and interrupts whatever my lecturers are saying. Now, for the first time, I'm anxious as I step into Gran's room, unsure whether I want her to say more so I can determine the truth from imagination, and terrified of what else she might have to say.

"Who's there?" her frail voice calls, and I spy a crop of gray hair peeking above the top of her armchair.

"It's just me, Gran," I answer, closing the door behind me. "How are you today?"

"Who…" She twists in her chair, and I move so she can see me better, coming to crouch in front of her. "You. W-what are you doing here?"

Frowning, I set my hand over hers. "I wanted—"

"No." The trembling in her voice startles me. "Get out!"

"Gran, it's me. Gray—"

"Get out. Get out! GET OUT!" She's screaming by the end, her eyes glassy and demeanor frantic as she grabs the closest thing to her—a ball of yarn—and chucks it at me.

I stagger away, hands going up in a placating gesture. "Okay. Everything's okay."

"You can't be here!" she continues in a panicked state. "I don't want you here. Help! HELP!"

"What's going on in here?" a nurse asks as she hurries into the room.

"I—" I'm at a loss for words. Sometimes, Gran has been confused or easily agitated, but nothing like this. She's never… "I don't know what to do," I admit.

"Grace," the nurse addresses, her tone soft and soothing.

"He shouldn't be here!" Gran insists, pointing an accusing finger at me.

"Okay," the nurse easily agrees, turning to me. "Perhaps you should go."

I swallow roughly, reluctant to leave her when she's in this state.

"He shouldn't be here," Gran repeats, on the verge of sobbing this time. Seeing her so upset breaks my heart.

"Okay." I sigh. "I'm going. I'll leave. I—" I stare devastated at my Gran. "I'm sorry."

Gone are the tears in Gran's eyes, replaced by a lost sort of hardness aimed at me. "You're not capable of feeling sorry." The facade cracks. "You killed my baby girl. I will never forgive you."

Everything in me shatters. My dad... she thinks I'm my dad.

"Grayson," the nurse says carefully. "It's best if you go. I'll get her settled. She'll be okay."

I nod absently, but my feet remain superglued to the floor.

"She'll be okay," the nurse continues, and I finally tear my gaze away from Gran's frightened face.

"Yeah. Okay." I shake my head, pulling myself together. "Okay, I'll go. I'm sorry," I say to the nurse before leaving Gran's room with a heavy heart and even more questions than I had before.

Numb, I climb into my car as my phone buzzes. Pulling it out, the number for Springview Federal Correctional flashes across the screen. I send it to voicemail.

For the next several hours, I drive aimlessly around as day turns to night, and my headlights pop on, lighting up the road in front of me. I barely even notice. Seeing Gran deteriorate like this... it's painful to watch the woman who was once my anchor, my lighthouse, fade into nothing more than memories —possibly not even real ones at that.

How am I meant to see her every week if this is going to become a regular occurrence... her thinking I'm my dad? I don't want her to be terrified of me. I don't want my visits to bring about such pain. She's already suffered enough, losing her daughter and husband. I don't want to add to that. Not when she's so frail and I don't know how much time she has left.

The weight of being mistaken for my father weighs heavily on my chest. It's not that she didn't recognize me. It's her reaction to thinking I was my dad. That fear... how can it be imagined? *Is* it imagined? Was I so oblivious when I was younger that I missed her terror?

The not knowing is driving me insane, but I have no way of finding out. It's not like I can ask my father about it. I can't trust Gran's version of the truth... who else is there to talk to?

My mood is heavy when I finally pull up outside the house. The windows are dark, and for the first time in a while, I'm disappointed that no one is home. Recently, I've felt like an outsider walking into my own house. Avoiding the guys and actually feeling more at ease when they aren't around. Tonight, though, I feel like I need to talk.

Inside, I walk from room to room, unable to settle, but there's definitely no one here. It's a Friday night... Logan most likely has a game, and Royce is probably there.

Or maybe they're with her.

"Ugh," I groan aloud. I can't even handle thoughts of her.

"Your dad raped me, Grayson."

Unbidden, her words echo in my mind.

No. Not possible.

It's not like my dad actually *killed* my mom, despite what Gran is saying. Mom was sick. Dad played no part in that. She probably meant it metaphorically. Perhaps she blames him for not doing more, or maybe their marriage wasn't what she wanted for her daughter... there are so many ways Gran's words could be interpreted that aren't outright murder because that's just... not possible.

My dad may not be perfect. He may not even be a good man, but he's not a murderer, and he's certainly not a rapist.

RILEY

CHAPTER THIRTEEN

My muscles hurt from being on stage all night as I grab my bag, calling goodnight to the girls still in the dressing rooms as I head for the door.

I haven't spoken to Royce all week, and I find myself almost looking forward to our cone of silence in his car as he drives me home. There's something so simple yet precious about it. How many people can you say you can sit in comfortable silence with?

After all the craziness of a busy week, it's exactly what I need, and I'm hurrying toward the exit when Ben slides into my path, not looking the least bit happy with me.

Just great. Exactly what I need when I'm two feet from freedom.

"Ben," I state with a small yet tight smile. "My shift is over. I was just heading home." Of course, he knows this already. The final stragglers have just been kicked out, Royce along with them, when the front doors were closed and locked for the night, and other girls move past us, waving their goodbyes as they head out.

He boxes me in with his larger frame so he's towering above me, a purely intimidating move. "I'm receiving complaints from the other girls about how you're not pulling your weight," he starts. "The fact that you refuse to stay late on occasion to help tidy up is not fair on everyone else who has to pick up the slack."

I stare at him in outright shock. "That is not... I haven't been *refusing*..." I stammer.

"Blindly following the dictations set out by a jealous boyfriend is not a healthy relationship, Riley," he states in a pitying tone that makes me want to drag my nails down his face.

"He's not..." I trail off, unsure whether I would say my boyfriend or jealous. Both would be true, but the first is information I don't want Ben to know. I'd rather he think Royce is my boyfriend if it means he mostly leaves me alone. As for the second, Royce put down that stipulation to protect me, because he knows what a sleazebag Ben truly is.

"You can either explain to the other girls why they have to cover your workload, or you can get over this little... spat and get back to work."

My teeth grind furiously against one another as I stare up at him. He hasn't given me a choice at all. Not really.

"Fine," I hiss. "I'll get back to work."

His toothy smile is slimy. "That's my good girl."

Shudders roll through me as memories rush forward like water through a faucet. Bertram's face overlays on top of Ben's, forming a grotesque monster, and I must space out for a moment, because the next thing I know, Ben is snapping his fingers impatiently in front of my face.

"Well, don't just stand there. Get back to work!"

Needing to get away from him as fast as possible so he doesn't see how badly I'm trembling or notice the sweat now dotting my forehead, I scramble onto the club floor and begin the task of cleaning up.

I've barely been at it for five minutes when I hear yelling coming from outside, followed by banging on the front door.

"What in the actual hell is going on out there?" Ben gripes as he emerges from his office, stomping toward the chaos.

With a sense of foreboding, I trail after him, not entirely surprised when he unlocks the door and Royce flies through it. "Where is she?" he snarls menacingly, fisting the front of Ben's shirt and raising his other hand. "Tell me where the fuck she is this second or so help me god…" He completes his threat by driving his fist into Ben's face.

"Royce!" I half gasp, half chastise, although ultimately, I'm happy to see him. To know he cared enough to come searching for me when I didn't appear out front after my shift ended.

Besides, Ben deserved that punch for how he spoke to me earlier. I'm sure as shit not about to feel bad for the asshole who is now cursing up a storm.

Hearing his name, Royce's head snaps in my direction, his ice-blue eyes blazing with… concern? Could I be reading that correctly?

His gaze drops, searching every square inch of me as if expecting to find me battered and bruised, and I realize that it *is* concern I see in his eyes.

"I'm fine," I assure him.

"Of course she's fine," Ben grouses, holding his hand gingerly over his eye. "You heathen! What did you think was happening in here?"

Royce only snarls at him, an inhuman sound that has Ben shuffling backward even though his shirt is still being securely held in Royce's strangling grasp.

"Why aren't you outside?" he barks at me.

"I, uh, had to stay behind to clean up."

At my explanation, his nostrils flare and he whirls on Ben. "I thought I told you," he begins in a disturbingly calm tone, "that she wasn't to be alone with you. That she wasn't going to be staying behind after closing anymore and that you sure as fuck weren't going to ogle her while she goes about her job."

"We're only working," Ben snaps as though Royce is being ridiculous.

Royce huffs out a disbelieving breath, and before things escalate further, I step forward and place a placating hand on his forearm. "We were," I assure him. "Ben was in his office when we heard you," I explain, knowing he needs to hear it if there's any chance of us ending this without more fists flying.

Seeming to forget about Ben's presence entirely, he lets him go and turns to me, dropping his face to mine so his intense stare can bore into my eyes while he searches for the truth behind my words.

Only when he finds it does he relax—which, by Royce's standards, means he's still coiled tightly, but at least he isn't one wrong word away from ripping out Ben's esophagus.

"Are you done with your temper tantrum now?" Ben snarks snidely. *Jeez, it's almost like the guy has a death wish.*

Any progress I'd made with Royce instantly vanishes as he glares at my boss. "If she's in here with you, then so am I."

"Absolutely not. That's against policy. All patrons have to be off the premises by 2 am."

With an unbothered shrug of his shoulders, Royce volleys, "Then I guess we're both leaving. Have fun doing the rest of the cleaning by yourself."

Wrapping his much larger hand around mine, he pulls me toward the door, but as we reach it, Ben throws his arm out, stopping us. His eyes bulge with unrestrained rage. "This is *my* club. *I* decide when my employees are done and when they can leave."

Lifting a haughty eyebrow, Royce asks, "So, which will it be? Am I leaving now with Riley, or are we both staying?"

The seconds tick down like the timing device on an explosive, before Ben finally hisses, "Fine, you can both stay." Pointing his finger at a table, he dictates, "You, sit your ass down there and leave her to get on with her work."

"I'm not the one who enjoys distracting his employees with unwanted come-ons."

Aaaaand that's enough of that. Tightening my hold on Royce's hand, I drag him toward an empty table and away from the impending fistfight.

"Sit there," I say under my breath, feeling Ben's eyes boring into my back. "I'll be done as soon as I can."

"No need to rush. I'm not going anywhere." He says it loud enough for Ben to hear as he makes himself obviously comfortable in the chair.

"God give me strength," I whisper aloud, earning a smirk from Royce as I turn away from him and get back to work.

It's safe to say the next half hour is one of the worst I've ever had to endure. Ben, most likely in an attempt not to appear perturbed by Royce's trespassing, doesn't return to his office. Instead, he lingers near the bar while I move around the room, wiping down tables and stacking chairs on top of them.

He and Royce spend the entire time in some weird standoff where neither of them actually says anything, but the tension is so thick in the room that it's like moving through sludge.

"All done," I finally call out, more than ready to get the hell out of here. Except, when I approach Royce, he makes no move to get up.

In fact, he ignores me altogether, his stare fixed on Ben where he's standing, pretending to rearrange the bottles of alcohol behind the bar.

"You're only a manager," Royce states. He says it casually, like he doesn't know he's starting something by saying it.

Internally, I groan.

"Excuse me?" Ben growls, spine stiffening as he glares at Royce through the large mirror that hangs on the wall behind the bar.

"You said earlier that this is your club, but that's not true now, is it?" At Ben's silence, he continues. "You know, the thing about working in an elite college town is that practically all of your patrons have money and connections. It wouldn't take much to remove the little bit of power you think you have here."

Spinning around to face the threat in front of him, Ben is simmering with rage as he spits, "Are you threatening me?"

Royce laughs, the sound cold and caustic. "Threatening? No, I don't need to threaten the likes of you. I'm simply reminding you that you're a bug I could flatten beneath my palm and replace without so much as lifting a finger." He finally stands, not once removing his gaze from my boss as he threads his fingers through mine, a clear message which Ben picks up on as his gaze darts to our joined hands before returning to Royce's face when he says, "You might be in charge within these walls, but out there, you're nothing. A nobody. In my world, nobodies have a way of vanishing without a trace."

With a final, searing stare, Royce pulls on my hand, and we cross the room. Ben's stunned silence trails us. "My bag," I say quietly as we approach the door, and he lets go so I can grab it from where I left it near the door. When I return to his side, he presses his hand against my lower spine as he pulls open the door, ushering me out into the night.

"I hate that smarmy fucker," Royce hisses once we're inside his truck. "What did he say to get you to stay behind?"

I blow out a weary breath. "He said the other girls were complaining about having to pick up my slack because I refuse to stay late, and even if it's not true, he makes a valid point. It's not fair to the others. If I don't stay, one of them has to. It's not like he's any worse with me than with them. Why should I get out of it when they have to suffer?"

"Fuck, I hate it when you get all logical," he gripes, face pinched in a tight frown.

A surprised laugh barks out of me, bringing a ghost of a smile to Royce's lips.

"The next time he corners you about staying late, text me, okay?"

I run my eyes over his serious expression. "I'd have to have your number to do that."

God, that came out way too flirty.

Not to mention, I shouldn't be asking for things like his number.

Except, when he came barging through that door tonight, I instantly felt safer. And the fact he barely wasted any time at all before coming to seek me out... I don't have to forgive Royce; I don't even have to like him. Nevertheless, I *do* trust him to protect me from Ben. For whatever reason, he's taken up that mantle, and Royce isn't the kind of man to take on a task without seeing it all the way through.

He holds out his hand, silently demanding my phone, and I pass it over with only a moment's hesitation.

The angel on my shoulder tells me I shouldn't be creating any more ties with these boys, and the devil on my other one whispers *do it.*

Royce didn't know me when Grayson started this little vendetta. All he knew was what Grayson told him, and with that knowledge, can you blame the guy for hating my guts? I'd hate me too... Especially given the lie I suspect was made against him. The damage something like that would have done... makes Royce's actions more than understandable.

And after he found out the truth... he kept Grayson and

Logan away, despite the fact I'm sure that put a strain on his friendships with them.

He's actively sought out my work schedule so he'd be here every night I'm on shift, and followed me home in the early hours of the morning.

So why shouldn't I give him my number? Why shouldn't I place this one bit of trust in his hands? I'm already trusting him not to tell the others about Aurora. If I'm entrusting him with her safety, then it's only fair that I trust him with my own.

"I sent myself a message from your phone, so I have yours if something like tonight happens again," he says as the phone in his pocket vibrates.

As he hands mine back to me, I notice the red abrasions on his knuckles. "Your hand," I gasp, reaching for it instead of the phone as I bring it closer to inspect. "You've cut yourself."

"Fucker has a hard face. It's nothing. Barely a scratch."

I frown at his dismissal. I get that he's a fighter and all, and this is probably nothing to him, but knowing he got it trying to protect me makes me feel guilty.

"They'll be a million times worse after my fight this weekend."

"You're fighting at The Depot this weekend?"

"Sunday, yeah. I'm up against Bruiser, a brute of a fighter. Got a body like granite. I always take a good battering when I'm up against him."

I gape in horror. It might have been hot watching him in the ring, but it baffles me how someone can so casually discuss getting beat up like that. But I guess, if you have the balls to step into that ring, how is discussing it any worse?

He shrugs it off, putting the car in gear as we finally exit the lot and drive to my apartment in silence. By the time he pulls up outside, I've made a decision.

"You're coming upstairs with me."

He blinks at me in surprise. *Yeah, can't say I blame him.*

I gesture toward his swollen knuckles. "If you have a fight in a couple of days, your hand needs to be in top shape. It's my fault you had to punch him. The least I can do is ice it for you and wrap it to stop any more swelling overnight."

Leaning across the center console, Royce puts himself in front of my face. "Let's get one thing straight. I punched that asshole because he had it coming, and because I wanted to. You are not to blame; do not take on that responsibility."

"All the same, I want to make sure it's okay for your fight. After all, according to Tara, you're one of the best fighters at The Depot. I'd hate for you to ruin your street cred over some swollen knuckles. Especially to someone called *Bruiser.*"

He huffs out a chuckle, shaking his head as he retreats to his side of the car. Still, his gaze bores into me with enough heat that I begin to sweat. "Fine. I'll let you play nursemaid if it'll make you feel better."

"It will."

He follows me out of the car, into my building, and up the stairs to my apartment. My anxiousness ratchets with every stair we climb until my hands visibly shake as I slide my key into the lock and open the door, inviting him inside. I expect him to run his eyes over every inch of the small, sparsely furnished apartment. Only instead he stands in front of the closed door, staring at me while I fiddle with my keys and stare right back.

This is... new territory.

I feel like I'm standing on the threshold of his bedroom all over again, except the roles are reversed this time. After everything I've shared, I shouldn't feel so awkward about having him in my apartment. The two of us alone. And yet, after the loud bustle of the club and even the hostile tension underlying every moment when I was in their house, the silence now is... immense.

Despite the excessive amount of time we've spent staring at one another across the crowded club floor... This is a new step in our dynamic. Another layer chipped away.

"Have a seat. I'll grab some ice," I say, gesturing toward the small two-seater breakfast bar that divides the kitchen from the living room. "Thanks to Logan, I have *bags* of it."

"He's still sending you food deliveries?"

"Every few days, despite me telling him not to. I'm pretty sure he has no concept of how much regular people eat."

"Well, he is an athlete, so he probably eats three times what you do. And with me and Gray in the house, we consume more food per week than the average household."

Chuckling, I say, "I bet that's true."

"Logan's been attempting to work his way back into your good graces?" There's a hint of a smile in his voice that has me looking his way as I grab the bag of ice from the freezer.

"How do you know about that?"

With a scoff, he says, "You think I don't hear all about *the best lunches of his life* every night when he gets home?"

"He does not!" I gape.

"Oh, he does. In excruciating detail and with far too many emotions involved. He's worse than a girl. If he had his way, he'd probably have us painting on our nails and devouring gallons of ice cream while we brainstorm ways to make it up to you."

I can't help the laugh that slips from me as I grin, imagining exactly that.

"I'm glad you find my suffering amusing."

"It could be worse," I say with a wry smirk. "You could have Barbie pink nails and braided beads in your beard."

He bursts out laughing. "Logan would be buried ten feet under if he even approached me with a nail polish brush."

Since he's brought it up, I dare to ask, "How, uh, are things between the three of you?" as I go about wrapping the ice in a clean dish towel.

The humor slides from his face, and his exhausting sigh tells me everything. "Strained. Awkward as fuck. Mainly between Grayson and me, and Logan and Grayson. I wanna throttle him and tell him to wise the fuck up."

Once the towel is secured around the ice, I walk over to where Royce is perched at the kitchen island. Resting my hip against the counter, I press the ice against his raw knuckles. "I'm sorry. I know I'm to blame for the two of you being at odds."

"Riley," he says with a sigh, leaning closer. Even seated, I don't have any height advantage. All it does is bring us face-to-face. "You need to stop apologizing for shit that's not your fault. As humans, we make enough mistakes that we have to apologize for, never mind taking on issues we have no control over."

"Don't I, though—have at least some control over it? I could have talked to him... Or—"

"Or nothing. You did try to talk to him. You tried to tell all of us, and we wouldn't listen. That's on us—on him. Not you."

"Yeah, but I just left your house and told you to keep them away..." I scrunch my nose.

"Yeah, after we kidnapped you and tried to make you our sex slave for the holidays." Royce's lips flatten. "I never did apologize for my role in all of that."

Glancing down at his hand on the worktop, I lift off the dish towel to inspect his knuckles before applying pressure again. "No, you didn't." I can't seem to raise my head to look at him. Honestly, an apology is the last thing I expected from Royce. He's not the kind of guy who apologizes. He's the type who proudly wears his mistakes. Boldly stands in the face of them. Yeah, he'll admit that he's wrong, but he won't apologize for being so.

Calloused fingers gently wrap around my chin, slowly pulling my face to his. "Then let me tell you now how sorry I am for not believing you. For thinking the worst of you. For forcing you to put up walls between us and for not having your back when you needed it the most." His thumb rubs back and forth across the angle of my jaw, making it almost impossible to concentrate on his words. "However, I can't say I'm sorry for bringing you into my house. If I hadn't, I never would have gotten to glimpse the real you. I'd have been left with this horrifically incorrect assumption of who you are, and what a travesty that would have been."

My throat is dry, and I have to run my tongue along my lips to moisten them. "What about the blow job and lap dances?"

His smirk turns devilish as he tilts his head, bringing his lips to my ear and dousing my senses in the rich smell of leather and something heady. *When the hell did we get so close?* "Can't say I'm sorry for those, either. Especially since I know you enjoyed them as much as I did."

His free hand rests on my hip before slowly caressing up my waist and over my ribs before sliding around to my back. All the while, he runs his nose up the column of my neck and presses the ghost of kisses along my jaw as my breathing grows more erratic.

"Riley, if you don't want anything to happen, then I need you to step away because I'm about to lose whatever self-control I have, and all I can think about right now is kissing you."

The rough rasp of his voice gives away how affected he is.

I don't move. Not even sure that I can.

He pulls back just enough to meet my gaze, and somehow, I find the coherence to speak. "This doesn't mean I forgive you."

Another one of those sinful smirks tilts his lips. "I know."

With a firm press of his palm against my back, I fall into him, my lips colliding with his in an electrified kiss. I forget that I'm angry at him. Forget that he played me. That he's Grayson's best friend and emotionally damaged.

I forget about everything other than how incredibly amazing it is to kiss him; in the unforgettable magnetism that has always existed between us. Chemistry has never been our issue. I've always wanted him, and he has always wanted me. The only thing holding us back before was that he thought I was someone I was not.

Now... Now, I'm not sure what's going to happen. What I *want* to happen. What I do know is that I *really,* really enjoy the feel of his skin against mine. His hand on my neck, pulling my body in closer.

The dish towel and ice are forgotten as the temperature soars, and I somehow end up between his legs, one hand pulling on his strands of hair as the other explores his chest and shoulder.

My body molds to his, my hormones going wild as my hips rock, desperate for some sort of friction. I'm on the verge of wrapping my legs around him and completely giving myself over to this insane need escalating inside of me when he eases back.

"I'll never get enough of kissing you, but we should probably stop." It's the deep rasp in his voice and pupils blown wide with desire that tells me the last thing he wants to do is stop, but unlike me, he hasn't completely lost all common sense.

"That's probably wise," I agree breathlessly. With his hands cupping my neck, he rests his forehead against mine and closes his eyes. "This is not at all where I intended tonight to end up, but I'm definitely not sorry. Kinda wishing I'd punched that asshole a week ago now."

I snort a laugh. "You're not very good at apologizing, are you?"

"It's the first genuine one I've ever given, so you'll have to cut me some slack. By the time I've earned your forgiveness, I'll be an expert."

"Is that so?" I ask with an arched brow. "You're so certain I'm going to forgive you."

His smirk is all self-assured cockiness. "I am. Wanna know why?"

I nod, my forehead rubbing against his.

"Because I couldn't stay away from you when I thought you were responsible for the ruin of Gray's family. Despite the type of person I believed you to be, you consumed my every waking moment. Drove me completely fucking wild dancing for me in the club.

"So long as we're around one another, this chemistry between us will keep pulling us into one another's orbit. Whenever I'm around you, I want to strip you down and take my time learning every dip and curve of your body, and I *know* you're just dying for me to push you to your knees and make you choke on my cock. I bet your panties are drenched purely from that kiss." He smirks knowingly, the asshole. Of course, he's right. The second he leaves, I'll be using the shower head to give myself some relief. Otherwise, I'll be tossing and turning all night.

"I'm sorry, what does our mutual desire to jump one another's bones have to do with me eventually forgiving you?"

At my teasing tone, his eyes shine with mirth and something softer and out of place on his usually harsh face.

"It has *everything* to do with it because it makes it impossible to elude one another. Unable to deny this attraction between us, which means whatever this connection is, it's strong." He grows serious, his expression unnaturally vulnerable. "I've never been this consumed by another person before. What we have is rare and powerful. With time and nourishment, it'll be a force to be reckoned with. *We* will be a force to be reckoned with. I don't believe even you can overcome it."

"So you're saying it's inevitable, and I should just throw in the towel and forgive you right now?"

"Definitely not. I'm saying *we're* inevitable, but you should absolutely make me work to earn your forgiveness. Only then can we enter this on equal footing, with no regrets or self-doubt." His fingers stroke down my cheek. "I have my own demons I need to work through, too, so take all the time you need, James. I'll be here when you're ready." He dives in for a lingering kiss. "And in the meantime, I plan on stealing as many of these as I can."

With my heart fluttering and breath uneven, I step away, grabbing the towel of ice and placing it in the sink as I gather myself. "I should wrap your hand," I say in a voice that is not my own.

"You don't have to." He clenches his hand, showing me just how okay it is. Still, I don't relent, grabbing the things from my little first aid kit.

"Do you want a hot chocolate?" I offer when I'm done, finding myself not wanting him to leave just yet.

His stare bounces back and forth between my eyes. "Sure."

I haven't had hot chocolate in the apartment since moving to Halston, but I've been dying to make a cup since it came in one of Logan's deliveries earlier in the week.

Making each of us a cup, I hand him his, and we sit on the sofa. He's careful to leave a gap between us, and I mentally applaud him for his respect, even if my body craves his closeness.

Bringing the steaming mug to my lips, I sip it with a sigh as I watch him over the rim of my mug.

His lips twitch in a wry smirk. "Something caught your attention?"

"Just realizing that *fuck off* on your forehead has disappeared."

He snorts. "Believe me, Ry, it's still there. Just not when it comes to you."

"Did you really think I was stalking you?" I ask curiously. "Isn't that a bit self-obsessed? You're not *that* desirable."

My attitude earns me an arched brow, one filled with sly seduction. *Really?* It says. *Is that why you couldn't stay away?* I promptly ignore it.

"Why would I go out of my way to invoke your wrath?" Drawing my finger in a circle around his face, indicating the mean mug he's perfected, I state, "No dick is worth that."

He chokes on his hot chocolate.

"In my defense, *no one* from Halston would be caught dead in The Depot."

"Except for you three." I counter.

He shrugs. A blatant, *well, yeah.*

"Why is that?"

"Fuck if I know, James. Maybe because we're all broken in a way the other students aren't. Our demons are closer to the surface. There's a weight, a darkness that sets us apart. I'm not saying no other student has their issues. Every single one of us is fractured, yes, but we…"

"—Your cracks are chasms," I finish when he appears stumped for words. "Your demons aren't content to lurk in the corners and bide their time. They whisper in your ear, piercing through the relative peace until they dance in the center of your existence. Making it so you can't function around them."

"Yes," Royce agrees, eyes shining with understanding. "And

when you carry those demons for long enough, your every breath becomes laden. Every step echoes of your battle fought in silence."

"It's in those ink-dark waters that the three of you became united," I piece together.

"Like recognizes like," Royce states, astute eyes on me. "But you know that as well as I do."

Because it's in those same dark, icy waters of isolation that I found each of them. Where the tendrils of the darkness encasing my soul unfurled and reached out to him. To Logan. To Grayson. And whispered *hello*.

A heavy stillness falls over us. An acknowledgment of the traumas wrapped like a silent shroud around each of us, impelling a solitude that most dare not touch. However, I am not afraid. Nor is Royce. We stare into the face of one another's trauma, and we do not recoil. For we appreciate what many others would not—the resilience of the human spirit, the embodiment of shadows turned to strength, the wisp of light that can be borne from the darkest of nights.

ROYCE

CHAPTER FOURTEEN

I can't stop replaying our kiss last night. How fucking good it felt. How I had to physically pull myself back to stop us from going any further. I wanted to. God, did I want to... and I know in the moment she wanted to as well. However, knowing she didn't trust me absolutely was enough incentive for me to stop it before it could go any further.

I shouldn't even have allowed myself to kiss her. That hadn't been on my agenda. When she's invading my senses like that, it makes it impossible for me to think straight. All I want to do is touch. Taste. Devour.

If that asshole boss of hers hadn't tried to pull a move last night, I never would have let her beguile me into going up to her apartment. She never would have gotten that close to me. Without the barrier of my truck's central console, I was helpless to stop myself from touching what wasn't mine.

And then I went and told her we were fucking inevitable, when what I should have said was that she needs to stay away from me. That I'm not good enough for her. That I'm irreparably damaged and unfixable and incapable of giving her what she needs.

And when she finds out the accusations that have been levied against me... she'll want nothing to do with me after that. She'll fall... and hit the ground when she learns how interconnected my past is with hers.

The trauma it might cause her... bringing up those memories for her is the last thing I want to do.

Which is why I should be staying away. Observing from a distance, protecting her from the shadows. Except, she makes it impossible to stay away. To resist. To deny.

"You're looking particularly tortured today," Logan teases as he walks into the kitchen, where I've been staring into my coffee cup for so long that it's gone cold.

"Lot on my mind," I mumble, standing up and emptying the contents down the sink before refilling it from the pot.

Logan is watching me with a frown. "Did something happen with Riley? You said that boss of hers is a sleazeball. Did he try to pull something last night?"

"It's not that. I... kissed Riley."

"Bastard." There's no heat behind Logan's insult, and when I glance up at him, he's smirking. "What the fuck are you looking so put out for, then? I can tell you, if I got the chance to kiss Riley again, I sure as fuck wouldn't look like someone pissed in my cereal."

"Because I shouldn't have kissed her," I blurt out in exasperation. "What's going to happen when she learns of my past?"

"Man, that was a false allegation. Riley will understand that."

"Maybe she will, although what seeds of doubt will it plant in her head? What triggers might it provoke? Memories that might resurface? She doesn't deserve to relive her trauma."

Logan has the good grace to grimace.

"Beyond that, what happened... it fucked me up. It's *still* fucking me up. The Ellingtons have proven that they can come back at any time and rip my dreams away from me."

"Royce, they can't take Riley away from you."

"Can't they? They took my football career."

"Yeah, but Riley isn't someone to be bought or easily swayed. If anything, her past makes it easier for her to differentiate the truth from the lies. Show her who *you* are, and she'll have no doubt that you're telling her the truth."

I shake my head, refusing to believe him. Refusing to give myself even that little speck of hope. "I'll only bring more baggage to her door."

"Maybe you should let Riley decide that. Isn't that what we're doing? Giving Riley control? Letting her make the decisions; letting her set the pace. Just focus on making it up to her. If she decides she wants more, then I imagine you'll be unable to say no, so there's no point beating yourself up about it."

"You give the worst advice," I grumble, leaning back against the countertop as I nurse my fresh cup of coffee.

"I give the best advice, but enough about you. I need your help, and since you and Riley are on kissing terms, you're in the best position to help me come up with ideas to prove to her that I'm on her team."

"No. Absolutely not. I'm not doing that."

"What? Why not?" he moans. "I need help! Something that shows her how much she means to me."

"You could try telling her," I drawl sarcastically before mentally slapping myself for engaging him at all.

"Don't you think I've done that? My words mean nothing, apparently. I have to *show* it. Actions speak louder than words and all that jazz. I'm still debating getting her a car. There's this cool pink SUV I found that I think she'd totally dig, though she's made it clear that she doesn't want me to pay for everything for her, so maybe I should save that for later..."

"That would probably be wise," I deadpan. "Riley's all about the small stuff. The meaningful everyday things," I tack on before once again chastising myself for getting involved. Logan's going to do whatever Logan is going to do. He doesn't need my help, and I don't want to be tossed to the dogs when whatever he ultimately lands on backfires.

"I know that," he argues with a pout. "I've been doing that. It just doesn't feel like enough. I feel like I need to do more. Do something that genuinely proves to her how sorry I am."

Oh, for fuck's sake. "Riley's not like you. She's not a showy person. You don't need to give her big, public gestures. She doesn't need you to announce to the world that you're sorry or fix every little problem in her life by throwing money at it," I try to explain to him.

"You're right," he says with a determined set to his jaw that has me internally groaning. "I've been thinking too small. I need to go bigger."

"That's not even close to what I said," I argue. However, it's obvious he isn't listening as his eyes light up with a gleam that alarms me.

"Thanks for the chat, man. I gotta go get ready for tonight's game."

As he walks away, I call after him, "I didn't fucking say anything! Whatever you're thinking, I want no part in it. This conversation never happened!"

Asshole doesn't even respond.

I'm only left in peace for a few moments before the front door opens and Grayson walks in, t-shirt sticking to him and hair soaked from his run.

"Hey," he says breathlessly before filling a glass of water and downing it.

"Hi." Silence falls between us, rare and out of place.

"Where were you last night," he asks, wiping the sweat from his forehead. "I was looking for you. Wanted to talk."

"What did you wanna talk about?" I ask, deliberately avoiding his question about where I was.

Of course, the asshole notices, his eyes narrowing in thought before he connects the dots. "Seriously? You're still stalking her at that club?"

"It's none of your business," I growl. Before this can escalate into an argument, I repeat, "What did you wanna talk about?"

He shakes his head. "Forget about it. It's nothing." He goes to walk away, but I yank him back by the neckline of his top.

"No, it does matter. You've been a moody bastard recently. You look like shit, and you're never here." I scour his face with a frown, trying to understand. "Tell me what's going on with you."

With another shake of his head, he says, "I can't right now. I've gotta go meet with my dad's lawyers. You going to Logan's hockey game tonight?"

I nod. "Yeah. You should come. He'd appreciate the support."

"Yeah, maybe," he responds noncommittally.

"What about tomorrow night after my fight?" I suggest in a bid to fix this shit between us. "The three of us sit down with a couple of beers and talk."

He pauses for a moment, debating before finally agreeing. "That works."

"I mean, really talk, Gray," I emphasize. "This shit has gone on long enough. We're a family, it's about time we started acting like one, yeah?"

Despite the shadows around his eyes, his posture straightens like a load has been lifted off him. "Yeah. I'd like that."

With a small smile, he walks off, and I call after him, "Come to Logan's game tonight!"

All I get is a two-finger wave over his shoulder as he climbs the stairs to his room. Alone, I check the time, deciding I have enough time to burn off some of these *tortured thoughts* as Logan so kindly put them before I need to get ready for his game.

I can berate myself for giving into my desires all I want, but at the end of the day, Logan's right. I don't plan on leaving Riley unprotected, and so long as I'm around her, what will happen will happen. Neither of us has any real control.

There might be some truth in his words... if I can bring myself to open up to Riley. If I can let her in, let her get to know me, then perhaps what we have won't end in disaster.

If there was ever a woman who stood a chance at getting to know me, it's Riley... I just have to figure out how to open up to her.

RILEY

CHAPTER FIFTEEN

"Girls' night!" Isabella squeals when I open my door on Saturday night. Since I wasn't scheduled to work, I suggested a girls' night to Ava when I ran into her at the dance studio during the week. We haven't had a chance to catch up recently. Between her spending Christmas with her mom and me hiding away from the world for the remainder of winter break, we are overdue a chill night in. Just the three of us.

Isabella is already in her pajamas with a fuzzy pink robe on and Monsters, Inc. slippers on her feet as she flounces into my apartment, a blanket in one hand and a new-looking tablet in her other.

I'm smiling to myself as I watch her get situated on the sofa, even as shards of glass embed themselves beneath my skin because I haven't seen or spoken to my daughter since Christmas Day. Nearly three whole weeks. Usually, by this point in the month, Mom is harassing me for money, and I can use that as leverage to get a few minutes with my little girl, but all I've received is the odd text telling me she's *busy*.

Hopefully, this week, she starts to get desperate for money.

The distance from Rora never gets easier. Perhaps I should have adjusted to it by now. After all, I've been away from her for six months, but it still hurts not being able to see her every day or talk to her. I don't know what shows she's watching at the moment or who her best friend is, and it's killing me.

"Whatever you're cooking in here smells amazing," Ava says, pulling me out of my dark thoughts as she follows her daughter inside.

"Thanks. It's nothing much, but since my cupboards are overflowing with food I thought I'd cook something up for us."

"It'll go perfectly with the wine I brought." She holds up a bottle of white wine for me to see before grabbing two glasses from my cupboard. Twisting the lid, she pours a hefty measure into both glasses, and we sit down in my kitchen to chat while I wait for the timer on the oven to go off as Isabella entertains herself on her tablet.

"Did you have a good time at your mom's?" I ask.

"We did. Isabella loved spending so much time with her."

"How is she doing after her fall?"

"She's great. I'd worried that was the beginning of a downward spiral with her, but she's recovered fantastically. Was running around after Izzy better than I can."

I chuckle at Ava's wry grin, before she asks, "What about you? Did you have a quiet Christmas? See any family?"

Shaking my head, I respond vaguely, "I mostly just stayed in and read."

"Mmm, several weeks of uninterrupted reading time... I could totally get behind that."

"Oh, dinner's ready," I say, changing the subject as the timer goes and I get up to plate the food.

When we've finished eating, I grab the TV remote and flick it on. Tonight's hockey game flashes onto the screen and Isabella cries out, "Mommy, look! Hockey!"

Ava chuckles at her daughter and says, "I see that, baby." To me, she explains, "Isabella is crazy about hockey at the moment. I gave her my phone to watch TikTok videos one day and she somehow ended up on ice hockey ones. The teams were doing these challenges and attempting to copy figure skater moves. Anyway, she found it hilarious and now she's obsessed."

"Is that right?" I chuckle and Isabella nods.

"They did this one where they had to step over their stick while in their skates, and one player kept falling on his bum." She laughs hysterically like it's the funniest thing ever.

"Have you ever watched a real game?" I ask her. When she shakes her head, I move to sit beside her on the sofa. "Oh, well, you've been missing out. I just got into hockey recently too, and I love watching the games."

"You have?"

"Yup. You wanna sit and watch this one with me, and maybe we can see it live next time."

"Oh, Riley, you don't have to do that," Ava begins.

"It's fine. A friend of mine is on the team at Halston. I'll have to ask him, but I'm sure he can wrangle us some tickets, even if they're nosebleed seats."

She smiles gratefully as Isabella jumps up and down. "Yes! Mommy, please. Can we go?"

"If Riley can get the tickets, then we'll go," she agrees, laughing.

"YESSSS!!!" Isabella squeals as the opening music thunders through the speakers in preparation for announcing the team's players.

"Oh, here we go. If you watch, you'll see the players emerging from the tunnel. They always do a loop of the ice so they can wave at their fans before the game begins."

One by one, the players spit out of the tunnels to thumping music and screaming fans. "See that one there," I say when

Logan appears, his charismatic grin fully on as he waves at the crowd. "That's my friend. He's going to play professional hockey one day."

"Wow, really?" Isabella gasps.

"Yup." He may not have had an offer yet—at least, that I'm aware of—but I just know he will. Before he graduates from Halston, Logan will have been recruited to a professional team. It's what he was born to do.

"Just a friend, huh?" Ava teases, and when I look at her, I find her watching me knowingly.

"Just a friend."

Her smirk says she's not buying my bullshit, and before she can ask any probing questions, I return my attention to the TV in time to see Logan skate toward where the cameraman is.

"What is he doing?" Ava asks.

I have no idea. He gets right up in the cameraman's face and stares into the screen leaving me no choice but to soak in his chestnut eyes, his pupils enlarged with the adrenaline pumping through his body. After a moment, he smirks, and I huff out a laugh as he winks at the screen.

"Why do I get the impression that's for you?"

Refusing to indulge Ava, I continue to watch the screen as Logan skates away, and I catch sight of the back of his jersey.

"Holy, Riley. Why is that boy wearing your name on his jersey?"

I can't answer her, too busy gaping at the screen as Logan skates over to join his teammates.

No. No way that just happened. Logan Astor *did not* just get on the ice tonight with my name stitched on his jersey.

Except he most definitely did because now even the sports-casters are discussing it, wondering who *Riley* is and what she means to Logan.

"Your pink cheeks confirm it's undeniably you and not some other Riley he's making a statement for."

Wide-eyed, I turn to Ava, who bursts out laughing. "Oh, next girls' night, I'm getting someone to babysit so I can ply you with alcohol and find out what spicy secrets you've been keeping."

"No, Mommy!" Isabella protests. "I wanna come too!"

"Definitely not, Izzy baby. These are adult secrets. Not for your ears until you're at least thirty-five."

The three of us are transfixed to the screen as the game gets underway. Logan has a new cheerleader in Isabella, who spends most of the first period standing directly in front of the TV, jumping up and down every time he has possession of the puck and screaming when he makes a goal.

By the time they leave, Isabella has exhausted herself and is fast asleep in Ava's arms. We had so much fun painting our nails and doing face masks once the game was over. Closing the door behind them, I saunter back to the sofa, picking up the remote and unmuting the television before pulling a blanket around me.

The station is replaying a post-game press event from earlier tonight, and I turn up the volume.

"Logan, I think everyone noticed tonight that you didn't have Astor written on the back of your jersey. Who's the special person you played tonight's game for?"

Logan, already grinning like he won the Stanley Cup, says, "Well, John, for now, I'll just say that she's a pretty special person. In fact, she's become the most important person in my life recently, and tonight, I just wanted to show her that."

The room erupts into chaos as everyone begins firing questions at him. I'm only able to make out a few, asking for a last name and if Logan is officially off the market, but Logan ignores them all as he lifts his hand, saying goodnight to the room before walking off the stage.

As the TV moves on to the next program, I get lost in my thoughts. I did tell Logan his words didn't mean anything, so I probably should have guessed he'd show me in an entirely Logan way.

Chewing on my lower lip, I grab my phone and pull up our message thread. I haven't texted him since the day Royce brought me home, and I take my time typing out a message.

ME

Interesting game tonight.

A split second later, his name flashes up on my screen as he calls, and I hesitate before clicking accept.

"I was hoping you were watching."

"Oh, you know, the TV was on in the background. So it just so happened to come on."

"Uh-huh, if that's the story you need to tell yourself, Shortcake."

Huddled up on my sofa, my blanket wrapped around me and my phone balanced on my knees, I say, "You put my name on your jersey."

I can practically hear the smile in Logan's voice. "I put your name on my jersey, Riley."

"Aren't I supposed to wear your name? Isn't that the thing that girls do?"

He groans. "Baby, don't go giving me mental images like that. I'm trying to be good here, and the thought of you in my jersey is like fucking kryptonite."

I chuckle, before bringing us back to the topic at hand. "Why did you put my name on your jersey, Logan?"

"Because I want everyone to know how gone for you I am. I don't give a shit about puck bunnies or other girls or any of that. I'm off the market. Even if it takes you years to forgive me, I'm still not interested in anyone else, and I want them to know it. I want *you* to know it. More than that, I wore your name on my jersey because it's you I'm thinking of every time I step out on that ice. You're the one motivating me to push harder, to go faster. To be better. And maybe I wanted a little bit of you with me when I'm out there, even if it's just your name on my jersey."

My throat is raw when I swallow.

"It sounds quiet where you are. Aren't you out celebrating?"

"Nah, I wasn't feeling it tonight. And might have been hoping you'd message. Royce, the asshole, deleted your number from my phone."

"He what?" I'm shocked, even as warmth floods me at knowing Royce went that far for me. "I was a little impressed with your self-control. I expected you to bang my door down my first night back here."

"Hey, I do have some self-control. Although even I can admit I wouldn't have been able to resist messaging you if he hadn't done that. I'm memorizing your number, so I can just put it back in if he pulls that stunt again." He falls silent for a moment. "He said you wanted space... I was trying to respect that."

"I know," I respond sincerely. "Have you heard anything from the scouts that came to your game?"

There's a momentary pause on his end, before I hear him clearing his throat. "Nothing that I'm interested in taking."

"Ah, already a high-maintenance professional hockey player. What, their perks aren't good enough? Only guaranteeing four-star accommodations on road trips? Oh, no, is the car they offer you a basic sedan? None of the bells and whistles fancy-pants Logan Astor is accustomed to?"

"Damn, woman, that's cold." He can barely get the words out from laughing so hard. "Nah, nothing so non-negotiable as that. Just not sure that the team is the right fit for me. Holding out for something more suitable."

"Well, I'm sure you'll get it."

"I plan on it, Shortcake. I plan on it."

RILEY

CHAPTER SIXTEEN

My initial response is a middle finger emoji while I debate my actual answer. The day has just turned to dusk and now night, I've been thinking more and more about Royce's fight. After reading the same page three times and not taking in a single word, I gave up studying a half hour ago.

I'd messaged him Saturday morning to check that his hand was okay, and the photo he sent me showed his knuckles looking as good as new. I wasn't sure what to say after that, and with Royce not being much of a talker, nothing else was said. Only that doesn't mean I haven't thought of him.

He mentioned what a tough fight this would be, and I'm

woman enough to admit that I'm worried for him. Which has me wanting to say yes to Tara's offer. Does that make me an idiot? For not wanting to stay away? To put heaps of distance between us?

Except, he was right the other night when he said we keep getting pulled into one another's orbit. The thing is... I kinda want to be dragged into his orbit. Royce is such a mystery. Is it so bad that I want to unravel him?

I sense that there is so much more to Royce than meets the eye. Already, he's proven to be a dichotomy. At first, he's abrupt and cold. His large, muscular build makes him instantly intimidating, and his stern glare does nothing to put you at ease. Yet underneath all that posturing is a sensitive soul. One that's taken a beating. One that resonates with mine, and perhaps that's why I can't stay away. Why neither of us can seem to resist the lure of the other?

However, it's not just Royce I'd be seeing tonight if I went...

Having already checked the school's website earlier, I know Logan doesn't have a game tonight. Meaning he'll definitely be there, and am I ready to see him after the stunt he pulled at last night's game? He asked me not to close my heart off to him, and after he stood up for me with Whitney and Grayson, I feel like I should give him a shot. Not let him all the way in. It's too early for that, but I could at least crack open a window for him.

That only leaves devil number three. The worst of them all. Grayson. What are the chances he'd be there tonight, seeing as things are strained between him and the guys? On the other hand, I'm done hiding from Grayson Van Doren. Done being his whipping girl. He's pitching for a fight, and honestly, after the shit he pulled over winter break, I'm more than ready to give it to him.

Between him and my mom, I have so much pent-up anger, and I'm sick of bottling it all up. Sick of swallowing it down. I'm ready to breathe fucking fire, and if Grayson wants to be the one in the blast zone, then by all means, he can come and get it.

My phone buzzes with an incoming text that solidifies my decision.

TARA

puppy dog eyes emoji

ME

Yes! Let's go!

TARA

Yay! Pick you up at 8. Wear something slutty.

Excited at the prospect of getting to see Royce in his element again, I head to my bedroom to find something to wear. Observing him in the ring last time had been exhilarating. I hadn't thought I'd enjoy watching men beat on one another, the violence and the aggression, but Royce made an art out of it. Just like when I watch one of Logan's hockey games, it's impossible to tear my eyes away from the action.

It takes me until Tara pulls up outside to pick an outfit and get dressed, and the dense thud of heavy rock music assaults my ears as we step into The Depot.

Tara's wearing a slinky black bodycon dress with bits cut out along her ribs and over her hips, her black hair pulled back in a sleek ponytail. Meanwhile, I went with a black leather mini-skirt and a maroon tube top. My makeup is on the heavy side, with dark red lips and smokey eyes, and my auburn hair falls around my shoulders in loose waves.

The bouncer gives Tara a chin tilt as we walk past but gives none of the snark Rome usually doles out, and the bustle of the warehouse washes over us as we step inside. Just like always, The Depot is packed. My eyes rake over the raw steel walls and exposed pipework as the mingling aroma of spilled beer and sweat assaults my nostrils before drawing my focus to the boxing ring in the heart of the warehouse, where a fight is currently underway. The nearby crowd shouts their encouragement, but it mustn't be popular contestants as most people are talking in small groups or huddled around the bar, and we have to squeeze through the throng to get to the front.

Xander, Tara's brother, spots us immediately. I suspect the bouncer gave him a heads-up that his sister was here. Handing a customer a beer at the far side, he ignores everyone else as he makes a beeline for us, smiling at his sister before his gaze shifts to me.

"Back again," he teases when he's within earshot before grabbing two ice-cold beers, popping off the lids, and setting them in front of us on the sticky bar top.

"It's hard to say no to this one." I point my thumb at his sister, who fake gasps while Xander chuckles.

"Tell me about it. I still haven't worked it out." Leaning in as though he's about to share a secret, he stage whispers, "If you ever figure it out, let me know."

Scandalized, Tara slams her beer on the bar top. "Riley is *my* friend!" She points an accusing finger at her brother, who pays her no attention.

"You got it." When I wink conspiratorially, Tara's head swivels and she gapes at me.

"You wouldn't!"

With a nonchalant shrug, I fight back my laughter as I say, "Better be nice to me then."

"Why did I bring you here again? This was a terrible idea. If I'd known you were both going to gang up on me, I'd have left you to waste away your youth alone in your apartment." She fake pouts, and both Xander and I burst out laughing.

"Alright, alright. We'll stop teasing you."

"Yeah, I gotta get back to work, anyway," Xander says. "Good to see you again, Riley." Turning to pierce his sister with a stern look, he states, "You know the rules."

With a mocking, two-finger salute, Tara smirks at her brother who rolls his eyes before moving back down the bar to fill orders.

Resting our backs against the bar, we look over the packed-in crowd toward the fighting ring, where two men are currently dancing around one another. We watch in silence as we drink from our beers, and I find myself not as sucked into the fight as I was with Royce's. Perhaps it's not the fighting that I enjoyed, but watching *Royce* fight.

Picking at the label on the beer bottle, I side-eye Tara as I hedge, "Do you know when Ruthless is up?"

She smirks knowingly. "Soon, probably. You'll know when his fight is up next." I nod. "So... he's been at the club every night you're on."

"He doesn't trust Ben, and he's been giving me a ride home after work."

"Oh really now? Do tell."

"It's not like that," I say with a roll of my eyes at Tara's teasing tone. "We... well, we sit in silence a lot, but it's a comfortable silence. And we've talked. He apologized."

Tara scoffs. "I'd damn well hope he apologized—ideally with his tongue between your thighs while you saw stars."

"Oh my god, Tara!"

"What? That man is *fine*, and you told me you can hardly keep your hands off him when he's around, so I don't see what the problem is."

"The problem is... Uhh—"

"See! You don't even know what the problem is. You're looking for an excuse to put up walls, Riley."

"I'm not," I protest. "He did a shitty thing."

"Yeah, he did, but he equally didn't know you then. You said so yourself that he softened toward you the more he was around you."

"He did," I agree. "And, yeah, I can understand why he went along with Grayson's fucked-up plan, but I have to think of Aurora. I need to know I can fully trust him before letting him in… before I can trust him with her."

"And I get that, babe. Believe me, I do. I'm just saying, there's no harm in you benefiting from his groveling and having a little fun in the meantime."

"Ugh," I groan into my palm. "Why am I such a mess?"

Tara barks out a laugh. "Newsflash, Riley, we're all fucking messes." She gestures with her bottle toward the crowd of people around us. "Every single person here is a mess in their own way. That's just fucking life. It's messy. You should know that better than anyone. The point is to find people who under-stand your mess, who get it because their mess matches yours."

"Damaged people call to damaged people," I murmur.

"Exactly," Tara agrees.

"Here's to being messed up, then," I say, lifting my beer bottle.

"At least we can be messed up together," she jests, knocking her bottle against mine before gulping it.

"Can I ask you a question?" she says after a moment. I arch a *get on with it* brow. "Do you think any of them—all of them— are worth a second chance? If they apologize or whatever— make it up to you—would you forgive them?"

I can't tell if she's asking for me or herself, but her question begs consideration. "I don't know. Logan hurt me when he just stopped talking to me. While I can understand his reasoning, that doesn't make it hurt any less. I thought we were building a solid foundation, and instead of talking about it, he just cut me out. I... I don't think I could go through losing him for a second time. But even if I thought I could, that easy, light-hearted relationship I thought we had no longer exists. Anything we would have now would come with strings attached..."

"Grayson."

"Exactly. He's in so much pain. It's agonizing to be around him, and I want to help him, but I also know he has to be the one to pull himself out of the darkness. He has to *want* to see the light. I've been there, I know how hard that is to do. I barely survived it myself. However, I can't let him drag me back into that. So until he can rescue himself... we're nothing. And even then, he'll probably still be an asshole."

Tara bumps her shoulder against mine. "I thought asshole was your thing."

Choking on my sip of beer, I snort-laugh. "Royce is a different breed of asshole. He's... not like how he seems. There's a sensitive side buried underneath all those protective asshole layers."

"Awww, Ruthless has a soft, gooey core," Tara teases.

"His core is *definitely* not soft."

"Hell no, that man is *all* muscle." Tara fans herself in an utterly over dramatic fashion, and the laugh that bursts out of me is light and free. "Well, if you want my advice, which you do since it's amazing... the way I see it, you've got three assholes who all have a hell of a lot of making up to do. If I were you, I'd let them. Make them grovel and take all the orgasms they're willing to offer. When it finally comes time to make your deci-sion, *then* you can decide if you're willing to forgive them. If there's a future there."

"You're forgetting one thing," I point out. "This grand plan of yours assumes any—all—of them *want* to be forgiven. *Want to be with me.*"

With a dismissive wave, Tara snorts, smirking. "Of course, they all want to be with you."

Quirking a brow, I argue, "What makes you think that?"

Tara's focus shifts over my shoulder before returning, that knowing smirk still in place. Using the neck of her beer bottle, she points. "The look on his face tells me I'm right."

I turn to see what she's talking about, and the air catches in the back of my throat when I spot Logan standing several feet away, staring at me as though he's seen a ghost.

"I'll just be... over here." I think Tara points somewhere, but I'm too pulled into Logan's gaze to notice. The entire room falls away—noises muted and distant—as Logan reels me in just like he did in Statistics that day. Except today he's not looking at me in disdain. The polar opposite, in fact.

His eyes scour over me in surprise before returning to my face, and the sheer intensity of the emotions shining back at me nearly brings me to my knees.

Desire.

Want.

Longing.

There is so much *longing* in those chestnut eyes.

The moment seems to stretch into oblivion, the two of us caught in a web that's entirely of our own creation before Logan surges forward.

In the space of a blink, his arms are around me, my feet lifting off the floor as he buries his face in the crook of my neck.

"Fucking hell," he laughs against my skin. "I thought I was hallucinating for a sec there."

All I can do is hug him back, soaking up his warmth as I press my face against his shoulder. Even in the sweaty, packed warehouse, he still smells like winter, and I inhale him like a woman starved.

"Can't say I ever thought I'd see you here. The Depot isn't exactly a popular hangout for HU students."

"Tara's brother owns the place," I explain.

"Tara? The girl you work with?"

I nod. "She's here somewhere." I can't tear my eyes away from him to point her out, not that he seems to care, as his hands come to frame my face.

He steps back, his gaze dropping to do a once-over of my outfit. "Fuck, Riley, you're killing me in that outfit. You look amazing. Sexy as hell." There's an amusing twist to his lips as he asks, "Please tell me you didn't wear that tonight for some douchebag here. I'll probably get my ass handed to me, but I'll totally take him on if you did."

The twinkle in his eyes gives away his teasing, and I shove playfully at his arm. "Royce said he was fighting tonight."

The corners of Logan's lips kick up. "Ahh, well, if he's the douchebag, then I guess I can let him have this one." His head cants to the side, eyes flaring with heat. "And you thought you'd cheer him on in that sexy little outfit? Or perhaps you're here to kiss his bruises better. Damn, perhaps I should get in the ring too."

"Don't you dare, you have a long and prosperous hockey career to think of."

"Mmm, would be worth giving up for a few Riley kisses."

"You're incorrigible," I grumble with a roll of my eyes.

Logan only grins brighter before taking my hand and pulling me through the crowd.

"Where are we going?"

"To find Royce. He won't believe me if I tell him you're here, and I wanna see the look on his face when he sees you."

"Grayson isn't here, is he?" I blurt, head swiveling as I push onto my toes to try and see above the crowd.

Logan shakes his head, glancing at me over his shoulder. "Nah, dude has been pretty absent..."

He leaves the sentence hanging but doesn't need to finish it for me to understand. I imagine it's been tense in their house since Christmas Day. It was already tetchy before then. Questions stack on the tip of my tongue, though I swallow them back for now and instead ask, "Shouldn't Royce be doing whatever he needs to do to get in the zone before his fight? Maybe we shouldn't bother him."

Logan's pace slows, a frown on his face when he stops and turns to look at me. "You're probably right. He's always at his moodiest before a fight. Best to wait until after."

As if on cue, the next fight is announced, and the crowd goes wild when they hear Royce's fighter name.

"Shit. I didn't realize he was up next. I promised I'd be back before he was called."

Looking torn, Logan frowns down at me.

"Go," I urge. "He needs you. I'll be fine."

Glancing around, his frown only deepens. "Yeah, not a chance, Shortcake. No way in hell am I leaving you alone in here. Where's Tara? Does her brother have someone keep an eye on the two of you when you're here? He better. No fucking way is it safe for either of you to be alone."

I huff in indignation even as warmth blooms in my chest at his concern. "Yes, he does. And we stick close to the bar."

He nods, seeming appeased as he marches me back through the crowd. Spotting Tara, I point her out, and Logan walks me over. She smiles when she sees me, arching a brow in a silent question that I deliberately ignore.

"You're Tara?" Logan asks, voice gruff. He waits until she

nods. "Don't let my girl out of your sight. I've gotta go babysit Royce's moody ass, but I'll be back as soon as his fight is over."

Tara nods, expression serious, and I don't bother to restrain the shake of my head.

"We'll be fine," I assure Logan, placing a reassuring hand on his arm. He nods, giving me one last lingering look before storming off through the crowd toward the ring.

"*My girl?*" Tara laughs the second he's out of earshot.

I shove playfully at her shoulder, not even trying to suppress my smile that probably shines brighter than the moon. "Shut up."

Shaking her head, she drags me away from the bar and toward the ring. "Come on, let's watch your other man beat the shit out of someone for fun."

RILEY

CHAPTER SEVENTEEN

"Ruthless reign, no pain, all gain!"

The crowd goes crazy as Royce, his expression stoic, eyes hard, and body slick with sweat and spattered with his opponent's blood, goes in for the kill. It's obvious to anyone paying attention that he's been toying with his opponent for the entirety of the match, and the cat-and-mouse game he's playing has had the crowd salivating as they scream for bloodshed.

Honestly, I've been right there with them.

I shouldn't have been worried since he is *dominating* his fight against Bruiser. I never would have thought I'd enjoy this sort of animalistic thrill, but I'm captivated, unable to blink as I watch. Similar to when I'm at one of Logan's games, there's an energy in the atmosphere, everyone united in their baying for blood. It's a palpable intensity that vibrates through you. The entire warehouse becomes a conduit for the raw power radiating from the ring until the air is thick with sweat, determination, and a primal energy that demands attention.

Just like the patrons at Lux watch enraptured during our performances, you can't help getting sucked in as the whole world shrinks to the fight happening before you. My entire focus has been on Royce as he delivered brutal blows to his opponent. The ferocity in his eyes is a testament to the unbridled anger simmering through him, driving him beyond his limits in pursuit of the pain he is seeking.

One thing I have uncovered in my sharp observation of him is that Royce fights not because he enjoys it, but because he *needs* it. He fights to press pause on his life. To lose himself in something other than his thoughts. He seeks out the pain as a distraction. Relishes in the burn, for at least it's a pain he's inflicted on himself instead of one cast upon him.

I read all of this in the hard lines of his face, in the splitting of his knuckles, and the tensing of his body before he launches his next savage attack. But most notably, I read it in the lack of victory displayed on his face when he throws the final knockout punch that sets the crowd ablaze. Everyone around me erupts into a cacophony of cheers, but not Royce.

His chest is heaving, tattoos shining from sweat beneath the floodlights, as he stares down at his opponent. There's no triumph in that stare. No sense of accomplishment. Only resignation that his brief moment of tranquility has come to an end.

Heart hurting for whatever it is Royce is running from, and the fact he feels the need to cause himself physical pain, I tear my gaze away and instead scan the rest of the crowd who are still screaming his name. I know none of them see what I do. Then again, the man in the ring is Ruthless to all of them, not Royce.

"Fucking hell, that was incredible," Tara yells in my ear.

"Yeah." That's all I can say in response. My own emotions feel as though they are bubbling just beneath the surface, and I'm not entirely sure what to make of it.

How plainly I can see Royce in a way no one else can. How comfortable I am in Logan's presence. How *easy* it is with both of them. Yet, the way I feel about them both is anything but easy. It's confusing and messy. On one hand, being around them feels so innately right, and on the other, I'm angry at myself for feeling that way. It shouldn't feel right. I shouldn't feel this undeniable pull toward both of them after what they put me through.

And yet, I do.

"Oh shit, girl. I think you're about to be in the best sort of trouble."

At Tara's teasing tone, I snap my head up, my gaze colliding with vibrant blue eyes. Royce is staring directly at me, his ever-present intensity searing me to the bone.

It's the same vehemence he wears at Lux, but it's also different. More, somehow. For the first time, there's a question in his gaze. A palpable longing. One I feel, too. It tugs on my core incessantly, and I'm so sick of fighting it. Of resisting. Of him sitting on one side of the room with me on the other.

I'm not sure who moves first; whether I nod or he steps forward as our chemistry reaches a boiling point and we finally succumb to the undeniable force.

He ducks between the ropes, and the crowd parts like the Red Sea as he strides toward me, his long legs eating up the distance between us until thick, muscular arms band around me and I'm thrown over his shoulder.

Heart racing, I squeak out a protest, which is swallowed up by a renewed roar from the crowd before we barrel through a door. It swings shut behind us, somewhat dimming the chaos, and in the absence of noise, I become acutely aware that Royce King is manhandling me.

"Royce, what the hell!"

He hitches my legs around his torso before sliding me down his front until his firm pecs press against my chest and my legs are wrapped around his waist. His hands grasp the tops of my thighs, the corded muscles bunching in his shoulders as he holds me up. My eyes drink in every inch of tattooed skin on display before I lift my head to meet his stare. Eyes that moments ago glinted with ferocity, now appear softer, warmer. Brimming with a different kind of passion.

I barely have time to notice the small cut on his lip from a hit he must have taken before my back slams into something cold and hard. The metal of a locker creaks beneath the strain before warm, supple lips descend on mine, and my mind is wiped clean of all thoughts.

The bitter taste of copper floods my mouth, the savagery of it sending me spiraling as every atom of my being narrows in on the six feet of tattooed muscle pressed flush against me. The raw heat that emanates from his body. The firmness of his hard lines pressed against my softness. The firing of neurons and exploding of endorphins set my body ablaze and have me pleading to the gods above that this moment will never end.

My hands slide over smooth skin as I pull him closer, my tongue dancing along his as I arch my back and moan into his kiss. The explosion of chemistry is indulgent, just as it always is when we collide. Royce and I are like opposing magnets—forever drawn to one another, and no matter how hard we resist, the overwhelming pull is ultimately undeniable. Each time, the impact is just as incendiary, and I'm only now beginning to understand that there is no extinguishing these flames.

Pressing me more firmly into the locker, his hand slides over my ass, my skirt riding up as I squeeze my legs, pulling him infinitely closer. His other hand perches flat against the locker door beside my head as he moves to scrape his teeth along my jaw.

His rough beard scratches at my skin, sending shivers of delight straight to my core where a pulsing has taken up residence, building with each tantalizing touch.

"What are you doing here?" The vibration of Royce's lips against my skin elicits goosebumps as he sucks my earlobe into his mouth before descending lower along my throat. "I felt your presence the second I stepped into the ring." My chest rises with heaving breaths. "All I could think about was getting to you." His hand palms my ass and he rocks his thick, hard length against my core. "I had to hold myself back from obliterating him with one punch." His tongue licks a path over my collarbone. "Couldn't even look at you because I knew, one look and I'd be rock hard for the entire warehouse to see." I gasp. "Still, I felt the radiant heat of your stare. Felt you watching my every move." Running his nose up my neck, his voice is a deep, seductive rumble in my ear as he whispers, "Did you enjoy watching me play with my food before I killed it?"

Head too clouded with lust, Royce barely gets a response from me until he nips on the sensitive skin of my neck, and I moan out a "Yes."

Cold air bites at my skin as he moves back, and my eyes snap open, finding him watching me closely. His fingers run along my collarbone before his hand rests at the base of my neck, this thumb gently rubbing back and forth across my pulse point.

"You really should have stayed away," he murmurs, more to himself. "Because I can't. I've tried... *fuck*, I'm trying, because I'm not what you need. You're all pure and healed, and I'm... not enough. Yet every moment I'm around you, I lose the will to stay away a little bit more."

"What if I don't want you to stay away?"

His gaze drops to my lips at my question, remaining there as he half-growls. "Then I guess we're going up in flames together."

Eyes dropping further, he stares at the point where his hand rests curled around my neck, his fingers flexing. I can tell he's holding himself back. The flicker of self-doubt that crosses his face only confirms it.

"Don't," I choke out, tears burning the back of my eyes. "Don't, please." At my plea, his eyes snap to mine. "Don't treat me differently. I'm not made of glass; I won't break."

He swallows roughly, eyes searing into mine. When he speaks, there's a huskiness that wasn't there before. "You're the toughest person I know, James, but I don't want to cause you any more pain."

"The only way you'll do that is by holding back from me now." Lifting my chin, I expose my neck. "I see your demons, Royce, and I am not afraid. I want this. I want *you*."

"Fuck, James. You're going to rue the day you said that when you realize just how *obsessed* I am with you."

Removing his hand from my ass, he grabs my hips until I'm forced to drop my legs. Spinning me around, he shoves me against the lockers and crowds me from behind. The second he does, my whole body tenses, my breath stuttering as black splotches appear in my vision.

"You're okay," he soothes, always so in tune with my body as his hand strokes down my hair. "I've got you. It's just you and me here, Ry. No one else." I give a terse nod, and he continues to touch me reverently, even as his tone takes on a stern edge. "Hands on the locker, Babydoll. Do you feel that cool metal beneath your palms?" he asks when I do as he orders, placing my palms flat against the door above my head.

I nod again, gasping in surprise when he roughly grabs my hair at the nape of my neck and pulls, forcing me to arch my back and press my tits into the locker.

"You've been such a naughty girl, James," he growls in my ear. "Coming here dressed like that and making me take on that wimp while picturing this exact moment." His hand runs over the leather of my skirt before sliding between my thighs. "Did you put this on with me in mind?"

"Yes," I rasp.

His chest vibrates against my back with pure, male satisfaction.

"Did you plan to seduce me, Riley James? Were you hoping I'd bring you back here and fuck you senseless?"

"Yes."

The showerhead did fuck all to alleviate the blaze left in Royce's wake after his kiss on Friday night. So yeah, perhaps on some level, I was hoping this would be tonight's outcome.

Sometimes a girl just needs to get off, you know?

And Royce can do it better than any showerhead or vibrator ever could.

And... I trust him enough to do this with him.

I'm acutely aware of the rumor I heard about him; the accusation levied against him, and I know we need to talk about it, but I firmly believe, hand on a bible and swear it, that Royce is not who those girls believe him to be.

In my experience, character says a hell of a lot more about a person than words spilled from someone else's lips, and not once has Royce given me a reason to doubt him. Even when he had every reason to hate me, he still stood up for me. He sat with me after Grayson choked me half to death. He's shown up at Lux every single night I've been working because he doesn't want me to be left alone with Ben.

He *punched* the guy because he thought he'd done something to me.

Do those sound like the actions of someone who's done what those girls accused him of? Because they sure as hell don't to me.

His hand between my legs clamps my inner thigh, his fingers firmly stroking the raised scars there.

"One day, I want to know about these." I swallow nervously. "I want every one of your secrets. Access to the inner workings of your mind. Absolutely no part of you will be safe from me. I'm going to make certain that every fiber of your being knows who you belong to." My throat works, but no words come to mind. "But for now, I want to hear my name on your lips as you come apart on my fingers like a good little slut."

Emphasizing his point, he curls his fingers, the tips brushing against the sopping fabric of my panties, and I shudder. He groans his pleasure before wrapping his fingers around the material and sliding it down my legs. They fall to the ground, and he drops to a crouch, tapping my inner ankles to get me to lift my feet.

"These are mine now," he growls, pocketing them before sliding his hands up the back of my calves as he slowly rises. His calloused fingers scrape along the skin of my outer thighs before he slides one hand between my legs, burying his fingers deep inside me.

"Royce," I cry as he penetrates my wet heat and my walls clench around him, desperate for release.

"That's it, Babydoll. Louder. I want everyone in this place to know exactly who is making you come."

His other hand rubs expertly at my clit while he pumps two thick fingers in and out, and I grind my ass shamelessly against the hard bulge in his shorts as I drown in pleasure.

My nipples pebble, my breathing ragged pants as I chase my release, and as I clamp down on him, Royce groans. "That's it, Ry. Scream my fucking name."

I do exactly that, throwing my head back and yelling his name to the rafters as I drench his fingers in my release and collapse against him.

I'm nothing but a boneless noodle in his arms as he slides his fingers from me with a wet pop. Holding my gaze, he brings his fingers to his lips and sucks them into his mouth, humming as his eyes dilate with carnal desire. "So fucking sweet." *Oh, god.* That one act has my body crying out for another round, but instead, Royce gently turns me to face him, and I stare up into the softest expression I've yet to see on him. His hand cups my face before his lips descend in a slow, languid kiss that tastes of us, and I can feel it to the bottom of my soul.

Oh yeah, I could get used to orgasms and kisses while I make these men grovel.

He pulls away slowly, reluctantly, and I mumble, "I'm not a wallflower."

Appearing confused, Royce's lips twitch in amusement at my nonsensical words.

"You know me as the wallflower beneath your thumb," I attempt to explain. "At the mercy of you, Logan, and Grayson, but that's not who I am. I know how to survive, but more than that, I know how to fight. What battles are worth fighting, and which ones to let go of. When I was under your roof, I mostly let it go because I had a bigger agenda to work toward."

"Your daughter."

"Yes."

His eyes search mine. "I haven't thought you were a wallflower since you pointed out the fuck off stamped on my forehead, and I know you wouldn't be standing here today if you weren't an absolute warrior. However, if beneath your thumb is where you want me, James, then that's where I'll be, but there are far better body parts I could be under."

"Yo, are you fuckers about done in there?" Logan's voice slices through the room, reminding me of where we are and what we've been doing as heat floods my cheeks.

I cut my gaze to the door as it creaks open, Logan popping his head in. His gaze instantly finds mine. He looks completely unbothered to find Royce and I standing so close together, look-ing... well... ruffled.

"Here, asshole." Looking into the room, Logan tosses sweats and a hoodie at Royce. "I grabbed your shit. The way you stormed out of there like a man possessed, I assumed you weren't planning on coming back for it."

Royce merely grunts as he steps into the gray sweatpants, pulling them on over his shorts before shrugging into the hoodie. I notice it's the same one he was wearing last time I was here, with the name *Ruthless* stitched across the back in large letters and again in smaller font across the front breast.

"We don't usually hang around after he's done," Logan says to me. "Do you want to come with us?"

"She's coming," Royce dictates, not even looking at me as he rummages through his locker.

I roll my eyes, but say to Logan, "Yeah, okay. I just need to tell Tara I'm leaving."

"Here." Royce shoves a leather jacket into my hands before tossing a duffel over his shoulder, and I stare down at the jacket before glancing up at him, arching a brow. He scowls. "You're not wearing enough."

Logan snickers and I open my mouth, hoping some witty retort comes to mind before words start falling, except Royce cuts me off with a masculine growl. "Put the damn jacket on, James. It's freezing outside."

My eyes narrow, not entirely convinced that is what he meant, but I let it go and slide my arms into his jacket. I'm immediately doused in the scent of leather and damp earth, and I have to fight the urge not to fill my lungs with the unique smell of Royce King.

Once we're ready, Logan slings his arm over my shoulder and tucks me into his side, and we follow Royce out of the locker room. I direct the guys toward the bar, and in single file, we push our way through the crowd, me sandwiched between the two of them.

When we near the bar, I press onto my tiptoes to try to spot Tara through the crowd. "She's over there." Logan points toward where he sees Tara. "She's with some guy."

"Probably her brother."

"Nah, we know Xander. It isn't him. Think I've seen the guy on the door, though."

"Oh, Rome."

Looking down at me, Logan arches an eyebrow. "You just know every guy here, don't you?"

I huff out a frustrated breath and try to jump in my heels to see over the heads of the people in front of me.

"Jesus, woman. You'll break an ankle carrying on like that in those death traps." Wrapping his arms around my waist, Logan effortlessly lifts me off my feet until I have a clear view of where Tara is standing near the bar, having what appears to be an argument with Rome.

"Looks like she's busy," Royce states.

"Yeah." I chew on my lip before making a decision and pulling out my phone. "I'll text her. Rome and Xander will make sure she's okay." I hurriedly fire off a message, tucking my phone away before we leave the warehouse. A zing of anticipation races along my spine as Logan helps me into the passenger seat of Royce's truck, and the three of us drive into the darkness.

LOGAN

CHAPTER EIGHTEEN

I'm on top of the world as Royce drives us down the dark country roads, knowing Riley is here. That she trusted us enough to leave with us. It feels like a huge reward after the work I've put in this week to not completely lose her. I've been an emotional mess, straddling the line between getting her to lower her walls and not wanting to barge all the way in and demand anything. I'm a hockey player, for god's sake. I'm used to slamming my way in there and taking what I want, but that approach won't work with Riley.

Hearing how I shattered her trust not once but twice flayed me open. It was the slap across the face that I needed. That I deserved. Seeing the hurt in her eyes... I never want to fucking see that again. Never want to be the cause of her pain.

Seeing her at The Depot tonight... was like seeing a mirage after days lost in the desert. For a moment, I thought my brain had conjured her after constantly obsessing about her for weeks.

It doesn't matter that she was there for Royce. The fact she was there at all gives me hope. Hope that all is not lost. That if she is opening herself up to my best friend then one day she might be willing to do the same with me.

"Where are we going?" Riley asks.

Leaning forward between the two front seats, I suggest, "I could go for a milkshake and fries," not yet ready to take her home and say our goodbyes.

All I get with her these days are tiny pockets of moments together. Guarded ones, at that. But tonight, there's a carefree air about her that I haven't seen all week. She always seems on edge at lunch, despite me trying to take it slow.

"Of course, you could," Royce grumbles as he reaches the T-junction, but I smirk when he puts his blinker on in the direction of our favorite fast food joint when we're at The Depot. "There's an all-night diner not far from here," he says to Riley, tone sweeter than one he's ever used with me.

"They do the best milkshakes," I inform her.

She turns in her seat to look at me, grinning. "Perfect."

A few minutes later, Royce pulls off the road onto a gravel parking lot, his headlights lighting up the small, fifties-retro diner. The vibrant cherry red and creamy white exterior has faded with age, the curvy letters displaying Leon's Diner on the glass of the door peeling off. However, the interior lights cast a warm and inviting glow at this late hour.

Climbing out of the car, the parking lot is empty as I move to hold Riley's door open for her and hold out a hand to help her as she jumps down. Royce rolls his eyes at me, and when Riley's back is turned I give him the middle finger. Fucker just laughs, and Riley glances between us, confused about what she missed.

"Come on, Shortcake. Milkshakes wait for no man." I usher her up the steps behind Royce. The door creaks on its hinges, acting as a replacement bell since the original hangs listlessly above. The musty scent of old grease brings back good memories of many a night here, myself, Royce, and Grayson sucking down some surprisingly good burgers and fries while Royce rode the high of his latest win and the three of us forgot about our real-world problems for a bit.

An older woman behind the counter gives us a weary glance. Her customer service smile is notably absent as she waits to see if we'll take a seat at the counter or one of the empty booths. I nod at her in greeting before placing a hand at the base of Riley's spine and directing her ahead of me down the narrow aisle between booths.

Royce slides into an end one, the vinyl upholstery creaking beneath his weight, and before Riley can slip in beside him, I push her toward the seat opposite and shimmy in beside her, smirking as she shakes her head at my antics.

Royce scowls, but I ignore the bastard as I drop my arm across the back of the booth behind my girl, my fingers picking up a strand of her hair and absently playing with it while I watch her peruse the extensive menu.

What? If I'm getting extra time with her, then you can bet your ass I'm going to hog every second of it. If Royce is already *kissing* her—plus whatever he was doing in the locker room that had her moaning his name for the entire warehouse to hear—then I obviously need these extra moments more than he does.

"What can I get ya's?" the woman from behind the counter asks, approaching our table several minutes later.

"Burger, fries, and a chocolate milkshake for me," I say with a disarming smile.

"Same for me," Royce puts in his order, his smile non-existent as he hands over his menu.

"I'll take a plate of fries and a strawberry milkshake, please," Riley says sweetly, passing over her menu too. The woman jots down our orders before leaving. Alone, every single question I've astutely held back since Christmas Day sits like an anvil on the tip of my tongue, ready to spill, but now that we're away from The Depot, she has tensed up, her fingers fidgeting with the napkin holder and her gaze on the chipped tabletop.

"So, what did you think of Royce's fight?" I find myself asking instead.

Her shoulders relax marginally, and she leans back against the booth as she lifts her head, looking at me before focusing on Royce.

"It wasn't actually my first time seeing him fight."

"It wasn't?" I ask, surprised.

She shakes her head, a secretive smile playing along her lips now. "Nope. Last time, Royce accused me of stalking him and told me to get on my knees since I must be so desperate to know the taste of his cum to follow him out here."

I choke on my spit and Royce actually *laughs*. A full-belly one that I don't think I've ever heard before. Smirking like a cocky asshole, he leans forward, eyes only for Riley. "If I remember correctly, James. I made you eat your words from that night."

Her cheeks turn a deep shade of red, but she doesn't lower her gaze from his as my dick twitches at the reminder of her on her knees, Royce's cock shoved deep in her mouth. The way she flushed beneath Royce's searing gaze is somehow even hotter than the act itself.

A silent spectator, I watch with a mix of curiosity and surprise as the two of them share a moment charged with electricity. I have no idea what exactly happened between them on Christmas Day, but clearly, things have changed. The way Royce is looking at her right now... I've never seen him look at *any* girl like that. He's barely given a girl a second glance as long as I've known him, yet here he is, looking at Riley like...

Fuck...

Like, she's the Vince Lombardi Trophy, and he's just won the goddamn Super Bowl.

I knew he believed her. Knew he kissed her, but this... I wasn't expecting Royce to fall in fucking love with her.

The moment is broken when the waitress returns with our food and drinks, and Riley fills me in on her run-in with Royce that night at The Depot while Royce and I eat our burgers and she dunks her fries in her milkshake.

If I didn't already know this girl was fucking perfect for me, that one act alone would cement it. Any girl who knows the only way to eat diner fries is by smothering them in milkshake is a keeper.

I wait until our plates are empty and Riley is curled up beside me, clutching the remainder of her milkshake and finally looking relaxed before I broach the topic.

"So... Christmas Day." I glance between the auburn-haired beauty beside me and one of my best friends. It's a topic we've put off for too long. Royce refused to discuss what occurred, and I sure as fuck wasn't going to broach the subject with Riley at school.

Now that the three of us are here, now that I've gotten Riley to agree not to shut me out, it's time to really talk. "You obviously know Riley's telling the truth," I say to Royce, deciding that putting the focus on him might make this easier on Riley.

Royce's focus doesn't waver from the hazel-eyed beauty, the two of them seeming to share a silent conversation. Since when did they start communicating with just their eyes?!

"I do," he eventually states, still staring at her.

"Okayyy... as much as I wanna believe you took her at her word, I know you better than that, man. You'd have needed..." I stall mid-sentence as the penny drops, and my head whips toward Riley, eyes narrowing in scrutiny. "Proof." Her eyes lift to mine, wide and anxious. "You said you had proof," I mutter, my brain going into overdrive.

Her hazel eyes dart to and fro between mine, beseeching, before she drops them to the table, her shoulders shaking with each exhale as she wrings her hands.

Hating seeing her so anxious, I wrap my hands around her fumbling ones and wait until she musters the strength to lift her eyes to mine. I catch a glimpse of the vulnerability there—a fear of what, I don't know. Doesn't she understand that I'm all in when it comes to her? I already believe her; what could she possibly have to say that has her this worried?

"Hey," I try to soothe. "It's okay. Whatever it is, it can't be that bad." I mean, if it was enough to sway Royce, then it's gotta be enough to convince Grayson, right? Maybe a video or an audio recording? Is that why she's so panicked looking? Does she think I'll wanna see or hear it? Fuck no! I dunno if Royce has listened to it, but I sure as hell won't. Her word is enough for me. I'm liable to kill Grayson's dad with my bare fucking hands if I hear a single goddamn thing on that tape.

She wets her lips, focus intent on my chest as she finally begins to speak, her voice trembling as the words tumble out in a rush. "Do you remember the photo you saw on my phone? Of the baby?"

Okay... not where I thought she was going to go with this.

She's shaking like a leaf now, and I flash Royce a concerned glance before answering, "Your niece?"

She nods, then just as quickly starts shaking her head. "N-not my niece." Her hands hold mine in a death grip, as though terrified what she has to say next will send me slipping through her fingers. Eyes brimming with tears, she takes a steadying breath, steeling herself as she meets my gaze before landing the punch to my gut I never saw coming. "My daughter."

The tortured look in her eyes kills me, and I'm so caught up in them that I almost miss what she said. It takes me a moment to react, the words running through my mind several times before I finally process them.

"The picture was of my daughter," she gushes, the words falling like a waterfall from her lips. "It was an old one, like I said. She's older now. But I lied to you. I-I couldn't tell you..."

She continues, seemingly unable to stop talking now that she's started, but my focus is stuck on that one word.

Daughter.

She has a daughter. A kid.

I'm so shocked by that admission that I don't immediately understand the significance.

Until I do.

No...

That can't be.

That would mean...

My head snaps up and I stare slack-jawed at Royce as the dots slowly connect, the jumbled pieces slotting into place and painting a sickening picture.

Expression grim, he nods, acknowledging that I'm not losing my ever-loving mind. If only I was, because the reality is so much worse.

"She's—" I rasp, throat closing over. Coughing, I lick my dry lips and try again. "She's—"

Fuck.

Fuck.

Swiping a hand through my hair, I tug on the neckline of my hoodie. *Fuck. I can't breathe.*

My eyes bounce around the diner, not taking it in as sweat beads along my skin. Sagging forward, my elbows rest on the table as I bow my head and mutter the truth aloud to the table. "*His.*"

Unbidden images of Riley, fifteen. Scared. Alone. And

fucking pregnant with her abuser's baby, flash through my mind. How in the fucking hell did this woman not succumb to all of that?

She truly is a survivor. A fighter. The strongest fucking person ever to have faced all that and still be *her*—sweet, caring, understanding.

Rage pummels through me, crashing like waves, tinged with sorrow and disgust at everything she has had to endure on her own.

And just when she thought she'd found her new start... we turned it into a fresh hell for her to endure.

Fuck, now I *know* I'm going to be sick...

Bile rushes up the back of my throat, and jumping to my feet, I push out of the booth.

"Logan," Riley calls, voice pleading.

Unable to look at her, I hold up a hand. "I'm sorry, Riley. I just... I need a moment. Just give me one moment." Not waiting for a response, I stride away from the table, throw open the door to the diner, and stumble down the steps before collapsing on the ground and dry heaving.

My stomach purges itself of its contents, but it does sweet fuck all to obliterate the self-loathing eating away at my insides.

RILEY

CHAPTER NINETEEN

Logan is green as he scurries from the table, taking my strangled heart with him. Fucking hell. If I thought Royce finding out was bad, it has nothing on watching Logan's face shift from confused to shocked to horrified as I told him my deepest, darkest secret.

"He's not okay." My voice breaks and cracks over the words, sounding more like that of a forty-pack-a-day smoker than mine. Wrapping my arms around myself, I realize I'm cold to the bone despite the warm food in my belly.

Sliding out from his side of the booth, Royce drops down beside me, shifting over until he can pull me in against him. His aftershave blends with the sharp leather of his jacket, and dragging in a long breath, I bury my face in his hoodie. "Give him a few minutes. He just needs to process." I nod into Royce's hoodie, sniffling. "It's a lot to take in and probably the farthest thing from what he was expecting."

"I know," I say, pulling back to wipe beneath my eyes. "I just... The look on his face. He was devastated."

"He's blaming himself," Royce explains. "Grasping the full

picture of what you've had to endure, and knowing he added to it... he's blaming himself. That's why he looked so distraught."

"How do you know that?"

He stares down at me with an open expression. "Because it's how I felt that day in the park."

"We never really talked about that day," I hedge, picking up one of the strings on his hoodie and absently fiddling with it.

He reaches up, tucking a finger under my chin to lift my face to his. "I think you know by now that it changes nothing for me." At my skeptical look, he chuckles. "Okay, that day changed everything, however not in the way you're thinking. Your truth shattered the flimsy excuses I clung to for why I shouldn't allow myself to give into the draw I felt toward you.

"If you're asking if it changed how I feel about you, then yes. How could it not? Knowing what you went through; what you've survived... and going through all of that while raising a daughter... it makes you fucking superwoman, Ry." My gulp is audible as I swallow, tears stinging my eyes. "As for everything else: the questions I have and what it means regarding Grayson... well, I think we're better off saving that discussion to have with Logan."

"Assuming this hasn't completely pushed him over the edge."

Royce scoffs. "He might be spiraling, but that's more about him than you. That man is obsessed with you. Believe me. I hear about it enough to know. He'd move heaven and earth for you if it were possible."

Staring out the large windows overlooking the dark parking lot, I worry my lower lip when I don't see any sign of Logan outside.

Royce forces my face to his with gentle but firm fingers, eyes scouring my face. "How are *you?* I doubt telling Logan was on your agenda for the night."

A weak laugh escapes me. "I wouldn't have left with you if I hadn't considered the possibility. Logan knowing… it doesn't scare me."

Royce's stare bores into me, identifying everything I'm not saying. "But the thought of telling Grayson does."

I swallow nervously. "He has the power to take her from me, and I don't trust him not to act out of anger. In an attempt to punish me, he could end up hurting her, and I refuse to let that happen."

He takes in everything I say with a quiet reserve, turning over the words before simply nodding. "For the record, I wouldn't let that happen either, but let's not worry about Grayson for tonight. Once Logan has had time to process, the three of us can talk. Figure everything out."

"I have a daughter, Royce," I repeat the words for the second time tonight, pride swelling in my chest.

I've kept Aurora a secret from so many people for so long that it feels good to stand up and say that she's mine. I'm so damn proud of the little girl I created, and I want the world to know it. I want *her* to know it. I've been keeping her a secret for her own protection, and admittedly because I was scared, but I'm so sick and tired of all the secrets and lies. I just want to live my life—with Aurora. To live in a world where I can claim her as mine and be so damn proud to call myself her Mom.

However, despite all that, I need Royce—and Logan—to understand precisely what that means.

"Yeah, Babydoll. I know. I was there, remember?" Royce responds, a teasing smirk pulling at his lips.

"Royce," I groan, giving him a weak attempt at a stern glare. "You know what I mean. You both talk as though we have a future, but you need to understand I have a daughter. She's a permanent fixture in my life, which I'm not sure you fully grasp since she hasn't been here, and you haven't had to see what a terror a three-year-old can be on a lifestyle."

"You're a package deal," Royce states bluntly.

"Yeah. And that won't ever change. Not even when she's thirty and has her own life."

His lips twitch in a semblance of a smile.

"I understand that, Ry. Believe me, it's all I've been able to think about these last few weeks. I won't pretend to know anything about children, or raising them, or tell you that I'm any good with them, although knowing you have a daughter isn't going to be enough for you to get rid of me." His hand glides smoothly up the side of my throat before slipping around the back of my head until he has a firm hold on the fine hairs at the base of my scalp, and his next words come out in a rasp that sends my heart leaping.

"I know there's shit you don't know, shit that we need to talk about... Hell, I know I should be telling you to run in the opposite direction because I'm not any good for you. Only I'm too selfish to do that, and I don't have the self-control to stay away from you, so instead, I'll say that, for the first time in months—fuck, in *years*—I feel something other than hate and bitter resentment. *You* make me feel something other than the cloying spitefulness eating away at me."

"Maybe I'm just a pretty distraction," I murmur, voice breathless. Our faces are so close now that I can feel his breath against my skin when he responds.

"That's what I thought at first also. I told myself I kept returning to the club to toy with you. Because I saw how uncomfortable it made you."

"And being you, you thought I deserved it," I whisper against his lips.

"Yes," he admits unapologetically.

"So if you didn't keep coming back to get under my skin, why did you?"

He tilts his head, his nose running along my jaw until his lips reach my ear. "Because staying away from you is impossible." Shivers skate along my skin. "You became an addiction. A craving I had to sate. I'd tell myself tonight was the last time, then the next night, I'd find myself right back in that booth, needing to learn more, to peel back another layer and see what lay underneath." My breathing hitches. "You were so defiant at the club. Put on such a tough girl act," he continues to whisper as I cling desperately to his every word. "But then I watched as you fell apart in that dance studio.

"I stood on the street and watched as you succumbed to your heartache and loneliness. As you allowed yourself to completely shatter and fall apart... I'd never seen anything so breathtaking.

"I didn't understand then what your pain was about, but I felt every acute stab as though it were my own. I felt your betrayal and helplessness only because I recognized them in myself."

Loosening his hold on the back of my head, he brings his hand around so his thumb brushes my lower lip. "Then watching you take everything we threw at you over winter break and stand up to Grayson. You could have demanded that we listen to your side of things. Could have thrown the truth repeatedly in Grayson's face... yet, despite everything he did, you tried to spare his feelings. You wanted us to make our own decisions instead of shoving the truth down our throats, even though, given the circumstances, you had every right to."

With both his hands cupping my cheeks, he stares earnestly into my eyes. "You are tough as nails, resilient, and strong-minded, but also kind and compassionate. You haven't allowed the shit you've been through to harden you. So many of us allow life to make us callous, but this world didn't break you, Riley. It sharpened you into steel and made you a warrior.

"Everything I've seen and learned about you has only made me want to know more. When I tell you that I've given this some thought, I mean it, and *I'm in*, so if you don't want this, then you'll have to be the one to end it, 'cause I have no intention of going anywhere."

My heart hammers against my chest as I reel from Royce's confession. I have never heard him say so much at once, and I know it's not a common occurrence. Which makes everything he's saying even more special. It's him opening up to me. Him wanting me to understand exactly where he stands, and despite his claiming earlier this evening, he's now putting the ball in my court. Giving *me* the option to pursue this chemistry between us or walk away.

My throat scratches as I attempt to swallow, emotions too thick to get words past, before I give up and instead reach up and pull his face to mine. With my kiss, I pour out my gratitude at having been seen so plainly by him and accepted for all of my cracks and fissures. He has seen me at my rawest and recognized my emotions for what they were. More than that, he *felt* them, too.

He saw past my pale skin and reddish hair. Past the freckles and loose clothing. He saw beyond the shields I placed around myself. Through the carefully constructed barriers and mask of confidence.

He saw *me*.

And here he is, telling me that he's all in.

Arms around his neck, I hold on tightly as I break our kiss.

"I see you, too." My voice is thick and raspy. "I don't know what happened to you, and I don't need you to tell me until you're ready. But I do see you too, and I'm not going anywhere. I don't know how long this thing between us will last. *If* it will last. However, I'm in it for as long as you are."

His chuckle is dark and seductive as he wraps his arms around me, lifting so I straddle his thighs. Bending his neck, he nips along my throat. "Foolish girl. You've just handed your heart over to the devil. There's no getting it back now. It's mine, and I plan to keep it for the rest of eternity."

"Even if Logan ultimately ends up owning a piece of it too?" Not that I've decided to forgive him, but a girl should know if the two men causing her to wake up horny every morning are opposed to the idea of sharing.

"I have no doubt Logan will. He's persistent like that. And I can certainly get behind the two of us working together to bring you to orgasm multiple times." My thighs clench around his. Yes, I could definitely get behind that, too. Or underneath it. Any position, really.

"Let's go check he hasn't gotten into a fight with my truck." Royce helps me out of the booth before pulling out his wallet and dropping a handful of bills on the table. Taking my hand in his, it's with anxious steps that I follow him out of the diner.

The cold night air hits me in the face as soon as I step outside, and I huddle deeper into Royce's leather jacket as I search the parking lot for Logan. I find him pacing back and forth behind our truck, so absorbed in his thoughts that he doesn't even look up at the crunching of gravel beneath our shoes as we approach.

"Logan," Royce barks when we're a couple of feet away.

His harsh tone snaps Logan out of his spiral, and he stops in his tracks as he stares at me. Eyes shining, his face is deathly pale in the glow from the diner's lights.

"Fuck, Shortcake." Swiping a hand through his hair, he continues, "I'm sorry. I just... *fuck.*" He roars his curse into the night. "This just makes it so much more... real." He's back to his pacing, although at least this time he's talking. "I mean, I believed you. I did, but it was like this event that happened in the past. I was aware that it had happened and how horrible it was that it had, yet I guess I hadn't ever really sat down and processed it. But this…"

He stops pacing, staring at me in utter devastation. "You have a daughter."

Silent tears scorch a path down my cheeks as I nod.

His expression is tortured, riddled with pain and anger, and his next words are a hate-filled rasp. "He raped you and got you pregnant, and he got. Away. With. It."

A wretched, broken sob rips from my soul as my knees give out. Before I hit the ground, a crisp winter breeze washes over me as Logan pulls me into his arms. "I am so fucking sorry, baby." His voice breaks, tears lining his words. "I'm so fucking sorry you had to go through any of that."

I cling to him like he's a lifeline, except there's no *like* about it. Logan *is* my lifeline. He's my light in the dark. My hope in the bleakness. My safe place when I'm lost in the cold.

And at my back, I feel Royce's reassuring warmth. My steady shadow. Always there, always watching, always looking out for me.

My daylight and my night, and encased between them, I've never felt more protected.

RILEY

CHAPTER TWENTY

The three of us somehow end up crammed into the back of Royce's truck, Logan on one side of me and Royce on the other.

"I'm sorry, Shortcake," Logan repeats for what must be the dozenth time.

"You don't need to be sorry, Logan."

"I shouldn't have walked out like that." His sigh is heavy and forlorn as he lifts a hand to scrub at the back of his head. "There's... a lot I shouldn't have done."

I shake my head. "You needed to process. I understand."

"I still shouldn't have left you alone."

"What am I, chopped liver?" Royce grumbles, but I see his remark for what it is—an attempt at levity. I give him a weak, appreciative smile, and his eyes bounce over my face before he sighs, lifting his gaze to Logan. "If it helps, it's taken me the better part of a week to wrap my head around it." Looking sheepishly away, he confesses, "If I hadn't seen her with my own eyes, it probably still wouldn't feel real."

"Wait, you saw her?" Logan asks, gaping at Royce before

directing his question at me, "What the hell happened on Christmas Day?"

"My mom was bringing Aurora up to see me—"

"Aurora—that's her name?" Logan interjects softly.

I smile, nodding. "It is."

"Like Sleeping Beauty."

I laugh because, of course, Logan makes that inference.

"It also means dawn in Latin."

"As in, the dawn of a new day?" Royce queries, and I nod.

"I was in a bad place before I found out I was pregnant. I—" My throat closes over, tears welling even as I fight to push them away. Just talking about that time is too much, and I can feel the shadows closing in.

Sensing I'm on the brink of crumbling, Logan reaches out to clasp my hand in his. "It's okay. You don't have to talk about back then. Not if it upsets you." I sniffle, and he brushes a hand over my hair. "You were meeting up with your mom and Aurora on Christmas Day."

I nod. "Yeah. I hadn't seen Aurora since I left for college, and I'd finally managed to get my mom to stick to her agreement to come—"

"We'll come back to that later, James," Royce growls. I give him a blank look, a thickness in my throat at the thought of explaining the control my mother has over me. Letting them see how I've let Aurora down.

When he squeezes my thigh in a bid for me to continue, I push thoughts of that conversation aside and go back to explaining to Logan how Christmas Day unfolded.

"—I'd planned to get up early and sneak out of your house and back to my apartment. Only I overdid it on the eggnog the night before."

"Fucking Grayson," Logan snarls.

"Ugh, let's not mention him, yeah?" I groan. "Anyway, I

slept in and woke up within ten minutes to get there and went banging on Royce's door, pleading with him to take me."

Royce snorts. "She practically dragged me out of the house in my boxers."

"You were wearing clothes!" I retort with a teasing smirk.

"I'm surprised you were able to convince him at all," Logan states, sounding surprised.

"Yeah, I didn't. He was an immovable bastard. I had to use my Gin Rummy favor."

"I still wanna know how you got so good at that game." Royce points a finger my way, his scowl very real. Clearly, someone is still pissy about losing.

Biting back my smug grin, I shrug a shoulder. "You learn a thing or two when you spend the latter part of your teenage years in a school for troubled teens."

"A school for what?" Logan splutters.

I smile at him, except this time it's cold and biting. "Mom had to hide me away somewhere where I couldn't cause any more trouble after I'd had Aurora."

"That's..." Logan begins.

"... Royally fucked up," Royce finishes.

"It is," I agree with a resigned nod and a casual half-shrug. "But it is what it is."

"I'm starting to really not like that phrase," Logan grumbles. When I roll my eyes, he thankfully continues. "So, Royce took you to meet your mom and Aurora..."

"Yeah. I knew it would mean he'd figure it all out, although I didn't care at that point. I'd have sold my kidney to get there on time."

"She practically dove out of the moving truck when we reached the park," Royce tells Logan, glaring daggers at me.

"And you saw Aurora?" Logan asks, a slight whine in his

voice. "Do you have any pictures?" he directs at me. "I wanna see her."

More of that happy warmth infuses me as I grab my phone and pull up my photo album. It's filled with screenshots I've taken while I've been on FaceTime with her, and if you scroll far enough back, there are ones of the two of us before I left for college. Bringing up the first one, I hand my phone to Logan.

He falls silent as he stares at the photo, and I watch his eyes widen as he scours the picture, drinking in every detail as a soft smile graces his lips.

"I know you said not to mention him, but I can't get over how much she looks like Grayson."

Royce leans closer, squishing me between them so he can get a better look. He nods in agreement. "I thought the same. She's got Ry's hair but Gray's eyes. His smile too," Royce tacks on as Logan switches to a photo of Aurora's toothy grin.

I sigh, relaxing into Logan's chest. "I know. I swear she looks more like him with each passing year."

"You know he's going to lose his shit when he discovers the truth," Logan states, face pinched as he continues to scroll through my photo reel. "He won't be able to keep denying the truth."

"It's fucked up that he so blindly believes his dad," Royce snaps, irritated.

I sigh dejectedly. "He's his dad. We all want to believe the best of our parents, even if they haven't always been the best people." My indifference falls away as my own painful memories surface, and I swallow thickly. "My mom and I have never gotten along well. I knew she wasn't a maternal person, yet when I finally found the courage to tell her what her husband was doing after she fell asleep..." My voice cracks, my lower lip trembling as I fight back the wave of emotion. "It never occurred to me that she wouldn't believe me. That she'd take his side over mine—a man she'd known less than a year."

The first tear overflows as I rip my heart open anew, recalling the devastation of that moment. It had taken months for me to gather the courage to tell her, and I'd pinned all of my hopes on it. I'd convinced myself that it would stop as soon as I told her. That she would somehow make it all better. Take me away, call the cops.

Something.

Anything.

I couldn't have been more wrong. "Until that moment, she was still my mom. We weren't close and rarely saw eye-to-eye, but I thought..." I sigh, sniffling as I wipe at my cheeks and stare down at my lap. "I dunno what I thought, but the second she told me to shut up and not to say anything that could ruin her marriage, she stopped being my mom."

Rough fingers wrap around my chin, his grip firm yet gentle as he lifts my head until I'm staring into stormy blue eyes. "You were thinking that she's your mom, and she was supposed to protect you," Royce growls, practically vibrating with his anger. "She's the one who let *you* down. The most important job as a parent, and she failed you. That's on her. You shouldn't feel bad for putting your faith in the one person who you're meant to undoubtedly trust."

I nod, eyes blurry with tears.

"When do you see Aurora next?" Logan asks, voice soft as he strokes his thumb to and fro across the back of my hand.

"Last Saturday of the month, so another two weeks—assuming my mom doesn't cancel."

Above my head, the two of them share a look. "Riley, have you spoken to Aurora since Christmas Day?" Royce asks with an edge to his voice that makes me wary of my response.

My resounding silence is answer enough. "Fucking hell, Ry, that's messed up." Royce practically vibrates with rage.

"It is what it is. It's not like I haven't tried to get in touch with my mom. She just likes to ignore my calls until it's payday."

There's an almost feral edge to Royce's voice. "You mean to tell me we're two weeks into the year, and you haven't gotten to tell your daughter Happy New Year?"

I shake my head.

"That fucking bitch."

I snort, in total agreement with his assessment of my mother.

"Isn't there anything you can do?" Logan asks, just as outraged.

There's a forced nonchalance to my shrug. "I could get on the train and go see her next weekend, although it's likely to do more harm than good. This is just something my mom does. Eventually, she'll come asking for money and I'll have my leverage to get a conversation or meeting with Rora."

"That's... I don't even have words," Logan empathizes.

"It's disgusting, is what it is," Royce snarls.

"If you still haven't heard from your mom by next weekend, I'll drive you to wherever she is," Logan insists. "Or maybe we shouldn't wait 'til the weekend. We could go after class someday this week. I have practice on—" I cut him off by placing my hand on top of his.

"That's a sweet offer, but you don't have to do that."

"I want to," he insists. "Besides, you think I can deal with this asshole having seen her and not me? Not a chance. I have a feeling we're going to be besties. I'm thinking friendship bracelets and matching braids in our hair."

"Dude," Royce interjects, struggling to fight back a laugh. "What are you gonna do, grow a beard and braid that?"

"Maybe."

I can't help laughing at their banter, which I'm sure is their intention.

"Let me try and get in touch with my mom this week. I don't want to rock the boat unnecessarily. She'll be pissed if I show up randomly, and life will be easier if I can avoid that."

"Alright," Logan agrees. "Well, whenever you wanna go, just say the word and we will."

"Thank you."

We move on to lighter topics of conversation after that, before Royce eventually moves to start the truck and we make our way back to Halston.

"I'll walk you to your door," Logan states when Royce pulls to a stop outside my apartment. I arch a brow since my building is *right there*, but he's already pushing open the door and climbing out.

Turning away, I meet Royce's heavy gaze in the rearview mirror, and leaning forward between the two front seats, I press a chaste kiss to his cheek. "Night," I whisper with a final lingering gaze before sliding out of the back of the truck.

Logan is there to help me down, keeping his hand wrapped around mine while walking me the five steps to my front door. Standing in front of me, he lets go of my hand to slide his around the back of my neck, his fingers tangling around the strands of hair at the base of my scalp as he tilts my head back and lowers his forehead to rest against mine.

His chestnut hues shine with so much emotion.

"Thank you for confiding in me," he rasps, voice thick. "I know it can't have been easy, and I'm going to prove that I'm worthy of your trust."

My fingers dig into his forearms, my hand wrapping around the corded muscle.

"You told me not to shut you out... this is me showing you

the real me. I'm trusting you with the most important aspect of my life. Don't let me down, Logan."

My heart hammers against my ribs. I don't regret telling Logan. I felt he deserved to know, and I'm done keeping my daughter a secret. Of shying away from her existence as though I should be ashamed. It's exposing her to the entire world that terrifies me because it makes her a weapon that can be used against me.

"I won't. I swear it," Logan vows ardently. He doesn't give me time to even suck in a breath before his lips cover mine in a ravenous kiss.

All I can do is cling to him, my nails digging into the skin of his arms as he pours every ounce of earnest gratitude into his kiss, soothing away the ragged edges left from tonight's conversation and brushing any remnants of worry into the wind like dandelion pappus on a breeze.

His hands frame my face; his lips firmly pressed to mine like I'm the buoy keeping him from drifting out to sea. Or maybe he's the one preventing me from drifting. Either way, I've never felt more reassured. I thought baring all my secrets to the world would be like stripping away layers of clothing. I expected it to leave me feeling raw and vulnerable. Exposed. Criticized. But in Logan's arms, and knowing Royce will always be at my back, the last thing I feel is judged.

My heart thumps against my chest, pounding with an acceptance that slides along my nerves until I feel it in the tips of my fingers and toes. My blood warms with it, my mind calming as it wraps around me like the softest of blankets.

Logan's long, slender fingers trail down the sides of my neck as he slows our kiss, as though he can't quite bring himself to end it just yet. With a resigned sigh, he finally detaches his lips from mine, and slowly opening my eyes, I find him already watching me, eyes soft and expression tinged with awe.

"I'll see you bright and early in the morning?"

Huffing out a laugh, I tell him, "You don't need to keep bringing me coffee every morning, Logan."

"Oh, but I do. I still have a lot of making up to do, and it's even more important now that I achieve it."

My lips quirk up in a smile. "Fine, but no more names on jerseys, yeah?"

His returning smile is devilish as he steps away. "No promises, Shortcake."

"Logan," I warn.

"Night, Shortcake." His voice is laden with emotion, and I find myself dropping the argument.

"Night, Logan."

He stands and waits as I let myself into my building, only walking back to Royce's waiting truck when I give him a final finger wave through the pane of glass before heading up the stairs.

I've barely gotten my key in the door of my apartment when my phone pings with the first text, more coming through in the time it takes to get into the apartment, pull my phone from the small handbag I brought tonight, and get comfy on the sofa with a blanket over my knees.

LOGAN

Kissing you outside your apartment tonight: 15/10

Been dreaming about that kiss for weeks, and it was far better than my imagination could ever have conjured.

I grin ridiculously down at the screen, a tightening in my chest as I realize just how much I've missed this. Missed Logan's jokey, easy side. The side of him I was privy to before everything went so horrifically wrong. It doesn't fix the issues, but no one act will. However, all the little things Logan's been doing... they do make a difference. And I'm starting to believe that maybe one day they'll be enough.

I glance down as my phone vibrates in my hand, and realize there's a bunch of others from him.

LOGAN

Watching you give Royce a blow job: 9/10

Way hotter than I thought it would be if I was to ever see his sparkling junk. It was a struggle not to blow my load right there and then and jerking off in the shower to the thought of your lips stretched around my cock, those bright eyes staring up at me was nowhere near as satisfying as the real thing will be.

And now I'm hard, and Royce is glaring at me like I dared to whip it out in front of him.

I burst out laughing, picturing Royce's dark glare and Logan's lopsided grin. Of course, the idiot couldn't wait until he was alone in his room to begin his antics.

LOGAN

Every night watching you dance: -10/10

I frown at the screen, anxiously awaiting his reasoning. However, my fears instantly dissolve as I read his next text.

LOGAN

Pure torture. Blue balls are a real and deadly thing, Shortcake. I don't know what genius plan Grayson thought he'd come up with, but I'm fairly certain he tortured us more than you with that nonsense.

Chuckling, I fire off my first response.

ME

I didn't hear you complaining at the time.

LOGAN

You mean, you didn't hear me grunting your name as I came all over my hand every night?

Before I can respond to that, he fires back with his next one.

LOGAN

Fingering you that night after my game: 7/10

I wanted to do so much more. Wish I hadn't been so conflicted. Wish I'd already known the truth. I'd have scooped you up and brought you to my bed and told you how brave and strong I think you are while worshiping every inch of your body.

. . .

My teeth sink into my bottom lip as another message pops up.

LOGAN

Not exactly dirty, so you'll have to forgive me.
Then again, my thoughts at the time definitely
weren't innocent, so… That first morning I
woke up to you in my bed: 100/10.

Nothing has ever felt more right.

I'm still basking in the glow from Logan's messages when I climb into bed. All may not be forgiven, but I'm optimistic for the first time in a long while. Hopeful even. Having told him about Aurora and having discussed everything with him and Royce, I feel as though an immense weight has been lifted off my chest.

Next step: Find a way to tell Grayson.

That's not a problem for tonight, or even this week, but it's one I should probably work toward.

GRAYSON

CHAPTER TWENTY-ONE

"Anyone home?" I call, listening for any sound of life as I walk through the door. My mind is fried after spending the day at the prison visiting Dad. I've been dodging his calls, trying to avoid talking to him while I sort everything out in my head, but after spending hours yesterday with his lawyers, I decided to bite the bullet today and go see him. It's not like I could put it off for much longer without him growing suspicious or asking questions. I've been able to claim I'm busy with the new semester and work, but that excuse will only hold up for so long.

I spent the entire time staring at my dad, wondering if he was not the man I always thought he was. Trying to envision him as the monster Gran depicted.

Except I couldn't.

He has his faults, of course. He's brusque and driven. Never one to coddle or comfort me, but once I grew up, I never needed him to.

I kept wracking my brain, trying to remember what he was like with Mom. I never recall seeing them laugh or witnessing any sweet moments between them. In fact, I hardly remember them spending any time together.

So lost in my thoughts and not listening to a word he said, I'd asked aloud, "Do you ever miss Mom?"

My father had just blinked at me. "What sort of question is that? Are you even listening to me?"

"You never talk about her."

"I've had more important things to deal with, Grayson," He'd snapped with a crease forming between his brows. "What is this all about?"

Debating for a second, I then told him, "I never remember the two of you spending any real time together, so I was just wondering why."

"Your mother and I had very different yet equally hectic schedules. She was busy raising you, and then she wasn't well while I was working long hours to build her family company into what it is today."

I'd stiffened at that remark because *I* have made the company what it is today. Sure, Dad grew and expanded it, but he also nearly destroyed it.

"So you had a good relationship? You loved one another?"

"She was my wife," he drolls as though the two go hand in hand. They *should*, but that doesn't mean they do. Especially not in the world of money, where everyone's goal is acquiring more wealth, regardless of the fact they already own more than they could spend in three lifetimes. "Now, can we get back to the more pressing issue of my parole?"

"Yeah," I'd reluctantly agreed, knowing I wouldn't make any headway with him. I'm not sure what I'd expected from the conversation. For him to choke up and tell me he loved my mom and missed her every single day... yeah, I knew going in that that was never going to happen.

However, his lack of a straight answer has stuck with me the entire journey home.

Honestly, I'm kinda glad Royce pushed to have this talk tonight. I've been wavering back and forth between confiding in them. With tensions being high between us recently, I've found myself biting back the words every time one of them asks what's wrong.

I just know they'll relate it to Riley and I don't want to hear about that. This is about my mom, about the terror I saw in Gran's eyes when she mistook me for Dad. For once, since I saw her in that godforsaken club, it is *not* about Riley fucking James.

Just seeing Logan with her last week. Watching him defend her... fucking protect her *from me...*

Then, finding out Royce is still stalking her every move like the psychotic creeper he is. I should have known she was where he kept slinking off to, but since he'd ordered me and Logan to stay away, I assumed the same rules had also applied to him.

Guess I was wrong.

Don't even get me started on that vomit-inducing shit Logan pulled at his game last night. I have never regretted going to a hockey game as much as I did last night. I never should have allowed Royce to talk me into that shit, and had I known Logan was going to pull that stunt, I'd have gladly stayed home. Except I was trying to make a fucking effort. To repair some of the damage between us. I scoff at my naivety.

Still, I'm fucking here, ready to talk to them because I can't keep analyzing this shit in my head. I need to speak to someone, and regardless of everything, Logan and Royce are the only two people I trust enough to have this conversation with.

Only it doesn't appear as though either of them is home. I check the time on my watch, noticing that it's still early enough. Royce is probably only getting into the ring now, which means it could be another hour or so before they're home. That gives me time to work out while I figure out how to coherently explain the jumbled mess in my head.

Thirty minutes later, I'm breathing heavily, sweat slicking my skin as I head for the bathroom. Turning on the shower, steam fills the room as I strip out of my workout gear before stepping beneath the hot spray.

The water sluices over my skin, washing the day off me, and with one hand pressed against the cold tiles, I duck my head, allowing the heat to ease the strain on my muscles as it trickles down my neck.

Closing my eyes, flashes of copper and russet assault my vision, whipping through the air and curling around me until the smell of my menthol shower gel is replaced with something fruitier. The auburn hues meld into achingly familiar hazel irises, and at the echo of her pleading voice, my dick swells with interest.

I groan, even as I fight the urge to give into my body's desires, but even though she's not physically present, Riley has wrapped herself around my mind, and all I can see is the way she looked that day in the field. The resounding silence that filled my mind when she reached up and kissed me. How sliding into her felt like I'd finally found peace.

Unable to deny myself any longer, I reach down and fist my straining erection, pretending it's her holding me in a death grip. I bite down on my lower lip the way she did, losing myself in that animalistic urgency the way we did that day in the field... I'm lost in the sound of my breaths, the phantom feel of her hips slamming against mine, and just as my balls draw up, an image of Logan on the precipice of kissing Riley slams into me, followed by ones of Royce watching her dance on stage, and that all-consuming need twists into undeniable rage as I roar out my release.

"God fucking dammit," I rasp, sagging against the tiles as I catch my breath. "What the ever-loving fuck was that?"

I frown at the wall as I recover from my intense-as-fuck orgasm, attempting to put the pieces together. It almost seemed as though I was... jealous of Logan and Royce, only there's no fucking way that's the case. A scoff renders through the air. No chance.

She's the bane of my fucking existence.

And the best fuck I've ever had.

I shake my head to dispel that pesky voice.

The only reason she popped into my mind right now is because she's *always* on my fucking mind—because she ruined my fucking family.

Not because I want to fuck her. Or because I'm jealous.

I'm not either of those things.

"I need to get laid," I grumble aloud.

Except, it's only auburn hair and hazel eyes I see when I picture that so, yeah, maybe not.

Not feeling as refreshed as I should after such a wrenching climax, I shut off the shower and climb out. Checking the time, I realize I wasted far more time than I care to admit daydreaming about *her*. Logan and Royce must be back by now, so I hurriedly towel off before pulling on sweats and a hoodie and padding downstairs.

However, the house is silent, and the kitchen is empty when I reach it. I call out their names, checking each room downstairs before knocking on their doors. I didn't hear any sounds from their rooms when I passed, but maybe I missed it, too busy thinking about everything we needed to discuss. Everything I need to tell them.

Poking my head into both their rooms, I find them empty. Huh, I guess they stayed a little longer than usual. Royce probably got caught up talking to Xander or roped into another fight. It's not unusual for that to happen, so I shrug it off and grab a beer from the fridge before flicking on the TV while I wait for them.

My thoughts once again drift to our ensuing conversation.

I'm still hesitant to tell the guys, to hear what they think. To have the life I thought I knew very possibly ripped out from beneath me.

But at this point, I don't see that I have any other choice.

The truth is, I'm... floundering.

I wake up every night to Gran's broken voice in my head and Riley's hazel eyes staring back at me. Wide. Pleading. Looking oh so fucking innocent.

I'm psychoanalyzing every childhood memory, wondering if the harshness in my father's face and the trembling of my mother's hands were real or a figment of my imagination.

I can no longer tell what's real from what isn't. The truth from the lies.

Up is down, and down is up, and nothing in my life is making sense anymore.

The beer goes down too easily, and I pop the top off a second one while I wait. It's only when I've downed that too that I realize how much time has passed.

Where the fuck are they?

I type the same question into our group chat and stare at the screen, expecting the little gray ticks to turn blue, letting me know it's been read. Except the color doesn't change.

Growling, I press the call button and listen as it rings three times before cutting off. *What the fuck?* Logan, the bastard just hung up on me. Getting seriously pissed off now, I call Royce, but his just rings out. *Are the two of them ignoring me?*

"Such fucking bullshit," I mutter aloud to absolutely no one because I'm all fucking alone in this house.

Deciding beer isn't strong enough, I switch to whiskey,

sipping at it over the next few hours as I stare unseeingly at the TV. The array of colors is the only light illuminating the room and casting shadows over my depressive thoughts.

The one night we're supposed to talk... Royce was the one that fucking insisted on this, yet where the hell is he? Not here, that's where. Not where he's fucking supposed to be. Where he said he would be.

It's then that it hits me... could they be with Riley? As soon as the possibility enters my mind, it's all I can fixate on. Of course, that's where they are. Wherever *she* is.

That goddamn bitch, stealing yet another thing from me.

She shouldn't fucking be here!

Halston U was supposed to be *my* fresh start. Away from all the bullshit from high school. Here, I'm no longer the son of convicted felon Bertram Van Doren. I'm just Grayson. Business major. Top of his year. These four years were my reprieve before committing myself fully to Van Doren Holdings and building a company that people would respect out of the smoldering ashes my father left it in.

And she just had to come in and tear it all down.

Rip away all the walls I carefully constructed around myself.

So many universities in the country and she just *had* to pick mine.

I've never believed in a higher power, but if there is one, he fucking hates me.

Slumping lower in my chair, something falls out of the pocket of my sweatpants, and I lean forward to pick it off the floor, my fingers curling around the soft cotton of a pink hair scrunchie. I stare at it for a long moment. For some reason, I've been carrying the damn thing everywhere with me lately.

My memory flashes back to a teenage version of Riley. She was wearing this scrunchie the day she walked into my life, all wide-eyed and luminescent smiles as she introduced herself.

"Hi, I'm Riley. I'm really hoping we can be friends and this isn't going to be like it is in some of the books I've read where you hate me purely out of principle."

All I can do is blink at the dainty girl in front of me, her wild, auburn hair restrained in a ponytail and hazel eyes radiant as she holds out her hand expectantly. It's at that moment that I discover I've been trapped in the Arctic my entire life, and she's the sun finally come to melt the ice encasing me. I'm instantly captivated, unaware that from this moment on, she'd be the center of my universe around which everything else would revolve.

Realizing I've been silent for too long, staring at her like a creep, I smile, slotting my hand into hers. Sparks zap up my forearm, a jolt of electricity going straight to my heart.

"I'm Grayson," I tell her, "And I'm pretty sure the last thing I could ever do is hate you."

I'm jolted from my memory at the sound of the front door opening, hushed whispers reaching my ears as I blink back into the room. I stumble to my feet, my gait unsteady as my head spins from too much alcohol.

Blinking away the lightheadedness, the room comes fully into focus. Royce and Logan are standing in the doorway, staring at me with expressions I can't decipher in my slightly inebriated state.

"Where the fuck have you been?" I bark, glowering at the pair of them.

"The Depot," Logan answers, but there's something off about his tone that makes me narrow my eyes on him.

"We went to Leon's afterward," Royce adds.

I grunt out a response.

"Dude, maybe you should go to bed," Logan says, and when my gaze snaps to him, it takes a few blinks before I'm able to see the worry etched onto his face.

"I'm fine."

He scoffs. "Yeah, getting drunk at home, alone... you're the picture of *fine*."

"I wouldn't have been drinking alone if you'd been here *like you were supposed to be*."

"Shit," Royce hisses, looking chagrined as he swipes a hand through his hair, brushing a loose strand back from his face. "I'm sorry, man. I forgot."

I scoff. "Too busy balls deep in that whore, I imagine."

Royce's expression hardens to steel as Logan snarls, "That's enough. If you're just going to insult Riley, then you can take your drunk ass to bed... or anywhere else but here."

"Whatever," I say, the words slurring, only I'm way past caring. I stagger toward them, the whiskey bottle swinging from my fingers. "I'm done waiting around for you two to pull your dicks out of her."

Logan growls in warning, but it's Royce who reaches out to stop me on the threshold. "Gray. Look, I'm sorry, but we're here now. We could... talk." He frowns, giving me a once-over. "Or just chill for a bit."

Fucking exhausted and in need of sitting, I'm about to agree when Logan shifts and I catch a hint of something sweet and fruity. "I thought you were at The Depot?" My voice is deceptively calm, blanketing the raging flames of chaos flaring inside me.

"We were," Logan throws back defensively.

"Then why do you both smell like *her?*"

I watch as both of them stiffen before Logan shakes it off with a shrug of his shoulders. "None of your fucking business."

My teeth grind, the noise like nails on a chalkboard in the otherwise soundless room. Eyes snapping to Royce, I say in a dead tone, "At least now I know where your loyalties lie."

I shove my way past them, ignoring Royce as he calls after me. "Come on, Gray. It's not like that. We ran into her there."

Yeah, and they *chose* to hang out with her instead of agreeing to the plans *he* made.

"Gray!" he calls again as I reach the top of the stairs, thankful when I can block out their murmuring with the shutting of my bedroom door. With the bottle still in hand, I collapse on my bed and stare absently at the ceiling as I drown my sorrows in top-shelf whiskey and pretend everything isn't crumbling around me.

I'm three sheets to the wind by the time I stumble out of the house later that night—or maybe it's early morning now. Who the fuck cares? I haven't the first fucking clue where I'm going; I just know I need to get out of my room. Away from the swirling whirlpool of my ever-depressing thoughts. Away from the rage coiling through me. The bitter loneliness. The hostility. The doubt. The anger.

Away from fucking *everything*.

I stagger drunkenly through the deserted streets of Halston, my bottle of nearly empty whiskey clutched like a lifeline in my hand. My surroundings are a blur, though at least the cool night air is a calming balm to the storm raging inside.

Tripping over a curb, I lose my grip on the bottle, and it hits the ground, smashing on impact. "Nooo," I moan. "Wilson!" I cackle at my joke before leaving the shattered remains on the sidewalk. Looking up, I blink blearily as a familiar red-brick building comes into focus.

It takes me a moment to recall where I am. However, once I do, I stumble toward the door and yank it open. If I were sober, I'd probably scoff at the lack of security in this place, but since I'm not, I simply smile at my good fortune. A smile that is abruptly wiped from my face when I catch my foot on the step and nearly fall flat on my face in the grimy tiled lobby.

What is with everything trying to trip me up tonight? Fuckin rude!

I catch myself at the last minute, eyes squinting on the rows of boxes until I find one with her last name. Apartment 7.

I spin around, the whole world going fuzzy and black at the edges, before my eyes narrow on the stairs. "Ughhh," I groan. "*Stairs.*" I conduct a thorough search of the lobby—if you could call it that—for an elevator but of course this shitty apartment building doesn't have one. What apartment block doesn't have an elevator these days? Who could live in such a state?

Guess there's nothing else for it.

Shaking my head in abhorrence, I glower at the flight of stairs. "Don't trip me up," I slur, before I begin conquering the stairway to hell. Another burst of laughter escapes me. "More accurately, the stairway to the devil herself."

With a death grip on the handrail, I grunt and groan my way up the two flights. By the time I reach Riley's floor, I pump both fists in the air like I just won gold at the Olympics, before squinting at the door numbers in search of apartment seven.

I find it at the end of the hall, swaying on my feet as I stare at the mundane door. *What am I doing here again?* Oh yes, I wanted to give the bitch on the other side of the door a piece of my mind.

Slumping forward, I peer through the eyehole, but nothing comes into focus, and I can't work out if it's me or the shitty doors in this place.

"Riley!" I bellow, banging my fist against the wood. "Riley!" Pausing, I squint at the red-chipped painted door. "Ry-lee," I try again since her name came out as more of a slur the first two times.

"What do you want, Grayson?" comes her sharp voice

through the door. My heart picks up speed as my molars grind. How can that voice simultaneously perk me up and piss me off?

"You," I slur.

No, wait. What? I shake it off. That's not what I meant.

"You're drunk. Go away, Grayson."

Instead of listening to her, I press my back against the door and slide down it until I hit the floor. Breathing heavily, my eyes feel like they have two-ton weights attached to them as I rest my head against the wooden door.

I swear I can hear her moving around inside before there's a soft thud. Is she sitting on the other side? I'm going to pretend she is, 'cause otherwise, I'm having a conversation with a door, and that's just too pathetic to comprehend.

"I have your scrunchie," I tell the door. "It doesn't smell like you anymore, though," I continue when my words are met with silence. "It used to smell of that body spray stuff you'd use, but it doesn't anymore. I don't like it."

Somewhere along the way, I forget that Riley is sitting on the other side and I just start rambling, not even fully aware of what I'm saying. They're just words I've kept bottled up for too long.

"Do you remember that dickhead who'd always pull your hair at school? I gave him a black eye for harassing you, and when he told me he liked you, I broke his nose."

"Why would you do that?" Her voice breaks through the silence, so close that it sounds like she's beside me. I get distracted, staring at the door unblinkingly for a long moment as I picture her sitting right there, her head pressed against the wood the same way mine is.

Lifting a hand, I flatten it against the door, imagining her doing the same.

"All I want is to hate you," I rasp so low I'm not sure she

even hears me, except a moment later she responds, sounding beyond exhausted.

"You do hate me."

I shake my head, forgetting that she can't see me. "Hate is the farthest thing I feel for you." I sag further into the wood as the alcohol courses through my system. "You've had all of my attention from the moment you stepped into my house all those years ago. And I wasn't the only one who noticed you. I had to declare you off limits to the guys on the team because they'd keep saying they were going to ask you out, and I couldn't fucking handle it." I sigh wearily. "You've always been mine, even if I could never have you."

Turning, I press my forehead against the door, the weight on my eyes becoming too much as they drift closed, and I release a long exhale. "I *can't* hate you, even when I want to. Even when I know I should. For a while there, I'd convinced myself I did, but all it took was one look at you on that stage..." My teeth grind, my pants growing tight. "And the last thing I felt for you was hate."

The world grows black and silent around me. Actually, I think I pass out for a bit, only startling back into consciousness at the sound of Riley's soft, tired voice. "Go home, Grayson."

I nod, my forehead rubbing against the rough wood of her door, but I can't seem to feel my feet, so I continue to sit there slumped on the worn carpet outside her apartment.

I'm not sure how much time passes. I'm pretty sure I doze some more, but finally, a voice in the back of my head nags at me that I can't spend the night sleeping out here, and I stumble to my feet, somehow managing to make it down the treacherous stairs without breaking my neck and stagger into the frigid night.

Making the ten-minute walk to my house seems to take a lifetime. Probably doesn't help that I keep forgetting where I'm supposed to be going and can't seem to remain upright unless I use a building to prop me up.

Fucking finally, home sweet home comes into sight, and I internally rejoice. "Mwahaha, I win this time," I sneer at the door after spending a good five minutes attempting to get my key into the lock before slamming the door behind me and lumbering up the stairs, all the while cursing them out. Stairs are the worst invention ever. We should get an elevator. *Mental note to self: contact someone about installing an elevator in the house.*

I don't think I run into either Royce or Logan as I make my way to my bedroom, but honestly, my vision is so tunneled and blurry at this point that I dunno if I'd recognize them even if I did.

As the darkness sweeps in and consumes me, I fall face-first onto my bed and pass out fully clothed.

I wake in the morning to sunlight stabbing me in the eyes. It tastes like something died in my mouth, and I wrack my brain trying to put together the pieces of last night. I remember getting home from visiting Dad. Waiting like a sad-sack for Logan and Royce to get home... only for them to smell of *her*. A fresh wave of hostility courses through me as I remember storming off to my room and downing the rest of the bottle of whiskey. I'm guessing I passed out at some point after that.

Scrubbing a hand down my face, I groan into my palm. Alcohol had sounded like a good idea last night, but this morning, my problems are as stark as the morning light currently blinding me.

Turning my face away from the window, I decide my problems can wait another couple of hours while I try to sleep off this hangover, except my phone chooses that moment to ring, the obnoxious noise like the slamming of cymbals against my ears.

Groaning, I roll over and reach blindly for the blaring device on my bedside table. Finding it, I squint through gritty eyes, cursing under my breath as the caller ID notifies me that it's my father calling. *Ugh, what can he want? I only spoke to him yesterday.*

My lips purse as I glare at the phone, undecided whether to answer. I'd wanted to talk to Royce and Logan before having to speak to my dad again, but after last night, I realize now that I'm alone in this. Just like I have been in everything else in my life.

With a bone-weary sigh, I collapse back on the bed and accept his call. Perhaps it's better this way. Better to ignore the likely paranoid ramblings of an Alzheimer's patient and the manipulative tactics of a liar. Better to ignore the uneasiness in my gut. The rapid uptick of my heart in *her* presence.

Better to shut down everything and remind myself that I can only rely on myself. I don't need to fall down the rabbit hole, questioning my entire childhood, my entire *existence*. I don't need to depend on friends. And I sure as fuck don't need to be thinking of *her*.

RILEY

CHAPTER TWENTY-TWO

My eyes are gritty when I wake the next morning—thanks in part to Grayson for waking me in the middle of the night with his drunken breakdown. What was he even thinking coming here in the middle of the night and spouting shit about how he doesn't hate me and I've always been his? *Ugh, I can't even with him.* I scrub a hand down my face as I roll onto my back.

However, even without his disturbance, my sleep was broken. I tossed and turned, replaying my conversation with Royce and Logan last night. Seeing Logan's face in my dreams the moment he put the pieces together.

Not yet ready to get out of bed, I stare up at my ceiling as I process the knowledge that Logan now knows everything. Every dark secret I've tried to keep hidden these last four years.

Beyond the initial shock, he seemed to take the news in stride. He didn't pull away or treat me differently, but I worry that today will be different. Now that he's had time to sleep on it, he'll realize what a colossal disaster I am and that I'm more trouble than I'm worth. I mean, most twenty-two-year-olds aren't interested in pursuing single mothers. We're a complex package. Anyone who is with me will never have all of my focus. Never be the pinnacle of my life, because Aurora already has that position, and even when she's in her forties and has her own family, she will *still* be the most important person in my life.

And because I'm crazy, I worry that if Logan hasn't pulled away... that if he behaves the same way today as he did last week, he hasn't considered that. Hasn't realized the significance of dating someone with a child.

I've given myself a headache stressing over the entire thing when I finally force myself out of bed to get ready for the day, and by the time I'm heading out the door, I can't figure out if he'll be waiting for me outside or not. If I *want* him to be waiting for me.

I can't stop myself from scanning the street for his car the second I step onto the sidewalk, my heart plummeting through my chest and into my stomach when I find the street empty.

Well, I guess that's that then.

"I know it's a Monday, but the week can't be off to that horrible of a start already, can it?"

At the sound of his voice, I spin around, finding none other than Logan Astor leaning against the side of my building, one foot kicked up against the wall, and a recyclable tray containing two coffees in his hand.

"I... What are you... Where is your car?" I finally settle on, deciding that's the question that will make me look the least unstable.

Pushing off the wall, he prowls toward me. "Since it's a nice day, I was hoping we could walk to campus together." He looks so hopeful, and the fact that he left me open to say no, even though he had already walked here, has me nodding in agreement.

The grin that lights up his face is enough to loosen the anxiety holding my chest in a vise.

"It's not campus coffee," he says, handing me one of the cups in the tray. "I stopped at a cafe on the way over so it would still be warm."

Bringing it to my nose, I inhale. It smells just as good as the coffee on campus, and I thank him before we start down the street, side by side.

"Not that I'm not happy to see you," I begin, cringing at the way the words come out. "But, what are you doing here?"

"I thought it was obvious. Bringing you coffee and walking with you to campus," he responds with a wry glance.

"You know what I mean, Logan. After last night... After everything you found out... Why are you *here*?"

His brows have pulled down while I talked until his features are pinched in a severe frown, and he pulls me to a stop in the middle of the sidewalk. "Do you really think that finding out you have a daughter would make me change my mind about you? About us?"

"It should," I counter. "Have you thought about how a relationship between us would even work with a kid in the mix? You wouldn't just be dating me—you'd also be a prominent figure in her life. She doesn't live with me right now, but once I've graduated and got a job, I plan on changing that. By then, she'll be in school, and you'll have your hockey career. I won't be able to fly out to your away games 'cause I'll have to stay home with her. I won't be there to support you at every game the way other players will have their partners and girlfriends. I won't be able to go to parties afterward 'cause I'll have to get home to relieve the babysitter. She will *always* come first for me, Logan, and I'm not sure if that's something you can handle. If it's something you've even considered."

He's silent for a long moment. So long that any thin shreds

of hope I'd been clinging to turn to dust and slip through my fingers.

"That was some speech, Shortcake. I'll give you that. Points for really trying to push me away." Stepping closer, his palm slides around the back of my neck, fingers slipping through my hair until he cradles the back of my head. "But you're not saying anything I haven't already considered. I've spent all night thinking about this—about you, her, us—and I get it. I would never ask you to make me a priority above her. I don't need you at every single game if I know I'll be coming home to you after-ward. To our family."

"What about when you're a big shot for the Puffins or Pigeons... I forget the name. It begins with a P."

"The Pacific Penguins," he says with a humorous smile, "And I'm not going to be a big shot for the Penguins."

I scoff. "You will be," I tell him confidently. "That offer is coming. Just keep playing the way you have been."

His smile turns warm and genuine as his thumb glides back and forth up the back of my head. "I love your faith in me," he murmurs softly. "I already got an offer from the Penguins... and I turned it down."

My initial joy for him turns to confusion. "You turned down your dream job from your dream team? Logan, what the hell?! Why would you do that?"

He gives a nonchalant shrug of his shoulder. "The Penguins are no longer my dream team."

"But, it's an NHL offer. What if you don't get another one? What if—"

"I'll get another one," he states confidently.

"I... don't understand."

He flashes me his white teeth. "My agent is in talks with the Springview Timberwolves."

"The Springview… as in less than two hours from here, Springview Timberwolves?"

"That's the one."

"But… are they a good team? I thought the Penguins were the best. If they're not as good, then you won't make as much money or have the same sort of prospects or career advancement—"

"They're good enough," Logan interjects. "And even if they weren't, I'd still say yes to whatever they offer me." He squeezes the back of my neck, ensuring he has my full attention. "If it means being close to you."

My lips part but no sound comes out as I stare up at him.

"I can play for the Timberwolves while you finish college, and after that, we can see what we want to do. If Aurora is settled in school here, we can stay here, and if we want to move somewhere else, I'll make sure I get placed with a team nearby."

"You make it all sound so simple," I mutter, shell-shocked.

"'Cause it is simple, Shortcake."

"I haven't even forgiven you yet."

He only grins as he drapes his arm over my shoulder and tugs me back into motion. "Good thing I'll now have an extra three years to earn it."

Logan meets me outside the dining hall for lunch, and I notice the lack of food in his hands as I approach.

"So," he hedges. "I was thinking today we could go to the food court since you should realize by now that regardless of where we eat, I'll be buying the food. But if you don't want to brave the students there, we can go to a cafe or something instead."

I chew on the inside of my lip as I mull it over. "I do like that spicy chicken dish the food court serves."

His answering smile is all light and sunshine. "Food court it is, then."

"Have you invited Royce?"

"Nah, the food court isn't exactly his scene."

"Well, you should still invite him to eat with us. We can always go somewhere else if he doesn't wanna eat there."

Still smiling, he dips down to kiss my nose. "Always thinking of everyone else," he murmurs admirably before pulling back. "Alright, I'll message him, but he won't come."

I lift one shoulder in a shrug. "At least we've invited him."

Together, we head to the glass structure that houses the food court. Following him inside, the low hum of chatter reaches my ears along with the delectable combination of scents from various food options, from Thai to sushi to good old burgers and fries. My mouth salivates as my eyes bounce over the multiple food stations placed around the perimeter of the court. Each is a masterpiece of modern design with gleaming countertops, state-of-the-art cooking equipment, and displays that showcase the drool-worthy offerings.

Natural light pours through the floor-to-ceiling windows, illuminating the entire space and offering panoramic views of the college's meticulously landscaped gardens and paths.

Most of the central space features sleek wooden tables and plush chairs, which provide inviting spaces for students to gather, work, and enjoy their meals. Cozy booths adorned with vibrant cushions offer more intimate spots for group discussions and relaxed study sessions.

"What do you feel like eating?" Logan asks at my side.

"Ehhh..." I'm too overwhelmed to narrow it down to just one option.

Realizing this, Logan says, "You wanted the spicy chicken,

yeah?" I nod and follow him to a Thai food station, where he loads up plates with various options before directing me to another. Just like always, he fills the tray with enough food to feed an army, and when satisfied, he leads me through the busy tables. People call out to him as we pass, but he doesn't stop, acknowledging them with a tilt of his head or one of his infamous smiles.

"Yo, Logan!"

He stops at a table overflowing with tall, broad-shouldered men, and it only takes a moment for me to recognize the other faces of the Halston U hockey team.

"You sitting with us?" the same man asks.

"Nah, I'm gonna eat with my girl today." All eyes snap to me, and I feel my cheeks heat as I smile and give the table a self-conscious wave.

"Good to see you actually exist," Anderson—I forget his first name—says with an amusing grin. "We were beginning to think our man, Logan, had gotten so desperate he had to invent a fake girlfriend."

"Nope, I'm perfectly real, but inventing a fake girlfriend does sound like something Logan would do."

"Hey!" Logan chastises with a teasing smile as the table chortles. "I haven't had to do that since junior high."

Another burst of laughter goes up from the table, and this time, I join in.

"Anyway, we're gonna go eat. I'll catch you guys later."

"Later, man," Anderson says, as the rest of the table mutters their goodbyes. "Nice to finally meet you, Riley."

I almost trip over my feet as Logan leads me away, not expecting any of them to know my name, but then again Logan did pin it to the back of his jersey for everyone to see.

"We didn't have to sit over here if you wanna eat with your team," I say when we sit down at an empty table along the glass wall that overlooks the expansive green at the front of campus.

"Nah. I spend enough time with them and not nearly enough with you."

My cheeks once again flush, burning brightly beneath Logan's attention, and I duck my head, picking up a French fry and smothering it in ketchup before placing it between my lips.

"I usually split my time between sitting with the team or with Royce and Grayson. Not that Royce comes here anymore, and Gray's more likely to stab me with a fork these days."

I frown at his dark tone. "Did something new happen with you guys?" I knew there was tension between them, but the way he says it, it sounds like something went down. *Could that be what had Grayson showing up drunk at my door last night?*

"It's nothing," he dismisses, shaking his head. "Just Grayson being his usual pigheaded self."

"Mmm." I know that version of him well. "Hey, my neighbor's kid is really into hockey at the minute. They were watching your game with me the other night, and I was wondering if it's possible to get tickets for your next home game? No worries, if it's not, I just thought I'd ask."

"Of course. That's not a problem. How many do you need?"

"Hmm, two? Three?" I deliberate briefly before saying, "Three so I can go too."

"Shortcake, there's always a permanent seat rinkside for you," Logan says, a goofy grin splitting his face. "I'll get tickets sorted so your friends can join you for the next game."

Blushing, I murmur my thanks before sampling the food in front of me as Logan's phone pings in his pocket. Pulling it out, he makes an incredulous noise. "Well, well. Mr. Hermit himself has deigned to grace us with his presence."

Arching a brow, I stare at him in confusion, having absolutely no idea who he's talking about.

"Royce is joining us for lunch."

"Thought you said this wasn't his scene?"

"It's not. He hasn't set foot in here all year."

"So why is he coming today?"

Logan pierces me with a stare that says I should know *exactly* why Royce is eating in the food court today.

"Because of me?"

He smirks, leaning back in his chair. "Well, it sure as shit ain't because of me."

I swear I sense when Royce enters the room. I could justify it on how the entire room momentarily goes silent. Voices drop to a whisper as all attention turns to him.

But that would be bullshit. I knew he was here before anyone else. The second his eyes settled on me, I felt it. The weight of his gaze. The intensity of his stare. We're connected in a way I've never been to anyone else. Our life forces are intertwined. I couldn't *not* sense him even if I was blindfolded.

Heads turn, whispers following in his wake as he crosses the court. Unlike Logan, Royce doesn't acknowledge a single person. His face is set in its typical hard mask, his *fuck off* shining neon bright for everyone to see.

"Holy shit, Royce King!" I hear a student at a nearby table gasp. "I haven't seen him since he won us the championship game last year. Does anyone know why he isn't on the team anymore?"

Out of the corner of my eye, I notice the rest of the table shake their heads. Royce's sudden disappearance from the team —and college life in general—appears to be a campus-wide mystery.

I hadn't realized until now that Royce was as infamous as Logan. Despite no longer being on the football team, girls still push out their chests and bat their lashes at him as he passes, and guys hold up their hands for expectant high-fives that Royce completely disregards.

The hall sits in stunned silence as he approaches our table and lowers into the seat beside me, deliberately sitting so he's angled with his back to the room.

This close, I can see the tense set of his shoulders, the way they sit close to his ears, and his facial expression is pinched. It's clear he's uncomfortable as fuck with all this attention on him.

Shifting closer, I slide a hand onto his knee beneath the table. Placing his on top of mine, he squeezes, although the harshness on his face doesn't lessen.

When the silence in the room lingers, the weight of hundreds of eyes on us, he shifts to glare at the gawking crowd. His expression is so foreboding that it has all heads snapping away, the room bursting into loud conversation once more.

Only then do his shoulders marginally relax, and when he turns back to face me, his expression somewhat softens. "Hi, Babydoll."

"Hey."

"Dude," Logan interjects. "See what happens when you avoid people for half the fucking year."

Royce glares at his best friend before ignoring him altogether. "How have your classes been so far?" he asks me.

"Good. I'm taking Psychology 101 this semester, and I'm enjoying it more than I thought."

His smile is small but genuine as he inches closer until his thigh presses against mine, our fingers interlocking where they rest on his knee.

"Have you eaten?" I ask, nudging the tray toward him.

"Hey, I bought that for you," Logan pouts.

"You have zero concept of how much a regular person eats,"

I tell him, pointing a fry in his face as Royce chuckles under his breath. "There's plenty to go around."

"So," Logan begins in between bites. "You brought it up this morning, and I didn't get the chance to ask you about it, but why does Aurora live with your mom?"

I glance warily around the food court in case anyone is listening in on our conversation.

Catching on, Logan leans in and lowers his voice. "Do you not want to talk about her here?"

"No, it's fine. I'd just gotten used to not talking about her so freely." Logan's mouth curls in dislike as Royce's nostrils flare. "And probably best that the entire campus doesn't know, but no one's listening. If we keep our voices low, we're fine." Fiddling with my fork, my stomach churns with unpleasant memories as I attempt to explain, "I was sixteen when I had Aurora. A minor. My mom had already played off everything with Bertram as attention seeking, and the nurses had made her aware of my, uh, scars." I swallow roughly. "Once Aurora was born, Mom used that to have me declared unfit and herself instated as Aurora's primary guardian."

"Okay, but that was back then," Logan says, looking confused. "What about now?"

"Mom won't willingly hand her over to me, and court cases cost money. I was able to save enough last year to consult a lawyer, and he essentially said it would be a waste of money."

Logan growls in disgust. "Fighting to gain custody of your child is a *waste of money?*"

"Why did he say that?" Royce asks, sounding much more reasonable. Only there's an unmistakable hint of violence simmering beneath his words.

"I was a high school graduate living at home with my mom and working two dead-end jobs with no money or prospects.

He said no judge in their right mind would choose me, even though I'm Aurora's biological mother."

"But you're her *mom*," Logan emphasizes, looking simultaneously pissed and confused.

I just shrug, not having an answer for him. It is what it is… and yup, Logan's right, that *has* become my mentality to everything in life.

"So that's why you're here," Royce muses before Logan can start into the tirade I see forming.

I nod. "Yup. I'm going to get a degree and a secure job, and I'm going to save the money to hire a team of lawyers. Whatever it takes to get her back."

Logan's mouth opens as he goes to say something, but one look from Royce and his jaw snaps shut.

"I don't doubt for a second that you'll achieve it," Royce says instead. At the sincerity in his voice, I peer up at him with a smile.

"Thank you."

It feels really nice to have someone believe in me.

An hour later, when we've finished lunch, Logan walks me to my next class. However, before I can untangle my hand from his, he whips me around, his fingers sinking into my hair as he cups the back of my head, pulling on the strands until I stare up at him. His other hand grasps my hip, tugging me flush against him as his lips descend on mine.

Flames erupt, and I happily burn to ash in their wake.

I'm breathless and soaked by the time we pull apart, my voice raspy as I ask, "What was that for?"

He huffs out a laugh. "I couldn't let you go without leaving you with the reminder of how fucking perfect we are together."

The tingling of my lips agrees with him.

"Get to class, Shortcake. I'll see you after."

Nodding, I watch as he saunters down the hall before I turn

toward my classroom. Movement out of the corner of my eye has my head snapping to the side, spotting Grayson standing at the far end of the hall in the opposite direction to where Logan disappeared.

His eyes burn into me, simmering with a possessiveness that I need to look away from. Instead, I scour his face, searching for any signs he remembers showing up at my door last night. He looks like crap after his bender, with dark shadows under his eyes and his hair ruffled in a way I haven't seen before. Like he rolled out of bed, giving zero shits about his appearance before heading to campus.

Catching me staring, his eyes narrow into their familiar hostility, and I find it impossible to compute the man in front of me with the drunk version sitting outside my door, telling me he kept a scrunchie I wore four years ago and that he broke some guy's nose because he liked me.

Looking at him now, I find it impossible to believe he truly meant it when he said hate was the farthest thing he felt for me. That glare... It looks a hell of a lot like resentment.

Whatever.

Until he finds the balls to come to my house sober and recite the crap he spouted when drunk, he's on my shit list.

Besides, it would be impossible for him to ruin this moment, so with a smirk, I give him my middle finger before striding into class.

RILEY

CHAPTER TWENTY-THREE

"T his is a nice surprise," I say, smiling as I step out of my psychology class on Wednesday to find Logan leaning against the wall opposite, waiting for me.

"I wanted to see you." There's a lazy smile on his face as he does a casual sweep of my body before pushing off the wall. He pays no attention to the other students milling out of the hall as he slides a hand through my hair and lowers his face to mine. Our lips meet in an explosion of tangled tongues and undeniable chemistry, and by the time we break apart, the hall has emptied. "*Really* wanted to do that."

I chuckle, a smile splitting my face in two. True to his word, finding out about Aurora has changed absolutely nothing for Logan. Well, if it's changed anything, he's even more determined to make it up to me. He still greets me every morning with a coffee and walks with me to campus. I've been eating lunch with him and Royce in the food court, and Logan has been joining me in the library when our free times overlap.

"Where are you heading next?" he asks, taking my backpack and putting it over his shoulder before slotting his fingers between mine without a care in the world. "Library. That was my last class of the day, but I've got a paper to write for my US history course."

"Sounds boring."

I chuckle. "Yeah, it's a little dry. It's definitely not my favorite subject, but it's better than Chemistry last semester... I don't know why I thought that would be a good one to take. It was like the professor was speaking a foreign language half the time."

He barks out a laugh. "I can imagine. So you'll be in the library the rest of the day?" He waits until I nod. "Awesome. I've one more class today, then I'll have time to kill until practice. I'll join you when I'm done."

"Sounds good," I say, smiling up at him as we make our way to the library.

"Still no word from your mom?"

He's asked me the same question every day. It's endearing how worried he gets when I give him the same answer—no. Logan is a fixer, and I can practically see the wheels turning in his head as he figures out how he can fix this. The problem is, this isn't a problem he can flash a smile or throw money at and solve for me.

Throwing money at my mom would only make the situation ten times worse. She's like a dog with a bone. If she had any inkling someone with money gave a damn about me, she'd dig her claws in so deep she'd shred Logan apart.

"I don't need you to find a solution to this for me, Logan," I feel the need to say. "This is *my* problem. Don't go doing something reckless."

He huffs in frustration. "I hate this for you."

I squeeze his hand, appreciating the sentiment. "Just, please. I know you want to help, but *please* don't interfere. If my mom finds out about you." I shudder. "It will only make things infinitely worse."

He blows out a breath, staring down at me with sad eyes. "I promise I won't reach out to your mom. I don't want to make life harder for you, Riley. However, promise me, if there ever is anything I *can* do, you'll tell me. I know you're not used to relying on others, but you *can* rely on me—and Royce. We *want* to be there for you. To help, if we can. So promise me you'll tell us if there's something we can do."

It's my turn to huff. He knows me too well. "Fine," I say with a small smirk. "If ever you or Royce can help me, I'll let you know."

His grin is dazzling. "That's all I can ask."

Outside the library, he leaves me dazed with another all-consuming kiss before passing me my backpack and striding off to his next class. I watch him go before I regain my common sense and head inside.

Walking past tables with various students sitting at them, I aim for the back of the library where it's usually quieter. As always, the tables back here are empty, and I have my pick of which to sit at. Choosing one, I set my bag down and lift my notebook out to check over the assignment along with the suggested reading list.

With the name of the textbook in mind, I go in search of it, finding it stuffed on a shelf in an abandoned corner where old, dusty, first-edition leather books that students rarely use are kept. Cradling the book in my arm, I exit the aisle, letting out a squeak when I'm grabbed from behind. The book falls from my arms and the world blurs as I'm hauled into yet another dusty-smelling aisle.

"HEL—" My yell is cut short as a hand clamps over my mouth, and I'm pulled more firmly against a firm chest. Writhing against him, I manage to turn in his hold, only to find myself shoved against a bookstack. With his hand still securely in place over my mouth, he buries his face in the crook of my neck, before growling in a low voice, "Do you have any idea what watching you with them does to me?"

Grayson.

Of course, it's him.

I suspected as much. He's the only person on campus who hates me and is insane enough to do something like this.

He growls frustratingly, and when he shifts, I feel his very hard length pressing against my abdomen.

"Don't you realize you were mine first?"

His hand lifts from my face, and I barely have time to suck in a breath before it's replaced with his lips. His kiss is bruising. The starting cry before a battle. His tongue infiltrates my mouth, a weapon he wields with precision as he cuts through my defenses.

Urgency undercuts every swipe of his tongue and I can feel his desperation in the solid grip he has on the back of my head, holding me in place as though terrified I'll disappear.

It's a kiss that speaks of unending hunger. His, but also mine. How is it I can loathe Grayson until our bodies collide, and then unfathomable need blasts through me, and any common sense I possess is obliterated?

I've caught him staring at me multiple times this week. Hell, only a few hours ago, he was glaring at me from across the food court, looking about ready to rip Logan's arm away as he escorted me outside. I'd been assuming his anger was directed at the fact his friends were spending their time with me instead of him, but as his words replay in my head, I wonder if I read him all wrong.

He presses me harder into the stacks, the feel of him everywhere scorching through my train of thought as our mouths move against one another, bruising and hard as they engage in a primal dance. Our touches are desperate, a union born from a craving that borders on madness.

It's only when his hands move beneath my clothes with fraught haste, that a sliver of sanity breaks through, and I bring my hands up between us, pressing against his chest.

I'm not sure if he misinterprets me, but he growls into my mouth, only kissing me harder as his hands continue their exploration of my skin.

"Grayson," I hiss into our kiss, shoving harder against his chest.

"I fucking need you, Riley," he rasps, sounding completely gone to this insanity that exists between us.

When he tries to capture my lips again, I sink my teeth into his lower lip hard enough to draw blood, forgetting that I'm dealing with a psychopath who finds my violence a turn-on and only grinds himself more insistently against me as copper floods my mouth. My own depravity raises its head, a whine escaping me before I can swallow it back as my hips buck against his. Need crashes through me, and I momentarily forget what an epically stupid idea this is. Grayson is just so... consuming.

Logan is sweet and loving.

Royce is filthy and crass.

But Grayson... Grayson is wild and untamed. He's a storm to be unleashed, and I'm helpless to outrun him.

Plunging head first, I succumb to the insanity.

Sensing my surrender, Grayson nips my lips in approval, his hands roaming over my ass in the skirt I wore today because I wanted to see the way Logan's eyes lit up when he picked me up this morning, and feel Royce's hands without the denim barrier of jeans when he inevitably placed his hand on my leg under the table at lunch.

I'm lifted off my feet as Grayson presses me deeper into the stacks, spreading my legs wider so he can wedge himself between them. With nothing except my tights and panties as a barrier, I can feel every inch of his hardness as it digs into my core, and a needy whimper spills from my lips as I shudder against him.

"You drive me crazy," he groans, moving so our cheeks are pressed together, his large hands clasping the backs of my thighs as he rocks against me. "The noises you make. The way you smell. I can't stop thinking about how good you felt squeezing the cum from me."

I make an incoherent noise of agreement as I rub against him, too far gone to pull back.

His hand moves between us, and he rips a hole in my tights with a growl before pushing my panties aside and shoving two fingers roughly inside. I'm practically dripping with need, the wet suction audible to the entire aisle as he curls his fingers.

"Fuck," he hisses at the same time I cry, "Oh, God."

A sharp pull on my hair, and my heavy eyes snap to his. "Not God, baby. I'm the one who has you dripping on the fucking floor while you strangle my fingers. You'll say *my goddamn name* when I'm the one making you feel so good."

To really drill his point home, he presses down on my clit while he massages my inner walls, and stars burst to life behind my eyes as I cry, "Grayson."

"Much better," he purrs, continuing his assault on my pussy. "I want you to remember whose taste is in your mouth, whose fingers are in your pussy while you come for me."

"Grayson," I pant deliriously. "Please. I need to come."

"What you're feeling right now... that desperate ache that you have no choice but to sate... that's how I've felt every fucking day since I chased you down in that field," he growls in my ear.

"Now imagine having to watch some other man satiate that need, knowing he's touching what rightfully should have been yours." I moan, feeling the beginnings of an earth-shattering orgasm scrape along my nerves. "I've wanted you since you were fifteen and had no idea how depraved my desires for you ran," he continues. "I've wanted you while hating you. While I watched you be with my best friends. I want you even while everything in my life spins out of control. You are the epicenter around which everything else revolves. I can blame you. I can hate you. But through it all, I can't stop myself from *wanting you*. Now, come for me so I can fuck you and finally think straight."

His words are delivered with an embittered, demented tone. Half-frustration, half-possession. All the while, his fingers continue their practiced ministrations, coaxing my orgasm forward until it barrels through my veins, clenching my muscles and bowing my back as I cry out.

My head is still in the stars when I hear the unmistakable snag of a zipper, and snapping my eyes open, I push against Grayson's chest. "Grayson, no."

He stops, gaze snapping to mine. "What?" he barks. "Why?"

"*Why?* Are you fucking kidding me? There are a million reasons why, the least of which being that the last time we were in the same room together, you knicked at my skin with a knife while fucking me and ignoring my protests for you to stop."

"You didn't," he argues indignantly.

"I did."

Frown lines bunch along his forehead. "You didn't mean it."

"You were being a psycho, Grayson!"

"You didn't!" he practically yells. "I wouldn't..." His eyes dart back and forth before a thought catches and he barks a shattered laugh.

Untangling himself, he steps back so abruptly that I'm left scrambling as I struggle to steady my feet beneath me. His previously lustful stare has hardened to granite as he sneers at me. "You wanted it," he hisses. "Just because you can't come to terms with that doesn't give you the right to place the onus on me. But thanks for the reminder of exactly what type of girl you are." Giving me a disgusted once over, he turns on his heels and strides away.

Hands coiled into fists at my side, I watch him disappear, wondering how the hell I can go from lusting after Grayson Van Doren to wanting to throttle him in the span of mere seconds.

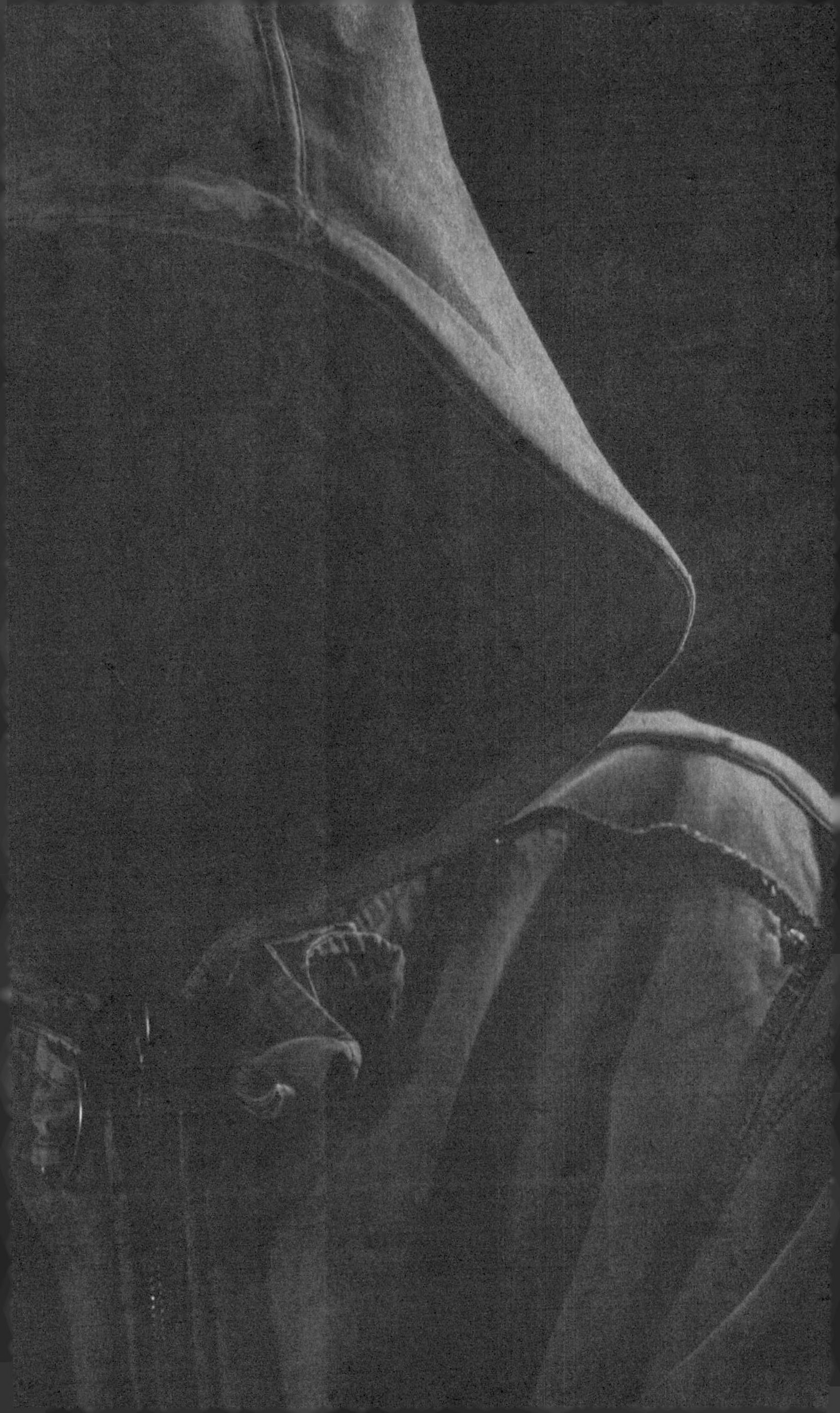

ROYCE

CHAPTER TWENTY-FOUR

olling my eyes, I swipe away from Logan's notification and instead pull up my chat with Riley—my non-existent chat with her. Staring at our last messages, the night after I punched her asshole boss, I try to think of something to say but come up blank.

Why is this so hard?

I want to talk to her, except I'm not the talkative type, and all I can think of to ask is if she's okay, where she is, and what she's doing... which all sound a tad stalkerish, even for me. I hate not knowing what she's doing, yet I also don't know how to engage in a text message conversation with her that doesn't come across as weird as hell.

Logan does it so easily—flirts and messages back and forth. He's constantly chatting to her when they aren't together, and especially when they are. Yet, I struggle to piece together a single sentence.

I'm not used to initiating this shit. To voluntarily put myself out there, but I want to try... for her.

Feeling like a total idiot, I stare down at my phone at a loss for words before giving up and stuffing the damn thing into the cup holder.

Forgetting about it, I pull on a pair of black leather gloves, flexing my fingers against the fabric as I do a final sweep of the quiet suburban street before sliding out of the truck. I take the time to silently close the heavy door behind me before slipping unseen into the night.

It wasn't hard to find Lydia's address once I tracked her down online and discovered the woman was *never home*. From my quick scan of her social media, she's a vapid narcissist who cares *way* too much about what people think. Her socials are filled with selfies taken at high-class restaurants and bars with fake friends, at the spa, and on dates. In every single photo, she was wearing a different outfit, dripping in jewelry, and her hair and makeup seemed professionally done.

After everything Riley had said about her mom, I'd decided I needed to do a little research on her for myself. Find out what sort of a bitch keeps a kid from her own daughter.

Apparently, the type perpetually suffers from a mid-life crisis where they pretend to be twenty years younger than they are. Meanwhile, Lydia is out living her best life, and her daughter is slaving away—attending college, studying, working, and doing everything she can to provide for herself and to keep up with her mom's ludicrous demands.

Seeing her mom's extravagant lifestyle splashed out before me only infuriated me more and sent alarm bells ringing. Riley mentioned that her mom comes looking for money every month, but from what I can see, she has plenty of it.

Riley might get paid well to dance at Lux, but she doesn't get paid *that well*. If she did, she certainly wouldn't be throwing her cash at her mom.

Which makes me wonder if Riley is even aware of her mom's galavanting. The extent to which she's burning through money. The entire situation is bizarre, yet I do fully appreciate that Riley is simply trying to do the best she can.

However, I'm here now, and I don't fucking like the setup with her and Aurora *one little bit*. No mother should be forced to be away from her daughter, and it truly sickens me that it's Riley's mom who is standing in her way.

Walking casually down the street, I glance both ways before heading up the drive to Lydia's house. I watched Lydia unceremoniously dump a half-asleep Aurora off with the neighbor before climbing into an expensive-looking sedan, dressed to the nines and looking as though she wouldn't be back until morning.

Still, it is with calculated steps that I creep steadily closer to the small bungalow. The thin black Henley I put on does nothing to diminish the bitter winter chill, but it, along with my black jeans and boots, enables me to blend seamlessly with the night.

Pulse steady, my movements are fluid as I crouch beneath a window at the side of the house and pull a set of tools from my pocket before sliding the necessary ones into the lock. My fingers work deftly, the latch unlocking with a soft *click* before I push it open.

It takes a few minutes for me to fit my large frame through the small window without getting stuck or making a noise, but eventually, my boots plant on the soft carpet. The room is cloaked in shadow, and I pause, giving my eyes time to adjust as I listen intently to the rhythm of my surroundings.

Outlines of furniture come into focus, and I glance around

the small room. Pink walls and sheets on the bed declare it as a child's bedroom, and I falter, realizing I'm standing in Aurora's room.

It's surreal, only driving home the reality of this entire situation as I take in the wall behind the bed, adorned with wallpaper featuring unicorns, fluttering butterflies, and vibrant rainbows.

A fresh, coarse wave of anger crashes over me. Who keeps a child from their mother? What Riley's mom has been doing is blackmail. She's essentially holding Aurora hostage... in exchange for money? It's gotta be more than that, but what?

The need to know drives me forward...

It's a paranoia born from having everything you thought you knew ripped out from beneath your feet. From having someone you'd known your entire life turn around and accuse you of such a disgustingly heinous crime that you can't even comprehend what's happening.

Now, I make sure I vet every single person I cross paths with.

It's become an obsession. The fear of being caught unawares like that again means I crave the control of knowing everything about everyone in my life. It's why I took it upon myself to not only harass Riley at the club but stalk her every move.

I know that, until this week, she ate all her meals in the dining hall.

I know that she lives off-campus because this year's scholarship didn't include accommodations, and it's a struggle for her to pay the rent monthly.

I know that her two friends are Tara from the club and a woman in her building, along with her five-year-old daughter —which makes a hell of a lot more sense now that I know Riley's secret.

I know that she keeps everything bottled up inside until she can pour every ounce of it out in the dance studio.

I know that her favorite color is pink, and her secret pleasures are fantasy books and pumpkin spice lattes.

And I know on which days her past is closest to the surface because those are the days when she's more withdrawn and wears makeup to hide the purple rings beneath her eyes.

This woman I know, like the palm of my hand, can read so intuitively that words aren't required... I saw the embarrassment in her posture as she discussed what she believed was her failing as a mother and her gritty determination to win Aurora back.

Which is why I'm here... standing in her daughter's bedroom in the middle of the night. To better understand a situation that I fear Riley has glossed over, so I can better ensure that the warrior of a woman doesn't have to wait four more years before she can *start saving* to get her daughter back.

Looking around the room, my gaze catches on a single teddy bear propped up in pride of place against the pillows, and I find myself drawn closer, my boots padding silently across the thick carpet until I can stretch out a hand and lift it.

My eyes run over the Halston U t-shirt he's wearing, and I'm hit with the sudden image of a teary-eyed Riley giving this to her daughter before heading off to college. The sacrifice she's making, being away from her daughter—trusting her mother with her care—while she works to create a better life for them.

I can't begin to imagine how challenging it must be for her, regardless of the good intentions behind her actions.

Setting the bear back where I found it, the toe of my boot knocks against something beneath the bed, and I lower to my knees. My fingers brush against a box and I grip it, dragging it out.

It looks like a shoebox that has been glitterized. Wrapped in pink paper and covered in sprinkles and stickers, the words *Aurora's & Mommy's box of memories* is scrawled across the top in Riley's familiar handwriting.

A lump forms in my throat as I run a humbled hand over the words, imagining the two of them working on this together before Riley left for Halston. A box of keepsakes and memories for Aurora to pull out when she missed her mom.

I hesitate, reluctant to intrude while also wanting to insert myself into their happiness, before gingerly lifting the lid and sinking onto the edge of the bed. Using the flashlight on my phone, I peek inside. My lips twitch at the top photo—Riley and Aurora grinning at the camera, covered in paint and looking like mischief incarnate.

Setting it aside, the next one is a photo of them at some sort of fair. Another is of her daughter's third birthday. In every single one, it's just the two of them, happy and laughing. Their happiness is infectious, and I find myself wishing I could have been there, lurking in the background, and seen these moments for myself. Amongst the photos are tokens—stubs from a *Paw Patrol* movie, tickets for what I'm guessing is the same carnival as in the pictures, and a bead bracelet, the vibrant colors faded as though it's been worn excessively.

With the box on my lap, I take another look around the darkened room, noticing how no photos are adorning the dresser or walls. There is nothing for the little girl to look at when she misses her mom. No remnants of these happy moments. In fact, bar a small pile of toys in one corner of the room and a few books stacked on the bedside table, the rest is surprisingly empty for a child's bedroom.

Frowning now, I replace the lid with care and slide the box under the bed where I found it. With a niggling in my gut, I move to the bedroom door, opening it a crack before pausing to listen for any sounds.

Blissful, empty silence.

Stepping out of the room, I navigate through the unfamiliar space, steps cautious and deliberate as I prowl through the house, peering into drawers and opening cupboards.

The final room I look into is a small office, and I step inside, closing the door behind me as I run my gaze over the shelves stacked with various files and folders. Flipping through one, it's filled with credit card bills. I snap a photo of them, but nothing raises any alarm bells—other than the fact Riley's mom has a serious spending habit. *Is that why she's consistently hitting Riley up for money?*

Setting the folder back on the shelf, I turn toward a laptop sitting on the desk. Pulling out of the chair, I lower myself into it and open the laptop.

When it comes to life, not requiring a password, I snort before scouring through the hard drive. Nothing jumps out at me, so I open the web browser and search through her history. I practically roll my eyes at the list of designer stores, skipping over those links. Nothing else stands out, and I'm about to give up when a website catches my eye—Craigslist. It's not exactly what I was looking for—not that I know *what* exactly I'm here for. But based on her shopping history, Riley's mom doesn't strike me as a *find second-hand bargains on Craigslist* sorta woman.

Her login details fill in automatically, signing me into her account, and I navigate to *searches.* It comes up saying there are no saved searches, but I notice a *(1)* beside the *postings* tab and click on it.

Person seeking key that unlocks hidden knowledge, where shadows whisper secrets and truth lies veiled.

. . .

What the fuck? What the hell does that even mean? I notice the cryptic message was posted earlier this evening and has not received any response. *Not to wonder.* Perhaps Riley's mom is delusional. Or has early onset Alzheimer's? There has to be something because whatever this post is, it's cryptic nonsense.

Still, I take note of Lydia's username—riches&glamor—then pull up the website on my phone and search for the post from my account. I stare at it for several moments until a notification pops up on my screen: *Three missed calls from Logan.*

It's followed a moment later by a text from him.

LOGAN

For real, man, where are you?! I need my potato chip fix.

Sighing, I get to my feet, knowing he'll blow my phone up every thirty seconds until I respond, and then until I get home.

I message him back, telling him I'll be home shortly and that I'll get him his stupid chips before doing a final scan of the room. Not spotting anything else, I sneak out the way I came in and jog back to my truck.

I think about that post the entire way back to Halston.

"Did you get the chips?" Logan calls the second I'm through the door.

"No."

"What the fuck, man? You said—Ha ha." He'd come stomping into the hall in a rage, but seeing me standing there, holding his bag of stupid chips with a grin, he scowls, snatching them from me before collapsing on the couch.

"Gray?"

"Who the fuck knows."

I blow out an exasperated breath. Gray has been MIA since we bailed on our chat. Which, admittedly, I feel like shit about. It wasn't done intentionally. I lost track of time after seeing Riley at The Depot. Then I was so caught up in everything she was saying and ensuring she was okay... it was only when we got home that I remembered Gray had been waiting for us.

I've tried to talk to him several times since, but he's shut me out. Shut both of us out. He's barely home anymore, and when he is, he holes up in his room, refusing to come out.

Sighing, I drop onto the couch beside Logan. "What are we gonna do?"

"Wanna play some NHL 24?" he asks, handing me a controller.

I give him a deadpan stare. "I meant about Gray."

"Why do we have to do anything? He's the one acting like a bag of dicks."

"Do you want to throw away four years of friendship? To live in this environment for the rest of the year—dating Riley while Gray hates our guts for it? What about the fact that he has a half-sister he doesn't know about and a dad manipulating him, and he needs our help more than he actually realizes?"

Logan frowns. "Alright, alright, I get it. Logan and Royce to the rescue, so what do we do?"

"That's what I'm asking you," I state, exasperated.

"Fuck if I know. We can't just tell him about Aurora. That would be breaking Riley's trust, and there's no fucking way I'm doing that again. He isn't going to listen to us if we try to talk to him about his dad..."

"There's something on his mind," I muse aloud. "He looks like shit any time I see him."

"Maybe it's his Gran," Logan theorizes. "Or his insides

slowly decaying because they know he's being an insufferable asshole."

I snort in agreement.

"He agreed to all four of us sitting down to talk on Christmas Day... maybe he'd do that again?" Logan suggests.

"Pretty sure I fucked up any chance of that happening when we left him hanging on Sunday. Besides, I don't know if he'd sit down with Riley now. His hatred toward Riley has only gotten worse." I've seen how he glares at her on campus. He's a walking disaster waiting to happen.

"Yeah, 'cause he's jealous," Logan scoffs. When I give him a quizzical look, he explains, "Have you seen the way that dickbag looks at our girl when he sees us on campus?"

I shake my head, not having noticed him watching us at all, but then I mostly only spend time with Riley in the food court, and I make a point of not memorizing the faces of the people watching us in there.

"He's got it bad for her. Pretty sure he wanted to stab me when I kissed her in front of him the other day." I arch a brow and he shrugs. "I was testing a theory... which was proven right, by the way."

I just shake my head, struggling to wrap my mind around that revelation. I was so convinced he hated her guts, but perhaps it's not as simple as that...

Sensing that my mind is elsewhere, Logan shoves the controller into my hand and starts a new game before I can argue. The mindlessness helps me work through everything he just told me before my thoughts shift to the cryptic post I saw on Lydia's laptop. I barely notice when Logan wins.

"Another round?" he suggests with a triumphant grin.

Checking the time on my phone, I agree. Before I put my phone away, I flick to Riley's messages and not stopping to overthink it, I type out: *Goodnight.*

A moment later, her response comes through: *Goodnight, Royce. X*

On Friday, I'm sitting outside Riley's apartment waiting for her to appear. My fingers tap absently against the leather steering wheel as I stare unblinkingly at her door.

I've been eating lunch with her and Logan every day, and we've been talking on and off since I worked up the nerve to text her on Wednesday night. Riley usually messages to say goodnight before she goes to bed, which results in a few texts exchanged back and forth before she falls asleep.

Since she came to my fight last weekend, there's this calmness that I can't quite explain. Braving the food court on Monday... after everything went down at the end of last year, I swore to myself I would never set foot in there again, but knowing she was there, I couldn't find it in me to stay away. Not like I ever can when it comes to her.

Didn't mean I wasn't shitting a brick when I walked in and all eyes turned to me, but I just focused on her, and it was enough. *She* was enough, and every day has been a little easier to bear with her sitting beside me. Hearing her laugh when Logan jokes around, listening to her enthusiastically talk about her classes...

For the first time in *months*, I feel alive.

And it's all because that stunning girl in there *sees* me.

Of course, she doesn't know the baggage I carry. The dark and twisted past that has permanently scarred my soul.

I should tell her. I know I should, but I also just want to sit in this moment where Riley is mine, and she looks at me like I'm someone worthy of her affection before I burst her bubble. I know once I do, she'll never look at me the same. She might not look at me the way everyone else does. Something tells me Riley will believe me when I explain the truth to her, but there's no way she'll look at me the same way. How could she?

Given her history, she'd be right to slap me across the face before telling me she never wants to see me again, but Riley is too good. Too pure. She has this capacity to empathize with people, which makes her soft-hearted. This does not mean she is a pushover—she's perfectly capable of standing up for herself, as evidenced by how she stood up to each of us last semester.

Despite her trauma, she still has this marvelous ability to sympathize. Her compassion is her greatest strength, a shining beacon to the dark shadows of my soul.

And I'm not yet ready to give it up. To give *her* up.

While I wait, I slide my phone from my pocket, navigating to the webpage I've repeatedly stared at for the past few days. Clicking refresh, there's still no response to Lydia's nonsensical message. I don't know why I keep checking. I still haven't figured out what it means, but something about it keeps me coming back.

Before I can decide what to do, movement from the corner of my eye catches my attention, and I lift my head as Riley steps out of her building.

She's dressed simply in leggings and an oversized hoodie. Still, the lycra material clings to her long, toned legs and tight ass, and her hoodie only sends my mind spiraling, thinking about the curves hidden underneath, the way her perky breasts would feel in my hands.

Groaning, I swipe a hand down my face as I mentally talk down the semi I'm now sporting. I might be so fucking gone for this girl, but I have no intention of sticking my dick anywhere near her. Not anytime soon. Not until she knows every dark secret I harbor.

Her gaze latches on to my truck and she pauses before making her way over. I lower the window.

"What are you doing here?"

"Driving you to work," I retort.

"Why?"

I fight the smirk trying to let loose. *This girl.*

"Just get in the truck, James."

She huffs out a breath, muttering something about stubborn-headed men as she yanks open the door and climbs in.

Her ass has barely hit the seat before I'm fisting the front of her hoodie and tugging her toward me. Our lips meet in a clash of swords and she melts against me, moaning into my mouth. *Fuck, I can't get enough of this girl.* Even with her lips on mine, I'm *starving* for her.

"Mmm, I could get used to a welcome like that," she says when we finally pull apart.

Smirking at her, I press another quick kiss to her lips before letting her go. "Get used to it, then."

"So this is what we're doing now?" she queries as I pull away from the curb and direct us toward Lux.

"Yup."

Riley nods. "Okay, cool. Just wanted to clarify."

And with that, it's agreed that I'll be driving her to and from work. Who knew a relationship could be so straightforward?

When we reach Lux, I walk her inside, the two of us parting with a smoldering glance before she saunters toward the dressing room. I stand and watch her go before venturing to my usual table at the back corner of the club, where I have a clear view of the entire room, including where her sleazy manager is standing behind the bar. He's glaring daggers my way and making it clear he just saw the two of us entering together.

Because I'm an asshole, I smile at him, and it's all teeth. Just a friendly reminder not to cross me. He instantly looks away, busying himself as I drop into my seat.

Not long later, the room descends into darkness. There's a moment of silence before the rhythmic snapping of fingers resonates throughout the room, followed by the first sultry notes of *Fever* by Peggy Lee.

A bright light illuminates the stage, my eyes instantly spotting Riley in the middle of the group. Her eyes are already on mine as she clicks her fingers, tilting her hips in time to the alluring beat. And for the next four hours, nothing exists except me and her... and the constant hard-on in my pants.

The second she steps outside after her shift, I'm on her, having been waiting by the door. I don't give a shit about the other girls walking past us, whistling and giggling as I lay claim to Riley's lips.

After the initial shock, she kisses me back with equal enthusiasm, her arms winding around my neck as her body presses against mine. A moan slips from her mouth when my hand slides under her hoodie and up her spine, the feel of her warm skin like heaven beneath my palm.

"Royce." My name is a low whine on her tongue, and I swallow it down, savoring her taste for a moment more before pulling back, breathless.

"Tell me you want this," I rasp, holding her gaze.

"I want this. You."

She's barely gotten the words out before I kiss her again. Her hands slide beneath my leather jacket as she clutches my belt in one hand, her other climbing up my front.

Before I completely lose my head and strip her naked in the middle of the parking lot, I grab her hand in mine and tug her toward my truck. She follows with a giggle that resonates in my chest, and I peer over my shoulder at her with a hunger burning in my gaze. That same need shines back at me, and I pick up the pace.

Reaching the truck, I yank open the back door and practically throw her inside. "Out of those clothes, Babydoll."

Her mouth parts in shock as she stares at me. "*Here*?"

"You've been taunting me all night. I can't wait even another second to taste you, James, so get out of those clothes, or I'll tear them from you."

Thankfully I'd parked in the back of the lot, and there's fuck all street lamps here, so I'm not worried about anyone seeing us. Besides, the windows will be steamed up in no time.

She makes an indignant sound, but as I climb into the back of the truck and close the door, she wriggles out of her leggings and panties before pulling her hoodie over her head.

It's dark enough that I can't fully make her out, but I see enough... the rapid rise and fall of her chest. The pink dusting of a blush racing along her skin. The stiff peak of her nipples as she anxiously waits to see what I'll do next.

"God, Ry. You're..." My throat closes over, and I lick my lips, at a loss for words. "Just come here."

Grinning coyly, she shifts closer until I pull her to straddle my lap. She has to duck her head to avoid hitting the roof of the truck, which brings her lips within perfect kissing distance. She moans greedily into my mouth as my hands explore her body, and I encourage her to rock against me, the rough fabric of my jeans scraping against her sensitive core.

"Use me to get yourself off." At my command, her thighs clench, and she grinds against me while I suck a path down her neck and chest, sliding my tongue around her nipple before taking it into my mouth.

"Ohh," she moans, back arching as she gets herself off. It's the hottest fucking thing I've ever seen, and I can't get enough.

I lavish her other breast with the same attention until she's trembling on top of me, and I know she's seconds away from coming. Kissing my way back up her chest, I tug and twist her nipple between my fingers, giving it a hard pinch when I bark, "Show me what a filthy whore you are and soak my jeans, James."

"Oh God. *Oh God. Royce.*" She comes with a shudder and a cry, and before she's had a chance to take a breath, I tug her lips to mine, devouring the last remnants of her pleasure.

Our kiss is languid as she comes back to earth, and careful not to bang her head, I maneuver her onto her back before crawling down her body. Spreading her legs, I rest one of her feet on the center console between the front seats, the other along the headrests above me as I bury my face between her thighs and taste for myself just how fucking sweet this girl is.

"Oh," she gasps, jumping at that first touch, but I wrap my arms around her hips, pinning her in place as I drink down everything she has to offer me.

"Royce! Oh my god, that feels so good. Keep going."

Like I had any intention of stopping. I could live between her thighs for the rest of my days and die a happy man.

Diving deeper, she bucks against me as I tongue fuck her channel before flattening my tongue and sweeping up her slit to suck on her clit.

"Oh fuck. Shit, yes. Yes! Right there." Sucking harder, I shift so I can slide two fingers inside her, curling them in the exact right spot. Back arching against the seats, she screams as she drenches my fingers.

Sliding them out, I lick them clean before gathering the rest of her release on my tongue. Each languid stroke has her whimpering, and when I'm finally done, she's boneless beneath me.

Pulling on my hair, she drags me back up until she can kiss me, sloppy and slow and so fucking sexy. "That was... Can we do that after every shift? The build-up has been driving me insane for weeks now."

I can't help laughing. "You'll hear no protests from me."

With another kiss, her hands roam down the front of my chest until they reach the waistband of my jeans. Knowing where she's going with this, I grab her wrists, stopping her.

"Tonight was about you," I explain.

"It can be about you, too."

I smile, pressing a quick kiss to the tip of her nose. "I know that, but tonight it's not."

"But, I want to," she argues stubbornly, cute little wrinkles forming between her brows.

"Next time," I promise her, stealing another quick kiss before pulling away so she can get dressed.

When she's good, I jump out of the truck and in behind the wheel while she shimmies between the seats. As I'm pulling the truck's door closed, I pause, noticing a car lingering in the lot even though it's well past closing. It takes me a moment to make out a figure sitting inside, and a second longer to realize it's Ben. *Creepy fucker.* Glaring, I give him the middle finger before driving us out of the lot.

As I navigate the quiet streets back to Riley's, one thing becomes crystal clear: This obsession... there's no stopping it now. I can't fight it anymore. She's too good. I want her too much.

She's mine, and that's all there is to it.

RILEY

CHAPTER TWENTY-FIVE

I pace back and forth across my apartment as the phone rings out. Growling in frustration, I jam my thumb down on the redial button for the third time. I'm not the least bit surprised that my mom isn't answering—same shit, different month. There are still another eleven days left in January, so there's probably another week before she starts blowing up my phone, demanding money.

Still, it doesn't mean I'm not frustrated and dying to talk to my daughter. Nor does knowing she's not going to answer stop me from calling her incessantly every other day. From internally screaming at her to pick up her fucking phone.

When it goes to voicemail *again*, I hang up and am about to redial when my intercom buzzes. Sighing, I toss my phone onto the sofa and go to answer it.

"Hello?"

"Hi, I have a delivery for a Riley James."

I frown at the intercom, having no idea what it could be. "It's not another food delivery, is it?" I grimace, knowing I'll have to donate it to the local food shelter if it is. There's no more room in my cupboards.

"Uh, no, ma'am."

Thank god. "Okay, I'm coming down."

Curious now, I trek down the stairs to the lobby and open the building door to find a man holding a nondescript paper bag and an envelope.

"Thanks," I say as he hands them over, and closing the door, I go back to my apartment. Setting the bag on the kitchen counter, I look at my name scrawled across the front of the envelope in what looks like Logan's familiar scrawl. I know his handwriting well enough after months spent tutoring him.

Opening it, tickets to tonight's game fall out, and a smile lights up my face. There's also a piece of paper inside, so I slide it out, unfolding it to read:

> *I could have just left the tickets at will-call, but I wanted to make sure you had them, along with some goodies for Isabella. There's also something special for you in the bag, but I'll understand if you're not ready. Regardless, I'll be the one with your name on my jersey. Can't wait to see you tonight.*
>
> *Yours,*
>
> *Logan*

I set the note aside and open the bag. There's a husky soft toy wearing a Huskies jersey and holding a hockey stick in his paw. It's so cute and I decide I will send Aurora one. There's also a pack of Huskies stickers and beanies for the three of us, and beneath all that are three jerseys. One is obviously for a child, so I lift out one of the others, unfolding it to read *Larsson* in big letters across the back.

I'm pretty sure that's the name of their goalie, and I'm

fairly certain that it's not for me. Folding it up, I lift out the other one, not the least bit surprised to find Astor stamped between the shoulder blades. I'm guessing this one is mine, and I can't wait to see the look on Logan's face when I show up wearing it.

———

"That thing drowns you," Royce comments as we navigate the crowd, everyone funneling into the stadium for tonight's game.

I glance down at myself. He's not wrong. The jersey is massive on me, but I equally don't care. It's not about how I look. It's about supporting Logan.

"You better hope Logan doesn't come in his pants in the middle of the rink in front of everyone. He'd never recover from that."

A shocked laugh escapes me and I gape at Royce. "Is that what you've been worrying about since you picked me up?"

Smirking, he merely shakes his head and I press onto my toes, searching for Ava and Isabella. When Royce found out I was coming tonight, he said he was coming too. Didn't even blanch when I said I had tickets for Ava and her daughter, even though I'm sure he'd prefer it if it was just the two of us.

Since I have to go to work afterward, it made sense for them to come separately so they can head home afterward and Royce can drive me to Lux.

"Do you see them?" he asks as I spot them standing near the ticket kiosk.

"Over there." I point in their direction and we push our way through the throng of fans toward them.

"Hey!" I call out, waving. Isabella spots me, pointing to her mom before racing toward me.

I bundle her into my arms. "Hey there, squirt. You shouldn't go running off on your mom like that. It's a busy place and you might get lost."

Ava gives her daughter a stern look when she catches up, and with her head ducked, Isabella mutters, "Sorry, Mommy."

"It's okay, baby. I know you're excited. I just don't want you to get lost and miss the game."

At that notion, Isabella shakes her head, and I put her down so she can hold her mom's hand.

"This is my... uh, this is Royce," I introduce, ignoring his smirk over my fumbling as he holds out his hand for Ava to shake.

"Royce, this is Ava and Isabella. Tonight's their first hockey game."

"And you came dressed to impress, I see," he teases.

"Gotta support the uh..." Ava looks down at her jersey. "Huskies."

The three of us burst out laughing before Royce urges us through the turnstile. "We better get inside so we can grab food before the game starts. Logan might miss the puck drop if you're not there."

I roll my eyes at him, catching Ava glancing between us, probably wondering what the situation between Royce, Logan, and me is. Yeah, that's not a conversation for little ears, so I'll leave it until we have our adult girl's night.

We queue up for food, and when it's our turn, Royce ushers me forward with a hand protectively on my lower back.

"Hot dog with all the toppings, nachos with cheese, and a beer, right?" he queries with a teasing glint.

"Ass." I playfully shove his shoulder, even as I grin. "You forgot the popcorn, though."

His lips twitch in a semblance of a smile, however his eyes shine with amusement, betraying his otherwise stoic expression. The one he dons for the world to see. His armor. Just like his leather jacket and tattoos. A carefully constructed shield to stop people from getting too close. Intended to have them casting displeased glances and steering clear.

He adds popcorn to the order he gives the student behind the kiosk, along with what Ava and Isabella want. Once stocked up with food, we shuffle toward our seats.

Ava is struggling to hold on to a bouncing Isabella in front of us as we wind through the busy hallways toward the entrance for our seats. Turning to Royce, I take the opportunity to ask, "Do you miss it?" I gesture toward the rink, but he knows what I mean.

"Parts of it," he admits honestly. "The game itself... all the time. But the rest of it. The popularity. The parties. The attention... no."

"You mean to tell me you don't miss girls hitting on the big-shot quarterback?" I tease. "Or maybe they didn't. Got one look at that *fuck off* on your forehead and decided you weren't worth the hassle."

He snorts a laugh. "Trust me, Babydoll. Plenty of people thought I was *worth the hassle*." Despite the teasing in his tone, I notice the slight tensing of his shoulders beneath his leather jacket. Refusing to let him get out of it that easily, I keep my eyes on him as we follow Ava and Isabella down the steps toward our seats. He sighs, the sound a near grumble in his frustration. "Girls were always throwing themselves at me."

"And you didn't like that?" I question, genuinely curious. I would imagine the fan-girling and admiration from others is part of the draw to playing sports.

His expression is carefully neutral as he states, "It became tedious."

Our steps falter and we come to a stop in the middle of the aisle. Life continues around us; people side stepping past us to find their seats, music pumping into the stadium, and the buzz of excited chatter. Yet, it all becomes irrelevant as my gaze brushes over his face, taking in the tight lines around his eyes and the thin press of his lips.

I'd bet Royce's aversion to female attention has everything to do with what I overheard, except here is hardly the place to discuss such things... assuming he would even want to tell me.

"Poor Royce," I pout. "Having to put up with all those girls practically begging to suck your dick. How terrible that must have been for you. Thank goodness I came along and flattened that ego before it grew too big for you to lug around."

He huffs out a laugh, a small yet genuine smile tilting his lips for the briefest of moments. "Get your ass in that seat, brat." His blue eyes burn with mirth as he brings his lips to my ear, eliciting a shiver as his breath fans over my skin. "Or I'll have *you* begging to suck my dick in front of all these people before the end of the game. I already know you like it when others watch, my dirty little slut." Somehow, he makes those four words sound like a caress, and I melt into molten lava on the spot.

His smirk, when he pulls back to meet my gaze, is pure masculine smugness, and with a nudge of his arm, I stumble in a daze down the next couple of steps.

The asshole, cool as a cucumber, munches on *my* popcorn as he trails behind as if he hasn't turned me into a ball of pure need.

"Wow," Isabella gasps from up ahead, and ignoring the ache in my pussy, I focus on where she's got her hands pressed against the plexiglass at the end of the aisle. "Look, Mommy. The ice is right there." She stabs her finger into the glass.

"I see it, baby."

"Our seats are just there," I tell her, pointing to four empty seats right by the rink and loving how her eyes light up.

Ava turns wide eyes on me. "These are amazing seats, Riley."

"Only the best for Logan's lucky charm and her friends," Royce teases before going to claim his seat and leaving me to deal with a grinning Ava.

"We are *so* having a girl's night soon. You've been holding out on me, and since my S-E-X life is dead in the water, I need to hear all about yours."

"What does that spell, Mommy?"

"Oh, look, baby. Here comes the Zamboni," she says, successfully distracting Isabella. Chuckling, I slip past them into the row, glaring at Royce.

"You'll point out And-son?" Isabella asks, joining me, although she doesn't sit. God forbid she be that far from the action.

"Anderson," I correct. "And, yes, I'll let you know as soon as he comes on the ice."

She's wearing his jersey tonight, and even though she has no idea who he is, she's already decided that her player is the best out of the three names we're each wearing.

As she babbles away to Ava, I watch her with a pained longing in my chest. It's great being with her, but *god* do I wish Aurora was here. That I could bring her to a game.

A warm hand slides into mine, and I spin to look at Royce with tears in my eyes. He gazes back at me with sympathy, leaning in to whisper. "One day, she'll be here. Wearing Logan's jersey and cheering him on, and you know he's going to eat that shit up."

I laugh, sniffling as I wipe at my eyes and Royce cups the back of my head, searing me with the promise of his words.

Thank you, I mouth, and not long after, the lights dim and the music builds in intensity before tonight's teams—the Halston Huskies and the UNH Wildcats—are announced. The stadium erupts into hoots and cheers, with signs being lifted into the air. I even hear howls from some of the spectators nearby.

One by one, the players' names are called over the speaker system, and they explode from the tunnel onto the ice.

Anderson is announced second, and Isabella screams her little lungs out as he does a loop of the ice. Royce squeezes my hand as I watch her. I dunno if Logan told him to keep an eye out for us or if it's just dumb luck, but as Anderson passes our section, he waves to Isabella, who nearly bursts with excitement.

When number seven is announced, I'm on my feet, screaming alongside Isabella and half the stadium as Logan bursts forth, hockey stick above his head as he grins and waves at the crowd.

Reaching our side of the rink, his eyes instantly go to mine, blown wide when he sees me in his jersey. He interrupts his lap of the ice, bringing himself to a sudden halt in front of me as his gaze rakes over my outfit.

"Turn around." He circles his hand in the air, and I play dumb, holding my hands up as if I have no idea what he's saying. Royce laughs beside me, and Logan glares as he bangs his fist against the glass. "Turn around, Riley!"

Giving him what he wants, I pull my hair over one shoulder as I do a slow spin so he can read the name spelled out between my shoulder blades, and when I turn back around, his chestnut hues have darkened with desire as they clash with mine. There's a predatory glint in their depths. It's a look that says, *be prepared to be fucked stupid tonight,* and my core tightens in anticipation, even as I return that voracious stare with a smug tilt of my lips.

I'm faintly aware of every eye in the arena on us. On our interaction. As if sensing it too, Logan smacks his gloved hand against the plexiglass, just like he did at my first game. This time, I know exactly what he wants. Know exactly what he's doing. And not giving a shit that the entire arena is watching—that undoubtedly Halston students are watching—I press my much smaller hand to his, the glass cool beneath my palm as I mouth *good luck.*

He grins, showing off his blue mouth guard, even as his eyes shimmer with desire and affection, that predatory glint turning more savage as his thoughts shift to his opponents. To the brutal win, I have no doubt he will achieve tonight. He hesitates a moment longer before tearing his hand away and turning in his skates, moving to join his teammates as everyone gets into position for the start of the game.

"You'll be lucky if he doesn't show up at Lux tonight and fuck you in the middle of the club," Royce drawls quietly in my ear as I collapse into my seat. I smirk back at him, not entirely opposed to that idea.

RILEY

CHAPTER TWENTY-SIX

The final buzzer goes off, the sound barely audible throughout the stadium over the eruption of joy and exhilaration. Everyone is on their feet, the roar of the crowd deafening as it fills the air, reverberating through the stadium and sending chills down my spine as I jump up and down, arms in the air. My voice is practically hoarse from screaming Logan's name, and a grin splits my face.

"YES!!" Isabella squeals, giving her mom a high five before turning to give me one too.

"He won!" I fling my arms around Royce's neck, even as I continue to bounce on my toes.

He chuckles softly against my skin, one arm banding around my waist. "Yeah, I noticed that."

I playfully hit his chest, my attention flicking back to the ice as the Huskies fist bump and do celebratory laps of the rink, helmets and sticks raised high in the air and infectious smiles on display. I scour the team, eyes bouncing over jerseys until I find number seven wedged in the middle of a group embrace. My eyes wander over Logan's grinning face as he pulls off his helmet and runs a hand through his sweat-slicked hair, before dropping to my name stitched onto his back. *My* Logan. *My* Husky. And damn, I could not be prouder of him. He performed triumphantly tonight. Made the other team look like amateurs as he darted swiftly between their defensemen, practically taunting them as he led the puck with practiced ease toward the net. He scored goal after goal after goal until it became apparent there was no way the other team could claw back the points.

Tearing my gaze from him as he celebrates with his teammates, my eyes lift to the still-cheering crowd. I drink it all in with awe. The sea of cheering fans clad in team colors, faces flush with elation. It's a breathtaking spectacle. I can feel the thudding of stamping feet and hollered yells vibrating through me. The collective energy of the fans has the very walls of the stadium shaking, and I can't stop smiling as I watch the joy and triumph on each of their faces.

The jumbotron flashes with images of the game's highlights, but a nudge on my shoulder has me glancing at Royce who juts out his chin, and I turn toward the rink as Logan pulls to a stop on the other side of the glass. Eyes dancing beneath the stadium lights, my grin only broadens at seeing his wide smile up close. He bangs on the glass with a glove-encased fist and mouths something I can't make out over the cacophony of noise around us. Pointing toward the tunnel where players are starting to disappear, his gaze darts to Royce who, seeming to understand Logan's silent demand, nods.

"What is it?" I ask, eyes still on Logan as he shifts those glimmering chestnut hues back to mine, their depths burning with adrenaline from his win and that same hunger I witnessed before the game. His gaze drops to my lips, pupils flaring, before falling lower, taking in the sight of me in his jersey, and I could swear I hear him growl through the plexiglass.

Beside me, Royce groans. "Asshole wants to see you before we leave."

With a roll of his eyes, Royce agrees to whatever Logan is saying, and with a winning smile directed at Ava and Isabella, he pushes away from the side and makes a beeline for the locker room.

The four of us shuffle out of our row and join the crowd of celebrating spectators as we slowly approach the exit.

"Thank you so much for tonight," Ava says once we reach the main concourse. "We had a blast."

"I'm just glad you enjoyed it. We'll have to do it again."

"Next week!" Isabella chimes in with a fist pump, making us laugh.

"I think Logan's game is too far away next week, sweetheart, but maybe the week after that, yeah?"

She nods, giving me a quick hug before the two of them disappear into the crowd.

Royce slides his hand into mine, pulling me in a different direction until we escape the crowds down a side hallway.

"Where are we going?"

"There's a room for friends and family to greet the team afterward," Royce explains.

"Do you usually come back here after a game?" I wonder aloud, recalling that we didn't after the last game I attended with him and Grayson.

"Not typically. Logan usually goes out with the team after, and we meet him at home later. Occasionally, if he's been badly injured or it's been a brutal loss, we've met him back here, but that's rare."

I shudder at the notion of Logan injured. Ice hockey is a violent sport; you never know what could happen. Logan always seems so invincible on the ice, but at the end of the day, he's only human. He bleeds just as easily as the rest of us.

I'm pulled from my dark thoughts by the faint murmur of sounds up ahead, and we halt as we round a corner and come face-to-face with a straight-faced security guard. Behind him, further along the corridor, people are milling about everywhere, cameras flashing.

"You're not allowed back here," the security man states.

"We're friends of Logan Astor," Royce explains. "Royce King and Riley James. We'll be on the list."

Lowering his gaze to the clipboard in his hand, the security guard scans the list until he finds our names. With a curt nod, he points toward the first door down the hall. "Friends and family room is there."

I give him a polite smile as Royce whisks me past and toward the room, pushing open the door and ushering me through. I'm immediately swamped in black and gold, the team's colors boldly on display with flags, banners, and various other pieces of memorabilia adorning the walls.

There's a plush couch pushed against one wall opposite a wall-mounted wide-screen TV, which is currently broadcasting highlights of tonight's game. In the corner sits a well-stocked refreshments table. Other than that, the room is... empty.

"Where is everyone?" I ask, taking it all in.

"It's a home game," Royce explains. "Occasionally, when one of the team has had a girlfriend or whatever, or if family comes into town for a game, they'd be in here, but for the most part, they meet friends afterward. This area will get busier as we get closer to the Frozen Four."

"Oh."

It's a whole other aspect to sports and Logan's life that I hadn't considered, and I'm suddenly hit with images of sitting in this room, anxiously awaiting Logan's smiling face after some big NHL win. My gaze slides to Royce as he wanders over to the refreshments table. Yeah, I can picture him here too. The two of us buzzing with excitement as we impatiently await Logan's arrival before going to celebrate. Together.

Because I won't have to rush away after each game to go to work.

Because there's nowhere Logan would rather be than celebrating every one of his victories with me... with us?

Is it too much to dream of such a reality? To hope for something so... mundane and ordinary, yet the farthest thing from either?

Before I can get too sucked into that faint glimmer of a possible future and pick it apart for issues, another door flies open, and Logan struts in, hair wet from his shower and the crisp scent of winter trailing after him.

His eyes go straight to me, not even looking to see if anyone else is present as he stalks my way, eating up the floor between us in three strides before his hands are on my thighs, wrenching my legs around his waist and lifting me off my feet before he presses me into the wall.

I think I hear Royce grumble something from somewhere nearby, but I can't make it out over the roaring in my ears. Over the rapid pounding in my chest. Logan's gaze eats me up like a lion starved, his voice guttural and flooded with emotion as he says, "You're wearing my jersey."

"Didn't seem appropriate to wear anyone else's," I murmur, unable to look away from his eyes.

He snarls before snapping forward, teeth digging into my lower lip before soothing the ache with his tongue. "You're wearing my jersey," he repeats, the words a near growl. "You're wearing my jersey, and all I can think about is taking that sweet-ass pussy of yours in it."

I moan against his lips, feeling the evidence of his desire pressing against my core.

Burying his face in my hair, he murmurs for only me to hear, "I didn't think you'd wear it."

"Figured it was only fair since you're wearing my name," I reply just as quietly. I feel the warmth of his chuckle against my skin before he returns his lips to mine, and I lose myself in him.

"Yeah, that's not fucking happening," a voice infiltrates, and it takes far too many seconds for me to recognize it as Royce's. Whipping my head around, I blink dazedly as I find him sitting on the sofa, munching on a bag of dried fruit as he watches us.

Heat floods my cheeks, and I try, pointlessly, to push Logan away. He refuses to budge, glaring at his best friend as his hands tighten around my upper thighs in a way that makes our crotches rub and sends skitters blasting through my nerves. It's a struggle to hold back my moan.

"You're welcome to leave," he bites out.

Royce merely smirks. "No can do, buddy." He jerks his chin at me. "I'm her ride."

Ignoring their sniping, I say to Logan more breathily than I'd intended, "Congratulations. You played amazingly out there."

Dismissing Royce, Logan's attention snaps to mine, some of that intense hunger dulling as he smiles proudly. Leaning in, he nips at the sensitive skin of my neck. "Only because my lucky charm was there, wearing my fucking number." He groans as though in pain, his eyes raking over said jersey. "Tell me I can see you tonight."

I reluctantly shake my head. Between classes, his hockey schedule, and my work, we haven't had a chance to hang out away from campus all week—other than our morning walks together when he brings me coffee. Until right now, I didn't think it was a bad thing. When it comes to Logan, it is very easy to end up speeding a hundred miles an hour into a relationship, and having already done that and been burned badly, I have no desire to repeat it.

Slow and steady is the name of the game.

... Although, at this moment, I hate myself for that. The way he's looking at me, I would love nothing more than to tell him to come over after I get off work.

"I'm working. I won't be home 'til late." I give his chest a light pat. "And I'm not ready yet."

Something shutters in his eyes, but he quickly disguises it. "Of course. Sorry."

Sliding my hand up his neck, I cup his cheek. "You don't need to apologize. I like how badly you want me. I want you too. I just... this needs to be slower this time."

I lean in, kissing him with light, unhurried strokes of my tongue, which he heartily returns.

"Can I take you out for breakfast tomorrow?"

Smiling back at him, I nod. "I'd love that. Go celebrate with your team tonight, and I'll see you in the morning."

"Alright." He gives me a final kiss before reluctantly letting me go, and I settle back on my feet as he turns to Royce. "Keep an eye on her tonight."

Royce's impassive expression says it all. *What the fuck else would I do?*

"Go play with your stick, hockey boy. I got this."

"Don't you have better things to do with your weekend than stalking me at work?" I tease as Royce pulls into the parking lot at Lux and puts the car in park. "It can't be all that entertaining to sit and watch me all night."

"More entertaining than anything else I'd be doing," he

retorts, leaning back in his seat and angling his body so he can see my face.

"What *would* you be doing?" I question, too curious for my own good, as I find myself wondering what Royce King does when he's not stalking me or exorcizing his demons in the ring. "Other than attending Logan's hockey games."

One shoulder lifts in a casual shrug. Too casual. And I tilt my head, watching intently as I patiently wait for his answer. "Nothing. I'd be in my room..."

"Drawing?" I push when he falters.

His response is a curt nod, the silence stretching between us until he ultimately confesses, "Weekends can be... hard." I can see the physical cost of voicing those four words etched into the tight lines of his face, and I don't need him to clarify to know he's talking about the weekends he used to spend on the football field.

It's on the tip of my tongue to ask him what happened. To hear his explanation. To finally understand the truth of what happened instead of hearing the accusing tone in my head from the girl in the library.

However, Royce is more shut down than I am. He physically recoils from putting his trust in another person, and I sense prodding at his wounds will only end up in him showing me his claws. I don't want to force the truth from him, either. I want him to trust in me. To know that his secrets are safe with me, as I know mine are with him. And to earn his trust, I'll readily put my curiosity on the back burner.

Just when I think he isn't going to elaborate, and I'm about to suggest that we get out of the car, he admits in a strained, low voice, "I spent a lot of my summer at The Depot, numbing the pain with bloodshed and alcohol. But that first weekend..."

First weekend... my eyes widen when I realize he's talking about the first game of the season since he was kicked off the team.

"I took on anyone who dared step into that ring. Even when my knuckles were a ragged mess, and I was so exhausted I could hardly remain on my feet. I fought until I could no longer lift my arms, and my legs gave out, and even then, I used words to ensure they kept driving their fists into my face."

His face is solemn, cast in shadows as he stares absently out the window, lost to the memories of his past. "By the time Logan and Gray showed up, they had to drag my unconscious ass out of there. They've made it a point ever since to not let me go alone, and after Logan threatened to miss a game to babysit my ass, I promised I wouldn't go on his game days."

I very much believe Logan's threat was genuine. As important as his hockey career is to him, his friends mean infinitely more. Logan is the sort of person who would set aside every one of his dreams to be there for those he cares about. Just look at how he's set aside his dream of playing for the Penguins to be near Halston for me.

I guess that's why I feel so protective of his aspirations. Why I want to be at his games, wearing his number and screaming his name—to ensure he knows that his dreams also matter.

Finally, painstakingly, his gaze slides to mine, tightened with anguish. "After Grayson pointed you out, coming here... tormenting you... it gave me the escape I needed and couldn't otherwise obtain."

"And now?" I ask thickly. "Do you only continue to show up because you've crowned yourself my self-appointed body-guard?" My light teasing drains some of the heaviness from the air, and it does all sorts of things to me when Royce's lips tilt up in the slightest of smiles. Knowing that I achieved that.

"I have to confess, my motives are not entirely selfless," he purrs, pitch deepening as his eyes blaze with dark fire.

Forgotten is his torment from a moment ago, liquid lust taking its place.

His dry charm is seductive. Sinful. *Delicious*, radiating temptation and promising unfathomable pleasure. I am left breathless and wanting when I murmur in response, "Oh?"

"How can it be," he continues, each word laced with cunning intent. "When I know the entire time you're on that stage, your eyes are on me?" Leaning in, his nose trails up the column of my throat, his breath like molten lava as it rolls over my skin, fanning the flames of passion he ignites within me. "Tell me, Ry," he whispers, his words a sweet caress and a sinful promise. "When you're up there, are you dancing for *them*... or for me?"

My heart pounds like a wild drum, the rhythm echoing in my ears and drowning out the world as the burning ice in his eyes holds me frozen in place. The scent of leather and something grittier wraps around me, intoxicating and heady, as I waver on the precipice. Dangling in the space between reason and pure desire, I resist the urge to lean in. The indecision is a battle I fight, my heart and mind locked in a fierce struggle. All the while, Royce's lips hover inches from my face, a tantalizing temptation tormenting me and slowly breaking down my resolve.

As the digital clock on the dashboard rolls into a new minute, it catches my attention, announcing the inexorable passage of time and the fact that I am officially out of minutes. Reality is waiting; my shift is about to begin.

My hand trembles, curling around the door handle as I put off reality for just a moment longer to remain with him, and as I'm about to turn away, his fingers latch onto my chin, holding me in place as firm, supple lips cover mine.

His kiss is so unlike our usual steaming intensity. While not lacking in its typical passion, there's a softness to it that we haven't shared before. A whisper of affection that carries the weight of newfound feelings blossoming between us.

His lips gently coax mine apart, his tongue flicking out—the first notes of a beautiful melody. Tenderly, he languidly explores my mouth, savoring each swipe like it's our first time.

Our breaths synchronize, any notion of work abruptly forgotten as I return his kiss with equal sentimentality. The usual chemistry that lies between us crackles, adding a heavy bass to our song.

So lost in his touch, in the rising tide of my feelings, I'm briefly dazed when he pulls away. His eyes, usually sharp and focused, now carry a gentle haze. A soft vulnerability, even as the intensity of his feelings radiates from his pupils, creates an almost ethereal glow. His usually guarded expression has unraveled, allowing a rare tender authenticity to surface as he drinks me in, and a secret smile tugs at his lips. One meant only for me. A hint at the man so very few are granted the privilege of witnessing. Of getting to know.

And yet, I want to know every facet, every cut and bruise, every scar and abrasion that has formed the man before me. A man who feels the need to lash out at the world before it can lash out at him. Who drives everyone away out of an innate need to protect himself. Yet, has gone out of his way to protect me—from Grayson, from Ben...

Where Logan would give up his life for those he loves, Royce would burn the world to ashes to protect the scant few he cares for. If I'm being honest, Grayson, too, would rip heads from shoulders for his family... the only difference is that I'm the one whose head he longs to remove.

Stroking a delicate finger down my cheek, Royce rasps, "I want you to think about that kiss while you're dancing for me tonight. Remember how it felt; remember how you could feel it all the way to your toes. And while you're watching me watching you, I want you to know that I'm imagining peeling off whatever outfit you'll be wearing and laying you out on that stage as a feast for me to devour."

After our moment in his truck, my shift at Lux is a test of endurance. The minutes tick by as though being dragged through sludge, each dance number lasting far longer than I remember it taking during rehearsals.

By the time the club closes and the last guest leaves, my body is crying out for Royce's touch. It remembers how good his tongue felt on me in the back of his truck last night, and it wants more. My nerve endings are begging to feel his coarse palms sliding over my skin, the wet warmth of his lips on mine.

With the look of a man being hauled to the gallows, Royce tosses me a lingering glance before he drags himself out of the club. He glares daggers at Ben in a silent warning as he passes him at the door, and at Ben's indignant smirk, my stomach flips with unease.

Last night and tonight, Ben has been glaring daggers at one or the other of us, clearly still pissed about Royce's fist finding a home in his face last weekend. It worries me. Ben is arrogant and doesn't take well to other men besting him, especially in what he considers his domain.

Perhaps it would be best if Royce stayed away for a while. He could sit outside in the car even for a week or two. Give Ben time to cool off. While I don't want Ben going back to his leering, I equally don't like the nasty gleam I've seen in his eyes this weekend.

As I saunter into the dressing room, I make a mental note to talk to Royce about it. He'll probably just say no and tell me not to worry. Only I do worry, especially if Royce is trying to look out for me, and even knowing that Ben is a pig, I still need this job. If the two of them come to heads, I can't afford to lose it. Which leaves me walking a tightrope as I struggle to balance Royce's wariness with Ben's whims, ensuring I'm performing at my best and pushing extra enthusiasm into every smile while I'm on that stage.

As soon as I've changed, I head for the exit. However, before I can reach the door, Ben slides into my path, appearing out of nowhere as he blocks my exit.

"Boyfriends aren't allowed in the club while you're working," he states, voice brimming with authority and that incensed fire burning in his glare. "It's bad for business and only leads to trouble."

"Ehh, okay," I respond, choosing to play dumb. Technically, Royce and I have not declared what we are. There has been no exchange of titles such as *boyfriend*, even if I imagine Royce's declaration from the night of his fight is his version of asking if I want to go steady.

"Your *friend*," Ben sneers, "can't be here when you're working."

"Royce and I aren't dating," I state. "And even if we were, he won't stay away because I ask him to." As politely as I can put it, I say, "You're the manager. Perhaps *you* should have this conversation with him."

Ben's fists clench at his side, his eyes hardening as he glares down at me. Despite my complacent tone, I know damn well Ben won't kick Royce out, let alone tell him to stay away. Not when Royce knows he profits from getting girls to perform private dances—willing or not.

"If you'll excuse me, I need to get going."

Looking like a volcano about to blow, Ben takes a menacing step forward right as the dressing room door opens behind me, girly laughter slashing through the tension. Eyes snapping over my head, Ben instantly relaxes his posture, his gaze dropping to mine in a silent *this isn't over* before he turns and strides away.

A breath loosens in my chest, adrenaline bleeding out of my system as I follow the two other girls outside, pasting on a smile as I climb into Royce's truck. His eyes linger on me, sensing something is wrong, but I wisely keep my lips shut, knowing it will only stir up more trouble if I tell him about my encounter with Ben. Eventually, he puts the truck in gear and drives me home.

"Hey," a soft voice whispers, thick and deep like chocolate. "Shhh, you're okay."

"R-Royce?" I hiccup, realizing I've been crying in my sleep, not just in my dream. Blinking, I wipe away the tears, his large body coming into view where he leans over the side of my bed, watching as I battle away the memories my nightmare elicited.

He'd come up to my apartment when we got home, and I remember falling asleep on top of him on the sofa, but he must have carried me to bed at some point.

"I didn't wanna wake you, but I felt weird leaving while you were asleep, so..." he shrugs, gesturing to a chair he carried in and set in the corner of the room.

"So you decided to sit and watch me sleep?"

He gives another unapologetic shrug. I should probably find it creepy as hell, and if it was anyone else, I would. However, coming from Royce, it feels almost... sweet. Like he was watching over me.

Gently rolling me onto my back, his movements are slow as he lies down next to me and wraps his arm around my shoulders. I rest my head on his shoulder, the steady *thud* of his heart grounding me in the present.

He's not here. He can't hurt you. He won't *hurt you ever again.*

"Wanna tell me what you were dreaming about?" Royce asks, his voice soft and soothing as he draws circles on the back of my arm with his finger.

Voice quivering, I tell him about the dream. About how it's always some variation of the same thing every time.

"How often do you have them?"

"Occasionally. Less often than I used to. Usually, something triggers them."

"What triggered tonight's?"

I chew on the inside of my cheek as I recall my run-in with Ben. That guy always makes the hair stand up on the back of my neck. And apparently, a simple confrontation with him is enough to trigger my nightmares. It's frustrating, but I know I can't always control my triggers.

It's on the tip of my tongue to tell Royce, but I know it will only piss him off enough to have him storming out of here, and selfishly, I don't want to be alone.

"I'm not sure."

"What sorts of things trigger them?"

I lift a shoulder. "Depends. When I initially started working at Lux, I had them after every shift. I was extremely nervous about dressing so provocatively on stage. But once I became comfortable with it, they went away."

Royce's tone is tighter than it was before as he says, "What else?"

"Ermm..."

I squirm against him, and sensing my discomfort, he intones, "Riley."

"Ben," I blurt. I'm not going to tell him about tonight, but that doesn't mean I need to keep previous instances from him. He already knows Ben is an asshole, I just don't want him to know Ben cornered me tonight—to discuss him no less. "There have been nights when Ben has told me to stay late to help tidy up. He'd always watch. Say some things or brush up against me." Royce has turned to granite, his breathing shallow. "I'd have a nightmare after that."

I can feel the beast coiling and stretching beneath his skin, and I hold my breath, listening to the rapid pounding of his heart against his chest as I wait anxiously for him to lose his shit.

My lungs are ready to burst when he finally exhales, his lungs collapsing and taking the tension with them.

"I'm going to kill him."

There's a very serious current to his words that has me leaning up on my elbow to stare into his face. "Royce King, you will not."

He glares at me, a raging fire burning in his eyes that speaks of untold violence, and I get the impression he's not seeing me at all. Reaching out a hand, I cup his face, running my fingers through his stubble until he slowly returns to me.

"You're never to be alone with him again, understand?" he says just as harshly.

"You've already given me this warning," I remind him.

"Yes, well, I'm making sure you remember it."

There's no chance in hell I'd forget it. Especially not after tonight.

"Just don't antagonize him. Please," I say, tucking myself back into his side and hoping he listens. However, I don't feel terribly optimistic when my plea is met with silence.

"You, uh, didn't have any when you were with us, did you?" he eventually asks, voice lower and less certain than it was before.

"There was the time Grayson chased me through the field, and for a moment, in my panic, I thought it was his father above me, but then I blinked, and it was Grayson. Other than that... no. Not once. I think I knew I was safe with you guys. I was furious, hurt, and admittedly rattled by Grayson, but I never feared *that*."

Silence falls between us. Royce's fingers continue their absent pattern, lulling me to sleep. My eyes drop to half-mast before eventually closing, and I'm drifting off when Royce murmurs, "Sleep, James. I'll be here to keep the demons at bay."

GRAYSON

CHAPTER TWENTY-SEVEN

For the first time, my palms are sweaty as I pull up outside the nursing home. Nerves churn in my stomach. Fear of what I can expect when I go in there keeps me sitting in the car long after parking.

"You can't avoid her," I tell myself. "You're all she has."

Hell, she's all I have.

I don't even have the guys anymore. That dumpster fire has exploded into a full-on rager. We're no longer talking at all. I can't even explain it... the *rage* that came over me when I realized they'd ditched me for *her*.

They're constantly fucking with her these days. I can't walk across campus without seeing Logan draped all over her or Royce sending her secretive little smiles. It's sickening. Infuriating. Leaving a bitter taste in my mouth and an overwhelming urge to storm over there and rip her away from them.

This feeling is like a venomous vine, coiling tighter around my heart until I'm suffocating on it. Yet, I'm helpless to stop it.

That's why I followed her the other day, needing to get her alone. Needing to... I don't even fucking know—fill my veins with her. Get that fix so I could put my head on straight again, and remind her that she can fuck my best friends but it doesn't stop her from wanting me.

The reminder of how it felt to be encompassed in her orbit, her fruity scent flooding my senses and wet heat clenching desperately around my fingers have my jeans growing uncomfortably tight right now, and the steering wheel creaks beneath my grip as my eyes close and I try to gather myself.

Too much time has been spent fantasizing about that, thinking about her... with them.

My teeth grind.

I'm losing my fucking mind. What am I even doing? Sitting outside Gran's nursing home sporting a hard-on as I daydream about a girl who accused me of... What exactly? She fucking wanted it. I know she did. I might have been half out of my mind, spinning out from what Gran had said and then finding her so at home in my kitchen, but I *know* she wanted it. The bitch just can't admit it to herself.

Anger licks along my veins, mixing with that unrelenting desire for her body and forming a toxic, potent blend that is going to be the death of me.

Needing to stop thinking about her before I whip my dick out in the middle of a public parking lot, I snap my eyes open and take a steadying breath before climbing out and walking into Sunnyside Nursing Home with laden steps.

"How is she today?" I ask the nurse at reception, recognizing her as the one who responded to Gran's cries last week.

"She's been well settled since your last visit. You know she can get confused sometimes and say things she doesn't mean."

"I know," I say defeatedly.

"Unfortunately, these are all signs of her condition worsening," she says as sympathetically as she can.

"You're saying she's going to keep thinking I'm my father and freaking out."

Her lips are pressed tight. "I'm guessing the two of them don't have a great relationship."

I bark a caustic laugh. "You heard her accuse him of murdering my mom."

"You have to understand, Grayson, that doesn't mean anything. She could be disassociating her feelings toward your father with something she's read in a book or seen on TV. Memories are confusing for her, and sometimes they blend together."

"I get that, I just..." I sigh dejectedly, and she reaches out to squeeze my hand. I stare at the warm gesture, momentarily stunned. When was the last time someone comforted me in such a way?

"I know. It doesn't make it any easier."

"It doesn't."

"She's in good form today and is in the TV room. Why don't you go spend some time with her."

I give her a wane smile before sauntering off. At the threshold of the TV room, I pause. Several other residents are here, some watching the television while others doze in their chairs. I spot Gran sitting by the large bay window and cautiously approach.

"Hi, Gran."

She doesn't look away from where she's staring out across the manicured lawns of the nursing home.

"How are you feeling today?" I watch her closely for any reaction but don't get any. "It's a beautiful day outside. Have you been out for a walk in the gardens?"

She remains silent and I settle myself into the chair for one of *those* afternoons. I'll take silence over her being terrified of me. Staring out across the lawn, I force myself to relax and just be in this moment with her. I know there won't be all that many more, and I want to be fully engaged in as many of them as possible.

"I know what you did," Gran eventually says, shaking me from my musings.

I turn to her with a frown, and she slowly twists to face me, her face a hard mask, even lined with numerous wrinkles.

"Gran?"

"I know what you did to that girl."

"Gran, what are you talking about?" I ask, throat going dry.

"Maybe I couldn't save her, but I did what I could to make certain you didn't destroy her like you did my daughter."

My mind reels, her words playing on repeat as I scramble to put together the pieces.

"You're a monster," she continues, eyes blazing with unfathomable hatred. "Someone had to put you down before you take another life."

"Gran," I rasp. "What did you do?"

This twisted grin that I have never seen on her pulls up the wrinkles on either side of her mouth as a vindictive gleam enters her eyes.

"You forget, Bertram, that this is *my* company. Do you think I had no idea what you were up to?"

I cringe at being called by my father's name, even though I knew that's who she thought I was. But then the pieces begin to fall into place—or at least, some of them.

"You gave the police what they needed to arrest him?"

She laughs, this brittle sort of noise that doesn't belong to the Gran I know. "When Grayson called me, I marched down there with everything I had. I'd waited too long to do anything, and another innocent girl got hurt, though I refused to let the cycle continue."

I gape at my Gran, attempting to figure out if what she's telling me could be true. The cops showed up at the door after Riley went to them, and several days later, Dad was arrested for embezzlement. After they'd escorted him out the door in cuffs, I'd called the family lawyer... and then I'd placed a call to Gran.

I'd assumed they'd investigated my father and found something incriminating... but could Gran have provided them with everything they needed to make the arrest?

Not to mention what she said about Riley... because that's the only person she could be referring to, except that would mean she believes Riley's story.

I shake my head, which is pulsing with a headache. There's too much to process to think about that. If what Gran is saying is true, then she's the one ultimately responsible for putting my dad in prison. Does he know that? He can't, he'd have said something if he had. I've always assumed that, like me, he placed the blame on Riley.

If I could find out the truth, though, it would prove that all of this isn't just in Gran's head. If she did send my dad to prison, she'd have had to have a good reason... it would mean there might be some basis to her claims about my mom.

That doesn't necessarily mean Riley wasn't lying... If Gran believed Dad did something to my Mom, then of course she'd believe Riley's lie...

Except, a niggle of doubt has firmly taken root...

I need to find out what the hell happened four years ago.

I need answers.

And with my father possibly getting released, I need them now.

RILEY

CHAPTER TWENTY-EIGHT

On Sunday morning, Logan meets me outside my apartment before we head to Urban Haven, a cute cafe near campus that serves breakfast all day. I've walked past it numerous times but never wanted to waste money by coming in.

From the street, the cafe boasts large, steel-framed windows that allow natural light to flood through. A hand-painted sign is propped up on the sidewalk stating, "When life gives you lemons, give them back and tell them you want coffee," with vibrant potted plants lining the doorway, adding a touch of greenery to the urban street.

I can smell the aroma of freshly brewed coffee and sizzling bacon wafting through the air as we approach, only growing stronger when Logan opens the door and ushers me inside with a, "They have the best waffles in the state."

The interior is just as quaint as the outside, with exposed brick walls, polished concrete floors, and overhead metal beams. Edison bulbs hang from the ceiling, casting a warm glow over the wooden tables and mismatched chairs. Rustic wooden shelves adorn the walls, displaying an array of books, and are decorated with succulents, antique coffee mugs, and tea sets.

The menu is written in colored chalk on a blackboard that takes up the entire back wall, each item sounding more delicious than the previous.

"Oh look, the artwork on the walls is for sale," I point out. "They must be displaying work from local artists. Royce could do something for them to display."

Logan scoffs beside me. "And let actual people see his work? Never gonna happen, Shortcake. Even *I've* never even seen one of his drawings."

"You haven't?" I ask in surprise.

Logan steers his focus away from the artwork on the walls to look at me. "You have?"

I go silent, not wanting to betray Royce's trust if it's not something he typically does. I knew he was reserved about his drawings, although I hadn't realized he was so private about them that even his closest friends had never seen any of them.

"Holy crap, you have. Damn, Shortcake, that's *big*. I hope you know that. That's like... a normal person's declaration of love."

"It's not like that," I protest. "I won a bet. He didn't want to."

Except he willingly handed over that drawing of me—that I framed and set on my dresser. Sharing that had absolutely nothing to do with a bet and everything to do with him sharing a piece of himself... a piece that I can now see he hasn't ever shared with anyone else.

"Nu-uh, not buying it. If Royce didn't want to, he wouldn't have taken the bet."

Hmm, perhaps he's right. A warmth settles in my stomach, knowing Royce feels comfortable sharing such a private part of himself. That he felt that way before he knew about

Aurora—before he knew for certain that I was telling the truth.

I'd known at the time that it was a big deal to him, but finding out even Logan hasn't ever seen one of his drawings brings a whole new depth to the significance of that moment.

"Welcome to Urban Haven," a waitress dressed in jeans and an *Urban Haven* t-shirt with a black apron around her waist says as she passes. "Take a seat anywhere. Someone will be with you shortly to take your order."

"Where do you wanna sit?" Logan asks. "There's a free table by the window?"

"Yeah, let's take that one."

As we make our way across the cafe, it buzzes with a relaxed yet vibrant energy. I recognize some of the patrons as Halston U students, enjoying their Sunday before the third week of the semester begins tomorrow.

A couple of them nod in greeting when they spot Logan, eyeing me curiously as we walk by. It's a look I've become familiar with this past week as I've spent more time with Logan on campus while he walks me to class and studies with me in the library. I've learned to mostly block out the stares and whispers. Of course, it helps that Whitney has left me alone after Logan had her shunned by the entire hockey team and their groupies.

Others are clearly locals, meeting friends for brunch and enjoying the laid-back ambiance.

"Do you know any of them?" I ask Logan as we take our seats.

"Nah, but I'm used to everyone knowing who I am and me not knowing any of them."

"That must be so strange," I muse aloud. "To have people greet and talk to you as though you're friends, yet not having a clue who they are."

"At first, I loved it—everyone knowing my name. It was flattering—having all my hard work validated and feeling like I belonged, like I was a part of something huge."

"What happened?" 'Cause I sense something must have occurred to change his outlook on it all.

He lets out a dry chuckle. "Did you know we nearly didn't make it to the Frozen Four my freshman year? We had an important game against Wisconsin, and we were tied, two minutes 'til the buzzer. There was this asshole who'd been on my case the whole game, pulling illegal moves that the ref wasn't doing a damn thing about. When he checked me into the boards for the fourth time, I lost my shit. Beat the crap out of him. Of course, the ref saw that, and I was thrown out of the game.

"In those last two minutes, we had two shots on goal and fumbled both, while they got a lucky shot and netted the puck right as the buzzer went.

"Of course, people blamed me. Not Coach or the team, though. We were all furious with how the game was handled, but not everyone on campus was as understanding. Even though I was a freshman, I'd already proven to be as talented as some seniors. Many believed if I hadn't been benched, we'd have scored those two goals and won the game." He shrugs. "They were probably right. But, as it was, it meant we had to win our game against Michigan—a tough-as-hell team—to qualify."

"So? You went on to win the Frozen Four that year."

He smiles now. "We did, but for those two weeks before our Michigan game, I was *hated*. People would glare at me or spit at my feet. One guy even told me he hoped I got hit by a car."

"Oh my god! What the hell is wrong with people? It's only a game."

Logan's casual shrug infuriates me. No one should have to

put up with that. We're only human. We make mistakes, and I don't honestly understand how anyone can hold Logan's actions against him, especially if his coach and team didn't.

"Hockey fans, like in any other sport, can get caught up in the drive to win. The highs and lows. It means everything to them in much the same way it does to the team. It had been years since Halston had even had a shot at making it to the Frozen Four, and they needed someone to blame. I was that someone."

He fidgets as he frowns down at the tabletop, running his fingers over the fork tines in an un-Logan-like gesture that illustrates how much the attitude directed toward him those two weeks still bothers him.

"But yeah, it changed my perspective. Made me realize how easily people's attitudes toward you can change. Then, after we won the Frozen Four, those same people who were spitting on me were now patting my back. I saw it all for what it was... fake. I smiled and pretended to soak it all up, but it was empty. Hollow. The only real things in my life are my family, my team, and Royce and Grayson." His eyes shift back and forth between mine, soft and vulnerable. "And you."

Swallowing past the lump of emotion in my throat, I'm at a loss for words as I drink him in.

"Good morning, folks. What can I get for you today?" a waitress interrupts, the heavy bubble of tension surrounding us popping with her appearance.

"Oh, erm..." I quickly scan the menu.

"We'll take your waffle stack with all the toppings, a plate of French toast, a portion of scrambled eggs, the breakfast burrito, fruit platter, and..." His eyes scour the menu board as I gape at him, wondering who the hell else is joining us. "The hash browns, two strawberry milkshakes, a pumpkin spice latte, and a cappuccino, please."

"Certainly. I'll get your drinks right away, and the food will be out shortly."

"Thank you."

"Logan," I hiss when the waitress walks away. "That is *way* too much!"

"Whatever you don't eat, we can box up and eat later."

"Later? Logan, you ordered enough food to feed your entire team."

He only smirks and I shake my head at him. "I really need to teach you proper portion sizes. The local grocery store is probably having a field day with you buying out half the shop every few days. You realize I end up giving half of it to food shelters?"

He simply shrugs a shoulder. "It's yours to do what you want. Besides, it's an integral part of my apology tour."

"There's an entire tour?" I tease with a half-smile. "And, uh, how many stops are you planning on this tour?"

"It's an open tour; the number of stops is undecided. I'll make as many of them as I have to to win you back."

Tilting my head, my expression is serious. "You know I'm not a trophy to be won, right?"

Logan's hand immediately wraps around mine on top of the table, and he leans in. "Fuck, baby, you are so much more than some stupid trophy. You're not a fleeting goal to achieve. You're the one who makes reaching those goals so much more meaningful.

"You're the only person I've felt this connection with. The only one who sees me. Who reminded me that amongst the fake smiles, there can be genuine ones too.

"You're the person I want beside me for every achievement and happy moment, but you're also the one I want to share my losses with, wallowing in the hard times. And I want to be that person for you, too. I want to be the one you talk to when you're angry, whose shoulder you cry on when you're sad, who you run to when you ace a test."

"You're my person, Riley, and I know I don't deserve to be yours yet, but I swear I'll prove that I can be that person for you as well."

After a breakfast that made me regret my decision to wear skinny jeans today, Logan and I spent the rest of the day wandering around Halston. Although I had done a bit of exploring when I first moved here, it mainly had been to find the local grocery store and laundromat and to get a feel for the area I was living in.

Nothing like today, where we stop to do some window shopping and wander into quaint little local shops. A bag swings from my hand, holding a gorgeous pink, herringbone weave blanket Logan caught me admiring.

My footsteps unintentionally slow as we pass a bookstore, and I spy the latest fantasy novel that has been blowing up a storm online since its release a couple of months ago. I haven't been able to justify the cost of buying it, but I pause to admire the gorgeous cover, fantasizing about how pretty it would look on my shelf.

"Why don't we go in?" Logan suggests, already stepping into the doorway.

"Oh, that's okay. I was just looking."

With a smirk and shake of his head, he tugs me inside, and I'm enveloped in the intoxicating aroma of aged paper, ink, and the subtle traces of countless stories just waiting to be read.

"You like to read?" Logan asks, perusing the shelf in front of him with curiosity.

"I do. Not that I get much of a chance to."

"What sort of books do you read?" He lifts a book off the shelf, studying the back of it before flipping through a few pages.

"Fiction. Fantasy mostly. I love the break it gives me from reality, the escape into another world that's so vastly different from the one we live in. Where the main female characters dance on the edge of despair yet emerge as warriors in their own right."

Taking his hand, I pull him deeper into the bookstore, scanning the shelves until I find the one I'm looking for, then search the titles on the spines of each book until I find one I've read. "Take her, for example," I say, pulling one out from the shelf and showing him the cover with a fierce, sword-wielding woman on it. "She's faced with the unimaginable—betrayal, loss, monsters that haunt both the world and her soul. Yet, she doesn't crumble. Characters like her... they don't just survive; they thrive in adversity. They teach me that strength isn't the absence of pain, but the ability to wield it. They dance through the darkness with grace, confronting nightmares with swords drawn and hearts unyielding."

I pause, my eyes meeting his as I search his chestnut hues for understanding. "They're my heroes. My inspiration. They face demons with a courage that defies the odds. They're not devoid of fear; they just don't let it control them. Their bravery keeps me going when life gets hard and feels pointless."

Sliding the book back onto the shelf, I explain, "Reading their stories, it's not about denying reality. It's about finding the strength to face it."

When I look up at Logan, he surges forward, hands on my hips, tugging me closer as his supple lips meet mine in a tender yet passionate kiss.

"The women in these books may be your heroines, but, baby, you're mine. What you've survived... the grace with which you face your trauma every single day astounds me. The fact you can still be so compassionate, loving, and caring after having experienced the worst of humanity... that right there is pure magic. Your strength knows no bounds, and if these books have helped you become the incredible woman before me, then I guess I better give one a read." He plucks the book I'd just returned from the shelf, scanning the blurb on the back.

"Logan," I rasp, gaining his attention. "Kiss me again."

A thud echoes in the aisle, my bag and the book hitting the floor as Logan's arms band around me, his lips sealing over mine as he fills my soul with the same strength I gain from reading my books.

Bodies flush, and the feel of his hard muscles flexing beneath me sends shivers coursing through my body as my lips part and our kiss deepens.

"We better stop before we get asked to leave," Logan reluctantly says, his voice a full octave deeper than usual.

"We wouldn't want that," I tease, leaning into him and soaking up his strength.

"Not before I buy this." He bends down to retrieve the paperback.

"You don't have to buy that, Logan."

"Try stopping me. If these characters have lent my girl strength when she needed it, then they're characters I have to meet."

"Do you even like fantasy books?" I ask, ignoring the flipping of my heart at his sentiment.

He shrugs. "No idea. We'll find out."

Taking my hand in his, he pulls me to the front of the store, where the shopkeeper is sitting on a stool behind the register.

"I'll take a copy of the book in your window, too," Logan tells the man, who goes to retrieve it.

"Lo-" His hand claps over my mouth.

"Shush, woman. Let me treat you." He's grinning like a loon. When he removes his hand, he smacks a quick kiss on my lips before turning to the register as the shopkeeper returns, paying for our orders before we leave.

<hr>

"Have you heard anything from your mom this week?" Logan asks as we enter my apartment building. We went for dinner after leaving the bookstore, and I had the best day ever with him.

"Ha. Nope."

"What do you wanna do? The offer to drive you to see her still stands."

I shake my head. "She'll call me this week. It's her usual MO."

He makes a disgusted noise in the back of his throat.

"I wanna talk to my family's lawyers about your situation—get their opinion. Would you be okay with that?"

I chew on my bottom lip as we climb the stairs. "You don't have to do that, Logan..."

"Riley," he says seriously, "I *want* to help. There's no reason for you to wait another four years until you can afford a decent lawyer, especially when my family has one on retainer. They're not family lawyers, so they might not be of any use, but I can at least see what they have to say."

I'm silent as we ascend the second flight of stairs. "Give me a few days to think about it?" I ask. "It's not that I don't want or appreciate your help, it's just... I'm used to being in this all on my own. This still doesn't feel real, and what you're offering... it's no small matter. I'd be in your debt for the rest of my life."

He tugs me to a stop on the top step. "Riley. I'm not doing this so you'll owe me one—"

"I know you're not, but that doesn't change how I'm going to feel about it. Just... give me a couple of days to think about it." I give him a pleading look and he folds with a sigh.

"Okay, Shortcake, but don't think you're going to distract me so I'll forget." There's a teasing lilt to his voice that draws a smile from me as I turn down the hallway to my apartment.

"What the hell?" Logan murmurs, and I glance up to see what's caught his attention. "Who the hell is that at your door?"

A body is slumped against the door to my apartment, and as we cautiously approach, whoever it is becomes clear.

"Gray?" Logan says in confusion. "Why the hell is Grayson passed out in front of your apartment?"

Isn't that the real question.

Sighing, I shake my head. "Apparently, this is where drunk Grayson likes to hang out," I mutter as I fish out my keys.

"Huh?"

I wave away his confusion. "We need to move him before I can open the door."

Logan hands me the couple of bags he was carrying from our day out, before bending down to haul a very passed-out Grayson off the floor. "Jesus, he weighs a fucking ton."

I huff out a breath as I hurriedly unlock the door before pushing it open. "You can put him on the sofa."

"I'm not bringing him into your apartment," Logan sneers.

Throwing my arms out, I ask, "What do you suppose we do with him, then? We can't leave him out here."

He looks around the hallway as if that is, in fact, a very feasible option.

"Logan. No. Just bring him inside. He's unconscious. What can he possibly do?"

Not looking the least bit impressed, he reluctantly relents, hauling Grayson higher into his arms before maneuvering him into the apartment and dropping him on the couch.

"Now what?" Logan asks.

Pulling the pink blanket Logan purchased today from the shopping bag, I drape it over him before grabbing a bucket from under the sink and placing it beside his head.

"Let him sleep it off, I guess." I turn away, pulling off my coat and hanging it up.

"Here?" Logan questions as though the idea is preposterous.

"Well, he's already here."

"He's not staying here alone with you."

At his stern tone, I turn to look at him, crossing my arms over my chest and arching a challenging brow. "I'm perfectly capable of handling Grayson."

"I know you are, Shortcake," Logan quickly insists. "Although I should at least stay. Just in case."

"You have an early training session in the morning," I remind him.

"I'm not leaving you alone with him," he reiterates with more firmness.

I roll my eyes at his ridiculous macho bullshit.

"I'll be fine. He's dead to the world and probably will be for at least twelve hours. Plus, he'll have one hell of a hangover when he wakes up. Doubt he'll be able to do much to me with that."

Logan gives me an unimpressed glare. "Not reassuring, Shortcake."

With a wry grin, I approach him, sliding my hands up the front of his chest.

"I'm at least staying for a while," he states in a tone that leaves no room for argument. "Make sure he really is passed out."

"I don't think he's faking," I comment, trying not to laugh at the way Logan glares at Grayson as if all of this really might be a ruse.

"Well, just in case he is, I'm going to keep an eye on him while we watch a movie."

"Is that so?"

"Riley," he growls, narrowing his eyes on me. "You will have to physically drag me out of this apartment. Let's finish this date day off with a cuddle on your bed where we can't hear this asshole's snores."

"Ahh, now I get it. This is all a grand ploy to get you into my bed."

The tension bleeds from Logan's features as he barks out a laugh, and I squeal as he launches forward and scoops me off the floor. "Baby, when I get you into bed, I can assure you, Grayson will play no part in it."

RILEY

CHAPTER TWENTY-NINE

"Call if he wakes up," Logan insists when I finally convince him to leave. Grayson hasn't stirred once while we watched our movie, and it's starting to get late, considering Logan has hockey practice early tomorrow morning. It has taken half an hour of me coaxing him toward the door, and now he's a brick wall on the threshold. "Are you sure you don't want me to stay?" he asks with a frown, glancing over my shoulder toward Grayson. "I won't try anything. I'll sleep on the floor. Or you can build a pillow wall. I don't care, I just don't like leaving you alone with him."

I smile sweetly at him. "I know. It's not that I don't want you to stay or that I don't trust you to do something I'm uncomfortable with. I simply don't think having you here when he wakes up is the wisest idea. Besides, if he wakes up halfway reasonable, Grayson and I have some things we need to discuss."

Logan snorts. "Grayson... reasonable? Maybe if he has a lobotomy in his sleep."

When Logan remains rigid in the doorway, I press, "I'll be

fine. I promise. Besides, you and Royce are only a few minutes away. I can call you if it sounds like he's waking up."

I can tell he still isn't happy about it, but eventually, he blows out a breath. "Fine, but call if he so much as twitches. I don't give a shit what time of the night it is." He finally kisses my lips before murmuring goodnight and walking down the hall.

I watch him disappear before closing the door and leaning against it as I gaze at the outline of Grayson sound asleep on my sofa.

What the fuck do I do now?

The first thing I do is move around the apartment, gathering the handful of photos of me and Rora and shoving them into a bottom drawer where he won't find them. I'm not ready for those questions if he wakes up and goes snooping around while I'm sleeping.

Once I'm done, I turn to stare at his sleeping form. He's been conspicuously absent since our... confrontation... in the library. Which begs the question, what happened that brought him to my door tonight?

I still don't know why he ended up here last weekend either, or what it means that this is where he comes to when he's drunk.

Stepping closer to the couch, I glance down at the face of the man who made my winter break miserable. Who blames me for everything wrong that's happened in his life. Even in his passed-out state, he still somehow manages to look angry. His face is pinched, and the frown lines along his forehead must be ingrained into the skin with how often they're present.

Despite all that, he looks so much like the seventeen-year-old boy I once knew, and I can't help reaching forward to brush a strand of hair off his forehead.

Several times now, he's implied he had feelings for me back

then. How different would our lives be if I'd known that? If we'd acted on them? If I'd confided in him? If he'd believed me?

Perhaps if we both hadn't avoided one another in an effort to ignore our feelings, we'd have gotten to know each other. He'd have known the type of person I was. Would have understood I'm not the type of girl to make something like that up.

So many regrets and what-ifs.

All of them pointless since this is where we're at. On opposite sides of a ravine with a fast-flowing river of everything we can't express rushing between us.

Aurora comes to mind, and my lips purse as I observe Grayson's sleeping face. How much longer can I keep her from him? The thought of telling him is crippling, yet it's reaching the point that it's selfish to keep her existence a secret. My reasons for not telling him are selfish and borne from fear.

Telling him would alleviate the tension between him and the guys. It would give Grayson irrefutable proof of his father's crimes. It would also give Aurora another family member. As much as I may wish that I could be all she needs, I'm not foolish enough to believe that. She needs more than just me. She needs more family, and while Grayson may have been an asshole to me, I know he's capable of being the brother she needs. If he knew... he'd step up. I *know* it in the very fabric of my being. The teenager I knew, he's still in there. He's just buried beneath layers of pain and hurt and betrayal, and not knowing who to trust.

Gathering my courage, I lick my parched lips before blurting in a voice barely above a whisper, "I have a daughter. You have a sister."

He doesn't stir. Not that I expected him to.

I needed to practice saying the words aloud to give me the courage to one day say them to his face.

I sit there another moment before I tuck the blanket tighter around him. "Goodnight, Grayson," I whisper before getting to my feet.

At my voice, his face scrunches and he shifts beneath the blanket. "Mom?" he rasps in a sleep-filled voice. I freeze, waiting to see if he says anything else. I know absolutely nothing about his mom. She was never talked about when I lived in his father's house. All I know is that she died when Grayson was young. Is he dreaming of her? There's something monumentally heartbreaking about this twenty-two-year-old man dreaming of his dead mother.

However, he becomes increasingly agitated, shifting restlessly on the couch to the point that I reach out to take his hand, feeling the need to offer him some sort of comfort. He grasps it like a lifeline, squeezing so hard that my fingertips go white. "I don't want him to hurt you," he whines, in a voice so small I can imagine it coming from schoolboy Grayson.

Not knowing what to do, I settle back beside him, reaching forward to brush my fingers through his hair. "Everything's okay," I murmur in a soothing tone. "No one is getting hurt."

My heart clenches at his concern for his mother, and a darker part of me can't help but wonder if he's having a nightmare or reliving a memory.

I continue to mutter reassuring words as I run my fingers through his hair until he settles back into sleep. Only then do I slide my hand from his relaxed grip, and with a final glance, I leave him alone to sleep off his hangover while I get ready for bed.

I'm burning up. My body is literally on fire as sensation after sensation rolls through me, a tidal wave of ecstasy building in intensity until I snap awake with a drawn-out moan.

It takes me a long moment to wade through the confusing pulses of pleasure, demanding all of my attention, to notice the head of hair buried between my thighs.

"Grayson," I gasp at the long, slow slide of his tongue along my slit before he assaults my clit with his lips and teeth.

Any outrage goes flying out the window as my spine arches off the bed and my eyes roll back in my head. *Holy shit, he's good at that.* He brings me to the edge of what promises to be one hell of an orgasm, before switching up his moves so that promise dangles just out of reach.

"Grayson," I snap when he does the same thing again, his vibrating chuckle against my sensitive parts causing me to shudder.

"Don't like being kept waiting, do you, little sis?"

"Don't call me that," I snap absently as he replaces his tongue with his fingers.

Stretching out above me in the darkened room, I can't make out anything more than his outline, but I can *feel* the clash of his stare.

"You don't like me calling you little sis? Only, isn't that what we are? Isn't that what made this so goddamn hard to resist when we were teenagers? Knowing we weren't supposed to be attracted to one another?" Bending down, he trails his lips up the column of my neck, sucking on the skin. "Watching you at family dinners, acting like you were my sister while I thought about spreading you out on the table, always had me nearly coming in my pants. I was so fucking hard for you." His breath tickles my ear before he sucks on my earlobe, his teeth sinking into the flesh and making me yelp.

"Telling my friends at school that you were my new step-sister while I fantasized about shoving you against the locker and kissing you so they could all see exactly how unsisterly my thoughts were," he continues in a gravelly voice.

"You drove me fucking wild without even trying, and all the while I had to pretend like you were nothing more than a new, unwelcome stranger living in my house."

Okay, yes, he's right. There was something incredibly hot in the forbiddenness of my attraction to him. In knowing I wasn't supposed to feel the way that I did.

"Tell me you didn't get off on that too," he rasps. "Tell me you never once acted like a sister in public while fantasizing about fucking me behind the nearest closed door."

"I did," I admit. "At your games. I'd cheer you on as your sister, but I'd be thinking about what would happen if I showed up in your locker room after everyone else left."

"Fuck," he hisses. "I wouldn't have been able to resist you."

He curls his fingers inside me while rubbing his thumb over my clit, and I'm on the verge of complete combustion. "Please, Grayson. I need to come."

At my plea, he pulls his fingers from me, and I whine in protest as he moves to kneel between my legs.

"Admit that you want this," he says in a sinister tone as his fingers undo his jeans, shoving them and his boxers down his legs. Fisting his cock, he pumps his hand up and down before swiping the spongy head through my folds. "Admit that despite everything, you want *me.*"

Holding his gaze, my voice is firm when I say, "I've never denied that I want you, Grayson. But wanting you doesn't mean demeaning myself into being the toy you turn to when you need something to break."

My admission is followed by a pregnant pause, and I'm highly aware of the stretch of my walls where his tip is pressing against my opening.

"I don't want to break you," he confesses in a broken tone. "I want you to piece me back together. To make me forget. To be my reprieve from the thoughts in my head."

He holds my stare as he pushes forward, filling me inch by inch until I'm stretched full, and he's leaning over me. His face hovers above mine. It's far more intimate than anything we've shared yet, and I'm grateful to the darkness for providing me with a modicum of distance. It would be far too easy for me to give myself over to this Grayson.

He begins to move, and I lose myself in the ripples of pleasure he elicits with every stroke. What starts slowly builds in intensity until I'm clawing at every inch of him I can reach, and he's ripped open my pajama top so he can suck on my skin like it's his sole focus in life to mark me.

"This," he rasps, breathing heavily as he thrusts into me. "This is what I needed. Do you hear that silence? Fucking bliss."

Call me crazy, for I know exactly what he means. Gone are the voices telling me how fucking stupid this is. Gone is the doubt. Leaving only the feel of his body sliding against mine and the crashing of his heart against my palm.

Yanking my arms above my head, he pins them in one hand as his other one glides over my chest before sliding around my throat. He gives it a testing squeeze, nowhere close enough to cut off my oxygen, and when I don't object, he does it again.

He repeats it with each thrust, getting progressively tighter, and the euphoria only heightens the sensations he elicits with every stroke. All of my awareness hones in on him. On the hard slam of his pelvis against mine. The slicking of sweat between our bodies. His harsh breaths against my cheek.

Switching up the angle, he drives deeper than before, and I ignite like a spark to a flame.

Pleasure courses through me in unending waves and I arch against his hold, my mouth opening in a silent scream as he fucks me through my release like a man possessed until his cum paints my inner walls.

I suck in a lungful of air when he releases my throat, not

even realizing that the splotches in my vision were from a lack of oxygen and not the world's most intense orgasm.

Tiredness crashes over me as I roll onto my side to face him, finding him already watching me. The euphoria from our release is intense enough still to keep any regrets at bay, though the weight on my eyelids slowly drags them down, and I'm asleep before I can ask him why he was outside my door earlier.

When I wake several hours later, I'm tucked beneath the duvet, and when I shuffle to a comfier position, I discover no sticky residue between my thighs. I even reach down to feel for myself, finding my inner thighs clean. I crack open an eyelid, and I'm not at all surprised to discover the other side of my bed empty, an indentation in the pillow from where Grayson lay.

GRAYSON

CHAPTER THIRTY

The plastic seat is hard against my ass as trepidation courses through my veins while I wait for the proceedings to get underway. It takes everything in me not to shuffle. I'm uncomfortable as fuck. The fact that I snuck out of Riley's apartment with Gran's accusations ringing in my ears makes everything ten times worse.

I don't even remember ending up at Riley's last night. After leaving Gran's, I went to the office, not needing to run into one of the guys and deal with that if I went home. Found a bottle of bourbon in my bottom drawer and knocked it back while going over everything Gran said... guess I must have finished the entire thing trying to figure it all out.

When I came to, it only took a second for me to piece together where I was. The smell of her was everywhere, and the little bits of girly shit sitting around... there's only one woman's apartment I could possibly end up in when blackout drunk.

With alcohol still sloshing around in my system, I'd stumbled into her bedroom. Intent on answers? I'm not sure what my thinking had been, but when I saw her sound asleep... so soft and vulnerable looking. So fragile. Seeming so much like the girl I remember...

I hadn't been thinking when I'd ambled closer. Or perhaps I was thinking clearly for the first time in weeks. Since seeing her in that club. My mouth was salivating for the taste of her. For the reprieve her presence offers.

When I'm inside her, the cacophony of life's chaos quiets to a gentle murmur. As if she possesses a magical touch, turning the disarray of existence into a fleeting symphony of peace. I can't make any sense of it, but I equally don't dare to question the miracle that is having her wrapped around me.

That respite she offers from the tempest that constantly rages at the borders of my sanity... I need it more with each passing day. Needed it with such a fierce desire in that moment that it drove me forward until I was pushing the duvet aside and curling my fingers in the waistband of her pajamas, pulling them down her legs.

The taste of her on my tongue, the feel of her spasming with each touch... nirvana. That blanket of deferment settled over me, and I lost myself to everything Riley. The girl I've never been allowed to have but have always craved with a passion I can't deny.

I shift on the chair, my pants growing inappropriately tight simply at the memory of our night together. I'd intended to talk to her afterward. I'd told myself I'd finally listen to her version of events five years ago. It might not be something I want to hear, but I need to hear it at this point. Need to see her face as she says it instead of shutting her out and refusing to listen.

Except, she'd fallen asleep almost instantly, and I couldn't find it in me to wake her. So I'd cleaned her up and spent the next few hours lost in my thoughts until I had to leave or I'd be late for Dad's parole hearing.

After months of working toward this day... I can't say I'm

the least bit excited about my father's possible release. I'm certainly not feeling the satisfaction I thought I'd feel.

Instead, I feel sick at the notion that I may be culpable in helping a vile, manipulative man get out of prison. The problem is I don't know for sure, and I don't know how to find out. Even if I do get to the bottom of the truth, is it too late? If my father is granted early parole, then he'll be released in a matter of weeks or months.

I run my eyes over the parole board, taking in the bland, expressionless features of the four members—three men and one woman. They look bored more than anything else, although I guess this is just another day for them. The outcome of this hearing won't change anything for them.

Not like it will for my dad.

Like it will for me.

Shifting my focus, I take in my father, who is looking sharp today in a tailor-made Brioni suit, his hair freshly cut and face cleanly shaven. The twisting in my gut intensifies as I imagine the fear in Gran's eyes when she thought I was him. What does she see that I'm missing? He looks so... *ordinary*. He doesn't seem evil. Doesn't look capable of the things Gran and Riley have accused him of.

Am I so biased by the fact he's my father that I can't see it?

Sitting beside his lawyer, he's the epitome of confidence, appearing collected as he straightens in his seat in front of the parole board, his posture tense yet resolute.

I've been putting on a good damn show in front of Royce and Logan, arguing that *they're* the idiots in all of this... only what if they aren't? What if *I'm* the one who has been a fool?

His lawyer pushes to his feet, garnering the attention of the entire room as he addresses the parole board.

"Members of the parole board," he begins, voice steady and sure, carrying a weight that seems to resonate around the room.

"I want to start by thanking all of you for giving up your time today to discuss the case of Mr. Bertram Van Doren. Throughout his incarceration, Mr. Van Doren has demonstrated a commitment to self-improvement and rehabilitation. He has actively participated in various educational and vocational programs within the prison system, displaying a genuine desire to better himself."

His spiel goes on, listing all the ways my father has demonstrated that he is rehabilitated and has learned from his mistakes. I zone out, losing interest until one of the parole board members asks my father if he'd like to address the room.

My father stands, flattening a hand down the front of his suit to iron out the non-existent wrinkles.

"Thank you. Members of the parole board, I stand before you today with a deep sense of regret for my past actions. During my time in prison, I've had the opportunity to reflect on the choices that led me down the wrong path. I've worked hard to understand the impact of my actions on those affected by my decisions. I know I can never undo the pain I've caused. However, I'm committed to making amends."

My brows furrow, creases deepening along my forehead as his words strike me. Not once do I recall my father expressing regret for embezzling company funds. Anger at having been caught—yes. Hostility for how everything came about—absolutely. But regret for the crime he did actually commit? No. Not once in the four years since his incarceration has he even mentioned the actual crime he committed.

A crime that nearly resulted in the demise of Van Doren Holdings.

One that broke our shareholders' trust. That nearly decimated our family name. *Mom's* family name.

If we'd gone under, jobs would have been lost. People left

scrambling when their paychecks stopped. Families thrown into chaos.

His hatred—my hatred—has always been pinpointed on Riley: the instigator. She may have been the one who set all of this in motion, but while I've been elbow-deep in shit regarding the company, cursing my father's name for being stupid enough to embezzle in the first place, I've never actually stopped to consider whether he's remorseful.

"What are your plans upon release regarding Van Doren Holdings?" the female member of the parole board questions, expression stern as her eyes bore into my father.

"My son"—my father gestures in my direction—"has been responsible for the welfare of the company and employees in my absence, and he will continue to have the final say, along with input from shareholders."

"Yes, but what about *you*, Mr. Van Doren," she pushes. "Do *you* intend to have any controlling interest in the company?"

"No, ma'am. My son has more than proven himself capable of managing the family business these last four years."

"A scrupulous eye has been kept on the company," my father's lawyer adds, observing the board. "And I have obtained reports from employees and shareholders who attest that Grayson Van Doren has done an adequate job of reviving the company in his father's absence."

Adequate, my fucking ass.

The muscle in my jaw flutters as I grind my teeth, wholly unaware that such reports were being gathered. Not that it would change anything—I like to think that I treat all of my employees with the respect they deserve. The people at Van Doren Holdings are practically my family. I grew up around them; I'm responsible for them.

"I will, of course, be at hand to consult should Grayson require it. Just as I have been during my incarceration." It's more like trying to run things from behind the scenes, but sure, spin it whichever way you please. "However, for the time being, at least until I can gain the trust of the staff and shareholders, I only wish to help where I can as a regular *employee* of the company."

"So you have no plans to return to your previous role as CEO?"

"No. All I wish is to spend time getting to know my son again and rebuilding my life."

I sit up straighter in my seat, wondering if my father means anything he's saying. It doesn't exactly fit with the narrative he's been telling me. It was only last month that he said he'd have to get the lawyers to undo my new green energy deal *when he was back in charge.* Yet, today, he's telling the parole board that he'll be a mere employee of his own company upon release?

Yeah, the board might buy it, but I sure as hell don't.

Seemingly satisfied with my father's answers, the woman nods, and the room falls into a preemptive silence while the parole board deliberates amongst themselves. My father and lawyer talk in quiet voices, leaving me to try and read the lips of the parole board members.

Tension bleeds into the air, and my palms grow sweaty. This is it. This is the moment we've been working toward for four long years.

My heart crashes against my chest in indecision, and I'm not entirely sure which outcome I'm hoping for.

Release, obviously. He's my dad. Of course, I ultimately want him to be free.

Shoving away the screaming voice in my head telling me to stop lying to myself, I cling to that belief as I lean forward in my seat, waiting with bated breath as the first member of the board eyes my father.

"Mr. Van Doren," he announces. "The parole board believes you have demonstrated significant efforts toward rehabilitation and have shown remorse for your actions. We hereby grant you parole."

A whooshing drowns out any further noise as my stomach twists itself into knots, so tangled that I'll need surgery to undo them all. *We hereby grant you parole.* The words hang in the air like a pillow, threatening to suffocate me.

Home. My father is finally coming home.

Yet, this tightness in my chest… it's not a feeling of relief.

My father turns to look at me over his shoulder, his grin bright and eyes shining with triumph and perhaps something more raw, vulnerable. Something genuine, or perhaps I'm only seeing what I so desperately want to see. Projecting my feelings onto him.

I force my lips upward while my insides explode into chaos and uncertainty, doubts clashing with rational thought as I internally spin out of control.

"Your release date is set for ninety days from today," the judge states.

Ninety days.

I have ninety days to determine with certainty if my father is the man I always believed him to be… or if he's the man Gran fears.

I'm still reeling from the news of my father's release as I walk across the Halston U campus that afternoon. I have class in an hour, although admittedly, the last place I want to be is in a classroom. Honestly, my focus hasn't been on my studies at all this semester. With all the other shit going on in my life, school has fallen to the bottom of my list of priorities.

With time to kill before my next class, I head to the food court to grab a coffee and a table while catching up on missed calls and emails from this morning.

Entering the glass building, I head straight for the coffee stand and order a double espresso before swiping my student card over the card reader.

"Have a nice day," the overly happy cashier says as he hands me the cup. I don't acknowledge him before turning away. Perhaps I should be as ecstatic as him, but all I feel is more weight being added to my already weary shoulders.

Coffee in hand, I scan the room. Since the lunch rush hour has passed, the usual chaotic bustle has dimmed, and most of the tables are now vacant. However, there are still people milling around, chatting, or working diligently.

Three people seated at a table against the glass wall on the far side of the room catch my attention, and I pause for a moment, taking a sip of the scalding liquid before striding toward them.

My heels clip against the marble floor as I close in on the table. I keep my eyes on Riley the entire time, watching as she laughs at something Logan says. She nudges him with her elbow before he throws his arm over her shoulders and drags her into his side. She goes with zero resistance. The apparent casualness of their intimacy causes my blood to boil and, with it, brings images of her stretching around me while she moaned my name.

It fills me with primal satisfaction when she cranes her neck, and I catch sight of a deep purple hickey on her throat. *I left that there.* Not Logan, with his fucking arm around her. I made a very firm point of marking her as mine last night for reasons I don't care to look at too closely. Still, the sight of my mark sends blood rushing to my cock, and the desire to strip her naked so I can explore the others and leave brand-new ones is all-consuming.

So what if I haven't been able to stop thinking about having her again since that first time in the field? It doesn't have to mean anything. Fucking her rebalances me. It hits the reset button so I can function. That's all it has to be.

Last night was about resetting my system. I'd lost control after visiting Gran, and I needed her to re-establish that because, apparently, she was the only one who could. She'd managed it that night in the field and again on Christmas Eve, although I barely even remember that encounter. I'd been in a haze after leaving Gran, her words spinning on repeat in my head until I didn't know what to feel. What was real, and what was imaginary. I was so distracted with trying to reconcile the dad I knew with the one my Gran fears, that I was caught entirely off guard when I stepped into the kitchen and saw her there.

I just needed her to tell me that she lied. I needed to know my father was who I'd always believed him to be.

But, of course, she couldn't give me that. She *wouldn't*.

I've been too fucking terrified to honestly look at what that might mean because acknowledging that truth... I don't think I can fucking handle it.

Each time Gran mistakes me for *him*, I splinter a little more. For how much longer can I dismiss her ramblings as paranoia? Especially now that my father is about to be a free man.

Shaking my head to dispel the downward spiral of my thoughts, I'm still watching the three of them as Riley says something that has Logan throwing his head back with laughter and Royce's lips twitch upward in a brief, genuine smile.

What the actual fuck, have I entered the twilight zone?

Royce doesn't smile. He barely smiles around us anymore,

and he sure as fuck doesn't smile in the middle of the mother-fucking food court. It's a miracle that he's even here. Neverthe-less, he's joined Riley and Logan for lunch every day for the past week while I lurked in the corner of the room and watched them.

He catches sight of me as I approach, and his lips flatten, eyes hardening in a silent warning.

Noticing his shift of attention, Logan glances my way, his jovial expression falling. *Fuck no*, I see him mouth as he gets to his feet, looking ready to deck me. "No fucking way," he says louder, pointing an accusing finger at me. "Get the fuck out of here."

"What did I do?"

He snarls. "You know exactly what you did." Turning, he points to Riley. "Look at her! She's fucking covered in your bites."

Like the smug bastard I am, I smirk, which only sets Logan off. With a curse, he dives for me, and only Royce's quick move-ments stop us from brawling in the middle of the food court.

"Sit the fuck down," he hisses, shoving at Logan's chest before turning to glare at me. His eyes blaze with a glacial intensity, and I know he's just as furious as Logan. He's just better at masking it. "You should leave."

I can't deny that cuts deeply. The sting burns away any arrogance and leaves me pissed.

"But I haven't shared my good news with you."

"It better be that you got an STD check and it came back negative," Logan snarls.

"Logan," Riley chastises, face burning red.

"Sorry," he mutters, seeming genuinely apologetic, which makes me roll my eyes. *Fucking pussy whipped.*

Still, guilt squirms inside me, and my gaze shifts to Riley. She's already watching me with a shuttered expression. "I'm clean," I find myself saying. My word probably won't be enough for her, although at least I've satisfied my own contrition.

Bar a marginal softening around her eyes, her expression doesn't change as she continues to stare at me, and I only manage to tear my gaze away when Royce asks, "What did you want to tell us?"

Ah fuck. I blurted that in the heat of the moment, and now I kinda regret saying anything. Here probably isn't the best place for this conversation.

However, we're all here, and I highly doubt I'm going to get them to meet somewhere else.

Sliding my gaze to Riley, I watch her closely as I disclose, "My dad is being released from prison." Her eyes widen, pupils dilating to pinpoints as her face drains of all color.

"He's *what?*" Logan explodes. "When did this happen?"

"Parole board met today," I answer, not removing my focus from Riley, who is as still as a statue. Her stare is locked on mine, her shoulders shaking with her erratic breathing. Her response isn't a fleeting startle of surprise... it's a visceral, bone-deep apprehension that seizes her features and strips away all pretenses.

I watch as her normal shields fold like a pack of cards, leaving her raw and exposed. Her fear resonating in the air.

"Logan," Royce barks, noticing the same thing.

"Fuck," Logan snarls, bundling her into his arms at the same time as I'm hauled away from the table.

My view of her is cut off as Royce unceremoniously drags me across the food court to the amusement of those watching us.

I shrug him off and he whirls on me. "What the fuck?" he hisses now that we're out of earshot. He shakes his head, his hands fisted at his sides and body vibrating with unrestrained anger. "Why didn't you tell us that was today?"

I scoff. "Because we've been all buddy-buddy lately."

He stares at me as if he's never seen me before. *That makes two of us.* I don't recognize him. I don't even recognize myself. In the span of several weeks, we've all become different people. Perhaps his change is for the better. He looks less consumed by his demons, more his old self than I've seen in a long time so I have to imagine so. I haven't been so lucky. My change... it's for the worse.

"You should still have told us," he states, each word ringing with his anger.

"So you could protect little miss stripper?" I sneer.

His brow arches like he doesn't know what to do with me. "So we could have been there for *you*, you asshole."

My responding snort is filled with disbelief, and the slight softness around his eyes hardens. "When?" he snaps, all coldness now.

"When what?"

"When is he getting out?"

My eyes bounce back and forth between his as I debate keeping the information from him, but as his hands tighten at his sides, I decide it's not worth the black eye he's itching to give me. "Ninety days."

With a terse nod, he states soberly. "What you just did is not fucking okay." His gaze skims over me before returning to my face, and the disappointment there slays me. "Get the fuck out of here."

When I don't move, he reiterates, "Get the fuck out of here, Grayson." Except, instead of stepping back, he moves closer, voice lowering. "If this breaks her, we're done. You've gone too far this time."

He doesn't wait for a response, not that I had one, before leaving me standing there as he strides back toward their table.

My eyes track him as he crouches down beside Logan, who

has Riley burrowed against his chest. I can't make out anything else from here, but I don't need to.

Turning on my heel, I leave the food court behind, but with every step I take, the terror in Riley's eyes remains with me. My chest tightens, an acute pang stabbing my stomach. Her reaction... it was the same as Gran's when she thought I was Bertram.

What the fuck have I just done?

RILEY

CHAPTER THIRTY-ONE

The world tilts on its axis.

Grayson's words, heavy and laden with an unbearable weight, seep into my consciousness like poison, branding themselves on my gray matter with a searing burn that renders all other senses void. I'm numb; every sensation deadened except the agonizing ache that takes root deep within.

He's getting out.

He's being released.

He'll be free to walk around, go where he pleases, talk to who he pleases, *touch* who he pleases.

What if he comes for me?

What if he finds out about Aurora?

I'm spiraling, the world spinning violently as a hollowness spreads outward from the pit of my stomach, an emptiness chilling my veins that threatens to consume me whole.

Pulsating waves of shock crash against the fragile shores of my mind, eroding through the walls and defenses I've worked so hard to put in place.

Black spots fill my vision, the pounding of blood in my ears and the chaotic rhythm of my heart prevent me from connecting with the world around me as I descend deeper into the dark pit of my desolate mind.

From some deep connection that is somehow still functioning, I register warmth wrapping around me, followed by Logan's crisp and calming scent. I feel the gentle caress of his hands stroking my hair. The soft whisper of words in my ear. Although I can't hear them, they *feel* soothing, and I sink into that sensation, clinging to it like a lost soul desperately clutching onto the last vestiges of light in a vast and unfamiliar darkness.

Gentle hands pull me away from where I'm hiding, burrowed in Logan's shoulder, and reluctantly, I turn my tear-stained face toward Royce, who crouches beside me.

His expression is anguished as he painstakingly reaches out to wipe away my tears. "Nothing is going to happen to you," he vows, his voice so sure and confident. "*We* aren't going to let anything happen. Not to you *or* Aurora."

"How can you claim that? You don't know what he's like, what he'll do once he's released. He isn't going to just let me go, and I—" My voice becomes strangled, fresh tears blooming as panic tightens like an elastic band around my chest. "I can't let him get to Aurora. I-I... How would I even know if she's in trouble?"

"You'd know," Royce argues, still with that assured tone that pulls me back from the ledge. "You would know because you're her mother. You'd know, in here." He taps my chest right above my heart, and even though it doesn't quell my fears, it eases the numbing panic enough for me to think.

"When?" I ask thickly.

He knows exactly what I mean, his expression giving nothing away as he bluntly states, "Ninety days."

Sniffling, I nod. "I-I've gotta go," I stammer, pushing out of

Logan's hold and locking my knees when they threaten to give out. I can't afford to lose my strength now. It's been heaven having the two of them to rely on, but I need to be able to stand on my own two feet. I can't allow this to destroy me. Not when Aurora needs me to keep her safe, now more than ever.

"Shortcake…"

I hold my hand up for him to stop, giving Logan an apologetic yet pleading look. "Please, Logan. I need time to think." When he still looks like he's going to follow me, I force a fake smile to my lips. "I'm fine. Really. This… shouldn't be such a shock. I should have expected it. I just need time to process. It's fine. *I'm* fine."

"Of course you do, Ry," Royce interjects before Logan can argue some more, always understanding what I need and ready and willing to give it to me, even when I can see how much it pains him.

Logan's lips purse, but he exhales before agreeing. "Fine. Call us if you need anything."

"I will."

I'm already grabbing my things and high-tailing it out of the food court. However, before I'm out of earshot, I swear I hear one of them mutter, "She is *not* fine."

No, I'm not, although it's not up to them to make me fine. Only I can do that. Only *I* can come up with a solution. Only *I* can protect my daughter.

In a daze, I speed walk across campus. The panic Royce and Logan's presence had calmed batters against my defenses, demanding to be acknowledged with every step I take away from them.

"Just a little bit longer," I mutter to myself, picking up my pace as I leave the campus grounds behind and hurry through the streets of Halston.

My hand is trembling, tunnel vision setting in by the time I reach my apartment, and I struggle with the lock before the door flies open and I stagger inside.

I have the wherewithal to shut and lock it behind me before I collapse on the floor, bringing my knees up and pressing my forehead against them as the panic attack I've been staving off knocks into me with a devastating force.

Tears stream endlessly, and I gasp for breath.

Always such a good girl for me.

"Please," I sob.

Have you been good for me, Riley?

"Go away!" I clamp my hands over my ears, but *his* voice is in my head.

I'll make you my sweet little girl again.

I only cry harder.

Aurora looks like she'd be good.

"No!" The broken scream bursts from my mouth. "No. No. NO! She's mine! You don't get to touch her!"

Stumbling to my feet, I stagger to the bedroom. I drop to my knees beside the bed and dig my fingers between the floorboards, prying up the loose one and pulling out the hidden manila envelope. Tipping it upside down, nightmares spill onto the floor as I fall back on my ass and stare brokenly down at each of the cards. Eight in total.

Birthday. Christmas.

Twice a year for four years.

The latest one was in my mailbox when Royce dropped me off on Christmas Day.

How is that for irony? Escape one Van Doren only to slam straight into another.

Hope you were a good girl for Santa this year.

That's what was written inside.

However, what I read was: *I'll always know where you are.*

How did he know I was here? Did Grayson tell him I was

attending Halston? It was one thing when he found me at Breakthrough, another when he learned I was living with my mom, but this was supposed to be my fresh start.

I didn't think it mattered when he was locked in a cell. However, now that he will be free in a matter of months, it changes everything.

Desolation crashes down on me as I wrap my arms around my knees, tears blotching my face as I stare at the cards in front of me. Each one is the same—Filled with its own sick taunt. A cruel reminder that I'll never escape. That he may be behind bars, but that doesn't mean I'm free.

Because the devastating truth is I'll never be free of him.

And I could live within this cage knowing he was locked in a separate one, but I can't go back to sharing it with him.

Curling in on myself, a broken, hopeless sob rips from my throat. My breath catches in my chest and I gasp, my lungs spasming. I sit there until I can't physically take the pain any longer. Until it feels like I might be crushed beneath the weight of it.

Falling back on old habits, I stumble to the bathroom, ripping open drawers and sending items flying in a bid to find what I'm looking for.

I know it's here somewhere.

Right when I start to think my lungs will explode from the pressure, I find the small metal blade tucked into the back of a drawer.

Just feeling the familiar weight of it in my palm brings a modicum of relief, even as part of me hates myself for resorting to this.

I just need to breathe.

To think.

To *feel* something other than this helplessness.

Hurriedly stripping out of my clothes, I turn on the shower before stepping beneath the cold spray.

Blade against my inner thigh, water beats down on me from above, mixing with my endless stream of tears. Life isn't meant to be this hard. Every step forward laden as my past tries to drag me back into that abyss.

Hopelessness echoes in the chambers of my mind, and everything in me begs to surrender. I don't want to, but how long can I continue on? I've been trying so fucking hard... I've been fighting... battling through the nightmares. Pushing through the triggers, but what's the point when the victories are ephemeral and the defeats are insurmountable? How can I overcome this? How can I fight it when the sheer notion of his release has the power to break me?

If I'm being honest with myself, I've been slowly fragmenting since coming here. Being away from Aurora and leaving her in my mother's care. It's slowly eating at me. Then being abruptly confronted with my past and having to face Grayson and the reminder he represents.

Now, today... it's more than I can handle.

With that knowledge, I slice the blade across my skin, watching as the red rivulets dilute in the water and run crimson tracks down my inner thigh.

There's no relief. No release.

I just feel empty.

The tears come harder, and clutching the blade in my hand, I fall to my knees, head bent beneath the stream of water.

"Riley." A voice calls to me through the darkness, but I'm too numb to fully register it. "Fuck. Riley! Shit, ROYCE!"

The shower door opens, cold air raising goosebumps along my skin before Logan sinks to his knees in front of me, fully clothed as the water turns his white top transparent.

His hands cup my face, lifting it to his, and worry shines

within his chestnut orbs. "Riley." Something catches his attention and he looks down, his expression shattering. "Fuck, Shortcake." His voice cracks as he tugs me to him, his heat seeping into my frigid skin. "Not like this. You're not alone this time. You have us, and we aren't going anywhere."

Pulling back, he grabs a hold of my hand, gently unfurling my fingers and plucking the blade from between them before tossing it toward the shower drain. "I know this was your escape before, but you don't need it. Not this time. You have us. Let *me* be your escape. I'll fill you with so much light and happiness and wrap you up so tightly that you'll never have to worry about *anyone* getting anywhere near you again."

He's already pulling me in for another bruising hug, and I bury my face in his neck, so damn grateful to have someone else holding me up for once. To have someone show up for me. Being here. Looking out for me. I've never had that before, and honestly, I'm so fucking exhausted of doing all of it on my own.

I sink into his warmth, losing track of everything around me. I vaguely register Royce's presence, a soothing balm to my wounded soul, as a towel is wrapped around my goose-pebbled body. One of them tends to the cut on my leg, the other holding tight to my hand the entire time, before I'm hoisted into the air and lowered carefully onto a soft mattress.

Heat envelops me as they each slide in beside me. "Sleep, baby," Logan murmurs as he snuggles into my side.

"We'll keep the demons at bay," Royce adds, the magical words that enable me to give in to the exhaustion pulling on my bones as I succumb to the inky depths of sleep.

"Daddy's little girl, aren't you sweetheart?" He strokes his hand down my long strands, oblivious or uncaring of my body trembling. I'm

shaking so hard that the bed vibrates. "So good at keeping our secret. We wouldn't want Mommy to get jealous now, would we?" He waits for me to shake my head. "And Grayson wouldn't understand. This is a special bond between daddies and daughters."

A special bond. That's how he always refers to it, yet it doesn't feel special to me. Not like the way I feel when Grayson smiles at me. Or when he slipped me a wrapped box under the table on my birthday. I tucked it into my jacket and didn't dare pull it out until I was locked inside my bathroom. Only then did I carefully undo the ribbon and lift the lid, revealing a colorful bead bracelet inside. It fit perfectly on my wrist. I wore it for a week straight before my mom caught sight of it. She said it was cheap and garish-looking and made me take it off, but I hid it in the bottom of my jewelry box. Then, sometimes, after he leaves, I lift it out and squeeze it to me, pretending it's Grayson's arms wrapped around me while I cry silent tears into my nightie.

He places a soft kiss on the back of my head. "I'll see you tomorrow," he whispers, before padding on quiet feet out of the room.

Alone. The tears I've been holding back spring forth, burning a never-ending path down my cheeks, because tomorrow always comes too soon, and I'm not sure how many more tomorrows I can force myself to face.

I startle awake with a gasp, skin damp with sweat as my eyes bounce over the dark bedroom.

He's not here. He can't hurt you. He won't hurt you ever again.

Except he's being released soon, and I can't delude myself into believing he's going to move on with his life and leave me alone.

Throat dry and too alert to go back to sleep, I smile wanly at the resting boy sleeping soundly on either side of me before ninja-climbing my way out of the bed.

Tiptoeing to the bathroom, I splash my face with water before staring at my reflection in the mirror. I'm wearing an oversized t-shirt that I know isn't mine, and lifting the collar to my nose, I inhale the faint hint of leather identifying it as Royce's.

Letting go, my shoulders drop as I exhale, the small act somehow making me look even more defeated.

"I've looked better," I admit to myself.

If I was being frank, I'd say I look like shit. Like I just got run over by a sixteen-wheeler. One who backed up over me for good measure. My eyes are hollow and haunted, bearing the weight of my anxiety, my hair limp and lifeless. It's as if my body has already waved the white flag in defeat.

Sniffing my armpit, I smell like fear. Like fear and desolation.

I fucking hate it.

I hate feeling this helpless.

"I think you look beautiful."

My eyes snap to Logan's through the mirror, finding him leaning against the doorway as he watches me. He's not wearing a top, and my gaze drops over his golden skin and chiseled muscles before lifting to his face.

I scoff. "If by beautiful, you mean beaten to within an inch of my life, then yeah, sure, I look *beautiful*."

Pushing off the doorway, his eyes remain locked on mine through the mirror as he moves to stand behind me. The heat of his body burns into me. Seeing us together, I look so much smaller by comparison, the top of my head barely reaching his chin.

"Where you see a battle lost, I see remarkable strength that shines through despite the adversities." Reaching out, his thumb brushes beneath the purple rings under my eyes. "These bruises speak of a battle fought bravely, of challenges faced head-on. A war you've not yet lost." His other hand slowly slides around my hip, fingers dipping lower until they disappear beneath the hem of my shirt and glide over the raised scars along my inner thighs—both old and new. Earnestly, he emphasizes, "You are *beautiful,* Riley. Not in spite of your struggles, but *because* of them."

My gaze rakes over his face, the sincerity blazing in his eyes that leaves no doubt about what he's saying as the back of his fingers brush my cheek before he wraps an arm around my chest and pulls me flush against him. His lips skim my temple, and we stay like that for a moment, clinging to one another.

"It's still early," he eventually whispers, his breath tickling the side of my face. "Come back to bed."

I follow him back to the bedroom, smiling at a still-sleeping Royce as I slip between the covers. Rolling onto my side, Logan and I lie face-to-face.

"Go to sleep, Shortcake."

"I can't." I never can after a nightmare. If it hadn't been the lure of being the filling in a Logan-Royce sandwich, he wouldn't have tempted me back to bed at all.

Brows pinched in concern, he asks, "What can I do to help?"

"Kiss me."

His eyes widen in surprise before uncertainty clouds them. "Ry," he rasps, adopting Royce's nickname for me. "I'm trying to take this slow. I want to gain your trust—"

"Please, Logan. I just need to forget for a little while, and you've always excelled at making me feel good."

His lips twitch before he leans in oh so slowly. He hovers above me, his proximity pushing me onto my back. The weight of his body on mine is a comfort.

Leaning in, he presses his lips to one of my eyelids, then the other. "So beautiful. So perfect." Our eyes clash as he rasps, "And all fucking mine," before our lips meet in a tender collision. A union of more than just flesh, but of souls.

Logan's touch is gentle but firm as he coaxes my lips apart, as if he held something fragile and precious, but not breakable. His kiss is a healing salve spread over scars that run deep.

Just as he always does, he sends my fears and concerns scurrying into the recesses of my mind; my anxieties are momentarily drowned in the softness of his lips. And as his tongue tangles with mine and he deepens the kiss, I taste his promise of unwavering support, of understanding, of love that could weather any storm.

It's a kiss that whispers of hope, of healing, not only for me but for *us*. With his lips, he pleads for forgiveness, and with each sweep of his tongue, I can feel the frayed threads of our relationship weaving back together.

He nips at my lip, the kiss turning from sweet and loving to dirty and hungry as my back arches into the bed. The move drives my hips forward, and I groan into his mouth when I brush against the hard length in his boxers.

"Shortcake," he rasps, pupils blown wide as he wrenches his lips from mine.

"Don't stop," I plead. "Please, Logan."

Face twisted in uncertainty, he stares down at me for a moment before cursing under his breath and slamming his lips down on mine. He fully lowers his weight onto me, and I hitch my leg over his hip, grinding against him in a desperate search of friction to ease the ache building between my thighs.

"Fuck, Ry," he rasps, voice choked as he buries his face in the crook of my neck, breathing heavily as he fights to gain control.

"More, Logan. I want to feel more."

Turning his head to look at me, desire darkens his chestnut hues. "I've wanted to devour you while you come on my tongue since I watched you finger yourself in my car. Can I taste you, Shortcake?"

Just the insinuation has me clenching my thighs as excitement drips out of me. "God, yes. *Please.*"

With a wicked grin, he helps me out of Royce's t-shirt before he shimmies down the bed and settles between my legs, forcing them wide. He stares at my pale pink cotton panties like they hide the secret to true happiness, before stroking his thumb up the front of them, pressing on the bundle of nerves until I'm soaked and panting.

"You gotta keep quiet, Shortcake," he says with a cocky smirk as he stares up at me. "Don't wanna disturb Royce's beauty sleep. Can you stay quiet for me, or do I need to gag you?"

Well, fuck. I don't know what the right answer to that is.

He must sense my indecision because he chuckles. "Royce is right. You are filthy-minded." Glancing down at the wet patch on my panties, he murmurs, "I don't give a shit if you wake him so long as I get to taste you."

With that, he rips my panties away and dives in. My eyes go wide as my hips leave the bed, and he has to clamp a hand on my stomach to keep me in place as his tongue explores every inch of me.

I try my hardest to remain quiet, but after one particularly incredible swirl of his tongue that has me crying out, I glance in Royce's direction, startled when I find him staring at me with hooded eyes.

The combination of Logan's tongue in my pussy and Royce's eyes on my face has me coming apart at the seams, and Logan readily laps up every drop of my release.

"Best breakfast ever," he declares, sitting between my legs and noticing for the first time that Royce is awake. "Sorry you missed out on it, man."

Smirking, Royce surges forward, his lips connecting with Logan's in a shocking kiss. It only lasts a few seconds before he pulls back.

"Mmm, you're right. Delicious."

Giving me a salacious wink, he swings his legs over the side of the bed and climbs out, his erection on display behind his *tight* boxers. Logan gapes wide-eyed at him before throwing his head back and bursting into laughter. "Who knew you were a good kisser?"

"Don't get used to it," Royce retorts. "I just wanted to start the day with the taste of strawberries in my mouth."

RILEY

CHAPTER THIRTY-TWO

I'm finishing off the delicious breakfast Logan cooked for us when Royce disappears into my bedroom, emerging with an envelope in hand. A very *familiar envelope.*

Not saying anything, he carefully sets it down on the table, eyes on me the entire time. He notices the way my throat bobs when I swallow, the slight tremble that takes over my hand before I wrap it firmly around my coffee mug.

"What's that?" Logan asks, apparently oblivious.

Royce isn't, though. I can tell by the sharpness in his gaze. The icy depths that look like they could burn me alive. Who knew ice could be so scalding? I know it's not aimed at me. It's aimed at the contents of the envelope. At who *wrote* the contents.

Silently, he tips it upside and the cards fall onto the table. All the while, his eyes remain on me, never once looking away. Just silently watching. Waiting.

Logan's eyes dart between me and Royce before lowering to the table, and he cautiously reaches out, lifting out the top card and opening it.

"Another year older, but you'll always be my little girl," he recites slowly, brow furrowed before he glances up at me, questions in his eyes. He reaches in for another card, flips it open, and reads aloud, "Remember, even though Daddy is far away, he's always thinking of you." Frown lines mar his forehead, and he doesn't hesitate this time before lifting the next one and reading, "No matter how old you are, you'll always be Daddy's little girl. What the fuck is this shit?" he snaps, already knowing.

My throat is raked dry, words unable to pass even if I knew how to convey the trauma that envelope retains. The nightmares it never allows to stray too far.

"There's one for every birthday and Christmas since his incarceration," Royce states, eyes still boring into mine with that all-consuming intensity. I can feel him peeling back the final layers wrapped around me until I'm left raw and exposed, and I pull my knees up, wrapping my arms around them in a bid for warmth.

"He's been writing to you?" Logan exclaims, mouth agape as he stares at the cards now spread out on the table before us.

"He's been reminding me," I correct, voice hoarse.

Logan's face snaps up. "Reminding you of what?"

"That I'll never be free."

Logan blinks, his mind taking a second to process before his nostrils flare, and he glares down at the table. "You should take this to the police. It's proof—"

My scoff cuts him off. "It's nothing," I counter. "Read them again, except imagine it's a heartsick father writing to his daughter."

Logan's brows bunch before his eyes drop to the open card in front of him. I don't recall precisely what that one says, but I can recite them from memory. "Even though Daddy is far away, he's always thinking of you. Hope you were good without me this year. You may be growing up, but you'll always be my little girl... *We* know the implication behind his words, yet to anyone else, it's a father missing his daughter."

"*Step*-daughter," Logan bites out.

"Semantics."

"Well, maybe we could show this to Grayson," he suggests instead. "It might—"

"No." My sharp tone cuts him off.

"Rather than telling him about Aurora, this could—"

"It won't!" I'm practically yelling, and my arms tighten around my knees as I force myself to take a calming breath. "It won't change anything for Grayson," I reiterate. "It won't be enough for him." I know it won't, and truthfully, Logan knows it too. That's why he doesn't argue any further. "What does it matter anyway?" I ask hopelessly. "It doesn't matter if Grayson believes me or not. A fate far worse is coming, and Grayson is the least of my concerns."

"Is this why you said yesterday that he isn't going to just let you go?" Royce queries, asking his first question since walking in with the envelope.

My nose stings with the threat of bitter tears, and I lift my face to the ceiling, swallowing them back and allowing myself to sink into the icy-cold tendrils of a reality I haven't ever allowed myself to accept. One I kept telling myself I'd find a solution for before time ran out—except the clock is ticking down now, and I'm no longer running out of time. I'm out. There are no more seconds left to spare.

Clawing deep for a resolve that feels like wisps of smoke between my fingers, I clutch a hold of it and wrench it up, wrapping it around me like armor. It's all I have as I lift my face to meet Royce's. "He's going to come for me, and when he does, I need to be far away from here."

I shut down any further conversation after that, telling the guys that I needed to get ready for classes, which sparked a whole new argument—one where they felt I should stay home and 'rest' and where I told them I would only drive myself more insane if I did that.

Thankfully, they seemed to realize that I had been pushed close enough to my breaking point and was likely to go on a homicidal rampage if pushed much further. Dropping the conversation, we each got ready in silence, before Logan drove us to campus.

They were both reluctant to leave me alone, but after promising them I wouldn't do anything stupid, they resigned themselves to the fact that they had classes to get to, and so did I.

My entire morning has passed in one hazy blur. I don't take in a single word any of my professors say, since my mind is too focused on where I go from here. I meant what I said this morning. I've been mulling it over all night and can't see any other way.

I need to get Aurora, and we need to run.

During my Written Communication and Information Literacy class, I pull my head out of the fog long enough to write down the date of Bertram's release. Ninety days. I have less than ninety days to pull together enough cash and resources to tide us over, then grab Aurora before we disappear into oblivion. I don't know what sort of resources Bertram will have. How far he'll go to search for me, only what else can I do? I have to try.

Flipping to a new page, I write down everything we'd need. Clothes. Toiletries. Food. Toys.

My hand shakes the longer the list grows. This isn't how it was supposed to be. I came here to better my future, but I won't risk it all for a piece of embossed paper. Ultimately, I came here to get Aurora back, so I'll readily run from this town if it keeps her safe.

I'm still lost in my head, going over my plan, tweaking parts and fine-tuning it when my morning classes let out, and I don't even notice Logan waiting for me until he steps directly into my path.

"Shortcake," he purrs, hands coming up to latch onto my arms before I crash into him. Blinking out of my stupor, I stare up at him, noting the worry hidden behind his coy smile.

"Logan." I glance around, taking in my surroundings for the first time. "What are you doing here?"

"Escorting you to lunch, obviously."

"Logan." I'm already shaking my head, attempting to pull out of his grip even as he tightens his hold on my upper arms. "I'm not in the mood to face the food court today."

His smile only widens. "Good thing I have Royce grabbing food for us then. We figured somewhere quieter would be better today." He's already directing me down the steps of the Hennessy building and across the quad, away from the food court.

"Where are we going?"

He winks down at me, wrapping an arm around my shoulders and pulling me into his warmth, utterly oblivious to how it seeps through my frigid skin, melting the ice that had been steadily hardening in my veins since yesterday. "Back to where it all began."

My head is in too much of a mess to piece together his cryptic reply, and instead, I let him lead me across campus until the library comes into view.

"Logan, we can't eat in here," I argue as we draw closer. "There's no food allowed inside the library."

He snickers, only continuing to urge me forward. "I'm sure Royce will find a way to sneak it in."

Once inside, we wind through mainly empty tables and along shelves piled high with textbooks until we reach the back of the building, where the private study rooms are.

"You booked a private study room?" I question, already knowing the answer, as he pulls open the door and ushers me inside.

"Yup. For the rest of the day, it's our little sanctuary away from the world."

He drops his backpack on an empty chair, moving to take mine when I merely stand there, too exhausted and braindead to do it myself.

As soon as he's removed it, he's back in front of me, hands in my hair as he tilts my face up to his. "Stay with me," he murmurs, his jovial facade momentarily dropping as he gives me a first-hand view of the worry swirling in his chestnut hues. "I can't lose you again."

"I'm here," I say aloud, knowing damn well it's a lie. My body is present, even though my brain is a million miles away, and my spirit is buried under so much pain and trauma that I'm not sure there's a shovel strong enough to excavate it.

"You're not," he counters. "Your brain has been working overtime since yesterday, trying to put as much distance between you and reality as it can. The only time you stopped running was when you were coming on my tongue." His last sentence is a near growl before he ducks down and seals his lips over mine.

Logan's kiss is like a gentle gust of wind, cutting through the storm raging within me. Tender, yet it carries an unwavering strength, a silent promise that everything will be okay. And for a moment, I allow myself to believe that. To fall into his reassuring comfort as the weight of my anxieties, the burden of uncertainty, all dissolve into the ether.

His kiss is a lifeline thrown to a drowning soul, and I cling to it with every ounce of my remaining strength because I'm so damn terrified of slipping beneath the surface and never reappearing.

With every firm press of his lips and warm slide of his tongue, he breathes life back into me, replacing the numbing cold in my bones with his perpetual happiness, unwavering warmth, and boundless light.

Hope replaces desolation, and for a brief moment, I believe. I believe he has the strength to hold me up. I believe I have the power to conquer my fears. I believe we can weather this storm.

"There she is," he murmurs, pulling back to stare into my eyes, and I know he sees it too. He also knows, just as I do, that it's a temporary fix. A Band-Aid on a gaping wound, but for now, we both ignore that, and I simply sit in the comfort he infused in me. In the knowledge that Logan is my anchor, my solace, and with him at my side, I'm capable of achieving anything.

Our moment is broken by the sound of the door opening, and Royce appears in the doorway carrying takeaway containers from the food court. His gaze immediately rests on mine, and I see a little of the tension drain from his shoulders as he takes me in, noting the residual light still lingering from Logan's kiss.

He sets it all down on the table, the three of us taking our seats before diving in. We're silent as we eat, and with each passing second, I feel the coldness seeping back in, a fog slithering over Logan's warmth and extinguishing it.

When I'm done eating, I pull study materials out of my bag, keeping my focus on the notebooks in front of me as I ignore the looks Logan and Royce share.

I'm only granted a handful of minutes to stare blankly at the open page in front of me, my thoughts racing as I go back to formulating my plan before rough, calloused fingers clasp my cheeks, wrenching my face to the side.

"What are you doing?" Royce growls, anger simmering in his icy-blues.

Stunned, I blink at him before finding my voice. "Studying."

His facial expression tightens in annoyance. "Try again."

At a loss for words, I simply stare at him, mute.

"You're running," he bites out. "Hiding."

"I am n—" He squeezes his fingers until my lips pucker, effectively shutting me up.

"Seems like you've forgotten one important thing," he continues, eyes boring into mine. Leaning in, my breathing hitches, goosebumps pebbling as his warm breath tickles my neck. "You have us."

His words are a repeat of Logan's from yesterday. Suddenly, for a split second, I'm yanked back to my bathroom, the water beating down relentlessly as Logan's warmth seeps into my skin, and he practically begs me to allow him to be my escape. To let him fill me with light and happiness.

A sob catches at the back of my throat. If only it was that easy.

"It is that easy," Royce growls harshly, making me realize I voiced my protest aloud. "We'll show you."

Before I can question him, his lips are on mine, hard and demanding. His kiss isn't soft and gentle like Logan's. It doesn't hold me together. It rips me apart. Tears me to shreds until the pieces of my soul are so scattered that I don't have a hope of piecing them back together.

He nips at my lower lip, tongue sliding past my teeth and branding the inside of my mouth. His other hand sinks into my hair, tugging on the strands and yanking me closer until I'm half in his lap. I melt into his claiming as he takes over my senses one by one until all I can feel, smell, and taste is him.

"That's it, Babydoll," he rasps against my lips. "Give your-self to me." His lips are back on mine as I crawl onto his lap, my hands sliding up the front of his shirt, feeling the rhythmic thumping of his heart beneath my palm. "I want all of you," he rasps, moving to kiss along my jaw as I arch into his touch, my crotch aligned with his so I can feel the truth of his words pulsing between my thighs. "Your body, your mind, your soul. Your good days and bad. Your strength and your tears." His hand tightens in my hair, pulling my eyes to his. "Tell me I have it all."

It's a demand. An order. A plea. I can see in his eyes how desperately he wants all of me. Every broken and fractured piece. Every jagged edge.

"I—" The words die in my throat, unable to give him what he wants.

I see it flash across his face, in the tensing of his jaw, when he realizes it. "That's okay, Ry. You will. I've waited five years for you; I can wait a little longer while I prove to you that you own all of me." Using his firm grip on the base of my skull, he turns me to face Logan, who is watching us, mouth agape and pupils blown. "All of us."

Logan nods mutely in agreement, eyes lasered in on mine.

My lips part, my tongue flicking out as my blood heats with their declaration. With the sincerity of their words, I can feel pulsing through the air and leaving no oxygen with which to argue.

"Now, I know your cunt is dripping with the thought of tasting both of us," Royce purrs, tone scraping like gravel against my skin. When I don't move, he nudges me out of his lap. "Get on your knees in front of Logan."

I blink down at him, desire whirling his irises into a molten cerulean blue that has me clenching my thighs. I might not be able to give him all of me, but I can give him this little bit of trust.

His eyes flare when I push out of his lap, and I get the sense my trust in him means more than he could ever express—at least not with words. Like I've said before, our bodies do all the talking, and right now they're singing.

Shifting my focus from Royce, I move around the table toward Logan. My eyes remain on his, watching as he lifts his hand to brush his thumb across his lower lip, dark chestnut orbs drinking me in as I approach. He turns in his chair, parting his legs so I can step between them.

"Shortcake," he rasps, "You're so fucking beautiful."

Placing my hands on his jean-clad thighs, I lower to my knees, and he releases an agonized groan. My gaze dips to the blatant bulge in his pants, and I lick my lips, suddenly desperate to taste him. Especially given he got his first taste of me this morning. I'm aching to return the favor.

"I've imagined how it'll feel when my cock disappears into that sweet, sweet mouth of yours since I watched you swallow Royce," he confesses, voice ragged. "Although I don't want you to do something you aren't ready for."

"I am," I assure him. Meeting his stare, I confess, "I'm broken beyond repair, but you showed me I'm not as wrecked as I once believed. I don't need you to treat me with kid gloves." One side of my lips tilts in a melancholy smile. "In the realm of brokenness, there is one advantage: the remaining fragments are immune to further shattering."

Reaching out a hand, he cups my cheek, his thumb skimming my bottom lip. "You make broken look absolutely stunning."

Holding his gaze, my hands creep up his thighs until my palm glides over his hard length and he hisses a pained breath. Reaching higher, I pop the button of his jeans, inching the zipper over his erection before tugging them and his boxers over his hips.

His cock juts proudly in front of him, already swollen with need and leaking precum, as I wrap my hand around the silky skin. Glancing up through my eyelashes, I hold his unblinking stare as I lower my lips, my tongue flicking out, desperate for that first taste. Sweet, just like him.

"Fuck, Shortcake," he groans, already losing it, and I've barely touched him. "Wrap your lips around me. I need to feel you."

I suction my lips around his head, flattening my tongue as I lower myself over him. My skin blushes at the hiss that slips between his clenched teeth, his eyes watching riveted as I take him into my mouth.

His head falls back, and I can feel his thighs trembling with the need to thrust before I pull back, swirling my tongue around his tip before taking him into my mouth again.

"Fuck, fuck, fuck," he curses under his breath, bringing his gaze back to mine as I bring him to the edge.

So absorbed in Logan's pleasure, I don't notice Royce move to crouch behind me until his heat envelops my back, his breath dancing across my skin and soaking my panties further.

"Do you see it?" he rasps in my ear, one hand on my hip as the other slides beneath the waistband of the leggings I haphazardly threw on this morning. "You're unraveling him. *You.*" His nose drags up the column of my neck and he inhales, his fingers pressing down on my bundle of nerves through the soaking fabric of my panties and making me whimper around Logan's length. "You hold all the power—over him. Over me. Over *us.*" His lips trail across my temple, fingers slipping beneath the lining of my panties and spearing my wet heat. He holds them still inside me, shredding me apart with his words. "Even on your knees, you wear your crown with grace, for strength isn't defined by standing tall but by rising every time you fall."

Tears that had been welling in my eyes overflow, partly from Logan's dick buried in my throat and partly from my breaking at Royce's words.

"You think you're broken?" Royce continues, fingers slowly sinking into me and sending my heart aflutter. "Then let us piece you back together. We'll create the most beautiful mosaic of resilience, of harmonious imperfection."

As if by magic, all the ripped apart shreds done by his decimating kiss slowly start to realign, threaded together with Logan's glowing strands and Royce's grit, the combination forming an unbreakable bond that fills me with light that shines from the inside out.

Or maybe that's the orgasm hurriedly creeping up on me.

"Fuck, yes, Shortcake," Logan groans, on the verge of coming apart. "Come with me in your mouth so I can fill you with my cum and lick the taste of us off your lips."

Fingers pumping into me, Royce swirls the pad of his thumb around my clit, and I explode. My cries are muffled by Logan's cock as he threads his fingers through my hair and buries himself in the back of my throat, grunting his release.

Limp and dazed, he effortlessly hauls me up his body, licking the remnants from my lips before twisting his tongue with mine and stealing the last of my resolve.

We're both breathing heavily by the time we break away, and he shifts me on his lap so he can tuck me protectively against him, and I curl into the comfort, my heart slamming against my ribs and a content sigh slipping up the back of my throat.

Royce gets to his feet while remaining bent at the waist, so we're at eye level as he steals my attention. "You're right, James. The advantage of being broken lies in the unbreakable nature of what remains. You are a testament to the endurance of the human spirit. Your pieces may bear the marks of struggle, but they also reflect the light of hope. It's in that light that I've found my salvation. That Logan sees his future.

"So, when I tell you that you are no longer alone, that you have us, they aren't just pretty words or empty reassurances. I mean it to the depths of my soul because we are so entangled in you that there is no us without you. You are our heartbeat, the strength in our unity, the undying flame lighting our path. Through the sunny days and the snowstorms ahead, we are at your side."

His gaze flicks to Logan before returning. "Whether you run, whether you stay. You will not be alone."

"What... You can't—"

"We can," Logan interrupts with unwavering resolve. "And we will."

"You have hockey," I point out, shocked and at a loss to comprehend what they are truly saying.

"Doesn't mean a damn thing if you aren't in the stands cheering me on."

"But, I can't stay. Aurora..."

My head swivels between the two of them, begging them to understand.

"No more playing by your rules, Shortcake," Logan states. "I've already set up a meeting with my lawyers for tomorrow. I'll give your mom every cent I have if that's what it takes to get Aurora away from her. I'm done sitting back and doing nothing."

My gaze shifts to Royce, who merely nods. "Your mom is done controlling this shit. One way or another, we are going to get Aurora."

ROYCE

CHAPTER THIRTY-THREE

My foot bounces against the library floor as I stare down at my phone. Logan is walking Riley to her next class. After what we walked in on yesterday, neither of us wants to leave her alone. She's vulnerable right now. Terrified. She's in fight or flight mode, and I saw the defeat in her eyes plain as day yesterday.

This isn't a war she knows how to fight. It's not a battle she thinks she can win. I saw the cogs turning in her head this morning. The flight plan she was stringing together with dental floss.

Only there's no way in hell either Logan or I will let her run. What she hasn't learned yet is that she doesn't need to face this fight alone. We will fight it for her. With her. We won't let her give up everything she's worked for because of that sick son of a bitch.

And I'm sure as fuck not about to let her deal with this by herself. Logan's solution is to go the nice, normal, legal route. However, I know how corrupt the system is. Not to mention how lengthy a case like this would be. We might have some time until Bertram's release, but not that much time.

I've been staring at Lydia's Craigslist post for a week now. No one has responded, but I keep coming back to it... it's the strangeness of it all. And the timing. The fact she posted this— seemingly her only post on the site—merely days before Bertram's parole hearing? That's one hell of a coincidence.

Maybe I'm better off ignoring it. No one's responded, so that could very well be the end of it...

... Or whatever she's after, she could look elsewhere for it.

Decision made, I type out, **I have the key**, only pausing for a second before hitting reply.

Fuck it. Lydia is a wild card that I don't like. She has too much control in this situation as it stands. Even if whatever this cryptic nonsense is has nothing to do with Bertram, Riley, or Aurora, it could be something I can use as leverage to get her to hand over Aurora to Riley. To ensure *we* can protect them both by the time Bertram is released.

I sit there for another half hour, not getting an ounce of work done since my attention repeatedly shifts back to the phone before I give up pretending to work and toss my books into my bag.

Riley is in class for another hour, so I should take this opportunity to run home and grab some clothes, knowing the house will be empty. There's not a chance in hell I'm leaving Riley alone after yesterday. She was already prone to nightmares before Gray threw this shit at her. No way am I about to leave her to deal with the fallout on her own.

Exiting the library, I cross campus to the parking lot and get into my truck, which has been sitting here since yesterday. I'd jumped into Logan's car when we saw Riley heading off campus after Grayson's little show. I'd wanted to give her the space she asked for, but the look on her face when she ran from the food court... Neither Logan nor I were happy knowing she'd be home alone while she fell apart.

Making it back to the house, I stop short when I step through the front door and find Grayson sitting in the living room with his head resting against the back of the sofa and eyes closed. Standing on the threshold, I debate leaving him to it, except worry has me stepping closer.

As I come into the room, I see how disheveled he is. His hair is a mess, looking like he hasn't showered today. He's wearing sweats and a hoodie, clearly showing he hasn't been to class.

I hate how fractured everything is between us. It's clear he isn't okay, and I don't know if it's everything between us and shit with Riley or if something more serious is going on.

He wasn't gloating yesterday when he delivered his news. In fact, if I had to guess, he only brought it up to gauge Riley's reaction. I don't know what he was expecting, or if he got what he wanted, but before I walked away, it wasn't the smug satisfaction I saw on his face. It was a man who looked like he was drowning in an endless ocean.

"You know you can talk to me," I say, settling into a seat.

He lifts his head off the sofa to look at me. His eyes are bloodshot, explaining his appearance. I don't see any spirit bottles, so I'm guessing he drank himself into a stupor last night and is suffering from the consequences today.

"Tried that, remember? You blew me off for *her*."

There's no snark in his tone. He just sounds bone-tired.

"It wasn't intentional. There's..." I sigh, leaning forward to rest my elbows on my knees. "There is so much I can't tell you, Grayson." I hold his stare, needing him to hear me. "I need you to get over this hostility you're holding on to 'cause I don't know what to do, and I could really use your help."

His eyes close as he drops his head back to the sofa. "I can't even help myself. I'm in no position to help anyone else."

"What has happened?" I ask him directly. "Because there's no way you're acting this way solely over Riley." I wrack my brain. "Is your Gran okay, or did something happen with your dad?"

The noise that leaves him concerns me. It's the sound of someone broken, and not once have I ever seen Grayson break. He is an insurmountable strength. Everything this life has thrown at him, he's dealt with it head-on. Taken it in stride, even if it struck him deeper than he'd allow anyone to see. His dad's arrest. His Gran's illness.

Riley's sudden appearance is the first thing to crack that facade, but somewhere along the way, he's completely fallen apart.

"Oh, you know," he says blasé, yet there's a manic cackle in his voice that has me seriously concerned for his sanity. "Just Gran thinking I'm my grandfather and telling me someone— pretty sure my dad—is killing her daughter. Then, mistaking me for my dad and looking at me like Freddy Krueger walked into the room.

"Oh, and I can't forget her latest revelation where she told me *she* gave the police the evidence they needed to arrest him." He emits a harsh, broken laugh as I stare at him wide-eyed. *Well, fuck. That's... a lot.*

"And I can't fucking tell if it's the insane ramblings of a woman whose brain is being ravaged by a disease that makes it impossible for her to differentiate reality from make-believe or if there's any actual basis to her words."

Falling silent, he stares at the ceiling, lost in his thoughts. "Yesterday, I watched my father all dressed up in his suit for court, and I couldn't fucking see it," he continues, tone devoid of any emotion. "If he's a monster, I don't fucking see it." With his head still resting on the sofa, he turns it toward me. "What the fuck does that say about me?"

"It means you're human, Gray. That you don't want to believe the worst of the only parent you've got," I say as reassuringly as I can. "The way this is eating you alive... you need to find out if what your Gran said about your mom is true."

"How?" he asks, defeated. "Can't exactly ask my dad."

"If your Gran had evidence of your dad's embezzlement, maybe she has something else?" I muse aloud.

"Wouldn't she have used that to send him to prison long before she did?" he counters, still sounding just as forlorn.

"She might not have anything conclusive, but there might be *something*."

He just shrugs his shoulders, and I drop it. Now isn't the time.

Since I have him, though, a pressing question has been nagging at me since I found that revolting envelope of cards scattered on Riley's floor.

"Gray," I hedge, aware I'm walking on thin ice. "Did you tell your dad that Riley was at Halston?"

"No," he answers bluntly, not looking my way.

"You're sure?"

He nods. "Yes."

Fuck. Then how did he know she was here? I scrub a hand over the coarse hair along my chin. Could her mom have passed it on to her on Christmas Day, and I missed it? Possible. It's not like I was in my right mind that day. Except, I saw how determined Riley was to run... the fear in her eyes...

I rub my palms down my jeans. *Just one more fucking puzzle to solve.*

Mind reeling, I decide to leave Gray to his thoughts. I stand, going to exit the room, when he asks, "Is she okay?"

I stop, glancing over at him. His eyes are open, trained on me, and I know who he's referring to. I momentarily debate not answering him. Would serve him right after the way he delivered that life-altering news to her.

Yet, after what he just told me, I find myself answering

honestly. "No, Gray. She's not okay. You decimated the already unstable ground she was walking on."

His throat bobs as he swallows, and I see regret flash across his eyes before he closes them and sags deeper into the sofa cushions.

"I'm gonna stay at hers for the next few days," I tell him. "I imagine Logan will be too."

He simply nods. "I think I'm gonna shower and head into the office. Might stay in the city for a bit—clear my head."

I think that's wise for now. Without saying another word, I leave him behind and head up to my room. Once there, I fill a duffel with enough clothes to last me the rest of the week, along with any notebooks and textbooks I need for class, before carefully setting my drawing tools on top and zipping it up.

With Grayson's destruction trailing me, I walk out of the house.

"What are the stakes this time?" Riley teases with a confident smirk later that evening. Logan is at hockey practice, so I have her all to myself for a few hours.

Even after our conversation in the library earlier, she still looked broken and defeated when I picked her up after class. I fucking hate that look. It's a look that makes me realize I'm as immoral as my father because I'd have done *anything* to take away the weight pressing down on her shoulders.

Beat the shit out of Ben.

Extort her mom.

Kill motherfucking Bertram.

Nothing is off the table when it comes to protecting this girl.

Riley James wholly *consumes* me.

Every single thing she does holds me captivated.

The way her eyes light up when she smiles.

How she chews on her bottom lip when she's anxious, or bites her nails when she's *really* nervous.

The blush that creeps over her skin when she's turned on. I fucking *love* that blush. Love when I'm the cause of it. How it turns a deep crimson when I talk dirty to her.

Even now, just sitting across the table from her, the chemistry between us is off the charts, practically reaching a boiling point.

A Gin Rummy rematch had sounded like a good idea when I'd suggested it. Especially with the way her eyes lit up for the first time since Grayson laid waste to her reality.

Now, I'm thinking we should have gone out somewhere public because it's taking everything in me to stop my hands from slipping to places they shouldn't.

"How about the winner gets to ask the loser a question?" I respond, subtly readjusting my junk beneath Riley's tiny kitchen table.

She smirks. "You sure about that, Royce? I could end up learning a lot of things about you tonight, and I can guarantee you're not going to learn *anything* about me."

I love this confident side of her. I never get to see it. Logan says she was the same way when she was tutoring him. Makes me wish I'd failed a freshman class so she could be my tutor.

Tapping my finger against the worn tabletop, I drink in the bright glint in her eyes. She's enjoying this... knowing she's going to kick my ass. It's a boost to her faltered confidence and the distraction she needed.

"I'm sure." I give her a cocky smirk in return. I might hate to lose, but honestly, I *want* her to ask me questions. She's so respectful of my boundaries, never voicing the questions I see brewing behind her eyes. She doesn't poke or prod at my wounds, and I'm so shut down that I don't even know how to open up to her. I want to, but years of keeping to myself, of trusting no one outside of Logan and Grayson, make it nearly impossible for me to flip that switch and tell her things.

So I'm using Gin Rummy as a way to get her to crack the casing surrounding me.

"Alright. Don't say I didn't warn you."

She shuffles the deck before dealing out the cards, and despite wanting her to win so she can ask me questions, I do give the round my all—because, like I said, I'm a sore loser.

"How?!" I bark when she knocks on the table and calls out *Gin*.

Her tinkling laugh is my only response, and I scowl at her. It only makes her laugh harder, knowing damn well there's no heat behind it.

Sinking back in my chair, I wave a hand. "Alright, ask your question."

Still smiling, she taps a finger against her supple, pink lips, eyes narrowing on me as she tilts her head in consideration.

"How long have you been fighting at The Depot?" she eventually asks.

"On and off since starting at Halston. I only used to do it in the off-season, not wanting to damage my hand while playing, but it's become a weekly thing since last summer."

Her eyes soften, picking up what I'm not saying—*since the end of my football career.*

"Do you enjoy it?"

"Nu-uh, one question per game."

Grumbling, she rolls her eyes. "*Fine.*"

Of course, she wins the next game and repeats her question.

"I dunno if *enjoy* is the right word," I answer. "It's a thrill. An adrenaline rush. Do I love it the way I loved football? No. It started as a way for me to let off the extra energy I carried in the off-season and has become a release that I *need* to function."

Although, as I say that, I realize I haven't been to The Depot in nearly two weeks—since that night Riley was there. It's the longest I've gone without feeling that clawing urge to replace the pain in my chest with the one in my hands.

It strikes me that Riley replaces that pain, except instead of covering one hurt with another, she soothes it. Like a balm.

She deals the next hand, and I'm not the least bit surprised —even if a little aggravated—when she wins.

"What about drawing?" she asks the second she declares *gin*. "Do you love it the way you love football?"

I have to think about her question. They're two very distinct things, yet they each calmed a part of me. Football helped burn off all that excess energy. The anger that I've always harbored but became almost unbearable after what happened during my senior year of high school.

While drawing speaks to my quieter, introverted side. It also gives me space to just be. To be alone with my thoughts and actually *think*.

"It's different," I hedge, an uncomfortable prickle settling over my skin. Still, I push forward. This is what I wanted. I *need* Riley to pry this stuff out of me because I suck at being able to just say it. "Both are a part of who I am, but they serve different purposes." I pause, running my thumb over the permanent indentation at the knuckle of my middle finger from too many hours hunched over a sketchpad.

"When I was on the field, running, tackling, giving it everything I had, it was a release. A way to take all the pain and frustration and transform it into something physical, something *I* could control." There's a lump in my throat as I confess, "Football made me feel alive. Powerful. In control. And it didn't hurt that the fans loved me," I tack on with a wry smirk, but it doesn't reach my eyes, which Riley astutely notices.

I force myself not to fall into memories of the roaring crowd, the feeling of coarse pigskin in my hands, or the adrenaline rush coursing through my veins during the game. Knowing that, for those sixty minutes, all eyes were on me. That the fans were screaming *for me*. It was a far cry from the cold, empty house I grew up in, where my presence was never recognized. Where my absence was never noticed.

"But, when I'm alone with my sketchbook, I can shut out the rest of the world. I'm in a sanctuary of my own making where no pain or hurt can reach me, but it's blissful silence instead of the crowd roaring in my ears. A contemplative space where I can think. Drawing is like meditating for me. It's a way to process everything that's happened, to make sense of the chaos. Unlike football, it's not about control; it's about letting go and allowing the lines and shapes to tell a story that words can't."

I chance a glance at Riley's face. Her lips are tucked between her teeth, her eyes shining with an understanding. She gets it—perhaps better than anyone ever has.

Dancing is to her what drawing is to me.

And Halston is her football. Her way of fighting back, of gaining control.

RILEY

CHAPTER THIRTY-FOUR

I'm half asleep when the first touch, a featherlight kiss, presses just below my ear, and it takes me a moment to recall moving to the sofa after I decimated Royce at Gin Rummy. I was reading silently on the sofa, curled up between his legs while he doodled in a sketchbook, and I must have drifted off.

The gentle touch is followed by another and another, slowly stirring me awake and coaxing my body to life. Each one serves as kindling, stoking the fire burning low in my belly to life. Loosening a breathless sigh, I arch into it as the thin top strap slips over my shoulder.

"Royce," I moan as his large, coarse, firm palms glide over the soft fabric around my ribs, clutching me with reverence as he presses me against the ridges of his body.

He continues to adorn me with light touches and barely-there kisses, which only serve to stoke the flames, building them higher and higher.

As if his earlier confessions hadn't already ignited a fire inside me.

I saw straight through his suggestion of Gin Rummy, and it

only has me falling harder for this man who is trying his hardest to open himself up to me.

"Please," I moan, hand on his thigh and feeling the sheer strength lying dormant beneath my fingers while I press my ass against the firm erection prodding my backside. My nipples are sharp peaks, poking through the thin fabric of my top in a demand for attention.

"Fuck, I love hearing you beg for me." Royce's tone is a guttural rasp in my ear. "I didn't mean to wake you, but I couldn't keep my hands to myself any longer. I needed to touch you."

"Touch me." The plea is a near-desperate whimper, my every sense consumed by him. I can smell him all around me. Can feel every hard, masculine plane sliding against my soft-ness. I'm fucking *burning* for him.

Tongue flicking against my skin, he sucks on my neck where Grayson's mark still lingers, replacing it with his own branding. One of his hands slips beneath the hem of my top, gliding up my stomach, and fingers trailing over my ribs until one heavy, full breast is cupped in the palm of his hand.

Back arching, I press it more firmly into his hold, whim-pering with need as he massages the skin.

He hisses into my ear. "You have no idea how badly I want to strip you naked and feast on every inch of your skin. Make you beg. Plead. Scream. Have you thrashing beneath me, so wild with desire that my name is all you remember."

"Royce," I utter, incapable of anything more as my body burns. Aches maddeningly with pulsing desire.

"I love what a needy little slut you are for me, Babydoll."

With a gush of wetness, I roll over and sit up on my knees before him. Chest heaving and eyes blazing, I know my cheeks are flushed with desire as I stare into his eyes that look as crazed and strung out as I feel.

"Logan?" I ask.

"Won't be here for another half hour or so."

I'm not sure I even care. After seeing Royce watch while Logan ate me out this morning, I would have absolutely no objection to Logan watching while Royce does the same.

Slowly peeling my top over my head, I drop it on the floor. Royce's gaze remains on mine for a moment longer before they drop, his nostrils flaring. Hand outstretched, he flicks his thumb over my nipple, my breath catching before he cups my breast.

"I love your breasts," he murmurs almost reverently. "It doesn't matter if they're on display in some slinky dress or hidden underneath a hoodie. They always look fucking perfect. I want to touch them. Lick them. Fuck them. Watch them bounce as I pound into you; see them glisten, covered in my cum."

"Yes," I pant, damn near coming as I squeeze my thighs together and picture him doing every one of those things.

As though pulled on an invisible string, his face lowers until his lips close around the pebbled bud, the scrape of his stubble along my skin eliciting a shiver. Releasing a moan, my hands slide into the thick, onyx strands of his hair as I hold him to me, soaking up every lick, every suck, every nibble until my nerves are flooded with want, basking in the glow of his attention and needing more.

His hand traverses the valley of my waist, fingers spreading over my lower spine as he pulls me to him, adorning every inch of skin with his touch, his lips, and his tongue until I'm a quivering mess before him.

Only when I'm panting and breathless and muttering incoherent pleas does his hand unlatch from my breast, fingers gliding over my smooth stomach until they reach the waistband of my shorts. He releases my nipple with a wet pop, lifting his gaze to mine, eyes portraying his silent question.

His fingers stall, waiting until I nod.

Eyes still latched onto mine, Royce devours my every reaction as his fingers slip beneath the fabric and slide through my folds, slicked with my wet heat. My hands go to his broad shoulders, steadying me as a finger circles my entrance.

Sensing that he is waiting for a final word of consent, I squeeze out a "please" between ragged breaths, and he spears me with a single digit. His movements are slow and deep, and I feel it fucking *everywhere.*

With one hand squeezing my hip, his gaze latches on to mine as he fucks me with unhurried, deliberate movements, building that ball of desire one stroke at a time until it *consumes* me.

I'm on the brink of unraveling when he pulls out, and I cry at the loss. His smirk is pure, masculine satisfaction as he brings his fingers to his mouth, holding my gaze as he wraps his tongue around them and hums at the taste of me on his skin.

"Fuck, Ry." His tone is guttural. Savage. Undoing. "I need to taste you. *Now.*" He's pulling down my shorts before I can even comprehend what he's saying. "Sit on my face," he orders, sliding down the sofa so he's lying on his back.

"W-what?" I ask, blinking in a stupefied daze.

"Sit. On. My. Face. *Now.*" His demand is a low bark. One that vibrates through me and has me moving on autopilot as I slide, naked as the day I was born, over his abdomen, leaving a wet trail in my wake that makes him growl like the savage animal he is until I hover over his face.

"Sit," he snaps, pupils blown and fixed on my hovering pussy.

"But—"

Strong arms wrap around my upper thighs, forcing me downward until I'm sitting firmly on his face. "I'll suffocate you!"

"And what a perfect fucking death it would be," he half moans, half growls, burying his nose in the neatly trimmed hairs of my mound. "To die with your thighs wrapped around me and your cum all over my chin."

Fuck. I might have died of mortification if it wasn't for his tongue running along the length of my slit, eliciting a gasp, followed by a moan as he sucked on my clit.

"Shiiiit," I groan, fisting his hair and riding his face as he fucks me thoroughly with his tongue. His arms are steel bands around my thighs, his hands grabbing a hold of my ass cheeks and squeezing as I rock against him. His tongue pistons in and out of my pussy as his nose rubs against my clit. It's rough and dirty, and I'm free falling over the edge in no time, head thrown back and his name a breathless prayer on my lips.

As soon as my legs stop shaking, I climb down him, driven by the need to make him feel as fucking incredible as he just made me feel. However, his fingers snag my wrist as I go to undo the buttons of his jeans, halting me.

My eyes snap to his, confusion and uncertainty filling me before I abruptly sit upright. "Do—Do you not want me to?" I ask, suddenly feeling exposed and hesitant as I take in his torn expression.

He's gotten me off several times since that night at The Depot, yet I haven't returned the favor even once. That doesn't seem... fair.

Pushing himself upright, he slides one hand to the back of my head, his other keeping its firm grip on my wrist as he says, "Ry, you have *no idea* how badly I want to feel your lips wrapped around my cock again. Know what it is to have your walls squeezing every last drop of cum from me." His hand wraps around my wrist directing my palm to his crotch, and I brush my fingers over the steel rod. "See how fucking badly I want you? Every inch is for you. *Because* of you."

"But then..." My face scrunches as I try to understand why he's putting a stop to this. It's apparent that he wants this. "Is it —do you not trust me?"

"No. Fuck, no, that's not it. It's—I—" he sighs, teeth gritted as he searches for the right words. Unable to meet my eyes, he states, "I haven't been with anyone in five years, and I don't want to rush anything between us. I don't want you to have regrets."

One beat of silence. Two beats of silence. Then I croak, "What? How is that possible? You said girls are always throwing themselves at you."

"They are." He grimaces. "They were."

"But... you were a football player," I state dumbly. "The quarterback." As if somehow being a football player and having regular sex go hand-in-hand.

Heaving out a sigh, his shoulders drop, and I realize he still hasn't looked at me. I take him in, managing to stop talking for longer than two seconds. *Truly* take him in. The defeated posture. The guilt in his eyes. The shame.

"Hey," I soothe, cupping his cheeks in my hands and slowly lifting his head until those piercing blue eyes, darkened with the sheer weight of the scathing emotions bombarding him, burn into mine. "It's okay. There's no rush. No pressure." I brush back a strand of hair that has fallen across his forehead. "We don't have to do anything that neither of us is ready for... You don't have to *tell* me anything you're not ready to discuss." Something shifts in those steely eyes. Softens. A fragile tenderness peeking through. It loosens some of the tightness in me, and I relax a little, continuing to run my fingers through his hair in a gentle, soothing motion. "But for the record, there's nothing I could regret with you."

Surging forward, his lips meet mine in a desperate kiss. A thank you and a promise all rolled into one. His hand slides into my hair, and when he pulls back just enough to meet my gaze, his voice is hoarse as he says, "I promise I will. I'll tell you everything. I just... I need a bit more time."

I nod, understanding. "Take all the time you need. Whenever you're ready, I'll be here. I'll listen."

His responding kiss is tentative, gentle, scraped raw with tenderness, and afterward, we cuddle on the sofa until Logan arrives. That night, when I startle awake from a nightmare, the two of them cuddle me between them, and for the first time, I manage to get back to sleep, knowing they're both there to keep the demons at bay.

GRAYSON

CHAPTER THIRTY-FIVE

Riley's face is all I see as I walk into Sunnyside Nursing Home that afternoon, with Royce's words playing on repeat in my head. *The way this is eating you alive... you need to find out if what your Gran said about your mom is true.*

Gran's room is my only hope. I'd debated it last time I was here, but it felt wrong going through her belongings without her knowledge. Now... Now, I just need to know.

She packed up her house before she came here, refusing to let me do a thing. Hell, if I'd had my way, she wouldn't be here at all, but she wouldn't hear of it when I offered to defer college so I could look after her in her own home.

I know she put some furniture in storage—heirloom pieces handed down from generation to generation—but she sold pretty much everything else. Which means anything of importance would be here... with her.

"Hey," the nurse behind reception greets. "Your Gran is just finishing up an art class, but you can wait for her in her room."

"Thanks," I say absently, signing my name in the visitors' log before tracing the familiar route to Gran's room.

Reaching her door, I pause with my hand on the handle,

second-guessing what I'm about to do, but the sheer terror on Riley's face drives me forward, and I slip into her room. With my back pressed to the door, I scour Gran's room with fresh eyes. Nothing immediately stands out, so I first move to her bedside table, pulling open the drawers. Nothing but tissues and hand cream. Getting on my knees, I look under her bed, finding nothing there either.

I bypass the dresser, really not wanting to have to rifle through my Gran's underwear and go to the closet next. There are a stack of boxes at the bottom and I flip the lids on each of them.

Shoes. Shoes. Sh—

I pause at a box that does *not* contain shoes. Instead, there is a small, black lockbox inside. With a wedge stuck in the back of my throat, I reluctantly reach forward and lift it out.

Trying the lid, I'm not surprised when it doesn't open, and I stare at the metal lock before I recall seeing a small key on Gran's bedside table. I hadn't thought anything of it, but...

Walking over, I pull open the drawer and retrieve the key. It looks like the type of key that would come with a lockbox, and my hands shake as I insert it, my breath shuddering when there is an audible click as the box unlocks.

I can barely feel my legs beneath me as I sag onto the carpet, placing the lockbox in front of me as I stare at it for a long moment. Am I sure I want to know what's inside? What if it changes everything?

Everything has already changed, I remind myself. *If this box contains the answers I need, can I really continue living in denial?*

Tentatively, with my heart slamming against my ribs, I reach out and slide back the lid.

Peering inside, I first notice a stack of photos and cautiously lift them out. My eyes go wide as I look at the top one. I recognize Gran, although she's a lot younger. Beside her is a tall, stern-looking man who must be my grandfather. He died when I was a baby, so I have no memories of him.

However, the smiling young woman beside him has all of my attention. It's been years since I've seen a photo of her, and she's younger and healthier in this photo than I ever remember, but there's no mistaking that smile.

"Mom."

Her vivacity shines from the photograph and I can't look away. In my memories, she's always so tired-looking. So exhausted. Her face gaunt and pale.

I stare at her face for several long moments before forcing myself to move to the next one in the pile.

There she is again, and just like in the first photo, she's smiling broadly, brimming with life and happiness. She's wearing a white dress, and beside her stands my father, stoic as ever.

Their wedding day.

With Gran's accusations burning through my mind, I scour both their faces, yet they seem like the picture-perfect couple. Mom certainly looks happy to be marrying him, and while my father is as unreadable as always, just because he's not good at expressing his emotions doesn't mean he doesn't feel the same way.

The next few photographs are similar. Family vacations. Mom when she was pregnant with me. As I go through each one, I can't find anything to justify Gran's allegations.

I'm in the next few photos as a newborn. Mom looks more tired in these, but that's only to be expected, right?

Flipping to the next photo, I pause, confused about what I'm looking at. What it means.

It's a close-up of a woman's side. Her top is pulled up, exposing black and blue bruising all down her ribs. There are no identifying features. Their face isn't in the shot, but an ice-cold chill seeps into my bones.

Turning it over, I recognize Gran's handwriting on the back. There's a date, and the words *pushed her down the stairs because she spoke back to him.*

What the fuck?

I quickly go to the next photo. There's more damage. This time, there's no mistaking that it's my mom. Her lip is split and her left eye is swollen shut and a deep blue color. Searching her one open eye, gone is the vivacious girl from the earlier photos. In its place is a broken woman. Someone who has given up on life. She looks... dead.

Turning it over, Gran has written another date and reason: *Didn't attend a gala because Grayson was sick.*

I physically recoil. He did this to her because of me? Looking at the date again, I wouldn't have been more than a year old.

My stomach spasms and unable to look at any more, I set them aside, mind reeling as I return my attention to the box.

Next, I lift out a bunch of pages. Scanning them, it becomes apparent that these are copies of the evidence Gran handed to the police that got Dad arrested. *So it wasn't the Alzheimer's talking.*

Sludge settles in my veins. Was Gran telling the truth about everything?

There's only one more item inside the box: a small, worn leather book. Lifting it out, a scent I faintly recall from my childhood wafts up to me, and I lean in to sniff the book. Lotus flower. Immediately, memories of my mom assault me. Her cheering me on while I swung on the swing. Her praising my fingerpaint artwork. Evenings curled up in bed while she read to me. Sundays spent watching TV on the sofa together.

Tears burn in my eyes as I stare down at the book—*her* book.

Reverently, I pull it open. Inside, in precise penmanship, are journal entries, and I flip to a random one.

Fear is an emotion I've become grimly accepting of. It's such a prominent part of my life that fighting it is only a waste of energy. Energy I'd rather put into loving my little boy. Grayson makes everything I endure bearable. He's my beacon of hope in the harshest of storms.

Swallowing roughly, I flick through to another entry.

I thought giving him a child would make him happy, but today, he looked at Grayson like he was nothing. How can a father look at his child with such apathy? It scares me in a way nothing else ever has.

Hands trembling, I move to another.

I read once that Ted Bundy was so successful as a serial killer because he was attractive and charming. I believe that. Late at night, I often find myself wondering how no one can see the monster lurking beneath my husband's smile, but then I didn't see it either until it was too late.

I don't even realize I'm crying until a tear drops onto the page, and I wipe it away as I turn to the last entry.

I'm sick. The doctors don't know what's wrong, but it's ravaging my body faster than anyone can figure out how to stop. I fear I'm not long for this world. I'm ready to go. Ready to shed myself of this existence. However, I worry about leaving Grayson. He's such a sensitive boy. What will happen to him if I'm not here to protect him? To show him what love is?

Dropping the book, I bury my head in my hands and cry. I cry for my mom. For my Gran. For myself. For all the people who my father has destroyed.

And I cry for the one girl who didn't allow herself to be beaten by him.

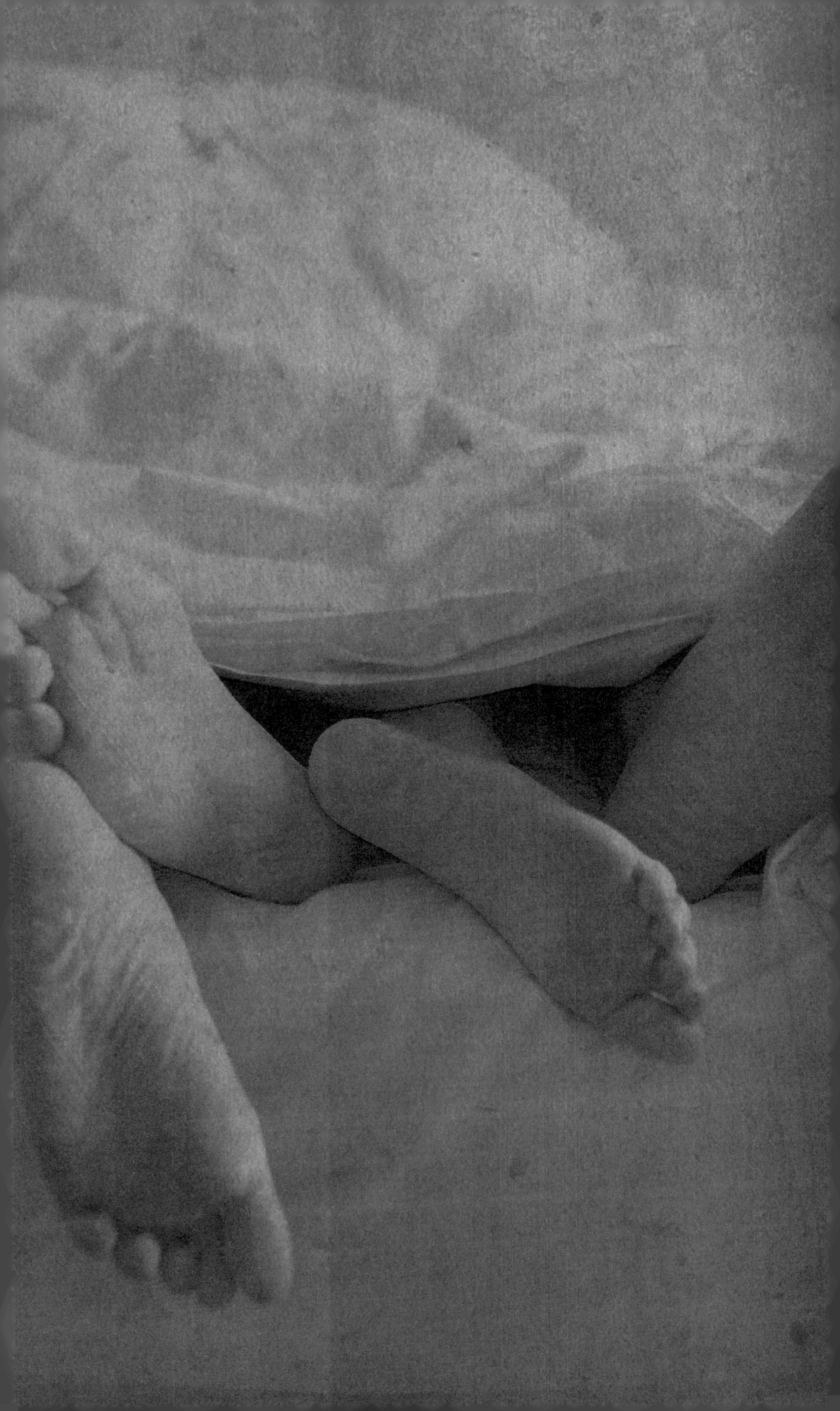

RILEY

CHAPTER THIRTY-SIX

"That could have gone better," Logan grouses as we leave his lawyer's office the next afternoon. Honestly, it went about as I expected. Actually, it was better than my last conversation with a lawyer about Aurora's guardianship.

At least this time, they said I had a strong case of regaining guardianship. Probably thanks to Logan offering to provide enough finances to sufficiently care for her until she turns eighteen. That was *not* something we had discussed before the meeting, but it turned the tide, and the lawyers went from being skeptical to confident that they could win the case.

The problem... is that a court case like this takes time. Especially if my mom contests it. The lawyers said they'd get the ball rolling immediately and that, in the meantime, they'd contact my mom about ensuring the agreement we made when I started college—that I'd have monthly visits and regular phone calls with Aurora—is abided by. If my mom refuses to agree to that, then we can take it to the courts and make her legally obligated to ensure I have that time with Aurora.

Even that is a small win, and after so many knocks down

recently, I'm taking it. I'd happily agree if I knew I could be guaranteed regular phone calls and visits for the next three and a half years without Mom messing with me.

Obviously, I always want my daughter with me, but I know not to overreach. To accept the wins life gives you because it could very easily take them back and decide to fuck you over instead.

"It could have been worse," I counter, earning a dispassionate glare from Logan. It's adorable how incensed he is, and despite the mediocre meeting, I find myself smiling up at him.

"Have I told you how much it means to me that you did this?"

His expression softens, the tension draining from his shoulders as he relaxes enough to wrap his arm around me. "Only about five times today alone."

"Well, I mean it. Even just organizing this meeting has instilled in me more hope than I've had in a long time. Don't even get me started on you offering to cover all costs and expenses. That's a conversation we need to have." I pierce him with a stern stare.

"No, it's not, Shortcake, because it's non-negotiable."

"Logan, do you even know how much it costs to raise a child to the age of eighteen? A quarter of a million dollars," I say, not giving him time to answer. "It is one thing for you to buy me food and cover my bills, but a *quarter of a million dollars,* Logan? No. Absolutely not. That's just... that's insanity."

He only grins like I'm not trying to make him understand exactly how much money he'd be throwing away. "Then call me insane, baby." Ducking his head, he kisses the tip of my nose before dipping lower to capture my lips. "Insane about you."

"*Logan,*" I groan, fighting back a laugh. *Dammit, how does he always manage to twist serious conversations until he gets his way?*

"You've taken one too many pucks to the head," I grumble irritably.

He barks out a laugh. "Shortcake, I wear a helmet when I'm on the ice."

"Then the team needs to invest in harder helmets because the ones they have aren't sufficient."

Grinning like a loon, he just shakes his head. "Do you need to get back to campus for class, or do we have time to grab lunch?"

"We can grab lunch," I say, looking up and down the busy street. The lawyers' offices are located in Springview, so Logan and I ended up skipping this morning's classes for today's meeting.

"Awesome. There's a perfect little Italian place near here that you'll love."

***

Early on Friday morning, I wake to the buzzing of my phone on the bedside table.

"Too early," Logan grumbles sleepily as he tugs a pillow over his head.

I can't help smiling at how adorable he is as I reach for my phone. After Logan fell out of my bed for the second night in a row, we decided it was just too small to fit all three of us—especially since they are both twice my size. So the guys drew straws and have been taking turns to stay with me. While I enjoyed having both of them here, I very much like having one-on-one time with each away from campus, too.

"Logan," I gasp, when I see my mom's caller ID flashing on my phone. His only response is a groan, and I hit his arm as I call his name again.

"Where's the fire, Shortcake?" he mutters, eyes still halfway shut.

"It's my mom," I tell him, showing him my phone screen. Instantly, he's awake, sitting up beside me in the bed. "Do you think she's gotten the letter from the lawyers yet?"

"Only one way to find out." He stares at the phone and then at me, and taking some of his courage, I answer the call and put it on speaker.

"Mom."

"Riley." *Oh, she does not sound happy.* "Care to explain this letter I received this morning?"

Chewing on my bottom lip, I stare at Logan with wide eyes.

"Since when do you have enough money to hire lawyers?" my mother snaps after a moment.

Of course, that's her primary concern.

"I had to find the money when you failed to uphold our agreement," I tell her.

She scoffs, affronted. "You saw your daughter last month, did you not?"

"And it was the first time since starting college, despite our agreement of monthly visits," I state, calm yet firm. "Not to mention that you've been ignoring my calls all month."

"I do have a life, you know."

God give me strength.

"We're less than a week from the end of January. I want to see my daughter."

"Our agreement stipulated that you'd financially reimburse me for taking care of your *problem*."

And now I want to murder her. Based on the way Logan is glaring at the phone like he can incinerate it with his eyes alone, he feels the same way.

"When I see my daughter, I will."

She huffs as though I'm being inconvenient.

"Today is the only day that suits," she snipes.

My eyes go wide as I look at Logan. He pauses for a second to think before nodding, mouthing *this morning* to me.

"Fine. This morning," I stipulate. "I'll be there in two hours." I hang up before she can argue, knowing she'll be there if only to get her money and to pepper me with questions about how I'm affording a lawyer. With an anxious but excited smile, I turn to Logan, finding him looking just as elated.

"I'm going to see Aurora."

His grin broadens. "*I'm* finally going to see Aurora."

With that, all of the tension in me dissipates and I fall into his arms with a laugh.

RILEY

CHAPTER THIRTY-SEVEN

"Thank you for driving me." I place my hand over Logan's and squeeze it. He flips his over, our fingers interlocking, and I smile at the sweet gesture. "I feel bad, though. Shouldn't you be practicing or doing some weird pre-game ritual before tonight's game?"

"Nah. I'll pop my earbuds in when I get on the bus this afternoon and zone everyone out until I'm on the ice. But, until then, I'm all yours." His flirty wink sends my stomach flipping and I look away from him as I fail to bite back a smile.

"Are you sure you're okay staying in the car? I don't want my mom asking questions or getting her hackles up if she sees you." I feel awful making him stay out of sight while I spend time with Aurora, but Mom will see his fancy sneakers and expensive jeans, and she'll just *know* he comes from money. Knowing I have a rich boyfriend would be bad enough, although a rich boyfriend who is willing to spend his money ensuring I get Aurora back... Yeah, that won't go down well.

I'd rather she knew nothing about him—or Royce and Grayson. Definitely not Grayson. Not that there is anything to know about Grayson, but she doesn't need to be informed of the fact we're both attending the same university.

"It's fine, Shortcake." It's his turn to give my hand a reassuring squeeze. "I understand. I'm just excited to see her, even if it's from a distance. I'm honestly super jealous of Royce getting to lay eyes on her first."

I huff out a laugh because only Logan could be jealous about something like that.

"I'm excited to see you two together."

"I can't wait to spend time with her," I admit.

"I can't imagine how difficult it must be, being away from her."

"It's unbearable. Saying goodbye to her last time was just as painful as when I left for Halston." Already feeling that ache in my chest, I add, "I know it's going to be just as agonizing today."

The hand Logan has on the steering wheel tightens around it. "Fuck the lawyers. Why don't I just pay your mom off, and we can bring Aurora back with us today."

I start to laugh, but it dries up when he glances my way, expression solemn.

"Uh, because you just can't."

"Why?"

"Uhhh… because my mom would probably demand more than it would take to raise Aurora for the next fifteen years."

"So?"

Realizing that this isn't a conversation he's going to let drop, I blow out a breath as I give it some consideration.

"She wouldn't accept your money," I state after giving it a moment's thought. "She has money. I dunno how much or where it comes from—her divorce, maybe? She's always hitting me up for money. Except for the way she dresses and the clothes she wears, there's no way she can afford those designer brands on the pittance I give her every month."

Logan practically vibrates in his seat. "Then why the fuck is she demanding money from you?"

I shrug. "Control. To make me miserable. I dunno."

"That's fucked up."

The most unladylike snort escapes me 'cause, yeah, it's seriously fucked up, but that's my mother for you.

"Alright, paying her off won't work," he says, defeated.

I stroke my thumb across the back of his hand. "Let's try the legal way, yeah? If that doesn't work, we can try bribing her. Money might not work, though maybe a pair of limited-edition Manolo Blahnik heels will."

I feel like I've won when his lips tilt up. "I'll start buying up everything I can find."

I burst out a laugh, and the conversation falls to easier topics for the rest of the journey to Springview. Once we reach the city limits, I direct Logan to a park near Mom's house where she told me to meet her. He parks in a space off to the side, where my mom is less likely to notice him.

"Which one is she?" he asks, scouring the play park for Aurora.

It takes me a second to scan the various kids rushing around before I identify Aurora, *still* wearing her too-small winter coat. "That one there, in the pink coat," I tell him, pointing out the windshield.

His eyes flare as his lips lift, and he follows her as she runs from the swings to the slide, climbing the ladder before sliding down it with her hands in the air and an infectious laugh on her face.

"She's gorgeous," he says admiringly.

"She is."

Tearing his eyes from her, he looks at me. "Well, go spend time with your baby girl, Mama. I'll be here."

I press a chaste kiss to his lips, but before I can retreat, his palm slides into my hair, holding me to him as he pries my lips apart so he can spear my mouth with his tongue.

By the time I stumble out of the car, I'm dazed, and the smug smirk on Logan's face as I close the door tells me that was his intention.

Thankfully, the crisp air douses my hormones as I walk over to the play park where my mother is waiting, sitting on a hard bench while Aurora circles so she can go down the slide again.

"Mom," I greet tersely, stepping up to her. Her head snaps toward mine.

"Riley." Glancing down at her Cartier watch—one I don't recall her having when she was with Bertram—she tacks on, "You're late."

"By two minutes." Jeez.

Lips pursed, her gaze hardens on mine, not appreciating my snark. "That college sure is changing you... And not for the better."

Her eyes narrow in scrutiny as she rolls them over me. "Did you sucker some guy into looking after you?" Her botoxed lips twitch in a cruel smile. "I always knew you were more like me than you admitted."

I blanch, both horrified by her insinuation and disgusted by how on-point she is. "What?! No! I told you, you forced me to have to take this step."

"Mmm," is all she says, eyes still astutely scrutinizing me.

With a dismissive wave of her hand. "Whatever. I have somewhere to be. I need you to look after the child for a few hours."

The child. God, this woman knows how to piss me off.

"My daughter, your grandchild? Why, of course, I can look after her."

I know I shouldn't be poking at her. It's a shock she's even allowing me to have alone time with Aurora. I imagine it's purely because I gave her no choice in the matter.

A thin, elegant eyebrow raises on her immaculate face, pumped with so many chemicals that the muscles have probably seized up. A little terrified she might change her mind, I soften my tone and repeat, "Sure, Mom. I'll look after Aurora. If you're going to be a while, do you mind if I take her to grab some food?"

"Fine," she says with a dismissive wave of her hand. "Just don't fill her full of sugar. I don't have time to deal with that all night."

My teeth grind because I'd *happily* look after a hopped-up Aurora every day of the week. Instead of pointing that out, though, I merely nod in agreement.

I don't watch my mother as she walks away. Instead, I turn my back on her and rush toward Aurora as she reaches the bottom of the slide.

"Mommy! Mommy! Did you see me?"

"I did, baby! You did so well! Do you wanna go again?"

She nods, immediately taking off to climb to the top of the slide. This time, I pull out my phone, snapping pictures of her the entire time before tucking it away so I can bundle her into my arms as soon as she hits the bottom.

"Do you wanna go on anything else, or do you wanna go get food?"

"Ice cream?"

I laugh, mentally giving my mother the middle finger as I grin and say, "Yeah, I'm thinking a large ice cream sundae with all the toppings."

"Yes!" Aurora fist-pumps the air, making me laugh before I

take her hand, and we walk out of the playground. She talks constantly, filling me in on everything I've missed.

As we approach Logan's car, he steps out, appearing both nervous and excited as his eyes dart back and forth between me and Aurora. I can't help but chuckle as I take in his wide, enthusiastic eyes and twisted, worried lips. He's cute as all hell.

"Aurora, baby, this is my... friend, Logan."

Logan crouches down in front of my daughter, eyes glowing with delight that makes my ovaries explode.

"I've heard so many good things about you, Aurora. It's so nice to meet you."

"Hi," she says shyly, her hand tight in mine.

"Mom had to run some errands, so I thought we could all go grab some food," I offer.

Logan's face lights up, and he nods. "Yeah, sounds perfect. Do you wanna take the car or, uh..."

"I don't have a car seat for her, but there's a diner just down the road we can walk to."

He nods, locking his car and standing to tuck his keys in his pocket.

"Aurora," he says as we begin walking across the parking lot. "I need your help with something. Your mom and I were trying to name each member of the Paw Patrol gang, and we couldn't remember them all. Do you think you could help us out?"

He waits until Aurora thinks it over before nodding, and I *swoon*, watching Logan make an effort with my baby girl.

"Alright, there's the Firefighter, the spotty one. What's his name?"

"Mars-all," Aurora states in a *duh* tone that makes me chuckle and Logan grin.

"Yes, that's the one. Really, Riley, how could you forget Marshall?"

I shake my head, feigning bafflement. "I have no idea. Silly me."

Aurora's laughter tinkles between us as we walk together down the sidewalk, Logan coaxing the names of each Paw Patrol member from her with ease. He's such a natural with kids. I remember him saying he has a bunch of nieces and nephews, so he's probably spent a lot of time around children. Somehow I bet, even if he hadn't, he'd still be a natural. He just has that type of personality.

By the time we make it to the diner, he and Aurora are cackling over their favorite Paw Patrol adventures, and I'm beginning to wonder if I've died and gone to heaven because this feels too good to be true.

Aurora picks out a booth by one of the large windows that looks onto the street, and she and I slide into one side, Logan opposite.

I thank the waitress when she delivers crayons and a coloring book along with menus, and Aurora squeals in delight before diving into covering the page in pink crayon, not even trying to stay within the lines.

Logan finds the entire thing hilarious, and I don't realize how big my smile is until he points it out. "You look beautiful when you smile like that."

And now I'm blushing.

"Doesn't Mommy look beautiful when she smiles?" he directs to Aurora, and I love how he includes her.

"Mommy always looks pretty."

"Facts," Logan agrees with a grin.

Ignoring the heat in my cheeks, I ask Aurora, "Sweetheart, what do you want to eat?"

"Ice cream."

"Yes, but do you need proper food? What have you eaten today?"

"Mrs. Garcia gave me powidge for beakfast." The way her nose wrinkles says everything about what she thought of that. Logan laughs while I simmer over the fact the neighbor fed my daughter instead of my mother.

When the waitress returns, I order actual food for Aurora plus lunch for myself, and Logan places his order, tacking on ice cream sundaes for all three of us.

The chatter and clinking of dishes is background noise to Aurora's light and vibrant giggles and Logan's voice as he regales her with stories of the antics his nieces and nephews have gotten up to while the two of them work together to eliminate every bit of white on the page until it's a mishmash of differing colored areas.

"Mac 'n' cheese for the little one," the waitress says with a smile when she returns with our food, setting a bright yellow bowl in front of Aurora, a club sandwich in front of me, and a burger and fries in front of Logan.

The conversation moves on to their favorite television shows, and I barely contribute anything to the conversation, too busy soaking up every second of the two of them laughing and getting on like idiots.

I pull my phone out to snap a few pictures of them, wanting to memorialize this moment so I can bring it out when I'm having a bad day and missing Aurora.

My attention is drawn back to the table when my daughter shrieks with laughter, and I snort when I notice Logan has smeared ketchup along his upper lip. I decide he's maturely closer to Aurora's age than mine, but we both burst out laughing when he acts like he has no idea what Aurora is talking about when she tries to point it out to him.

"It's there!" she exclaims, pointing at his face.

"Where? Here?" Logan points to his ear, swiping his finger along it and shrugging when it comes away ketchup-free.

"No, silly. There!" Her little body is practically sprawled across the table as she reaches for his face. I've already had to make a last-minute dash to save the mac 'n' cheese bowl from clattering to the floor.

"Ice cream!" Aurora squeals, getting distracted when the waitress returns with our ice creams, removing our empty plates.

By the time we're done, I'm full, Aurora is half asleep on my knee, and Logan has swapped his ketchup mustache for a chocolate one.

"You've been so good with her," I say quietly across the table, one hand stroking through my daughter's hair as she snuggles her face deeper into my side.

"She's amazing," he responds, his voice filled with awe as he watches her. Lifting his eyes to mine, he says, "You've done such an incredible job raising her."

Blushing, I duck my gaze, staring at the top of Rora's head. "I've barely done anything. I've hardly been present in her life at all. The year I took off between high school and college is the most I've been with her."

"One day," he says, the determined promise behind his words drawing my eyes upward. The fire in his chestnut depths gives me hope that he's right. That one day Aurora will be all mine. I'll have her all day, every day.

Tears stinging the back of my throat, I swallow. "We should probably go. Mom will be back soon, and you need to get back to campus in time for the bus leaving."

He nods, slapping a handful of bills on the table as I bundle Aurora into her coat.

We're quiet and contemplative as we walk back down the street toward the play park. Aurora's small arms are wrapped around my neck, her face buried in my coat, and Logan keeps one hand at the base of my spine, his eyes darting between the little girl sleeping in my arms and the sidewalk in front of us.

"I promise you, Riley," he says, stopping me before we round the corner to the park. "Whatever it takes, I will make sure Aurora is all yours. That no one will ever take her away from you again."

There's a lump in my throat preventing me from responding, not that I even know what to say to that. To the enraged look in his eyes. So I simply nod before he ushers me forward, ducking away before I round the corner and the play park comes into view.

My mom is already there, standing beside her car and tapping her shoe impatiently as she glares at her watch as if that will make me magically appear.

"Where have you been?" she chides when she sees me striding toward her.

"Sorry. I didn't realize you were waiting."

She sighs impatiently, but I ignore her as I open the back door and settle a sleeping Aurora into her car seat.

"Thanks for letting me spend some time with her today," I say after quietly closing the car door. "It meant a lot."

"Yeah, yeah. Just make sure you send me that money. I can hire lawyers, too."

Not letting her see the sting from her verbal snap, I stick my hand out, preventing her from getting into the car. "Answer your phone when I call this month. I don't want to go without speaking to my daughter until we next meet."

My mother's lips purse. "You realize I don't spend every waking minute with her?"

Eyes narrowed, I counter, "Then call me back when you are with her."

"Fine," my mother snaps, but a thought strikes before I

remove my outstretched arm. Knowing her, she will deliberately call when I'm in class.

"Every weekend," I stipulate, changing the agreement somewhat. "I want to speak to my daughter every weekend."

My mother's furious glare tells me I'm treading in shark-infested waters. Tough shit. I'm done playing her way. Perhaps it's knowing that Logan and Royce have my back, that there are now lawyers working in my best interest, but I suddenly don't give a flying fuck about my mother's hostile glare aimed my way.

"If you prefer, I can arrange to have this conversation with the lawyers involved."

My mother's smile is sharp. "So quick to throw your hard-earned cash around. You must really be making bank at that strip club of yours. I'd love to know what your lawyers would make of that..." Seeing the fear on my face, a gleam enters her eyes. "However, I'll agree since I have better things to do with my day."

"Every weekend," I emphasize.

"Yes, Riley. I heard you perfectly the first time."

Eyes drawn in skepticism, I press, "Starting this weekend. Tomorrow or Sunday."

My mother sighs. "Fine. Now get out of my way."

Reluctantly, I step aside, and she gets into the car, reversing out of the space. Just like on Christmas morning, I watch as she drives away, taking a significant piece of my heart with her. The difference is, this time, I'm not alone. The second her taillights disappear from view, Logan appears, wrapping me up in the deepest of hugs and letting me cling to him as tears leak from my eyes.

RILEY

CHAPTER THIRTY-EIGHT

Staring up at the brownstone in front of me, I swallow around the lump in my throat as I wipe my sweaty palms on my oversized jersey. I haven't been back here since Christmas Day, and the memories roll through me like a slideshow playing on repeat as I stare at the hunter-green front door.

Grayson's cold, hard eyes filled with hatred.

Logan's pained gaze when he believed I'd duped him.

Royce's ambivalence the first day he stared down at me on that couch.

Grayson's hand around my throat, choking me.

Royce crouched in front of me while I came through my panic attack.

Logan's world crumbling when I confessed the truth to him.

The feel of hard soil beneath my socked feet.

Nights spent sleeping in Logan's bed.

Afternoons curled up on the couch between Royce and Logan.

Good and bad, traumatic and cathartic, the memories flicker through my mind. I lost a part of myself in this house, to these boys, but I also found a long-buried strength I'd forgotten I possessed.

The front door opens, jarring me from my memories as a stoic-faced Royce appears before me. His gaze drops to take in the Huskies jersey I'm wearing, one corner of his lips quirking.

"At least this time, I don't have to watch Logan maul you in his jersey."

My returning smile is wide, and it is with zero hesitation that I climb the steps and walk into the house.

"Admit it," I tease, "You were getting hard watching us."

He only smirks in response, following me inside. "The only thing I was thinking, James, was how much hotter you'd have looked in *my* jersey."

I pause in the hall, turning to face him as a pang cinches my chest. He's teasing, but he's also not. "I'd have worn your jersey to every single game, too."

His smile is small but genuine, fleeting. "I know."

Before I can comprehend what he's doing, he snaps a photo, and barely a minute later, my phone rings with a FaceTime from Logan. When we got back to campus yesterday after seeing Aurora, he had to head straight for the bus. I had to work last night, meaning I missed his game. So when Royce suggested watching it together tonight, I jumped at the opportunity—once he assured me Grayson wouldn't be there. Apparently, he's been staying in an apartment close to his office for the last few days. I feel both relieved and guilty, knowing that. Relieved that I don't have to see him after the Bertram bomb. Guilty because if he's not even living here at the minute, then how dire is the situation between him, Logan, and Royce.

Despite what Grayson thinks, I don't want to come between him and the guys. I sense he needs them more than ever. He looked like a shell of himself in the food court that day. He's falling apart at the seams and incapable of stitching himself back together. I know the guys see it, too.

"Hey," I say, answering Logan's call and bringing the phone to my face.

"Let me see," Logan growls.

It takes me a moment to catch on, before realizing that Royce must have sent the photo to Logan, knowing exactly what it would do to him.

I flick my gaze to Royce, his soft expression warming me as he slips past me and toward the kitchen, offering us a moment of privacy.

Bringing my eyes back to Logan's heated ones, I fight back a smirk as I move into the living room, sitting down on the sofa and bringing my feet up. The TV is playing pre-game footage, but my entire focus is on the golden-haired man staring at me like I'm all he sees. "See what?"

"Riley." My name is a low rumble, a decadent promise, and god do I wish he was here right now.

"Oh, you mean this?" I angle the phone so he can see the black and gold jersey, eliciting a predatory vibration from the back of his throat that resonates through my entire body, settling low in my core.

"Fuck, baby. All I'm going to see tonight is you in my jersey. I'll be lucky to spot the puck never mind score a goal."

"Logan Astor," I say in a mock stern voice. "You better dominate on the ice tonight." I lower my voice, listening for noises of Royce moving about in the kitchen before hastily blurting, "Or I won't let you fuck me in this jersey."

My cheeks are bright red, but I ignore them. I've been thinking about it a lot recently, especially with the fooling around we've been doing the last couple of days. Both Logan and Royce have proven themselves. These last few weeks, they've made me feel special. Cared for. Protected in a way that

I've never felt before. I want to take this next step with both of them. Honestly, I'm not sure how much longer I can ignore the chemistry between us. It's practically begging for us to get naked and fuck.

"Fucking hell, Shortcake," Logan groans, looking visibly pained as his hungry gaze eats me up through the screen.

"When you get home tomorrow," I promise. "Come over then, and for every goal you score in tonight's game, I'll let you fuck me in a different position... with the jersey. If you want."

He groans, eyes closing as he swipes a hand over his face. It looks as though it takes monumental effort to compose himself. By the time he focuses back on the screen, that desire has been replaced with lethal determination. "I'm going to make a hat trick look like child's play. I'll score so many goals, your legs will be nothing but jelly by the time I'm through with you."

Well, fuck.

"Great one, Babydoll," Royce drawls, startling me where he's leaning against the doorframe, having caught the tail end of our conversation. "You just waved a red flag in front of a bull."

Based on Logan's feral grin through the screen, I'd have to agree. And I'm not sure if I should be thrilled or terrified.

Someone calls his name in the background, and he turns away, giving whoever it is a lift of his chin in acknowledgment before returning his attention to me. "I've gotta go. Have fun watching the game with Royce, Shortcake. Don't do anything I wouldn't do." I wish him good luck and he ends the call with a filthy wink that does nothing to diminish the need unfurling in my belly.

Royce sets snacks and drinks on the coffee table before joining me on the sofa. His gaze slides over my jersey, and reaching out a hand, he toys with the hem. A sadness seeps into his eyes, his voice quiet as he confesses, "I never gave a damn about seeing a girl wearing my number. It did absolutely nothing for me." He's silent for a moment before dragging his eyes away from the jersey and up to my face. "I wish I could see you in the stands, wearing my jersey, cheering me on."

That's twice today he's brought up football. It's surprising because he very rarely talks about it, and I haven't wanted to push or pry too deep and cause him unnecessary pain.

"Oh, yeah?" I intend for the words to come out teasing, an attempt to lighten his mood, but the weight of the conversation, the despair in his gaze, sucks any brightness out of them. "What was your number?"

"Seventeen."

Reaching out to touch the back of his hand, I say with sincerity, "I would have loved to have worn your number." The lines around his eyes soften as he holds my gaze, his hands banding around my hips as he pulls me to straddle him. There's nothing sexual about it. Purely a need to feel close to one another.

A teasing smirk comes to my lips as I place my hands on his chest, feeling the tensing of his muscles through his t-shirt. "I'd even have paired it with a big foam finger and screamed like a lunatic. In reality, the whole thing would have been highly embarrassing for you."

That cracks a smile, some of that anguish he permanently carries dissipating as his hands squeeze my waist.

"Probably just as well that we didn't know one another back then."

Leaning in until we're a hairsbreadth apart, he whispers, "Never," before closing the distance and kissing me. It's deep and passionate, slow and filling. "There is no existence where I'm not better for knowing you, James," he says, pulling back to rest his forehead against mine.

Running my hand through the hairs at the back of his neck,

I tell him earnestly, "You are a far better man than you allow yourself to believe."

Pulling away, his gaze drops. "You wouldn't say that if you knew everything about me."

I hate seeing him put himself down like that. I suspect I know what he's referring to, but even if he's talking about something else, he still couldn't say anything that would make me change my mind.

Cupping his cheeks with my hands, I lift his face to mine. "I would because I know you... in here." Sliding one hand down to his chest, I rest it over his heart. "Whatever has happened in the past, I know the person you are at heart. That doesn't mean you always do the right thing, or that you don't do the wrong thing for the right reasons. Hell, you could confess to killing someone, and I'd tell you he deserved it because I know that's the only reason that would justify your actions.

"It doesn't matter what you have to tell me, Royce. I will never think the worst of you."

"I don't deserve you," he rasps, throat bobbing with emotion. "But I'm too selfish to let you go."

"Good," I say with a smirk. "Because here with you is exactly where I want to be."

Loud cheering from the TV pulls us from our moment, and I glance over my shoulder to see the players coming onto the ice. Royce sighs before shifting me off his lap and pulling me into his side instead, and together, we watch the puck drop and the game begin.

Logan is like a man possessed every time he hits the ice for his shift, scoring multiple goals and assisting others. And after every single one, he stares directly into the camera—at me. It sends a shiver of anticipation down my spine, my legs trembling with how hard I'm clenching them.

The Huskies are decimating their opponent, and it's mostly

thanks to Logan. Their defense is on point, and their goalie has done a fantastic job of catching most shots, but Logan is the clear driving force of tonight's success.

Winning 6-1, Royce turns to look at me while the team celebrates on the ice before heading toward the locker room to change.

"Huh." He chuckles, glancing down at me. "Looks like your incentive worked. Guess Logan was right when he said you were his lucky charm."

"That was all him," I contest.

Royce shakes his head. "Logan is an amazing player, but the way he plays when he knows you're watching... it's next level. He's practically unstoppable. You do that. You give him a sense of purpose he's never had before."

He leans in closer with every word, tone dropping an octave.

My brows furrow. "Logan has always known what he wants and worked to obtain it."

"Sure, but there's a difference between going after something for yourself and doing it because you want to make the other person happy. To have them look at you with a gleam of pride, to imagine them standing beside you."

Eyes searching mine, he states, "He's no longer purely doing it for himself. Logan wants to be the best not only because hockey is his dream, but because he wants you to look upon his achievements and know they're an extension of his love for you."

My mouth is dry as I swallow, struggling to wrap my mind around what Royce is saying.

"How do you know that?"

Royce tucks a stray strand of hair behind my ear, the pad of his finger lingering on the corner of my jaw. "Because I see the way he looks at you, as if you're his whole world. His future has always been hockey. Although if I were to guess, I'd say, even if he ended up a fourth-line forward for some shitty team, he wouldn't care as much as he once would have."

His fingers curl around my jaw, the strokes light and reverent. "I'm not trying to scare you off. I'm just saying that Logan's future is no longer solely hockey. It's you."

My heart thumps heavily against my chest. Only, it's not with anxiety, but with steady assurance. A confirmation of what I've known deep down inside for a while but have refused to look too closely at. Logan wears his heart on his sleeve, and while no *I love you*'s have been exchanged, it wouldn't surprise me if that's where he's at.

Is it where I'm at? I'm less sure of that answer. Unlike Logan, I don't believe in soulmates and love at first sight, but I do believe in love, and if there is anyone I could fall in love with, it would be Logan Astor.

And if I looked inside myself, I might also admit that I could fall in love with the mysterious bad boy currently looking at me as though *he's* the one confessing I'm his future.

We fall into easy conversation after Royce's declaration. He orders food, and we munch on Chinese as we talk about lighter topics. When I bring up the sketch of me he'd drawn over winter break, he asks if I want to see it, and I follow him up to his room.

Just like last time, I pause on the threshold.

"Scared, Babydoll?" he teases, breath tickling my ear as he notices my hesitation.

"No," I tell him honestly. "Just taking a moment to appreciate the privilege that it is to be allowed into your inner sanctum."

His thumb and index finger grasp my chin, gently turning

my head to face him. The brief brush of his lips is reverent. Deep. Monumental.

"You're always welcome in my room, Ry. I'd hide away from the world with you any day."

We've spent many nights over the last days and weeks, typically after my shifts or, more recently, on the nights he stays at mine, curled up on the sofa. Him drawing while I read. I can't think of anything better I'd rather do. There's something to be said about sharing a space with someone, both of you doing your own thing. Simply being together because you enjoy one another's company but not feeling as though you need to fill it with words or lavish the other with attention.

"It's a date," I murmur against his lips. With a stroke of his finger along my cheek, he pulls away, placing a gentle yet firm hand on my back to nudge me into his room.

I go easily, breathing in the scent of leather and something gritty that is uniquely Royce. It wraps around me, a protective shield that both comforts and fortifies.

Keeping this hand on my back, he directs me over to his desk, nudging me into the chair while he grabs an A3 drawing pad.

He pauses with this thumb at the corner, his first sign of uncertainty.

"You don't have to." I glance up into his face, the war within playing out in the shadows of his eyes before he snaps his gaze to mine. In an instant, whatever was troubling him lifts, and he latches onto my gaze like it's an anchor as he pulls open the book.

"I told you I would, James. I don't break my promises," he states, lifting his spare hand and running his index finger along my lower lip. "Besides, I want to show you. I'm just not used to being so..."

"I know," I assure him, giving his wrist a gentle squeeze.

"Your trust is hard won. I like that about you, and I'm more than up to the challenge of proving you can trust me."

His exhale shudders, something loosening in his shoulders, and he nods before turning his attention back to the drawing pad. I linger a moment longer, taking in those dark, angry eyebrows, the sharp angles of his jaw, and his long, straight face. All of it paints a picture of a strong man used to depending on only himself. I so badly want to crack that impenetrable exterior, to see what lies underneath and show him that I'd happily protect him as fiercely as he's willing to protect me.

Tearing my eyes away, I tilt my head to look down at the open drawing pad. As I lay my eyes on the intricately detailed sketch, a rush of emotion sweeps through me, leaving me breathless. Awestruck.

Before me lies an imperfect, scarred, beautiful woman. It's me, and yet it's a version of myself I don't recognize. With every pencil stroke, Royce has woven a portrait that transcends mere physical resemblance.

My fingers reach out to trace the lines, almost as if I'm touching the delicate strands of my own identity. The drawing serves as a mirror that reflects not just my appearance, but the depths of my heart, my experiences, and my emotions. The way he's captured the pain lurking in the corners of my eyes, it's as though he can see to the inner sanctum of my soul, laying bare the facets of myself that I keep shrouded from the rest of the world.

There's not just pain in the drawing, though. There's also love and a vitality for life, a gritty determination I recognize intimately from the planes of Royce's face.

In the gray lines, I can make out my undying love for my daughter, the passion I feel for dance, my drive and ambition. And in the dark shading lies the hidden crevices—the shadows, the fear, the scars that are my companions in the quiet of night.

A reminder that I'm not just light but also a complex tapestry of darkness and resilience.

Beautifully broken and strikingly scarred.

Love and life and shadows and trauma all rolled into one.

Radiant yet haunting.

I'm laid bare in the sketch, every layer of my identity exposed. Every insecurity, every doubt, every fear and neurosis noticed by Royce and drawn so intimately that it leaves me with the stark realization that this brooding, complex enigma of a man sees me. Truly *sees* me. The dancer, the dreamer, the scared girl, and the protective mother.

Every aspect of who I am.

He sees it, and he's enthralled by it. It's drawn into every stroke of his pencil, every shading done by his finger, every hard line and gentle brush.

His affection.

"Royce." His name is a scratch at the back of my throat.

"What do you think?" he asks, voice carefully guarded.

It's beautiful.

Mesmerizing.

Transcendent.

Perfect.

Lifting my head, my eyes scan his face with a new awareness. He deliberately avoids my penetrating stare, glaring unblinkingly at the drawing pad, yet in his eyes, I see a reflection of his soul—a soul that has been shielded, sheltered, and hidden away from the world's gaze.

But not from mine.

He's lowered his shields—for me. For this moment. Because he wants me to see him as exposed as he sees me.

Doesn't he already know that I do?

Placing one hand on the table, I slowly rise to my feet, lifting my other one to cup his cheek and direct his attention to me. He doesn't come willingly, but he doesn't resist either, putting it off for as long as he can before he dares to lift his eyes to mine.

In those blue depths, I see the anger, the masculine force that has become his armor against a world that wounded him. Yet, there's also a flicker of vulnerability buried deep into the edges. A yearning for understanding that he guards with an iron resolve.

I stroke my thumb affectionately across his cheek, and brick by brick, his guard crumbles, that shield of apprehension disintegrating into dust, those ice-blue eyes melting with a warmth reserved solely for me.

Through his sketch, Royce has demonstrated that his gaze doesn't just skim the surface; it delves deeper, and in return, he allows me to do the same to him. It's a privilege to witness the cracks in his armor, the vulnerability he's allowing me to glimpse.

I place my palm over his heart, feeling the rhythmic thud beneath my palm. There's a quiet intensity in his gaze as it bores into mine—a yearning, a curiosity.

With Logan, everything is so simple because he says what's on his mind and tells me how he's feeling. There's none of that with Royce, and yet I don't feel as though we need words to identify what this is between us. I'm not even sure if words could accurately define it.

Royce might not know how to express his feelings verbally, but he does it with these sketches. With the fact he faithfully shows up at Lux every weekend. When he crawls into my bed at night to quell my nightmares. By bringing me home on Christmas morning.

With all the small and big gestures he makes every single day.

"You see me." My voice is barely above a whisper, but we're

standing so close that I don't need to talk any louder.

His throat bobs, and I trail the hand that rests over his heart up his chest, along the side of his neck until I'm cupping his face in both palms. "I see you too. I see the shields you keep around you, the haunted look in your eye when you talk about the past. I see your desolation, but I also see the hope you keep hidden. I want to be your hope. The one who pulls you out of the darkness. Not so I can claim I converted the bad boy, but because you deserve to live in the light, Royce. You deserve to be free of whatever pain it is you're carrying."

An audible gulp fills the space between us. "What if I'm not ready to come into the light yet?" he asks in a broken tone.

"Then I'll readily hold your hand and navigate the darkness with you." My eyes dart to and fro between his. "You have it all." His muscles go rigid as his eyes bulge. "My body, my mind, my soul. My good days and bad ones. My strength and tears." I swallow roughly. "You have all of me."

"Fuck, Ry," he rasps, somehow managing to make my name sound as though it's his undoing. His hands circle my face as he stares down at me with such devout admiration. "You own all of me. Every broken and jagged piece—even the parts I don't know how to share with you yet." He sags forward, our chests fused as he drops his forehead to my shoulder and his arms come around me, fingers fisting the back of my jersey. "I want to tell you. I know I need to." His exhale is a shudder I feel against my bare skin at the juncture of my neck.

While one hand is pressed flat against his back, I bring my other one up to stroke through his hair in slow, tender strokes. "I don't want you to think differently of me," he confesses so quietly I barely hear him.

"Pretty sure I already know what an asshole you can be." He huffs out a breath but remains perched against my shoulder, leaning against me for support but not putting any of his weight on me since I'd likely crumble beneath him.

I continue running my fingers through his hair, silence reigning between us. It's not awkward or uncomfortable. However, it *is* filled with all the things he is unable to say.

So I decide to help him out and say them for him.

"Does it have anything to do with the rumors that you... raped some girl?"

He turns to stone.

For long seconds, he doesn't so much as breathe. Then, with stiff movements, he lifts his head from my shoulder and steps back so he can see my face, his expression guarded as he searches my eyes.

"How do you know about that?"

"I overheard two girls discussing it in the library before winter break. They mentioned your name. At the time, it didn't mean anything to me. It was only when Logan brought me here, the day I woke up to you standing over me and he said your name, that I put the dots together.

"That's why you asked me for my last name," he croaks, shell-shocked.

I nod.

His hand shakes as he brings it up to swipe through his hair. "I don't understand. You stayed. You... Why didn't you freak the fuck out?"

"I did," I assure him. "Came close to a full-blown panic attack until I forced myself to calm down and think. That's when I realized it didn't add up."

"What didn't add up?" he asks in bewilderment.

"The you that those girls described and the you that I'd gotten to know at the club. I couldn't reconcile it in my head."

He's staring at me like I've turned purple and grown three heads. "James, I was a complete asshole to you."

I give him a wry smirk. "I'm not saying you weren't, but there's a difference between being an asshole and... what they claimed."

Taking a step forward, I hope he can hear the sincerity in my voice as I say, "You pushed my buttons. You tested my limits. You drove me right to the brink of my comfort zone, but not once did you push me over it. Every time I stepped out of my box, it was because *I* wanted to. Because *you* gave me the courage to do so. Despite the circumstances at the club, I never once felt uncomfortable with you. I was never concerned that you'd take things too far or do something I didn't want."

I slide my palm over his heart. "You gave me a safe space to explore my sexuality. You challenged and baited me, but not once did you force or coerce me into anything."

"But..." he trails off, looking even more baffled than he did a moment ago. "You hardly knew me."

I give a shoulder shrug. "I knew all I needed to know. You're forgetting I know what it is to stare into the face of someone who would take advantage of a person that way." Some of his shock gives way to red-hot hostility. "I know what it is to stare into the face of evil, and despite the impression you like to give the rest of the world, you, Royce King, don't have an evil bone in your body."

"That's where you're wrong, James, or are you forgetting that I spend my spare time beating the shit out of strangers? That I punched your boss."

"You're ruthless," I counter, earning a small smirk at the mention of his fighting name. "But those men know what they're up against when they step into the ring. And outside of it... you use your ruthlessness for good. I'm not scared by your violence. It comforts me."

My eyes shift back and forth between his. "Your compass

may be skewed, but unlike the Bertams of this world, it is far from broken."

With another step forward, I close the distance between us. "And that readiness to destroy the world to protect me is why I'm not afraid of handing over my heart to you."

His eyes are on mine, an indecipherable turmoil of emotions whirling within as his hands slide up my arms, across my shoulders until his fingers curl around my neck.

With his thumbs pressing beneath my jaw, he pushes my head back, the pads stroking across my skin in a tantalizing touch.

"I don't know what the hell I must have done in a previous life to deserve someone like you, but I'm selfish enough not to question it. You're mine, Riley James. Today, tomorrow, for the rest of our goddamn lives. And I'll always be yours. Even when I piss you off. Even when you get sick of my moody ass. Whether I'm at your side or lurking in the shadows. I'll always have your back."

With tears threatening, I press onto my toes, and wrapping my arms around his enormous shoulders, I pull him down to me and seal his vow with a kiss.

RILEY

CHAPTER THIRTY-NINE

Pressing against his chest, Royce submits to my silent demand, allowing me to push him back toward the bed. All the while, our lips remain interlocked, tongues entwined in a hungry, heated kiss that tastes of salvation and hope.

When the back of his legs hit the bed frame, he drops to the mattress, and I move to straddle his lap. His large, calloused palms land on my thighs, inching higher as our kiss deepens.

I rock against his growing erection as he palms my ass, fingers digging into the fabric of my jeans and pulling me closer. I moan into his mouth, and he eagerly swallows the sound of my pleasure.

"Fuck, Ry," he hisses, ripping his lips from mine to lick along my neck. "I love the way you taste. I'm constantly thinking about those sweet sounds you make when I'm eating you out or fucking you with my fingers."

Shivers race down my spine as my pussy clenches around nothing but air, and I grind harder against him, desperate for friction.

He growls, the sound wholly predatory, before grabbing me

in a bruising grip and flipping me over. My back hits the mattress, and before I can process what's happened, he's above me, his fingers making quick work of my jeans as he undoes the button and drags them down my legs.

"I need to taste you," he rasps, tugging off my sneakers and tossing my discarded jeans aside before he pushes my thighs apart and climbs between them.

I hurry to pull the jersey over my head, leaving me in just my bra and panties as he drinks in every inch of exposed skin with unequivocal hunger.

Lowering his face, he licks and sucks and nibbles a tantalizing path from the back of my knee to the inside of my thighs, and I'm quivering with need by the time his nose brushes against the sopping fabric of my panties.

"You smell divine." His voice is husky, primal, barely contained as he buries his face between my legs, inhaling deeply. "Look at you, all wet and needy for me."

He takes another deep breath before hooking his fingers in my panties and dragging them down my legs. I lean up on my elbows, watching with a hammering heart as he kneels between my legs. The sight alone is erotic—this broad-shouldered, unrelenting man *kneeling* for me.

A girl could get used to this.

Predatory eyes meet mine, the typical pale blue of his irises now molten as his fingers sweep lazily through my wet folds, his touch light, and teasing—nowhere close to what I need. "I'm going to devour this tight little pussy, and when I'm done, you're going to come on my tongue like the filthy slut you are." He rims my core before pushing a single digit inside. I gasp at the intrusion, arching into the sensation as he slides deeper. "You got that, James?"

"Yes," I pant.

He smirks, his expression pure masculine satisfaction dripping with desire.

I expect him to put his head back between my legs, but he takes his time, slowly fucking me with one finger before adding a second, massaging my inner walls and driving me completely wild. The entire time, he stares at the spot where his fingers disappear inside me, and watching him watch us only pushes me higher.

His other hand rubs tight circles around my clit until I'm mewling and writhing on the bed, panting and near delirious with the need to come.

"Royce," I plead.

Hearing his name jolts him out of whatever trance he was in, and he snaps his head up, pupils blown as he drinks me in. "Such a dirty girl," he purrs. "Already greedy to come. Not until I've had my fill, though."

I groan, slapping my palm against the bed sheets in frustration as he eases out of me. His warm breath sets my nerve endings alight as he chuckles against my swollen, sensitive clit, before running his tongue along my slit.

Back arching, I fist the bedsheets as I moan. Lifting my legs over his shoulders, Royce wraps one arm around my thigh, his other hand splaying across my stomach as he goes to town, devouring my pussy with vigor.

I go feral. Incomprehensible words fall from my lips as I grind and writhe and buck against him.

"Royce! Oh, God. I'm going to come!"

He doesn't let up on his ministrations as ecstasy radiates outward from my center, burning a path along my nerves, and I throw my head back and scream his name as my release barrels through me.

Extending my orgasm, Royce continues to lap at me until I physically pull him up, my fingers in his hair dragging him away from my sensitive core and up my body. Still fully clothed, the rough fabric of his jeans scrapes against my lower half, and my already weakened legs tremble.

"I need to feel you inside me," I state breathlessly, already clawing at his back, shoving his t-shirt up.

He locks into place above me, eyes burning with a glacial fire as they bore into mine. "Say it again," he demands in a choked voice.

I still my movements as I focus on his face, letting him see just how serious I am. "You have all of me, Royce. No matter what. I don't need to know everything to know I want this. That I want *you*."

"I've never wanted *anyone* the way I want you. For five years, I found it easy to live without sex, but since the day you crashed into me, fucking you has been all I can think about. I've never jacked off so much in my life."

My cheeks heat, even as a smug smile blooms.

He doesn't move, still seeming torn, so I ask, "Do you trust me?"

His answer is immediate and unquestioning. "Yes."

"Good. Then kiss me."

Sliding my hand around the back of his neck, I pull him to me. Our lips meet in a twining of souls. Royce and I are opposite sides of the same coin—contrasting yet identical. We've been forged in twin fires, our stories unique but our pain and scars matching. Inextricably linked. Bonded in a profound way that defies the disparities of our personalities.

The echoes of anguish resonate between us like the hidden harmony in a symphony. In his darkness, I see the reflection of the shadows I've battled, and in my light he finds a sliver of the hope he's been unwittingly seeking.

Our paths were always destined to intersect. To pull us from our solitary existence. To peel back the darkness. So that, in our weakest moments, we can lock hands and know we aren't alone.

Dragging my fingers down his spine, I slip them beneath his top. His skin burns against mine like a brand as I run my fingers over every ridge and valley, tracing the lines of his body. His top inches up, exposing his tattooed skin as I slide my palms over his chest before fisting the material and pulling it over his head.

Our kiss breaks as he tosses it away. The second it's gone, his mouth is back on mine, hungrier than ever as he licks at the seam of my lips, tongue prodding in demand for entry.

A symphony of fireworks goes off in my core, my body humming with anticipation as I thumb the waistband of his jeans. He pulls back before I can undo them, eyes running over me.

"I'm not sure I can be gentle," he says, some of that hesitation still lingering in his features.

"I don't want you to be gentle, Royce. *We* are not gentle. You constantly test me, and I love it. I love exploring beyond my comfort zone with you. I want all of you, just as you are."

He fights it for a moment longer, but I see when his restraint snaps and the ruthless animal that slumbers beneath his skin lurches to the forefront.

His eyes darken with predatory hunger, his voice dropping several octaves and eliciting goosebumps along my skin. Seriously, if I was standing, my legs would be jelly.

"Bra off. Now," he growls, kicking off his jeans while I unclasp my bra and carelessly toss it aside. My breasts heave with each exhale, my skin flushing beneath his appraisal. "Fuck, you're beautiful, Ry."

Ducking his head, he runs his tongue along my collarbone, peppering my feverish skin with kisses as his hands move to cup my breasts. I groan as he flicks my peaked nipple with his thumb, the rough calluses on his fingers scraping along my skin and igniting sparks in their wake.

His lips descend the front of my chest until he sucks my other nipple into his mouth. My cunt is weeping, my body damn near sizzling beneath his ministrations.

"Holy shit, Royce. Yes. That feels incredible," I pant as he sweeps his tongue over my areola, before clamping down on the nipple with his teeth.

I scream, dampness gathering between my thighs, and when I look down at him, he's smirking up at me. "I can't wait to hear you make that noise when I tear you in two."

"Big words for someone who is still wearing his boxers," I tease, earning a wolfish grin.

"If you think taunting me is going to get you anything other than a bright red ass, you don't know me at all, Babydoll."

My teeth sink into my lower lip, a grin stretching across my face. *God, I hope that's a promise.* I want him to be rough with me. To devolve into his baser self. I want to watch all those carefully constructed walls crumble until nothing lies between us. Until *we* are nothing but thrusting hips and panting breaths, a building ball of unending ecstasy.

He slowly climbs down the bed, and I lift my head so I can watch as he stands, covetous gaze raking over every inch of my flushed skin as he pushes his fingers beneath the waistband of his boxers, slowly pulling them over his hips before allowing them to fall to his ankles, leaving him naked as he fists his engorged, pierced cock.

Fuck, I forgot he had a piercing.

My pussy clenches in anticipation of how that's going to feel, scraping against my inner walls and prodding at my cervix. I want it. I want *him.*

As though reading my mind, he asks in a husky voice, "Tell me what you want, Ry."

My nipples harden into glass.

"I want you to fuck me senseless. To decimate my pussy with that jumbo-sized dick of yours and fill me full of your cum."

His lips twitch into a carnivorous smile. "Such a dirty girl, Ry. I should wash out that filthy mouth of yours with my cock, but I need to be inside you too badly."

"Please."

"Condom?" he questions, looking like the devil himself as he stands at the foot of the bed, legs apart and every ounce of tattooed skin on display as he slowly works himself over.

I shake my head. "No. I have a contraceptive implant, and I'm clean. I got tested after Grayson... and I haven't been with anyone else."

I've barely gotten the words out before he's back on the bed, prowling toward me with graceful ease. Hovering over me, he plants one hand beside my head. His other is wrapped around his shaft as he drags the head of his cock up and down my slit, lubricating it while simultaneously teasing me.

"Fuck, Ry. I don't think I can hold back."

"Don't," I rasp.

With a final lingering glance, he slams into me in one deep thrust, knocking the air from my lungs and all rational thought from my brain.

"Oh *fuck*," he hisses, the veins in his neck bulging. "You feel even better than I imagined."

How can he even string a sentence together, right now? My brain is too scrambled to do anything more than moan and whimper as I rock my hips against him in a silent plea for him to move.

Pulling nearly all the way out, he snaps his hips forward, his piercing dragging along every sensitive inch of my inner walls before knocking against my cervix and causing me to see literal stars.

His thrusts are punishing, each one a bursting bubble of rhapsody that fizzes along my nerves until I feel as though I'm having an out-of-body experience.

Seeking a deeper angle, he sits back on his heels, slipping his hands beneath my ass and hauling my lower half off the bed.

"Oh, *god,*" I moan as he slides impossibly deeper. My legs quiver, my body feeling like it's about to tear apart at the seams. "Royce."

"So fucking perfect," he grunts, focus zeroed in on where our two bodies join. "Cream my cock, Babydoll. I wanna feel those walls strangle my dick."

"Oh, god." The two words are a soundtrack playing on repeat in my head. One that turns into white noise as he flicks his thumb over my clit before pinching it.

I *scream.*

The sound ravages my throat as I throw my head back. Something inside me gives as rolls of pleasure rush through me in a tidal wave.

Royce continues to fuck me the entire way through my orgasm, cursing and praising me. Somehow, he manages to stave off his release, and I'm still in a post-orgasm stupor when he flips me onto my stomach.

His hands grip my hips, hauling me onto my knees, which tremble beneath my weight.

Whack.

A sharp slap snaps me back to the moment as pain and pleasure mingle and heat radiates from my left asscheek. Another smack has me yelping as I shift forward, only to be tugged back by unforgiving hands on my waist.

"Stay with me, Ry," Royce grunts, threading his head

through my dripping pussy as he slams back into me. His thrusts are unyielding, the harsh way he manhandles me, winding my body up for a second orgasm as I press my ass back against him.

Gliding a hand up my skin, goosebumps erupt along my skin, and I cry out when he fists my hair at the base of my scalp, yanking my head and forcing my back into a deep arch.

"Fucking you is my new favorite thing," he rumbles.

"Royce," I plead. "I'm going to come again."

"Come for me, James. Show me what a bad girl you can be."

My arms shake with the effort to stave off my release. "I want you to come with me."

"I will, Ry. I'm right here with you."

Using his grip on my hair, and an arm wrapped around my abdomen, he hauls me upright with my back pressed against his sweat-slicked chest. The angle is tighter, and I can feel every drag of his piercing as he continues his relentless pounding.

Twisting my head to face him, he captures my lips with his, his other hand sliding between my legs to circle my clit.

Once.

Twice.

On the third loop, I explode, trembling against his solid form as he follows me over the edge. I can feel our combined release seeping out of me, the thrashing of his heart against my shoulder blade.

The only sound in the room is our haggard breaths as I sag against him, the two of us enjoying the last remnants of our high.

"I can't feel my legs," I eventually push out between breaths.

He huffs a breathless laugh, gently lowering me to the duvet before dropping onto the mattress beside me. Staring at the ceiling, his left hand rests over his heart, and I roll onto my side, watching him.

After a moment, he turns his head toward me. His eyes are back to their usual color, but the frigid coldness that normally resides in their depths is gone. The warmth shining back at me steals my breath, and I lie there, frozen in place as I wait to see what his next move will be.

He reaches out an arm in a silent invitation, and I huddle into his side, my hand resting on his stomach as his heat bats away the chill that was starting to seep in. He presses a kiss to the top of my head, but otherwise, we don't say anything. Neither of us feels the need to fill the space between us with words. Not when our bodies have already done all the talking.

My eyes grow heavy, exhaustion tugging me down, yet sleep remains elusive.

"He used to call me his *good girl*," I whisper in a fragile voice, noting how Royce tenses beneath me. "I think that's why I like it so much when you degrade me." I swallow roughly. "What he did… he was so tender in his violation. It confused me. Made me feel as though what he was doing wasn't wrong, yet it never felt *right*…" I trail off, trying to remember where I was going. Did I even have a point when I began? I'm no longer sure. Weariness is tugging at my bones, my words a faint whisper. "It feels right with you. I like being your dirty slut."

In my half-asleep state, I feel him press another chaste kiss to my hairline, one hand stroking along the strands. "Go to sleep, Ry. I'll be here when you wake up."

"Mm, so good," I mumble. After we woke up and went for another hard and fast round of incredible sex, we needed to refuel. It must be after midnight, and we're sitting on the kitchen countertop, sharing a tub of ice cream between us—okay, so I'm mostly eating the ice cream while Royce watches me with a hungry look in his eyes that I'm pretty sure has nothing to do with Rocky Road ice cream.

I hold the tub out to him, but he shakes his head, a raw vulnerability in his eyes before he says, "Melissa was a cheerleader at my high school." The ice cream turns sour in my mouth as I set the tub down on the countertop, watching him intently and knowing how hard this is for him to tell me. "We grew up together. Had classes together. Partied together. I... *knew* her." His brows furrow as he frowns. "I *thought* I knew her." He sighs despondently as he stares into space. "It was our senior year, and she'd been flirting with me for several months, but I wasn't interested in starting anything with anyone when I was about to leave for college."

"So, what happened?" I ask when he trails off, my voice sounding loud in the otherwise silent room.

His gaze shifts to mine, his face pinching with the memory. "We'd just won the championship game, and there was a huge party. I was wasted and riding the adrenaline high of our win when Melissa came over. She flirted the way she always did at these things, and instead of politely turning her down like usual, I reciprocated." He sighs, shaking his head. "The next thing I remember is waking up naked and alone the next morning in a stranger's bed with the hangover from hell. I didn't think much of it at the time. Not until Dad called me into his office and chastised me for *not cleaning up my own mess.* He was more furious at having to pay off Melissa's family and the potential scandal of it all than he was concerned about hearing me out or getting to the truth of it all."

My nose wrinkles. "So wait, you don't actually remember having... sex with her?"

He shakes his head. "It's a total blank in my memory."

"So you don't actually know if you did…"

He shrugs. "The evidence would suggest that I did. She claimed she hadn't realized how drunk I was, and that when she said no, I got angry. That I used my weight to pin her to the bed…" His shoulders curl in as he shrugs. "I mean, it's possible."

"Royce King," I bark, jumping down from the countertop and closing the distance until I'm standing directly in front of him. "Even black-out drunk, there is no way in hell you laid a finger on that girl to hurt her. Just because you have the ability to do something like that doesn't mean you *did*." Reaching up, I press my palm into his chest over his heart. "You might physically have the power to hurt others, but you don't have the heart to do it."

He shakes his head, his weight leaning into my touch. "For some reason, Ry, you somehow see something in me that no one else sees, even myself."

Pressing up on my toes, I wind my arms around his neck, bringing our bodies flush. "That's because I'm the only one who dares to look past the bulging muscles and frowning face and see you for who you really are," I murmur. "But you're wrong, Logan and Grayson see it." I give him a small, optimistic smile. "And with time, you'll see it too."

He reaches a hand up to brush a strand of hair away from my face before stroking his thumb along my cheek as he stares reverently into my eyes.

"I don't understand, though. If that all happened your senior year, then why were you kicked off Halston's football team last year?"

He sighs, pulling me closer until my cheek is pressed against his chest, and he rests his head on mine. "Because Melissa's family didn't like seeing me doing so well. When they saw me on the TV after our championship win, they contacted the school and tried to get me expelled. My father stepped in and got it reduced with a generous donation, so I was only kicked off the team." He huffs out an aggravated breath as he squeezes me tighter.

We stand there in silence, holding one another together as I process his words, trying to make sense of it all. I knew Royce wasn't capable of what those idiots in the library accused him of, but this... For all we know, that girl could have set him up!

Eventually, he sighs, loosening his hold on me, and when I step back, I find him frowning down at me. "I actually wanted to talk to you about something."

"Sounds ominous," I muse as I haul myself back onto the counter and retrieve my ice cream and spoon, sensing I'll need it for this conversation.

"I won't force you to do something you don't want to, but we haven't ever really talked about it—"

"You want me to tell Grayson," I interject before spooning the chocolatey goodness into my mouth.

"Yes," he answers, sighing.

I arch a brow at him. "You do remember that he tried to choke me to death the last time I tried to speak to him?"

Royce has the good grace to grimace. "I won't let him lay a finger on you."

My eyes narrow on him as I think. "Why are you suggesting this now?"

Looking away, he rubs at the back of his neck. "I don't want to betray his privacy, but after that day in the food court, I ran into him when I came to grab some things so I could stay at yours, and well... He's a mess."

Yeah, I'd noticed that for myself.

"Doesn't that just make him more unpredictable?"

Royce blows out a breath, and I tilt my head at him in confusion, curious as to what Grayson told him. I won't ask. I respect their friendship too much to put Royce in that position.

"He said something. A bunch of things, really... but I think he's starting to doubt his dad."

My eyebrows hit my hairline. "How? Why?" Why now? Why, after all this time, would Grayson suddenly be questioning his father?

Royce shakes his head, pinching the bridge of his nose before he exhales. "His Gran is sick—Alzheimer's. She's been saying things—not about you, but about his dad... It's got his head all messed up, but from the way he was talking, I think he'd be open to listening. If he knew about Aurora, it would confirm the doubts currently eating him alive."

Searching his face, the corners of my lips tilt up in a small smile. "You're a good friend, Royce."

Jumping down from the counter, he stands between my legs, taking the ice cream tub from my hands and setting it on the counter. I'm only wearing his t-shirt, so when his hands land on my outer thighs, I feel the intimate brush of skin against skin.

"I'm worried about Grayson, but if you tell me you don't want to tell him, Ry, I won't bring it up again. I swear. No matter what you choose to do, I'm on your side in all of this."

"But?"

"*But* is keeping her from him really the best thing for you? For her? What's your long-term plan here? For Grayson to never find out? Do you genuinely think that's achievable?"

Releasing a strained breath, I lean forward to rest my forehead against his shoulder, and he winds his arms around my waist, bringing the two of us chest to chest. "I don't know," I admit. "Before I discovered Grayson was also at Halston, I had no intention of ever telling him about her. But now... everything has gotten so complicated."

Royce coaxes my head from his shoulder, his fingers stroking my cheeks as I stare into his eyes. "I'm scared," I confess. "What if he still doesn't believe me? Or what if he tries to take her from me? I'm already fighting a battle with my mom. I can't take on one against him, either."

"He wouldn't," Royce states with confidence, one side of his lips quirking up. "You think me or Logan would let him do anything that would hurt either of you?"

My responding smile is small and fleeting.

"I know you've only known the worst of Grayson since you got here, but he wouldn't do that to you. To either of you," Royce promises. "I think if he knew, he'd want to help. It might help the two of you find some closure."

Shoulders dropping, I admit, "I don't know if there can ever be closure for me and Grayson."

Silence wraps around us as Royce pulls me in for a hug. "I'm not saying no," I mumble into his shoulder. "Give me a few days to think about it, and we should have this conversation with Logan and get his stance."

"Okay," Royce readily agrees, and when he pulls back, there's a wicked smile on his face and a predatory sparkle in his eyes. "We have a far more urgent matter to attend to, anyway."

"Oh, is that so?" My lips are already lifting in a smile. "And what might that be?"

"The fact that you can sit there without wincing means I haven't done a good enough job of destroying your pussy. That's a problem we need to rectify immediately."

I don't get a chance to respond as he tosses me over his shoulder, and I squeal when his hand smacks against my ass.

"The ice cream!" I call, remembering that we didn't put it back in the freezer.

"Forget the ice cream, James. I'd far rather watch you swallow my cock."

Ugh, me too.

RILEY

CHAPTER FORTY

Buzz, buzz. Buzz, buzz.

The noise pulls me from the best sleep I've had in years, and I hastily sit up, grabbing my phone and silencing the call before it can wake Royce.

Despite the tiredness tugging at me, I'm instantly awake when I see my mom's name flash on the caller ID of an incoming FaceTime call. *Holy crap, she's actually upholding her end.* When I didn't receive a call from her yesterday, I'd half convinced myself she wasn't going to follow through.

Sliding quietly from between the sheets, I glance over my shoulder at Royce's peacefully sleeping form before I grab his discarded t-shirt from the floor and hurriedly pull it on before slipping from his room.

I accept the call as I step away from his door, the phone screen coming to life as I descend the stairs and showing a freckle-faced, gap-toothed three-year-old grinning at me in a bright pink leotard. "Mommy!"

"Rora!" She waves manically at me as I tuck my feet beneath me on the sofa in the living room. Instantly, my day is made.

"Lyda said I could call you before I go to Mrs. Garcia's."

My teeth grind at the knowledge that the neighbor is babysitting my little girl today while my mom is off doing god knows what. The only thing that stops steam from pouring out my ears is hearing Rora's butchered version of my mom's name —because, god forbid, anyone hears her being referred to as *granny*.

"Guess what, Mommy? I saw a unicorn yesterday at the park!"

I put on my best-surprised face, unable to suppress my smile at having this moment with my daughter. It has been less than forty-eight hours since I last saw her, and I was already missing her. "You did?"

Aurora's head bobs so vigorously that I worry she's going to strain her neck. "Yes, Mommy, a big, sparkly, rainbow unicorn with wings. Just like the one on my wall!"

"Waw! That's incredible! Did you ask it for a ride?"

Another nod. "Yep, I did, but the unicorn said it was busy spinking magic dust on the fowers."

I chuckle lightheartedly. "Busy unicorn. Maybe you'll get that ride next time."

Her face scrunches into sheer determination that oddly reminds me of Grayson when he looks at me sometimes— except far less menacing and much more adorable. "Oh, I will, Mommy! Next time Mrs. Garcia takes me, I'm going to bring carrots!"

"Good thinking, baby. Unicorns love carrots."

A noise behind her has Aurora turning around, and I faintly hear my mother's sharp tone in the background.

"I gotta go, Mommy. Lily's picking me up."

"Okay, baby. Have fun at gymnastics, okay?"

"I will, Mommy. Love you."

"I love you too," I say with tears in my eyes. "To the moon and back."

She leans in and kisses the camera. "To the moon and back."

The camera swings away from her face as she works out how to hang up before the screen goes black, and alone, I sag against the couch cushions.

My heart clenches painfully, that relentless, gnawing grief that's always present, sharpening into a knife as the overwhelming sense of missing her threatens to tear me apart. Especially now with the threat of Bertram's release hanging over my head.

Tapping the screen, my phone lights up, and my eyes widen when I realize it's after midday. Logan will be home soon. He suggested grabbing lunch when he got back, and I have an assignment I need to finish that is due this week.

Squeak.

The creaking of a floorboard has my head snapping up as I turn to find Grayson standing in the doorway. Dark eyes bore into mine, his drawn expression inscrutable as he tilts his head, gaze assessing.

Fuck. I thought he was staying in the city this week. How long has he been standing there?

"Who were you just talking to?" His voice is carefully contained, and I can barely form a response over the chaotic *thumping* against my ribs.

Fuck. Fuck, fuck, fuck.

I know we talked last night about maybe telling Grayson, but even if I was entirely on board with Royce's idea, I wouldn't want him to find out like this.

He takes a calculated step forward, and I jump to my feet, feeling the need to gain as much height as possible before I stand off against him. The hem of Royce's t-shirt falls to my knees, making me self-conscious as I rake my eyes over every taut inch of his body.

"Riley." My name is a warning, one that has the desired effect as my brain snaps into action.

"My f-friend." I swallow back the anxiety compacting like a dam in the back of my throat. "She has a kid; she wanted to say hi before we hung up."

His nostrils flare, jaw pulsing, and a fresh wave of fear floods my body, making it near impossible to breathe.

"She called you Mommy."

Oh shit. Oh fuck. So much for hoping he rocked up right as I ended the call, and his hostile demeanor was because of my unexpected presence in *his* house.

Which he's not supposed to be staying in at the minute!

"You must have misheard," I force out in a rasp, voice trembling and betraying the lie as it slips from my tongue.

He's on me before I can process the heat of his hand wrapped around my throat, forcing my face up to his as he pushes me into the wall with his larger, more powerful body.

"Don't lie to me," he hisses, voice venomous.

I tremble, acutely aware of every point in which his body is pressed flush against mine. There's fear, naturally, but as I'm flooded with memories of the last time he was pressed against me like this, I realize it's not *only* fear that has every nerve in my body standing to attention.

I still remember the way his lips melted against mine. How he demanded control and fucking *owned* me in that field. In my bed.

I still have faint yellow bruising from his hickeys, and despite how inappropriate it is, my core clenches with the need to be filled by him.

It's probably fucked up the way my body responds to him.

Actually, there's no *probably* about it. It is *definitely* fucked up that I am lusting after this man who looks at me like I'm the destroyer of his world. The man who is my daughter's fucking *half-brother.*

Jesus, Riley. What the hell is wrong with you?

I stare defiantly back at Grayson, refusing to be cowered. Refusing to allow my guilt over breaking him makes me feel inferior. He has *deliberately* inflicted just as much hurt on me.

For the first time, *I* hold all the cards, and I'm no longer afraid of showing him my hand. Royce said that he's been doubting everything, and from what I've seen of him in recent weeks, Grayson is undoubtedly crumbling. Yet, despite whatever his Gran has said, he's still living in delusion-ville. Denying the hard facts even when they're shoved in his face.

Not anymore. This isn't how I wanted to do this, except I'm fucking done. He knows anyway, even if the look in his eyes begs for me to offer an alternative explanation.

The rest of us have to live in the real world. It's past time Grayson fucking joined us in it.

"You don't need me to spell it out for you, Grayson. You already know the truth. It's been staring you in the face for weeks now, and you've been too damn stubborn to see it."

"Tell me anyway." His words are barely coherent, nothing more than a shattered rasp. There's no anger. Only desperation. A plea— for me to give him irrefutable evidence or for me to give him an out?

"You mean you're finally ready to listen?" I taunt. "Or are you going to choke me as soon as I tell you what you don't want to hear?"

Nostrils flaring, his dark eyes drill into me. His hand around my throat doesn't so much as loosen.

Lips pursed, my body coiled tight as I dare to spill my truth for Grayson to hear—and I hope that he truly will listen this time.

Perhaps I expect him to cut me off immediately, but instead

of simply confirming Aurora is my daughter, I tell him everything. From the first night my door creaked open to the day that stick turned blue.

"Your father raped me. Repeatedly. In my bed, in your house. For months. On the nights when you were gone or out late. He hollowed me out until I was nothing but an empty shell, going about the motions yet never really alive. When I finally worked up the courage to tell my mom, she essentially told me to shut up and stop spreading lies. That's when I started self-harming. It was my only escape. It was the only time when I felt alive. The only bit of control I had over my life."

My voice begins to wobble, even though the need for him to hear every brutal detail, to feel this pain the way I do, has me forging on. "Eventually that stopped being enough. I was so done. I just wanted it to stop."

My voice breaks, and still, we remain locked in place. His wide eyes bore into mine. Anchoring me while simultaneously making me feel like we're lost at sea together. "I planned it all out," I tell him, confessing what I've never told another living soul. "I stole some of my mom's sleeping pills and I planned to slice my arteries open in the bathtub. Figured I'd bleed out or I'd drown. Either way, I won.

"Only, the week before I intended to do it, I started getting sick. Every morning, I'd roll out of bed and have to dash to the bathroom, and my breasts were tender all the time. I think I knew at that point, but I ignored it at first. Coughed it up to nerves. But on the day I was due to... I couldn't go through with it without making certain, so I bought three different pregnancy tests on my way home..." My breathing is shallow as I confess, "And all three of them were positive."

Grayson's eyes slam shut, excluding me from his inner turmoil as his chest expands with a shuddering breath. He's trapped in a war.

With himself.

With his father.

With me.

His fingers reflexively twitch against my skin, the urge to tighten his hold almost overwhelming as his hips jam against mine.

I suck in a gasp before a surprised laugh barks out of me, and instead of flattening myself against the wall like he probably expects, I slide my crotch along his.

"Even knowing the truth, you *still* have a hard-on for me."

"Shut up," he hisses, eyes snapping open and *blazing* with rampant emotions too raw and exposed for him to navigate.

His hand around my throat shakes with the restraint of holding himself back, and knowing I'm probably bringing about my own demise, I lift my chin and repeat the action, slowly dragging my clenching core along the thick rod of his erection.

He hisses in a breath, the chaotic maelstrom of emotions whirling within him, stuttering out one by one. I do it again, smirking when I discover he's even harder than he was before. His thick cock pumping with blood.

My head tilts to one side. "Huh."

His eyes narrow on me. "What?"

With another torturous drag of my pussy along his length, I muse aloud, "I'm wondering if your issues aren't so much to do with what you thought I did to your father, and more to do with the fact that, even believing I screwed over your family, you *still* wanted me—still *want* me."

With a snarl on his face, Grayson leans in. My heart thumps in anticipation as his warm breath dances over my skin, before the wet heat of his tongue scrapes along the column of my neck. Goosebumps erupt up my arms, shivers racing down my spine.

"You drive me in-fucking-sane."

My back arches when he wraps his lips around my ear, my words coming out huskier than I intend, "Right back atcha."

The dam breaks. Crumbles into rubble.

I'm not sure who makes the first move, but in the next second, my hands are beneath his shirt, nails digging into the muscles of his back as his fingers press into the skin of my upper thighs hard enough to leave bruises as he hauls them around his waist.

Our lips collide like opposing armies on a battlefield, a tumultuous clash for dominance that neither of us is willing to concede.

His shirt is torn from his body, without any recollection of whether I was the one to destroy it or him, and my top gets shoved up to my neck, baring me fully to him.

His hand comes to cup my pussy, a feral growl reverberating between his lips as he curls his fingers between my folds before sliding into me knuckle deep.

I groan, back arching and pressing my peaked nipples against his hard chest as I writhe on his fingers. I'm already halfway there when he pulls out, and I whimper at the loss. He chuckles arrogantly, the sound of his pants being ripped open echoing through the room before I feel his blunt head at my entrance.

He keeps us both on the edge as he brushes the tip up and down my slit, my heels digging into his ass and fingers leaving crescent-moon shapes in his shoulders.

Right as I'm about to snarl at him to hurry the fuck up, his eyes snap up, clashing with mine, and his grip on my hip turns painful as he slams into me to the hilt.

"*Ohmygod,*" I garble, all of my muscles locking as he pistons ferociously into me. Pain skims pleasure, sending me teetering on the edge of euphoria. My head falls back against the wall, eyes hooded as my hands roam Grayson's alabaster chest.

Shifting me in his grip, his new hold forces my knees up and farther apart, enabling him to hit deeper.

I whimper, babbling words that make no sense as our hips meet in a fierce collision of primal urgency. A ferocity born of frustration as much as attraction.

There is an undeniable urgency to our meeting. One that speaks of paths untraveled, futures that could have been, romances that were never had—if only life had played out differently for us.

"Grayson," I moan as that first spark shoots outward from my core.

"Right now," he grunts, eyes on mine filled with feral possession. "Come, right now."

As if my body is programmed to respond to him, that initial spark turns into a ripple. A rush. A crashing wave that *consumes* everything in its path as it washes over me, leaving only sweet, sweet bliss in its wake.

It's only as reality creeps back in, jarring me out of my high, that the complications of our situation seep in through the cracks.

"Is it at all possible to leave you two alone in a room together without you fucking her against the nearest hard surface?" A voice drawls from the doorway, and my cheeks flame crimson as I catch sight of a smirking Royce leaning against the doorframe wearing only a pair of gray sweats.

My hands fly out, shoving at Grayson's chest and forcing him to drop me as he steps away. I instantly regret that decision when our combined release slips out of me, running down my inner thigh, and I grimace.

"Here," Royce offers, holding out a roll of toilet paper, and I accept it with a muttered thanks, cleaning myself before darting out of the room to throw it away and take a moment to collect myself.

My bare feet are silent as I pad down the hall toward the living room, their murmured voices becoming clearer with every step.

"Surprised you didn't feel the need to rip me away from her this time," I hear Grayson drawl.

"Don't think I wouldn't have if I'd thought for one second she didn't want it."

There's a moment of silence where I wish I could see their faces before Grayson sighs. It's an exhausted, weary sound, as though he's been carrying the weight of the world on his shoulders for years and has grown inexplicably tired of it.

"I'm guessing you know."

"Know what?" Royce responds cryptically, tone giving nothing away. Ducking my head, I grin to myself. My burly protector.

"You know what I'm talking about, asshole."

"I think you should have this conversation with Riley—without your dick finding its way inside her."

"Har har."

"I'm serious, dickhead. The fact you're not losing your shit right now tells me that you either haven't fully processed what she told you, or you're not taking her seriously."

I can sense the escalating tension from out here, and before words can be said that can't be taken back, I make my presence known, stepping into the room, bright red face on display as I avoid both of their eyes.

"I need to use the bathroom," Grayson mumbles, clearing his throat before he leaves the room. Twisting the hem of Royce's top in my hand, I stare steadfastly at the floor even as I hear Royce approaching.

"James."

"Mmhmm?"

"James, look at me." At his soft, demanding tone, I steel my spine and lift my head. I expect to find judgment or anger in his, or at worst his typical icy mask. Instead, it's the same soft expression he wore when he was buried deep inside me, staring down at me as though I was the only person in the world who mattered.

His understanding throws me completely off-kilter. "Why aren't you angry at me?" I ask quietly.

"Why exactly would I be angry at you?"

I stare at him in bewilderment. "Because I just—" I wave my hand toward the wall he just found Grayson fucking me against. "And we—" Now my hand flaps stupidly between us, causing him to chuckle as he steps into me. One hand goes to the back of my neck, giving it a possessive squeeze, while the other brushes still-sweaty strands of hair back from my face.

He waits until I meet his stare. "You. Me. Logan. Grayson. That's the unit. No one else."

"But—" He must see the confusion written on my face.

"You and Logan are perfect for one another," he explains. "He makes you smile when you don't feel like it and brings a light to your dark days.

"You and Grayson have a complicated history, but there's no denying there's chemistry there. Maybe even feelings." Thankfully, it's not a question.

"And you and me?" I ask tentatively.

One side of his lips twists in a wry smile. "I'll be the shadow watching your back. The steady presence at your side."

Frowning, I ask, "What do I give you?"

Giving the back of my neck another squeeze, he steps even closer, eliminating any space between us. "The question is, what *don't* you give me? You provide me with a purpose, pull me out of my head when I spiral. You've given me a reason to trust again. You keep the darkness at bay, and on days when it threatens to overwhelm me, you simply sit in it with me. You don't judge. Don't ridicule or push. I can be myself around you —good qualities and the bad—which is something I haven't been able to say in a long time."

Leaning into him, I press onto my toes, wrapping my arms around his neck. "You give me all of those things, too."

He presses his lips to mine in a chaste kiss. "I have no issues with you being with Logan. Or with Grayson. Logan has no issues with you being with me, and without having talked to him about it, I know he has no issues with you being with Grayson. Grayson... well, he can go fuck himself if he has any complaints."

I snort, resting my forehead against his chest. "What happens now?"

"Now, you and Grayson need to have a *real* conversation."

I nod, my face rubbing against the soft fabric of his t-shirt. I know he's right. "He needs space first. Time to process."

Lifting my head, I stare into Royce's face. "I should go. Logan will be home soon. The three of you should talk. You're his friends, you should be there for him."

"What about you? Someone should be there for you too."

I shake my head. "I'm not the one who just had their life ripped out from beneath their feet. Despite putting it off, I've known for a while that this day would eventually come. I'm fine, honestly." Placing a hand on his chest, I finish, "Just be here for Grayson, please."

Wrapping his hand around mine, he nods. "I will, but I'm driving you home first."

I smile up at him before sliding past, heading up the stairs to get showered and dressed. I already know I'll be spending the rest of the day in the dance studio until Royce or Logan—but probably both after today—inevitably sneak into my bed later tonight to keep my nightmares at bay.

GRAYSON

CHAPTER FORTY-ONE

Under the guise of needing the bathroom, I slip from the room and sneak up the stairs. I need a moment to think. To breathe. To decompress.

Fucking hell. I came home figuring Logan would be back from his away game soon and hoping to talk to them both. To tell them everything. To admit that I know. That I believe Riley.

I've spent the last four days drinking myself stupid in my apartment in the city while I stared at Gran's lockbox of horrors, reliving that moment in the food court when Riley looked like she'd been slapped. Like *I'd* slapped her.

I can admit it to myself: After that, I believed her.

Jesus... how could I not?

The shit I found in Gran's box... that was just the vomit on top of the cake.

Now, today... *Fuck.* I didn't expect to find her in my living room on the phone to her daughter.

Mommy.

Fuck. I will never unhear that word.

Never forget the way it shuddered through me.

"Fuck," I roar, pulling on the ends of my hair until the pain is unbearable enough to distract me from the chaos unraveling inside me.

Wiping a hand down my face, I pace back and forth across my bedroom floor. Riley's words play on repeat in my head, a taunting melody that slices through me until I'm bleeding profusely.

It wasn't just that I finally listened to her. It wasn't even that she has a kid. It was... everything.

The self-harm.

The hollowness in her eyes.

The way she choked over the words.

The very raw pain I could feel emanating from her.

My stomach rolls dangerously, the stress of the last hour taking its toll. What the fuck am I meant to do with this knowledge? What is it supposed to change? Somehow, everything and nothing.

It all feels surreal. My *life* feels surreal. A nightmare I wish to God I could wake from.

A daughter.

One that is also my father's.

That has half of my DNA.

A fucking half-sister.

The sound of the front door slamming startles me from my thoughts, and when voices reach me from outside, I step over to the window, peering down as Riley and Royce step onto the sidewalk. She's saying something to him, her words too muffled through the pane of glass for me to hear, and as she steps around the far side of the truck, I catch a glimpse of her face as she smiles.

Fucking *smiles.* As though she didn't just obliterate my entire world. Except, hadn't it already crumbled to dust around me?

Gran's words have been tormenting me for weeks.

The not knowing if her fears and paranoia were born from reality or made-up memories.

Without anyone to talk to about it, my thoughts have been spinning precariously in my head without giving any sort of insight.

Taunting me.

Torturing me until I find myself stopping in my tracks any time I spot Riley on campus, watching her from afar as I struggle to piece it all together. Questioning everything. Questioning *her*. Questioning *myself*.

Then that sick little box destroyed any hope I had that Gran's accusations were an Alzheimer 's-driven paranoia.

The final nail in my coffin of naivety: Riley's confession.

All of it is true.

Every. Fucking. Thing.

If there was any denying it before, there sure as fuck isn't now.

The laugh that leaves me is wrought by someone who is slowly losing their fucking mind.

I collapse onto my bed, staring unblinkingly at the ceiling and too lost in my memories of back then to make out the white paint or still ceiling fan.

She said she'd been planning to... I swallow, the image of Riley lying dead in a bathtub of blood water, eyes glazed and sightless with her wrists slashed open, rocking me to my core. My stomach spasms so violently that, for a moment, I think I'm going to throw up.

Is that when she went to the police? Because she found out she was pregnant. Why didn't she come to me? It stings that she didn't, but equally, I know I'm being a hypocrite. Would I have believed her if she'd come to me teary-eyed and soul-weary instead of hearing the accusation from my father's lips?

Fuck, I can't even think of my father.

Closing my eyes, images of that little girl's face embed themselves behind my eyelids. I didn't get a good look at her, but I could hear the happiness radiating from her as she chatted to Riley. To—*fuck*—her Mom.

My teeth grind, boiling rage and wretched sorrow shredding me to pieces.

It was my only escape.

The only bit of control I had over my life.

I will never unhear those words. The way her voice broke over those syllables. The unending sadness in her eyes.

It slayed me to see, and it tears me open now to relive it.

I can question everything else, but there's no arguing with that. No faking that level of emotion. That despondency. The anguish and shattered pain.

The exact same breaking I saw in the food court that day.

It makes me wonder how I never saw it before, except I know why... because I was too chicken shit to properly *look*. Point blank refused to acknowledge it. It was easier to live inside my hatred for her—for what she'd done—than to admit there could be an alternative truth.

Even in my denial, she was spot-on with her accusation. From the moment I laid eyes on her in that club, I've *wanted* her. Even knowing who she was and what she'd done. I didn't care, because all those long-buried feelings I'd had for her so long ago came rushing forward with a newfound vengeance. A thirst to be buried between her thighs, to hear her pleasurable moans and the sound of my name on her lips as she comes.

It's easier to hate her. It's *always* been easier to hate her.

But that doesn't mean I don't *want* her.

Even now. Even just having had her.

I can still smell her scent on me. On my dick, which is already pumping with vigor. Sweet. Enticing. Juicy. *Salivating.*

I was convinced fucking her in that field—wild and uncontained—would get it—*her*—out of my system. Instead, it was the first bite into the poisoned apple. One taste, and I was hooked. Primed to come back for seconds. Thirds. Fourths. Fifths.

Will I ever get enough?

In the next instant, my hand is around my cock, which is still damp from the remnants of us. It only heightens my desire as I stroke along my length, remembering the feel of her pressed up against me. The fire in her eyes as she taunted me.

Even knowing the truth, you still have a hard-on for me.

Damn fucking right.

It was like my dick and my head were functioning on entirely different brain waves—still are.

My brain says everything is so fucked up. That I've caused her enough damage. That my *family* has inflicted enough pain.

Yet my dick is screaming *mine, mine, mine,* loudly and repeatedly until it infiltrates my senses, taking over every reasonable thought as I plunge into her.

What is it about this woman? No one else has ever gotten to me the way she does. She's drop-dead gorgeous, but good looks aren't enough to drive me this fucking insane. She's shy and reserved but also sassy and fierce. One moment, she'll be cowering beneath my anger, and the next, she'll be tossing me on my back with her own flames. I never know what I'm going to get with her. I love to hate her, and maybe... just maybe, I hate to love her, too.

I remain lost in my thoughts, processing everything, yet nothing at all. I hear Royce's truck coming down the road and parking outside. Hear the slam of his door as he gets out, followed by the sound of his key in the lock.

He bangs around downstairs for a bit before all falls quiet. I don't expect him to knock on my door or anything. That isn't

Royce's style. He'll leave me to brood until I'm ready to show my face. Thank god Logan isn't in the house, or he'd have followed me up here, talking non-stop about what an idiot I've been and how much groveling I will have to do if I want to be in Riley's good books.

Do I even want to be in her good books, though?

Is that somewhere I want to be?

I don't even fucking know.

Hours pass, spent staring at my ceiling. At some point, I heard Logan come home, the two of them probably talking downstairs.

I realize now that they both knew. That must have been what spooked Royce on Christmas Day. It explains why he was so bent out of shape that day in the food court.

With a bone-tired groan, I shove upright. Resting my elbows on my knees, I cover my face with my hands and take a moment to gather myself. I know I need to go down and talk to them. Before I can muster the courage myself, Logan's voice bellows up the stairs.

"Yo, fuckface! Stop being a chickenshit and get your ass down here!"

Rolling my eyes, I know there's nothing else for it as I push to my feet and exit the room. Each step is laden as I descend the stairs, following the sound of their voices into the kitchen.

Both of them turn to look at me as I step into the room and Logan smirks. "About time, asshole."

I'm not sure whether he's referring to me showing my face, Riley spilling her guts to me, or the grim acceptance probably etched into my solemn expression.

Royce shoves an ice-cold beer into my hand and gestures for me to sit at the island before he leans against the kitchen counter, watching me as I settle on the bar stool beside Logan.

It's nice having the three of us in the same room together

and not barking at one another, but I'm under no illusions that this is going to be a friendly discussion. There will be no apologies and friendship bracelets. Their priorities have forever changed... which I can now finally understand and grimly accept.

I take a sip of the bitter beer, the coolness barely touching the scorching heat tearing up my insides as I feel both of their stares on me.

"So everyone is Team Riley now that we all know about Aurora, yes?" Logan questions with absolutely zero tact.

"Aurora?" I croak.

"Riley's daughter," Royce supplies, as if I couldn't possibly piece that together for myself.

Jesus. Hearing her name aloud brings it home, and I nearly fall off my stool.

Is this real? I subtly pinch my inner arm to make sure I'm not actually passed out in my office after one too many whiskeys.

"Is this fucking real?" I say aloud when the pinch doesn't change my reality. Swiping my hand through my hair, I glance at Royce and practically beg for him to laugh and call April fools, even though it's only January.

When he only stares back at me, I drop my stare to the countertop, shaking my head. "How?" I ask no one in particular. "How is any of this real? She has a kid?" It still blows my mind. Except I saw it. I *heard it. Mommy.* "It's definitely my dad's?"

I feel a little sick even asking that question, what with Gran's words floating around in my head. *Another innocent girl got hurt.*

"Dude," Logan growls, that one word dripping with warning as he tenses beside me. "*She* is the spitting fucking image of you."

"He's right," Royce agrees more calmly, but a warning still

rings in his words. "Ask Riley to show you a picture. The second I laid eyes on her, I put the pieces together."

"If she's not your dad's, then she's yours," Logan says far too casually. "Either way, that kid has Van Doren DNA in her blood."

"Fucking hell," I rasp. Somehow, that knowledge has me struggling even more. That was the last wall standing in my way, the one thread I was clinging to that would make all of this not real.

I almost fucking wish she was mine. It would be an easier pill to swallow than the reality.

"You realize acknowledging this means accepting that your dad has been lying to you?" Royce says with an edge in his voice.

"No shit, Sherlock." I swipe a hand down my face, completely wrung out.

"I know you were struggling the other day when we talked," he hedges, waiting until I lift my head before he continues. "This is the proof you needed to see for yourself who your dad truly is. What he's capable of."

My bark of laughter is ice cold. "Thanks, but I didn't need the proof." I drop my head between my shoulders, and the room goes silent. I know they're waiting for me to explain, except I need a moment to gather myself before voicing it all aloud.

"I found a box in Gran's room at the nursing home," I begin thickly. "It had photos. A journal of my mom's." My jaw pulses, and I can't look at either of them. "My dad... he abused her. Beat the shit out of her. Sucked the life out of her."

"Jesus," Logan gasps.

Finding some inner strength, I lift my head and pierce Royce with a deadened stare. "You said earlier that I wasn't losing my shit because I hadn't fully processed what she told me or wasn't taking her seriously, but it was neither. I already knew." I shake my head. "I didn't need her proof. I... I never wanted this."

His features are etched in pain as he nods.

"Just when I think it can't get any worse..."

"That's... Fuck, that's..." Logan shakes his head, at a loss for words. "I'm sorry, man. I'm sorry you had to find that. That you had to learn all this about your dad. That you felt like you couldn't talk to us."

I lift my shoulders in a casual shrug. It is what it is, and I get it. I get why they were on Riley's side in all of this.

Taking a swig of my beer, the bitter liquid does jack shit to lessen the turmoil shredding my insides. I feel ill. Drained. Like I've just come off a four-day bender.

Pushing off the counter, Royce comes to lean his elbows on the opposite side of the breakfast bar, his expression drawn. "I'm sorry, Gray. And I'm sorry for asking this, but I need to know that you're done tormenting her. Either be there for her or stay out of her life. She's got enough other shit going on. She doesn't need to be the target of your baggage too."

"What do you mean she's got enough other shit going on?"

His stark stare burns into me, giving nothing away before he shakes his head. "I need to know if you're in or not, before I can say anything. 'Cause if you're not in, it's none of your business."

"And if I am?"

One side of his lips tilts in the smallest of smirks. "Then you better get yourself some knee pads 'cause you're going to be spending the next however long on your knees begging her to forgive your sorry ass."

I scoff, pulling back with a frown and taking a sip of my beer to hide my unease.

"So, what'll it be?" Logan pushes. "Are you Team Riley or Team Sad Sack All Alone In The Corner?"

Rolling my eyes, I search both of their faces as they wait for my answer.

"Yes, fine. I'm Team Riley. No more hating her. No more going after her."

"No more covering her in fucking bites," Logan snarls, and I smirk at the possession in his eyes.

"Can't promise that one. Riley certainly seemed to like it when she was coming all over my cock." Logan morphs into a Rottweiler in front of me, but before he can take me to the floor, Royce's arm snaps out, and he yanks Logan away.

"We have more important things to discuss," he barks. When Logan goes to argue, he glares at him. "Whatever happens between him and Riley is their business. Riley can handle him."

I scoff, even as Logan's eyes light up and he grins evilly. Shaking away Royce's hold, he settles back into his chair, looking smug as fuck. "I need to stock up on popcorn. This is going to be one hell of a show."

I roll my eyes, giving him my middle finger. I am not a fucking groveler and I haven't even decided if I want anything to do with her, let alone earn any fucking forgiveness.

Although even as I think that, a begrudging respect for everything she's endured takes root inside me. The grit, determination, and resilience it must have taken to put down that blade and choose to stand up and fight. To go up against my father. Against her mother. Against me.

That day, she took up the battle cry, and she's been screaming it ever since.

"There's something else we need to talk about." The ominous edge to Royce's tone interrupts my internal musings, and I focus back on him, clutching his mostly full beer bottle between his hands as he glances between me and Logan. "I went to Ry's mom's house."

"You what?!" Logan splutters, hacking up half a lung as he chokes on his spit. I slap him on the back—hard.

He gives an unapologetic shrug. "I wanted to check her out."

Of course, he did.

Intrigued, Logan leans forward. "And? Was she in? Was Aurora there? Wait... When did you do this?"

"The other week. The house was empty. Aurora was at a neighbor's and the mom was out for the night."

Logan sneers. "I fucking hate that bitch." He sounds practically venomous, and I stare at him with raised eyebrows. Logan rarely has a bad word to say about anyone, yet it's clear that he has a lot of bottled-up resentment toward Riley's mom.

"Tell us how you really feel," I drawl, earning a sharp glare from him.

"That woman is a bitch. I don't give a shit what you think you remember from when they lived with you and your dad. She's a bitch. She's been keeping Aurora from Riley. Using that kid to control and manipulate her own daughter. Riley has to fight to see her once a month and barely gets to speak to her in between visits. I've got my lawyers involved, but they say it'll be a lengthy process for Riley to regain custody."

"She doesn't have custody of her own child?" I question, thoroughly confused. Although, I guess that explains why I've never seen any indication of a daughter. Even in her apartment, there were no signs of a child being present.

"Her mother had her declared unfit after she gave birth, then shipped Riley off to a school for troubled teenagers where she couldn't even be around her own kid."

That does sound fucked up.

"Maybe she was unfit?" I supply. I mean, after everything she'd been through, it would be understandable.

Logan scoffs in derision, like I just told him hockey was a stupid sport.

"Riley would do *anything* for that little girl, and the way her mother is keeping her from her is disgusting."

I can't exactly argue with that, and Logan looks like he'd be ready to flatten me if I even tried.

"You were breaking and entering," I say instead, focusing on Royce.

"It was weird," he says with a frown, eyes on the beer bottle in his hand. "Aurora's bedroom had been painted with care and love—a perfect bedroom for a little girl—but there were no pictures anywhere."

"What do you mean?" I question, brows furrowed.

"I mean, if you couldn't see your mom every day, wouldn't you have photos of her all over your room? Wouldn't Riley want to know that her daughter can see pictures of her at any time, know that her mom is with her in spirit, watching over her while she sleeps? Instead, any mementos of their time together were tucked away in a box as though they had to be kept hidden."

"Dad removed any photos of Mom after she passed away," I muse aloud. "Wouldn't let me hold on to any keepsakes of hers. Said it was unhealthy to form such attachments."

"Yeah, but Riley isn't dead," Logan bluntly points out, before acknowledging Royce's comment. "That's definitely weird."

"Right?"

I agree, but I'm guessing that's not the reason Royce brought up the topic.

"What else did you find?" I ask, moving on from the topic of bare walls.

Royce rubs at the back of his neck, brows pinched. "I went through her laptop and found an ad she'd put on Craigslist." He pulls his phone from his pocket, tapping at the screen before sliding it our way. Logan and I nearly bump heads in our eagerness to see the screen.

"Person seeking key that unlocks hidden knowledge, where shadows whisper secrets and truth lies veiled?" Logan reads. "What the hell does that mean?"

Royce shrugs, seeming as baffled as Logan. "No idea." Pulling the phone from Logan's hand, I re-read the cryptic message again. "But I, uh, responded."

"You did *what*?" Logan exclaims. "What did you say? What's even the appropriate response to something like that?"

With another shrug, Royce says, "I told her I had the key."

"The key to what, though?" Logan questions, as though one of us will suddenly have the answer to that when we didn't a minute ago.

"Did she get back to you?" I interject before Logan can start spouting off a list of euphemisms for *key*.

"Yeah. I woke up to a message from her this morning."

"And?" Logan.

Pulling up a new message thread, he hands it over, and I note an address somewhere in Springview.

"That's tomorrow," I point out.

A moment of silence settles over us.

"What if it's some weird sex thing?" Logan interjects, making me want to smack him over the head. "No, seriously," he continues at the dark glower on Royce's face. "What if key means like *giant, magical penis,* and hidden knowledge is a euphemism for *mind-blowing orgasm?*"

"Do shadows whisper secrets and unveil truths while you're nutting into a sock?" Royce drawls.

Logan's face scrunches. "Well, no, but maybe it's different for women."

I snort. "I don't think it's that different."

Logan merely shrugs. "Well then, what does it mean?"

"Where shadows whisper secrets and truth lies veiled," I murmur, mulling it over as my eyes scan the sentence for the dozenth time. "Sounds like she's looking for information on accessing somewhere where, maybe, secrets are held?"

"Like a safe or a vault?" Logan supplies.

I shake my head. "I don't think so."

"I'd guess whatever it is is illegal or dodgy as fuck at best," Royce states, and I have to say, I agree. The cryptic nature of it all would imply as much.

"Do you think it has anything to do with Riley or Aurora?" Logan questions, brows pinched.

"No idea, but even if it's unrelated, I plan on using it to get Aurora away from her."

Logan nods thoughtfully. "If it helps us protect Aurora, then I'm in."

I glance between them, getting the sense that I'm missing something. "Why does Aurora need protecting?"

Logan scoffs. "You mean other than the fact her caretaker is a narcissistic bitch?"

I merely arch a brow and wait.

"Your dad, obviously."

"You think my dad will go after Aurora when he's released? Does he even know she exists?"

"We dunno," Logan answers, "But, Grayson, your dad..."

His eyes slide to Royce, who finishes, "He's been sending Riley cards from prison."

That hits me like a slap to the face, and I gape at him. "He's what? Are you sure?" That doesn't make any sense to me. "Other than when he was first incarcerated, he's never even mentioned Riley. And he's certainly never said anything about Aurora."

"I'm sure. We saw them."

"Creepy shit, too," Logan interjects. "The sort of fucked up shit that looks perfectly decent on the surface, but when you look deeper, it's just crawling with ick."

Reeling, I slump further into my stool. It's a struggle to hold myself upright with all these revelations. I'm not entirely sure I'll be able to handle any more.

Perhaps sensing I'm on the verge of slipping beneath the surface, Royce brings the conversation back on track. "Let's just see what Lydia has to say tomorrow and go from there."

Logan nods in agreement. "Okay, so we go tomorrow night and find out what she's after. And if it has anything to do with Riley and Aurora."

"I'm going alone," Royce states, tone brokering no argument.

"Like hell, you are." Logan levels him with a flat stare.

Casting a side-eye my way before sliding his gaze back to Logan, Royce says, "Gray can't come with me in case she recognizes him, and you need to stay here with Riley."

Eyes slightly widened, his stare drills into Logan in a wordless conversation.

Jesus Christ, what now? "Why does he have to stay with Riley?" I question, interest piqued, but mostly, I'm just exhausted and hoping this isn't one more horrific thing that's going to make me feel like shit. I mean, surely, she will be fine by herself for one night?

Their gazes remain locked for another moment before Logan relents, sighing. "You're right. It'll be late before you're back. We can't leave her alone."

"Why can't you leave her alone?" There's an apprehensive edge to my voice, and I can sense it, another dark revelation I'm not mentally prepared for.

The two of them share a look I can't decipher before Royce says to me, "Riley is having nightmares."

I stiffen, reading between the lines. *Because I threw my dad's release in her face and probably made her life a hundred times worse.*

My gaze drops to the table, ashamed, and I swallow.

"She was fucked up after that," Logan says softly, and I know he doesn't intend for his words to slay, but fuck, they do. "She'd probably murder me for telling you this. However, fuck, I think you should know, just so you can understand that Riley puts on a tough front, but she's only human, and well, the news of your dad... it broke her." Logan's voice catches before he clears his throat, and I still can't look up from the countertop. "We found her in the shower, after... attempting to harm herself." His sigh is heavy. "I've never seen her look so... lost. It's like she wasn't even there. Her body was, but her mind, her spirit, her *soul*, had fled the building."

A rushing silence swoops in on the trail of his words, clogging my throat and paralyzing my tongue.

After a moment, Royce clears his throat. "So, I'll go to the meet tomorrow. Grayson will stay here, and you'll stay with Riley."

"No way, I'm coming with you," I argue before they can agree to anything else. I'm done being out of the loop, sitting on the sidelines. I'm a fucking mess, and I know I haven't fully processed any of this—hell, I'm probably in a state of shock right now, but I'm fucking in. Whatever it is, from now on I want in on it. "I'll stay in the car, out of sight. It'll be dark, and you can park a bit away so she doesn't see me."

Royce mulls it over, eyes scouring my face. He must see that I'm not going to back down. No matter what happens, I can't keep burying my head in the sand and pretending none of this is an issue directly affecting me.

"Alright," he eventually agrees. "We'll go meet Lydia, and Logan will keep our girl company."

His eyes are on Logan and I know he means *their* girl, but fuck if I don't include myself in the sentiment too, and in the sea of chaos, that notion brings a little bit of calm.

RILEY

Pulling my slouchy sweater over my shoulder, even though it falls off not a moment later, I adjust the bag on my back as I stride down the street toward my apartment. Despite the bitter wind, sweat clings to my scalp as I pull my hair from the elastic band and shake it out.

After Logan left for an early morning practice, I changed and headed to the dance studio, where I barely stopped to gulp down a few sips of water for the last several hours. The burning need to push all the uncontrollable emotions out from under my skin had me spinning, dipping, and weaving across the room, even after my legs started to shake and my breathing grew heavy.

I'd like to say it had nothing to do with the fact there are now eighty-four days until Bertram's release, but it does.

That and my confrontation with Grayson.

And the fact I had sex with him *again*.

Seriously, when am I going to learn? That man might be fantastic for my pussy, but he is *bad* for my brain. I can't keep allowing him to press me up against the nearest hard surface whenever he has issues expressing his emotions.

I don't even know what comes over me whenever he's around. My brain completely turns off when he pins me in place with that molten gaze. It's ridiculous.

Lost in my thoughts, I fail to notice the fancy-as-hell car parked along the curb just down from my apartment, and I'm already fishing out my keys by the time I hear my name being called.

Turning around, a casually dressed Grayson rounds the front of an ostentatious black car and steps onto the sidewalk.

"Grayson?" My eyes dart around him, expecting to see Royce or Logan with him, but it appears as though he's alone, which instantly has me on alert. "What are you doing here?" I ask as he steadily approaches.

I haven't seen him since yesterday when I blurted out every traumatic drop of my past. He looks like he hasn't slept, with dark rings under his eyes, but he's freshly showered and appears more pieced together than in recent weeks. Less... tortured somehow?

He stops a couple of feet in front of me, eyes dropping down my body before flicking to the door of my apartment building. "I, uh, was hoping we could talk?"

"Talk?" I parrot.

He nods, appearing uneasy as he shifts on his feet. "About... *things.* Maybe, inside?" When I simply blink at him, he points at my building.

Inside. He wants to go inside... my apartment? "Oh. Erm... Yeah, okay, I guess."

I stare at him for a moment longer before forcing my legs into action and turning to walk toward the building. I hear him behind me, his proximity causing the keys in my hand to jangle as I go to insert the key into the lock.

It's not fear that has me so shaken. Honestly, I'm not sure

what it is. Anxiety? Apprehension? The not knowing—not knowing where we go from here or if this changes anything for him.

My hand jolts as the key hits the lock and drops to the ground. Grayson swoops in before I can, picking them up. "I've got it," he murmurs, successfully unlocking the door and pushing it open for me to enter.

He trails behind, still holding my keys as he follows me up the three flights of stairs to my apartment, and I step aside when we reach my door so he can unlock it.

At the *snick* of the lock, he looks my way before pressing down on the handle and pushing open the door, gesturing with his arm for me to go ahead.

Sucking on my bottom lip, I nervously step into my apartment, sensing him at my back. Standing awkwardly in the middle of my small space, I watch as his eyes roam the open-plan kitchen-living area, taking in the shabby furniture and outdated walls. He takes note of the tiny home comforts I've added, like the blanket Logan bought me and cushions I found in a charity shop, the pile of books on the coffee table, and the scented candle on the windowsill, as though he didn't crash on my sofa only a week ago.

God, how was that only last week? So much has happened since then. Every bit of stable ground I'd worked so hard to achieve feels like it's come apart beneath my feet.

"Do you mind if I, uh, shower first?" I ask, plucking at my sweater, the strap of my leotard visible through the oversized neck hole. Sure, I want to wash the sweat off my body, but mostly, I need a minute to prepare myself. Interacting with Grayson is always a violent battle and I need a moment alone to gather my armor.

The sound of my voice draws his attention and he slowly

turns to face me, gaze cascading down my body like rainwater. "No," he answers, voice lower than it was before. "That's fine. I'll... be here."

I stand there a moment longer as he turns away, grabbing one of my books off the pile and sinking onto my old, worn sofa as he flicks through the pages. The way he's lounging, he looks so at home. It's a weird juxtaposition, and unable to wrap my head around it, I turn and head for the shower.

Half an hour later, I'm freshly showered, my damp hair in a messy bun on the top of my head as I walk into the kitchen wearing a pair of old sweatpants and a hoodie Logan left behind.

I stop two feet through the doorway, staring at where Grayson is standing, gazing down at a photo frame in his hand. "She looks exactly like I did at that age," he says without looking up, voice hoarse.

I pad across the floor in my socks, and he tilts the photo frame toward me. Then I smile as I look down at a photo of Aurora wearing a bright pink princess dress, complete with a tiara. I remember that day like it was yesterday. I spotted the dress in a shop window on my way home from work last summer. It was only a couple of weeks before I was due to leave for Halston, and I was spoiling her rotten to ease my anxiety about abandoning her again.

We had a princess tea party, and she got dressed up in the dress and crown, filling the other seats at her small table with her teddies before putting on a Disney movie and cuddling on the sofa until she fell asleep.

I only have a few photos dotted around the place of her or

the two of us. Most of them are on my phone, which I unlock and navigate to my Aurora album before handing the device over for Grayson to swipe through.

Minutes tick by, the air so thick it makes it impossible for me to get oxygen into my lungs. The room is deathly silent as Grayson swipes through photo after photo until he reaches the ones of Aurora as a baby. I don't have many of them. I was rarely allowed to see her, and we weren't permitted cell phones at Breakthrough Academy. Plus, getting my mom to send me any physical pictures was next to impossible.

Unable to stand the silence any longer, I begin talking. Rambling, more like. "Her name's Aurora. She's three—four next month. Her favorite colors are pink and purple. She claims she can't pick between them and will throw the world's biggest temper tantrum if you try to make her. She loves Disney movies and Paw Patrol. Right now, she's really into gymnastics, and last Christmas she asked Santa to bring her a big brother."

Grayson's head snaps up, his eyes shining with unshed emotion as they bounce back and forth between mine. "She doesn't know about you," I tack on. "It was too complicated to explain. She has just always wanted a big brother. For whatever reason, she thinks it would be the best thing ever—she says a younger brother would be a baby and he wouldn't listen to her, and for some reason, she believes an older one would happily play dress up and attend teddy bear tea parties with her."

Grayson merely blinks at me, and for a moment, I worry I've broken his brain. I wouldn't be altogether surprised if I had.

"Shouldn't she want a sister to do that with?" he eventually croaks.

I chuckle half-heartedly. "You'd think so, especially given what a girly girl she is, but nope, she's only ever wanted a brother."

His throat works as he swallows, the bob drawing my eyes as he slowly turns back to the photo staring back at him from my phone.

"I don't know what to make of all of this," he admits, the honesty catching me by surprise. Frankly, I was anticipating a lot more yelling. Blatant denial. Accusations being thrown, and cutting remarks lobbed like sharp blades.

Shock. He must be in shock. It's only reasonable and explains this uncannily agreeable side to him I'm witnessing.

His head slowly cants toward me, and I can feel his eyes perusing my face as I continue to look at Aurora's cheesy smile. "You're not the first woman he's hurt," he confesses so quietly that I almost wonder if I misheard him.

Stunned, I lift my eyes to his, catching the inner turmoil churning in their depths. Pain. Confusion. Hurt. Remorse. It's all there to see.

"My mom," he explains, seeing the question written on my face.

Fuck.

If that's the case, no wonder he's a mess. How long has he known that? He can't surely have thought that when he convinced Royce and Logan to go along with his half-baked kidnap plan, which means something new has come to light that has him suspecting...

Is that what Royce was alluding to? What his Gran has been implying in her sick state? I have so many questions, but I don't dare voice them, not wanting to break whatever fragile tendril of hope is currently stretching between us.

"I'm sorry," is all I whisper instead.

His gaze drops to the floor, his Adam's apple bobbing as he nods before clearing his throat, standing taller as he regains his composure. Awkward silence reigns. I guess this is usually where we end up fucking one another, but there's no sizzling chemistry in the air to distract us today. Only scraped raw emotions.

"The food court that day," he begins, unable to look at me. "I shouldn't have told you like that."

Swallowing around the lump of emotion in my throat, I tell him, "I doubt it would have mattered how the news was delivered."

He finally looks at me, his stark gaze skating over my face. It's jarring not to see it pinched in anger. For those dark hues not to be spitting fire. He both resembles the Grayson from my past and yet looks nothing like him. He's older. Hardened, though somehow still the same.

"I also wanted to give you this," he says, pulling a piece of folded paper from his back pocket and holding it out to me.

I glance between it and him before taking it. Unfolding the page, it takes me a minute to realize I'm looking at test results.

"You already told me you were clean," I murmur, forcing my eyes from the page to look at him.

He gives a too-stiff shrug. "I haven't given you a reason to take me at my word." I'd gotten tested after winter break, however it doesn't mean I don't appreciate his sentiment.

"I have the implant," I supply. "In case you were worried."

Eyes searing into mine, he simply nods, the silence stretching between us.

"I should go," he says eventually.

"Okay."

God, I sound like an idiot, I internally groan, biting back any more stupid retorts I might blurt as he sets the photo frame down and heads for the door.

Opening it, he pauses on the threshold, looking back at me over his shoulder. For a moment, I think he's going to say something, but he gives a slight shake of his head before walking out, closing the door, and leaving me alone.

Well, that could have gone a lot worse.

At least we didn't hate fuck each other this time. That's gotta count as a win, right?

Hot Shot
HUSKIES

RILEY

CHAPTER FORTY-THREE

"Ugh, I'm so full," I moan as we leave the restaurant. Logan insisted on taking me out on a date night, and I have to say, it's been perfect. "That was delicious, but now I need to go home and nurse my food baby."

Logan chuckles, draping his arm over me. "No can do, Shortcake. The date isn't over yet, and I have somewhere I want to take you."

"Is that so?" I tease, grin blooming. It amazes me how easily he lifts my spirits. I was surprisingly relaxed after spending my morning in the dance studio and chatting with Grayson. Something about our conversation felt cathartic—or perhaps it's the knowledge that he now knows everything. That he seems to believe me, or at least, he isn't calling me a manipulative liar. *Small wins.*

Still, being out with Logan tonight... bathing in his lightness that casts everything else in shadow. It's exactly what I needed.

"Yup." The way Logan looks at me... somehow makes me feel like a teenager going on her first date whenever I'm around him. I feel like I'm getting all the typical *teen crush* hormones that I never experienced when I was at school.

And I'm not complaining one little bit.

I'm relishing every blissfully ordinary moment. Even with everything that's going on, for the first time in my life, I don't feel irreparably broken. When I'm around Logan, it doesn't feel as though my past is clinging to me like an unwanted ghost. There are no chains shackled around my ankles.

Logan makes me feel free. Fresh. Untarnished.

"So, where are we going?" I ask once we're in his car.

"You'll see," he responds cryptically, giving me one of his cheeky, up-to-no-good grins.

"So long as this isn't another kidnap attempt," I half-tease.

"Next time I kidnap you, Shortcake, it'll be to hide you away in a remote cabin, just the two of us."

"Mmm, that sounds much more pleasant. And what exactly would we get up to in this remote cabin of yours?"

Flicking his gaze my way, he levels me with a dark, hungry stare, his intentions crystal clear. I struggle to swallow around my suddenly dry throat, and it's an effort to keep my voice neutral as I say, "Board games?"

His laugh is light and musical, soothing my soul in a way no other sound can. "Sure, baby. *Board games.*"

I'm grinning by the time he pulls through a set of gates, and I arch a brow. "Don't you spend enough time on this campus?" I tease. "You really want to spend the time you're not in class or training here, too? If you're not careful, Logan, you'll get your-self branded a nerd."

"Someone's feeling bratty tonight," he retorts with a heat in his gaze. Bypassing the student parking lot, Logan continues driving us around the campus edge toward the sports stadium.

"Is there a training session tonight?" I question, assuming that's why he's brought me here.

"Not exactly," is his only response, and I stare at him in confusion as he parks the car and gets out. He's pulling a duffel bag from the trunk as I step out, swinging it over his shoulder before taking my hand and leading me toward a back entrance into the stadium.

I take in the long, gray hallways lined with jerseys and photos of previous years' teams, only pulling my focus when I hear the unmistakable sound of children laughing up ahead.

Glancing at him from the corner of my eye, Logan grins knowingly but still doesn't say a word as the hallway opens into a tunnel, spitting us out beside the ice rink.

Children are laughing and playing, bundled up in layers of clothing as they chase one another on the ice, while others are sitting in the stands, their parents helping them into their skates. Peals of laughter ring out around the otherwise empty stadium, and with wide eyes, I spin to look at Logan, finding him staring out over the rink with a softness in his eyes I've only ever seen when he looks at me.

"What is this?" I ask, my voice low so it doesn't carry.

Tearing his gaze from our surroundings, he looks down at me with that same softness. "Hot Shot Huskies," he states proudly.

Brows furrowed, my eyes bounce over his face, then out over the rink. "You teach hockey to kids?" I ask, unable to believe what my eyes are seeing.

"Wouldn't be fair of me to keep all this talent to myself," he says cockily.

I laugh, the sound loud enough to draw the attention of some of the kids nearby.

"Logan!" one little boy yells, wobbling in his skates as he moves to the side of the rink. He looks as if he can't be more than eight or nine, and casting my eyes over some of the others, I notice there's quite a variation in ages. A couple of kids look like they're the same age as Aurora, while most appear to be the same age as the child currently looking at Logan like he hung the moon. Still, a couple seem older—ten or eleven, perhaps.

"Hey, J, my man," Logan greets. "You been practicing your crossovers?"

"You know it! Wait til you see, I'll be as fast as the Flash," he says with all the arrogance of a child.

Logan chuckles, and spotting me for the first time, the kid shifts his attention my way, head tilting slightly. I give him a self-conscious wave.

"Who's that?" he bluntly asks.

Throwing his arm over my shoulder, Logan pulls me into his side before proudly stating, "This is my girlfriend, Riley."

Everything inside me melts at those words, and I momentarily forget about the cute little dark-haired kid watching us with a look of distaste as my eyes snap to Logan's. Unfazed, he grins down at me, knowing damn well the effect his admission will have had.

The stadium falls away around us as I stare into his chestnut hues, shining with pride and warmth and all sorts of soft emotions that I've never felt directed at me before.

"Eww," the kid interrupts, causing Logan and I to snap out of our trance. "Girls have cooties."

I chuckle, and Logan grins knowingly. "I'll remind you of that in five years, bud. You ready to show me these mad skills of yours?"

The kid nods, and it's only when he pushes away from the side of the rink, spinning in his skates, that I notice he's wearing a *Hot Shot Huskies* jersey, complete with a husky puppy and the name *Furlong* printed across the back.

Well, fuck, if that isn't the cutest thing I've ever seen!

"Sorry we're late," a familiar voice calls behind me, and I turn in time to see Ava and Isabella running toward us.

"Don't worry," Logan reassures. "I still need to put my skates on too. Do you need help getting Izzy booted up?"

Ava shakes her head. "I think I've gotten the hang of it now."

"Cool," Logan says before switching his focus to Izzy. "What are we thinking tonight, Izzy? Think we can skate *and* hold the stick?"

Isabella's head bounces up and down with determination. "Yup."

Logan's face lights up. "That's what I wanna hear. Alright, I gotta get my skates on. Ice in five minutes," he calls loud enough for everyone else to hear. "Sit with Ava, and I'll catch you in a bit, Shortcake," he murmurs, pressing a kiss to my temple before sauntering off to chat with the other parents and putting on his skates.

Dumbstruck, I watch as Ava pulls a pair of child-sized skates out of a bag and gets Isabella into them, and when Logan calls for everyone to get on the ice, she helps her walk over to the rink and step onto it. Logan is right there, though, ensuring she's okay.

"I'm so confused," I admit when Ava comes to stand beside me.

Chuckling, she grabs my arm and pulls me down onto the bench as we watch the kids warm up. I notice that coats have been shrugged off, and everyone is wearing the same jersey, with their last names printed across the back, including Isabella.

"How did you know about this?" I ask Ava as we watch the kids skate around the rink, working on various exercises depending on their age and experience.

"Logan stopped by the studio the day after we went to his game. Mentioned this kids club and asked if Isabella would be interested in joining. She loves it. Even had me taking her to the rink out of town to practice in between sessions. It's incredible, Riley. Covers everything, including the costs of the jerseys and skates. I haven't had to pay a penny."

I turn to look at her with wide eyes. "I know," she says, chuckling. "Finding free activities for kids in this town is impossible, but Logan explained that the whole point of Hot Shot Huskies is to ensure everyone has an equal opportunity to participate in sports."

"That's... Wow," is all I can think of to say as I watch the sweetest man I've ever met move from group to group, correcting stances and doling out advice.

Ava nudges my shoulder. "He's a good one."

"I know," I tell her, unable to take my eyes off my man.

We observe from the sidelines for the next hour as Logan teaches the children. I barely blink as I watch him adapt his teaching style to each child, pushing while simultaneously encouraging and supporting them.

In the final half hour, they break into two teams—one side donning bright yellow bibs over their jerseys—and play a friendly game. Again, I notice how he evenly splits the teams, ensuring there are younger kids on each side. He places them in positions where they are away from the brunt of the action and less likely to get hurt while simultaneously shouting for the older kids to give the game their all.

I barely feel the cold around me, so captivated with seeing Logan in this role and occasionally fantasizing about him teaching Aurora how to skate and play hockey. *FYI, the image has my ovaries nearly exploding.*

I'm still gaping in shock at the ice when the session comes to an end. "Did you see me, Mommy?" Isabella yells as she comes running toward us with her skates still on.

"I did, baby. You were so good!" Ava sets her daughter on the bench beside us, undoing her skates and putting them away while Isabella regales us with everything that happened as if we weren't watching every minute.

"Well, I'd better get her home," Ava tells me when they're packed up. "Girls' night soon?"

"Definitely," I agree, hugging her and saying goodbye to Isabella before they disappear. The other parents are in a hurry to get their kids home for bath and bedtime too, rushing out the door with thrown goodbyes and thank yous.

When we're alone, Logan stalks toward me, his skates banging against the hard floor as he holds a second pair out for me.

"What do you say, Shortcake?"

I laugh, even as I stretch my hand out to accept the skates. "As long as you're prepared to catch me. I'm fairly certain most of those kids can skate better than I can."

He holds on to the skates even after I've grabbed them, and I glance up at him. "You fall; I fall, Shortcake."

There's so much meaning behind his words. It goes way beyond a simple skating session, and all I can do is gaze at him until he releases the skates and breaks eye contact. Then I bend to put them on and lace them up.

Clinging to Logan's firm arm, I step onto the ice like a newborn foal testing its legs for the first time. Logan laughs as I flap my arms, my body twisting like a noodle as I struggle to maintain my balance.

"Shut up," I laugh, hitting him pathetically in the chest. The move sends me off balance, and I waver, arms spinning until he grabs a hold of them, holding me upright and on my feet.

My fingers dig into the soft fabric of his Huskies hoodie as he slowly skates backward, and I allow him to lead me further out onto the ice. He looks so at home, moving in his skates as though they are merely extensions of his feet, and I can't help but relax as I stare up into his languid smile, his features void of creases and furrows.

After we've circled the rink a few times, he loosens his grip but remains close as I skate on my own.

"You're a natural," he says, seconds before my blade hits a wedge on the ice and I nearly fall flat on my face. Logan's fingers clasping the back of my jacket are the only thing that saves me from eating ice. "Maybe I said that a little too prematurely," he mutters, making me laugh.

"Give me a sec. It's been years since I was on the ice. Not all of us can so easily adapt to balancing on sharp blades attached to the bottom of our feet."

He holds his hands up before he shoots past me, showing off now as he spins to face me, skating backward at a pace I wouldn't dare test. The asshole proceeds to literally spin circles around me as I find my feet until I can skate confidently around the rink.

"Tell me about Hot Shot Huskies," I prod after his latest adrenaline burst, which had him racing around the perimeter of the rink like the ice was melting beneath his feet. Slowing his pace, he matches my tortoise crawl. "How long have you been teaching them?"

He shrugs casually, but I notice a glint in his eye when I dare to glance his way. "Since freshman year. They're a good group of kids. They all come from families who otherwise couldn't afford for their children to learn to skate or play hockey. It's an expensive sport..."

"... and this program covers the cost of their equipment," I voice aloud what Ava told me. "Their skates, the jerseys they were wearing, their sticks."

He nods. "And the lessons are free."

I gape at him. "You donate your time?"

He gives another too-casual shrug. "Seems like the least I can do to give back."

If possible, my heart swells with affection for this man who gives so much of himself and asks for nothing in return.

"I'm surprised Halston doesn't advertise it more. Use programs like this for PR."

Something passes over his face, too fast for me to decipher. "They probably would... if they knew."

I puzzle over that, brows furrowing until pieces start to make sense. "Logan," I gasp in awe as my arm snaps out to grasp a hold of his. "Is this... *your* program? Did you set it up?"

He doesn't verbally answer, but his eyes drop to mine, shining with so much emotion that it's an answer all on its own. "You did," I murmur in astonishment. "Holy shit, Logan." I've never seen him look as bashful as he does now, and I can't stop watching him. "You set up a program all on your own to help disadvantaged families have the same opportunities when it comes to hockey as those with money. You've given those kids a chance to achieve something they otherwise never would have. You've helped those parents make dreams and wishes come true."

One shoulder lifts in a shrug that carries too much emotion. "I'm just teaching them hockey."

I dig my heels into the ice, squeezing his arms as hard as I can. "You know damn well you're doing more than that. You're making a difference in their lives. Those children love you. They love being on the ice, learning the game. *You* gave them that."

"Coach helped. He okayed using the stadium." I narrow my eyes in a stern glare that makes him chuckle. "But okay, yes, I set up the rest. I donated the funds, bought the gear, and got Royce to design the jerseys. I started the program, giving up my time each week to teach them—although some of the other guys help out occasionally, too."

Tugging on his arm, I steer myself closer, my skates coming to reside between his larger ones as my body presses against his. I stare into his gorgeous chestnut eyes with a new appreciation—a fresh understanding. I always knew Logan wore a front, I just hadn't realized how much he kept hidden underneath. Until now, I've only been seeing the surface of the real Logan. Now, for the first time, I'm staring directly at him. No masks. No nonchalance. No pretenses.

And he's absolutely glorious in his unmasking.

One hand curls around the front of his black hoodie and I pull, drawing his face down to mine and blotting out the world around us until nothing exists except the pounding of my heart in my chest, the strength of his body beneath my hand, and this exhilarating charge in the air between us.

When his lips hover inches above mine, his eyes darkened to a burnt umber as they bore into mine, burning with hunger and a raw vulnerability as if he feels this precarious whirlpool of emotions as strongly as I do, I murmur, "Kiss me." I'm not sure if it's a plea or a demand, and I don't care.

Seemingly as desperate for me as I am for him, he wraps those strong arms of his around my waist, my skates offering no resistance as he drags me infinitely closer, eliminating any space between us as he lowers his lips to mine and steals the air from my lungs with a single brush of skin against skin.

Despite the fierce passion in his gaze, his kiss is gentle and intimate, sending shivers down my spine. Every nerve in my body is on edge, our next brush of lips firmer yet soft. Sweet. Palpitating.

On our next meeting, his tongue sweeps past my lips, his groan meeting my moan before our kiss descends into something more profound.

Anticipation burns in the air around us. My arms move over his chest to wind around his neck, and in the middle of the ice rink, I hand my whole heart over to Logan Astor, knowing without a doubt that he'll protect it with his entire being.

"Riley," he groans against my skin, my name a plea on his lips.

"Logan," I return, my voice just as strained and breathless.

"You're pushing at the last threads of my restraint," he rasps, face buried in the crook of my neck and breath teasing my heated skin.

"Good. I don't want you to be restrained with me." I press a kiss to the sharp angle of his jaw. "I want every real and genuine part of you." Another kiss. "The kind and generous and loyal man before me." Another kiss brings me to the shell of his ear, and I begin to work a trail down his neck, smirking against his skin as his throat bobs. "And the ruthless, untameable man on the ice who won his team the Frozen Four three years in a row and will do the same this year."

He growls, the sound vibrating through his chest and spurring me on. "Be a Husky with me, Logan. Show me that fierce determination when you set your sights on what you want and refuse to let anything stand in your way."

His muscles vibrate beneath my touch, and with a final whisper in his ear, "Take me, Logan. I'm yours," he snaps. His hands roughly grasp the back of my thighs, and I'm lifted off my feet, my legs hurriedly wrapping around his waist as he expertly skates without even looking toward the edge of the ice.

His searing gaze remains locked on mine, navigating the rink with a precision that only someone who has skated on it a thousand times could achieve. Reaching the edge, he stomps off the ice and carries me down the tunnel. I don't care where he's taking me as I thread my fingers through his feathery, soft blond hair and relish the feeling of being in his arms, knowing that soon—very soon—Logan will be mine in every conceivable way.

A door is roughly kicked open, and I only lift my head long enough to take in the empty locker room before I lower my lips to his and kiss him with every ounce of tender affection, burning desire, and tentative love I feel for him.

I only pull away when he drops to his knees, and I feel the hardwood of a bench beneath my ass. Blinking, I stare agape at Logan on his knees before me, this mountain of a man gazing at me like I'm the only thing standing between him and insanity.

"You better know what you're doing, Shortcake," he growls, hungry eyes unmoving from mine. "'Cause I've never wanted anyone the way I need you, and once we cross this line, you'll be irrevocably mine."

The first flutter of nerves tingles against my ribs, and the only word that comes to my lips is "Royce." I'm aware that I already crossed this line with him, and he promised he was good with this—and with Grayson, which I'm refusing to give any thought to at the present moment. Only I never clarified with Logan that *he's* okay with this. I mean, it's been weeks of eating in the food court together, and they've both been spending their nights at my apartment. However, before we cross this line, it feels important to clarify where we stand.

Logan's lips twitch. "I am quite clear on Royce's feelings regarding you."

My eyebrows hit my hairline. Somehow, I cannot imagine the two of them sitting down for a heart-to-heart.

He chuckles, and it's dark and seductive, scraping against my skin in the most delicious of ways. "Royce is not as mysterious as he makes himself out to be. If you know how to read him, he's an open book." Sliding his hands along my jean-clad thighs, he continues, "He's been through so much shit. If you bring him even an ounce of happiness, then I'm not going to stand in the way of that. Besides, if there's any woman capable of handling Royce King, it's you, Shortcake."

He seals any response I might have come up with behind his lips as we sink into another heated kiss.

"Stop distracting me, Shortcake," he rasps when we break apart, chests heaving. "I need to get these skates off before I can start on all the dirty things I've been dreaming of doing to you."

I chuckle breathlessly but manage to keep my hands to myself as he deftly undoes the laces of my right skate before sliding it off my foot. I watch as he diligently moves to my other foot, noting the care he takes and the gentle touches he uses. Does he know that every drawn-out second is torture on my frayed nerves, which are screaming to feel his hands on my skin, his lips, his breath?

After what feels like an eternity, he sets the skates aside, hands roaming over my calves, thighs, and hips. Reaching the zipper of my jacket, he slowly lowers it until I shrug it off my shoulders. My breasts ache with the desire to be touched; my nipples sharpened peaks that scrape tantalizingly against my bra.

My whole body comes alive as he slips his hands beneath my top, pressing his palms against the soft skin of my stomach. My breaths come in heaving pants as he takes his time exploring, my top lifting inch by inch as his hands roam over my ribs, abdomen, and back.

At the first peek of my baby pink bra, he groans, some of that notorious control crumbling as he rids me of my top, leaving me in my jeans and bra.

"Fucking hell, Riley. You've no idea how beautiful you are."

I blush beneath his compliment, not that he seems to notice as he leans in to kiss a blazing trail up the center of my stomach, between the valley of my breasts, and across the heaving expanse of my chest.

When his hands come up to cup my heavy breasts, I groan, arching into his touch as I wrap my fingers around the edge of the bench. "Logan," I moan, my core clenching hungrily as blasts of heat emanate from my lower belly, screaming for exactly one man.

He nips at my collarbone. "Patience, Shortcake. I've waited a long time for this moment, so let me enjoy it."

Well, fuck, how can I argue with that?

His large, calloused palms knead my breasts, his thumbs flicking over my nipples. The barely felt sensation only serves to drive me mad, and I squirm on the bench as my panties grow wetter.

He takes his time, exploring every inch of exposed skin before his hands slide around to my spine, undoing the clasp. My bra falls away, and Logan dives in, tasting the sensitive flesh with his tongue.

Lifting one hand from the bench, I twist my fingers through his hair, gasping as he rolls his tongue around my nipple before sucking it into his mouth.

"Logan," I groan, growing impatient. "You're killing me."

He chuckles against my skin. "Good. Now you've some idea how I've been feeling."

"Please," I plead. "I need you."

"Mmm, I like it when you beg. Where do you need me, Shortcake?"

"Everywhere," I pant, half-delirious.

"Hmm, here?" He runs his tongue along a rib, and I huff out a frustrated breath. "Or maybe here?" He blows a breath of warm air over my stomach. "Or were you talking about down here?" His fingers trail along the waistband of my jeans before he pops the button.

"Yes," I pant, greedily lifting my hips to help him along.

He chuckles at my unsubtle movements. "Is someone getting a little impatient?"

"Yes," I snap. Grabbing my jeans and shoving them down my thighs when he takes too long.

At the sight of me before him in only a pair of pink panties, his teasing falls by the wayside, his eyes drinking me in with a reverence that leaves me feeling exposed. Naked in a way that goes far deeper than skin.

"Perfect," he murmurs, leaning in to kiss the inside of my knee. He chases it with another one just above it, then another, and my heart lodges in my throat when he reaches the tops of my inner thighs and his tongue flicks out to run along the pearly-white scars. He lavishes each one with the same appreciation as he does the rest of my skin, to the point where I'm on the verge of tears. Not only do I feel seen in a way I never have before, but I feel accepted, too.

With tears brimming in my eyes, I grasp his face with both of my hands and drag his lips to mine, kissing him hard and deeply. Time stands still as our lips move in perfect harmony, our tongues a tangle of all-encompassing passion. His fingers slide beneath my panties, slipping between my slick folds, and I groan into his mouth as he sinks two long fingers inside me.

His other arm rests against the bench at my back as his lips and fingers send me spiraling, and I break apart with his name on my tongue and tattoo on my heart.

"More," I rasp, still floating in the aftershocks of my release. "Need more." I pull and tug at his hoodie in a desperate need to make it disappear, to feel the burning heat of his skin directly against mine.

He chuckles dazedly, but with an arm reached behind his back, he helps me out, removing his hoodie and t-shirt with one firm tug. My hands slide reverently over his smooth, chiseled, tanned skin, committing every dip and ridge to memory. The pads of my fingers circle the tattoo on his ribs, the EKG strip with the hockey player drawn into it, before trailing over his ribs to the defined V at his hips.

Reaching the buckle of his jeans, I pop it open and pull down the zipper before pushing them down his thighs. I tug on his boxers but stop when another tattoo is revealed beneath the waistband.

12.18.2023.

I frown, staring at it in confusion as I try to figure out if anything specific happened on that date only six weeks ago. When I can't figure it out, I lift my eyes to his face, finding him watching me closely, expression unusually vulnerable.

"What's this?" I ask, my voice barely more than a whisper.

He reaches out, his fingers brushing my cheek and sending shivers down my spine. "The day you told me your truth."

I blink, mind reeling. "The day you believed me."

He nods. "The day I knew without a doubt that you were my everything, and I'd do whatever it took to prove it."

Tears burn the back of my throat, and I stretch my neck and spine until I can press my lips to his. "If you're not careful, you're going to make me fall madly in love with you," I whisper, hardly daring to put a voice to those words.

He smiles against my lips, quick and tentative. "I'm not doing anything that you're not already doing to me, Ry."

His hand slides into my hair and his lips seize mine, my body melting into every hard demand and gentle stroke of his touch.

"Please stop teasing me. I need you now." My voice barely sounds like my own as he gets to his feet.

"Ah, fuck," he growls, stumbling, and it takes me a second to realize he's still wearing his skates. An obstacle we both forgot about. He moves to undo them with quick, nimble fingers, chucking them, along with his jeans and boxers, aside faster than I would have thought possible.

In the span of a breath, he's back in front of me, towering over me as he pushes me down onto the bench. My panties disappear in the next blink, and I can't look away from the endless pools of his eyes as the blunt head of his cock probes at my entrance.

We both still, understanding this moment for what it is— the meeting of two souls. And with a raw reverence, he pushes inside, and our souls become one.

My walls stretch around his thick, hard length, my back arching as neurons I didn't know existed spark to life.

"Fuck," he grunts, his body quaking. "You're unbelievably tight."

My responding chuckle is strangled as he splits me open. "God, Logan, that feels so good."

"Incredible," he rasps in agreement. "Pretty sure I can die happy now. Can't imagine anything else the world has to offer beating this."

I straight up laugh, which causes me to squeeze him tighter, and he grunts, arms straining either side of the bench beside my head. "Just kiss me, you idiot."

Sweeping in, he sucks my tongue into his mouth, and I lose myself in all things Logan Astor. He plays my body like he does hockey—with determination and passion, each move performed with perfect precision until his name is a breathless plea falling endlessly from my lips.

"Fuck, fuck, fuck," he growls.

Each stroke has me quivering, and one look at Logan lets me know he's on the verge of completely shattering, too. Seeing him so unraveled is my undoing, and I come apart on his cock as he continues to pound into me. One, two, three more thrusts before he pulls out, his seed exploding over my stomach as he comes with a roar.

Breathing heavily, he rests his forehead against my chest,

likely hearing the pounding of my heart. "Fuck." He sucks in two more heaving breaths. "I completely forgot about a condom until I was about to come."

I'm too exhausted to laugh, but my chest vibrates with the semblance of one, and he lifts his head, gifting me a cocky yet endearing smile. "Just in case you didn't yet realize how obsessed I am with you, I haven't had sex with anyone since you started tutoring me, and I got myself tested after that first session."

"That was awfully presumptuous of you," I say, at a loss for a better response. Even as heat blooms in my chest, it is a struggle to suppress my smile, knowing that even with the ups and downs we've had, he never sought out anyone else.

He huffs out a breath, but his grin only brightens.

Lifting my arm, I point to a minute, barely noticeable scar. "Implant. And I'm clean, too. Although, I did, uh, have sex with both Royce and Grayson the other day."

His eyebrows arch in surprise. "At the same time?"

"What?" I ask, aghast. "No! Separately. Royce was..."

"Inevitable," Logan finishes, understanding.

"And Grayson was—"

"Grayson."

With a small smile, I nod. "I haven't slept with anyone else, though. Not in a long time."

His grin turns positively savage as he leans in until my entire field of vision is filled with his looming face. "Glad we cleared that up. So next time, I am going to paint your inner walls with my cum, then watch as it drips down your thighs, marking you to the whole world as mine."

Fuck.

At his possessive tone and dangerous words, my body clenches, coming back to life from the embers of that earth-shattering release. His smirk is hungry and smug, knowing exactly the effect he has on me, and before I can do something stupid like demand he put his cock back in me and prove his point, I scooch back to sit upright.

Still looking far too full of himself, Logan reaches for his t-shirt and uses it to clean me up before mumbling about using the bathroom. Pulling on his boxers, he strides toward where I presume the showers and toilet stalls are.

When he's out of sight, I slip into my panties and bra and search for my top amongst the disarray of our discarded clothing when my gaze catches on the name *Astor*, and I pause, staring at what is presumably his locker. Hanging in it is his jersey, in all its black and gold finery. I smile coyly as an idea comes to mind. Abandoning my mission to find my clothes, I move closer.

My fingers brush over his name stitched across the back before I pull it from the hanger and slip it over my head. It drowns me, stopping mid-thigh, and the sleeves fall past my fingers, but it feels like butter against my skin. I smile into the fabric as I breathe in the unique winter scent that is uniquely Logan.

A sharp inhale has me spinning to find Logan standing in the doorway leading to the showers, staring at me with ravenous hunger. "Fucking hell, Shortcake, do you even know what you're doing?"

I cock a brow. "Trying on your jersey."

His laugh is strangled. "More like making every single one of my fantasies come to life."

I recall the way his eyes lit up with a feral possession the first time he saw me wearing his number. The way he practically pounced on me in the family room after his game. The promise I made to him before Saturday night's game...

My gaze dips to his boxers, or more notably, the long, hard rod making itself known, and my teeth sink into my lower lip.

Glancing up at him through my eyelashes, my smile is coy. "You're saying this does it for you, Astor, seeing a girl in your jersey?"

He shakes his head, taking a step toward me as if being pulled on an invisible string. "Not just any girl." Another step. "*You*, Shortcake." Another step, and he's mere feet from me, his gaze hot enough to scorch my skin. "Seeing *you* in my jersey is my every fantasy."

"Just seeing me?"

"Baby, be careful. You're asking to get fucked."

Smiling like the cat that got the cream, I tilt my head and stare at Logan directly. "If your fantasy is to fuck me in your jersey, Astor, then why don't you come over here and make that dream a reality."

He pounces, all gentleness gone, and I'm left facing the Logan that his opponents face on the ice as my panties are ripped from my body and I'm hauled off my feet. This time there's nothing sweet or tender about our union as Logan drives himself into me in one hard thrust and proceeds to fuck my brains out, emptying himself inside me just like he promised.

ROYCE

CHAPTER FORTY-FOUR

"You're taking all of this surprisingly well." I side-eye Grayson as we make the drive to Springview for my clandestine meeting with Lydia. He hasn't said a word the entire journey, and I'm curious to know what he's thinking. After our conversation yesterday, he went for a walk to clear his head and has barely said a word since. However, Riley's revelation on top of the shit he's found out about his mom can't be easy for him.

His only response is a grunt, and I roll my eyes, deciding if he doesn't want to talk, then that's fine with me. Silence is my MO, anyway.

Instead, I reach forward to turn on the radio for some background noise, Bad Things by *The Phantoms* playing softly through the car as I relax back in my seat, my foot resting on the accelerator as we head down the freeway.

"I went to see her," Gray eventually blurts.

"Went to see who? Riley?"

"I see what you guys were saying. Can't argue with those looks."

I cast a glance his way. "You saw a picture of Aurora?"

He nods, scraping his hand through his hair as he turns to stare out the passenger window. "Thought it would help if I saw her."

"And?" I query when he trails off, sounding lost and defeated.

Slowly, he turns back to face me, exhaustion etched into the hard lines of his face and bruised beneath his eyes. He shakes his head.

"I feel like I'm the world's biggest idiot. How could I not have seen it? I mean, he was beating the shit out of my mom, and what, I just didn't notice?"

"You were only a kid, Gray."

"What about with Riley? I wasn't a little kid then and I still missed the signs. What sort of person am I related to? Whose blood is in my veins? If my father is this monster, does that make me one too?"

"You're not your dad, Gray," I state resolutely.

He only shakes his head, not believing me. "The most fucked up part of it all is that I still can't compute the two. In my mind, there's this man who did these awful things to people I care about, and then there's my dad. The man I've known my entire life. How does that even make sense?"

"It's a fucked up thing to try to understand," I tell him. "You won't be able to in a day or two. Hell, you probably need a lifetime of therapy to fully acknowledge that shit."

My dad has always been an asshole. He made no attempts to hide it. He was never really interested in having children. Only agreed to have me because he felt like he had to—both for social reasons and to continue the King line. I have never been anything other than an asset to him, one which lost a hell of a lot of credibility after the rape scandal at the end of my senior year of high school. The one that's been tailing me like a case of Gonorrhea that won't go the fuck away.

"There's this person that did... *that*... the one Gran is petrified of and believes hurt my mom... Then there's the dad that I know, that I grew up with, that I learned from and see every month at the prison... that's not... How can they be the same person? How could I not have seen it? He's always been cold and aloof. Driven. Demanding. He's not the easiest to get along with, and we don't have the best of relationships, but that's a far cry from... *this.* "

His resounding sigh is born of profound exhaustion, the sound of a soul that's adrift at sea; a concession to the relentless struggles and uncertainties that plague him.

"I never took a psychology class," I tell him, "but your dad is incredibly good at hiding his true self. At convincing everyone around him to see what he wants them to see... including you."

Sighing, he turns away from me, absently watching the fields pass by outside his window. "Yeah. I have no idea who my father actually is."

We lapse into silence, the radio the only sound as I speed along the freeway, inching closer to Springview.

"What are you expecting to happen tonight?" he asks sometime later. "What do you think Lydia's up to?"

"You tell me, you know her better than I do."

He scoffs, the sound caustic and cold. "I already told you the vague impression I had of her from back then, and based on what Logan had to say, I was completely off base." He shakes his head, muttering bitterly, "Clearly, I don't know anyone."

Lips pursed, I stay quiet. I feel bad for the guy. What must it be like to find out your dad isn't who you thought he was? I do understand what it's like to question your ability to deduce someone's character, though.

I fell victim to the same crime—thinking someone was a completely different person from who they turned out to be.

Melissa had been outgoing, flirty, popular... a cheerleader, and a fellow senior. We'd been in some of the same classes over our four years in high school together and ran in similar friendship cliques. I knew she had a thing for me, and one night at a party, I'd had a couple of beers and made the worst mistake of my life.

She was someone I thought I knew.

I thought it was no big deal.

Until the cops were putting me in handcuffs...

"Are you sure this is the right place?" Grayson asks as I pull the car up to the curb and stare down the wide, cobblestone street. We're in the old, historic part of Springview, which has been gentrified recently and is now bustling with numerous restaurants, clubs, and bars.

Old meets new as the brick buildings weathered from the passage of time clash with large glass fronts and steel beams, each establishment busier than the last, the Springview nightlife alive and vibrant.

I double-checked the address on the GPS, which matches the street sign. "Yup, this is the street."

"Doesn't exactly speak secret, back-alley meeting," Gray muses.

"No, but there are plenty of people around, which is why I'm guessing she picked it. Right, stay here. Keep your head down." I toss him a Halston U ballcap, waiting until he puts it on, pulling it low over his eyes as he slouches down in his seat.

"Good luck," he calls as I exit the car. I walk past rowdy restaurants and bars as I amble down the street, passing groups of people and the occasional couple. Antique lamp posts adorned with orange ironwork cast a warm, flickering glow, creating an inviting ambiance that coaxes you further into the bustle.

Halfway down the street, I stop outside a nondescript building. Three stories tall, the lights are off in each of the small, narrow, paned windows.

There is a railing around the edge of the building, with stairs leading to a basement level. At the top of them is a small, almost missable cast iron sign embossed with gold music notes on an S-shaped staff—the only hint that the building is anything other than vacant.

Looking around the busy street, no one seems to be paying me any attention as I descend the old, uneven steps to a small, open doorway. I'm met with more rickety stairs, these steep and narrow.

With every step I take, the air grows thicker, musty as though, wherever I'm headed, time has stood still. Brass lanterns emit a soft glow, providing just enough light for me to see as the distant sound of music reaches my ears.

Reaching the bottom, I'm met with a low ceiling, the rich scent of aged wood and cigar smoke hitting me hard. The music is louder now, the sultry jazz notes pulling me down the claustrophobic hallway and through another doorway.

A loud, lively room opens before me, dimly lit with antique chandeliers that shine and sparkle beneath the mahogany ceiling, the walls adorned with shimmering gold wallpaper and dark blue paneling. In the center of the room is a spacious dance floor where couples sway to the smooth jazz melody currently being played by a live band in the corner.

Plush, low-slung sofas and velvet-covered armchairs are scattered throughout, providing cozy corners for intimate conversation. Walking further into the room, I notice smaller, private rooms and cramped nooks hidden behind discreet archways and velvet curtains, offering a more intimate space away from prying eyes. Some have nameplates above the doorway or arch, the closest reading *Jazz Crypt.*

I wander through the numerous rooms and labyrinthine hallways lined with vintage photographs and antique sconces that wind through the speakeasy, leading to secret bars, lounges, and even a hidden cigar room. As I explore, I become more and more impressed with this secret hideaway as I search the crowd for Lydia, and despite the reason for my visit tonight, I make a mental note to bring Ry here. I think she'd really love it.

Not spotting Lydia anywhere, I begin to wonder if this was all a waste of time as I approach one of the various bars and order an Old Fashioned from the dapperly dressed bartender— because you can't not order a drink in a place like this.

With my drink in hand, I lean against the bar, listening to the hum of hushed conversations, laughter, and clinking of glasses around me. Doing a final scan of the room, I reach into the back pocket of my jeans when my phone vibrates.

GRAY

Did she show?

ME

No sign yet.

The phone vibrates again. This time, the notification says I have a photo from Logan. Opening it, I smile into my whiskey glass as I stare down at a selfie of him and Riley tucked up on her sofa beneath a mountain of blankets and nursing hot chocolates topped with cream, marshmallows, and sprinkles.

After staring at Riley's happy face, I close out of the photo and open the browser to my message thread with Lydia. I perk up at the new comment which was posted thirty minutes ago.

Riches&Glamor: *Meet me in the Whispered Hideaway room at 10 pm.*

Checking the time at the top of my screen, I realize I only have two minutes. Knocking back the last of my drink, I set the empty glass on the bar top and go in search of the Whispered Hideaway.

I find it tucked off a dead-end hallway, the small room barely big enough to contain a dark green velvet booth and a neat wooden table. The walls are wrapped in that same hunter-green velvet, with brass sconces and accents dotted around the room. Candles flicker on the unoccupied table, and I frown as I turn to face the archway I just walked through.

Checking the time, I slide into one side of the booth, keeping my gaze focused on the door. While I wait, I fire off a text to Gray to appease him so he doesn't get any crazy ideas about coming in here and blowing our cover.

I hear the clip of heels seconds before a shadow darkens the doorway, Lydia's sharp gaze landing on mine.

She's far more appropriately dressed for this high-end establishment, in a slinky, shimmering green dress that clings to her curves and hugs her boobs, the miracle bra she's wearing doing its job of ensuring those things are shoved in your face and impossible to ignore. It's a dress intended for someone half her age.

"Ruthless?" she questions with an air of authority.

I merely nod, watching her with suspicion as she sets her

wine glass on the table and slides to the opposite end of the booth.

Her eyes slowly take me in, the two of us assessing the other. I obviously don't see what she does, based on the way her pupils dilate and one side of her lips hitches in a coy smile. She bats her eyes seductively, and it takes effort to keep the cringe off my face.

"You're after the key?" I grunt, spreading my legs and leaning back on the sofa, making myself appear as intimidating as possible as I flick an unbothered glance her way.

She nods. "Yes. I was told you would be able to help me."

I stare directly at her, gaze hard and cold. Ruthless—that's precisely what I am. "I might be able to."

With a grin touching her lips, she shuffles closer. I tense for a brief second before I manage to force my muscles to relax.

Placing a manicured hand on my forearm, she purrs, "I didn't think you'd be quite so handsome."

I force myself to lean into her as my gaze drops over her lithe form blatantly on display. It's agonizing to wrench my muscles into a seductive smirk. "I can't say I often get the plea-sure of dealing with pretty young women in my line of work." I lick my lips, zeroing in on her lips. "Maybe we'll be able to mix business with a little pleasure."

My insides seize up simply at the suggestion. Except Lydia buys it, shimmying even closer as she drags one nail over my bicep, gaze trailing my tattoos before she smiles up at me through her fake eyelashes. "If you're able to help me, I'll let you do whatever you want with me."

I don't think she'd be on board if she knew just what I wanted to do with her.

Unless she's not opposed to permanently going to live with the fishes.

Instead of saying any of that, though, I merely chuckle.

"Darlin', you don't wanna go promising something like that to a man like me. I'm not like your uptight suit-wearing men. I like my sex rough and hard."

Her eyes gleam while I fight back the urge to wrinkle my nose. "You can be as rough as you want with me." Leaning in until her lips are inches from my cheek, she whispers, "I like it."

Bleugh. Someone bring me a bucket, quick.

With monumental effort, I force my features into a smirk as I pull slightly back, grateful for the modicum of distance as I get down to business. "Before we get carried away, we should discuss business. Why don't you tell me what you're after?"

For a brief second, that look of desire twists into suspicion before she smooths it out. "A girl needs her secrets, Mr. Ruthless."

Bringing my face down, my breath fans over her ear as I drop my voice, "How can I know how best to help you if I don't know what specifically you're looking for?"

Watching her, I can see the uncertainty in her eyes as she drags her siren-red lower lip into her mouth and hating myself for every minute of this, I reach out and trace her jaw with my fingers. "A gorgeous woman like yourself," I say, putting on my best seductive tone and disgusted that I'm using it on this bitch. "Could easily end up in a sticky situation if she doesn't know what she's doing. There's a lot of depraved people out there." I drop my gaze down her body. "People who would be more than happy to take advantage of a pretty little thing like you."

With that lip still trapped between her teeth, a smirk appears on her face. "How do I know you're not one of those people?"

My focus drifts to thoughts of Riley in my arms, how it felt finally being inside of her, having her wrapped around me in the most intimate of ways. My gaze grows heated, the bitch in front of me ignorant of the fact my desire is *not* for her, but for her daughter. "There's only one thing I want to take advantage of when it comes to you," I state with a cocky smirk, deliberately dropping my gaze to her obviously fake tits spilling out of her too-tight dress.

Placing her hand high on my thigh—as if she has any fucking right to touch me—she emits this stupid girly giggle that has my entire body wanting to recoil. "Alright." Shifting so her leg presses against mine, she lowers her voice to a near whisper. I'm not sure if it's because she's worried about someone in the hall possibly overhearing or if it's an excuse to get closer. "I'm looking to sell something rather... sensitive."

My hackles instantly rise, and my fingers fold into my palm to restrain myself from demanding *what* she is looking to sell. That sort of outburst would only raise her suspicions, which is the very last thing I need to do.

However, her admission gives me a bit more of an idea of what she's expecting from this meeting: someone to help her get onto the black market, or a similar platform.

Told you it would be something highly illegal!

Instead of strangling the information out of her like I want to, I force my lips into a small, easy smile. "There are many controversial items for sale if you know where to look—drugs, antiquities, humans, organs. You looking to sell an organ, gorgeous?"

Her face scrunches. "Definitely not."

"If you help me narrow it down," I say lowly, "I'll know who to put you in touch with."

Staring up at me, she pushes her lips out in a pout. "What if you think less of me?"

I see her question for what it is—distrust, still.

"Baby, whatever it is, I've seen worse. You have no idea of the depravity of the world I live in. The twisted shit I've seen and participated in. Everything from underground fighting—

which, trust me, is nothing like the MMA shit you see on TV—to participating in auctions of all sorts: rare artwork, weapons, even humans." I force my lips up. "Ever fancied getting yourself a male sex toy?"

Another manicured finger is scraped along my bicep, this time followed up by her other hand sliding around to the inside of my thigh, precariously close to my *very* flaccid dick. "I'd much rather have your company," she flirts, buttering me up.

I give her another fake as fuck cocky smirk. "All I'm saying, gorgeous, is that I can meet *all* your needs."

"Mmm, I don't doubt that."

I allow her to paw at me for a moment. She's on the fence, I can tell. Not sure whether she can trust me or not.

"Look, sweetheart, trust goes both ways," I state, sliding out of the booth. "No hard feelings if you've changed your mind, but if that's the case"—I thumb the doorway—"I have other work I need to get to."

I barely make it a single step toward the door before she reaches across the table, her talons digging into my arm. "No." I pause, staring down at her as she anxiously flicks her tongue out. "I'm looking... to sell a... person—a child, to be exact."

Everything in me locks up. I swear, even the blood is frozen in my veins. *This* is the confirmation I needed. The confirmation of what I'd already presumed. I think I suspected it the second I saw that post. It's why I couldn't let it go. Why I blindly agreed to tonight's meeting.

I'm sure my grin is garish, all teeth as I place my hand flat on the table and lean down. "Then I'm exactly the person to help you do that."

Sliding back into the booth, I tolerate every second of her hands on me, because now I know what the stakes are. I'll tolerate anything to ensure she trusts me. Trusts me enough to hand over Aurora and let me walk away with her, no questions asked.

"Tell me about the child. Buyers and auctioneers will want basic details—height, weight, hair, and eye color. A photo is best if you have it."

"Oh, uh, no. I don't have one, but, erm, I can get one."

I nod, listening silently as she describes Aurora to a T, utterly oblivious of the storm brewing inside me with each bitter word she spews. Thankfully, I can pretend to be focused on the job instead of her, as my face is a blank mask to contain the fury coursing through my body. Any flirty looks would portray how close I am to snapping her neck.

Every detail she spills is gasoline, fanning an already raging flame, stoking it into an uncontainable bonfire.

When she's done, I choke out, my voice a barely recognizable growl, "Alright. I'll get a profile put together and reach out to my contacts. What about papers?" I ask. "Birth certificate, passport, that sort of thing?"

She nods emphatically. "I have her birth certificate. She doesn't have a passport."

"I'll need all that too."

"I need this dealt with swiftly," she states, that air of superiority returning. "I don't have much time."

My facial expression remains neutral, although my mind spins in a hundred different directions, attempting to put together puzzle pieces I don't even have.

Why the urgency? Why now? Does this have to do with Bertram's parole hearing? The timing seems too coincidental, yet I don't have enough information. Only stacking questions with no answers in sight.

"Of course."

With our business concluded, her coy expression returns. She practically glues herself to my side, her hand possessively on my thigh, nails digging in. *Remind me to burn these clothes when I get home.*

"Well," I state, gently untangling my arm from hers as I rake my hand through my hair. "I believe that is everything. I don't see us having any issues getting this little girl off your hands." My smile is slimy and savage as I slide out of the booth and stand.

"Y-you're leaving?" she asks, stunned. "B-but don't you want your payment?"

I flash her a haughty smirk, my eyes falling to rest on her chest. "I prefer to receive my rewards at the end of a job well done."

Not hanging around, I stride out of the room. My steps quicken, and I'm practically shoving my way through the busy underground rooms, rushing up the stairs so fast that I bang my head on the low ceiling more than once.

Stumbling onto the street, I press my hand against the side of the building and vomit my guts up.

Fuck.

Fuck.

Straightening, I wipe the back of my hand along my mouth, ignoring the stares from passers-by as I move away from the building. I brush my hands down my arms as I walk, still feeling that vile, disgusting bitch pawing at me.

How she can think for one second that I'd actually be interested... and yet I led her on. I *let* her touch me. Fucking flirted right back.

I know I did it for the right reasons. That, knowing the situation, Riley wouldn't hold my actions against me. However, it doesn't alleviate the nausea churning in my stomach as I make a beeline for my truck and climb in behind the wheel.

"Well?" Grayson asks.

I don't speak. Can't. Can't voice aloud what I just sat in on. What I fucking contributed to.

"You not gonna clue me in?"

"Not yet," I manage to choke out as I navigate back onto the freeway, only half of my attention on the road. The other half is still in that room, replaying that conversation and trying to work out what the fuck I can do to prevent Riley's daughter from being sold on the black fucking market.

"Well, can you at least tell me where we're going?"

"The Depot," I grunt. "I need to talk to Xander."

"What's up?" Xander asks, eyeing me from behind his desk with his arms crossed. The three of us are crammed into his small office at The Depot.

"I need you to put me in touch with someone good with computers. A hacker. That sort of shit."

His eyes widen in surprise, unused to such a request from me. Typically, I come here to fight and get paid, occasionally to get shit-faced. "Why?"

Mimicking his pose, I state, "Can't tell you."

His sharp stare holds me in place. Xander is a smart guy, quick on his feet, and observant as hell.

"What makes you think I know someone like that? I'm just a lowly barkeep." His tone is measured. Xander and I may be friends by association, but we're not best buds. I know fuck all about his personal life and he knows crap about mine.

I snort. "Yeah, sure you are." He arches a single eyebrow in challenge. "You think I haven't noticed the fact that you've never once been bothered by the police? No unannounced drop-ins. No cops bursting in and busting any of us even though *everyone* around here knows *exactly* what goes on in here."

His lips press into a thin line, but he remains silent.

"Or how about how you've always got good fighters? Men that belong on the circuit. Names that *mean* something in certain circles. Who wouldn't give a shit about some little bar out in the sticks."

Still, silence.

"Look, man." I sigh. "I don't give a shit. You know I don't care. But I could really use your help. You'd be doing me a solid, and saving a life in the process."

Grayson's wide eyes whirl on me, though I blatantly ignore him. He peppered me with questions the entire drive here *despite* me refusing to answer a single one. No fucking way am I reciting this twice. He can just wait until it's the three of us, and I only have to say aloud *once* that I had to flirt with Riley's bitch of a mom just so I could find out that the same bitch is trying to sell off her granddaughter to make a quick buck.

Xander's lips flatten, his stare softening marginally. "Fuck, fine. I know someone who can get you what you want."

"Thank you." He nods, and I tack on, "I need the info quickly."

"Yeah, yeah. I'll reach out tonight, alright?"

With another nod and shake of his hand, Grayson and I follow him out of the office, declining his offer of a beer before we make our way through the busy warehouse to the door.

I tilt my chin at Roman, who is on the door tonight as we step outside, and he grunts a goodbye before we climb into my truck and drive off.

"Are you finally going to tell me what this is all about?" Grayson asks as I navigate the back road home.

I shake my head. "Not 'til Logan is here too. I can only repeat this shit once."

LOGAN

CHAPTER FORTY-FIVE

Riley is sound asleep in my arms when my phone lights up. I glance down at her, but she doesn't stir. After showing her my community program—my single greatest achievement—and the two rounds of mind-blowing sex we had, we came back to hers. We crashed on the sofa, binge-watching TV until she passed out, and I tucked her into bed, climbing in beside her in case she had a nightmare.

Shifting my attention to the screen, I read Royce's text.

Fuck, that can't be good. The only reason I'm not asleep right now is because I was waiting to hear about how his meeting went tonight with Riley's mom.

Absolutely nothing is making sense, and with Bertram up

for parole, the last thing we need is Riley's mom stirring up trouble—assuming that's what she's doing. I still maintain her post was some weird sex thing. I mean, that's what most people on Craigslist are after.

ME

Is this about tonight?

ROYCE

Yup.

I roll my eyes at his one-word answer. Man has such a way with words. Bet he has Riley swooning for him.

ROYCE

Is Riley sleeping okay?

I huff out a laugh. Dude is so fucking gone for our girl. And I'm totally okay with it. He could do with a bit of sunshine in his life, and Riley is the perfect fit for his stubborn broodiness.

I've seen a difference in him these last few weeks. It's small, barely noticeable if you don't know the guy, but I see it. There's a lighter air around him, a brightness in his eyes that I haven't seen in months. I've even caught the dude smiling. Fucking *smiling!* It's small. Looks more like a grimace. But it's fucking there!

I snap a picture of the woman herself curled up beside me in bed and send it to him, attached with the words *like a baby.*

It's sweet how he worries about her. It's not a side of Royce I've ever seen before. Sure, he loves me and Gray, and we have one another's backs, but we also know we can hold our own, too. It's different with Riley. *He* is different with Riley.

Setting my phone back on the nightstand, I snuggle deeper in the bed, the smell of vanilla swirling around and lulling me toward dreamland.

***

"She *what?!*" I bellow, gaping at Royce in horror. It is way too fucking early for this shit! "She can't do that, can she? No, there's no fucking way she can do that. She's not even her fucking mother. What right does she have to give up—no, not give up, fucking *sell* a child that isn't hers."

God, I am angry. Beyond angry. I am fucking furious. I have half a goddamn mind to drive to that bitch's house and wring her entitled fucking neck. Thinks she can sell my girl's daughter and get away with it. I'm going to bury her six feet under.

"Logan, calm down." Grayson sighs wearily.

I spin to glare at him where he's sitting in a chair in our living room. How can he be sitting right now? I can't even stand still. "*Calm down?*" The words come out in a near shriek. "Don't fucking tell me to *calm down,* Grayson." I fling a hand in Royce's direction. "Did you even listen to what he just said? Or is your head so far up your asshole that you're living off your own bullshit? This is so fucking far beyond you being pissed about something she didn't even fucking do. Get over yourself, you shithead. This is her *daughter.* Her fucking daughter. *Your* half-sister. Doesn't that mean anything—"

I'm shoved into the living room wall, Grayson's hands fisted in the front of my shirt as he glares murderously into my eyes. "Of course, I give a fucking shit. I might be struggling with all of this, but despite what you may think, I don't want to see Riley or her child hurt. Not like that."

Teeth gritted, I huff out a breath before shoving him off me. "Then what the fuck are we going to do about it, then?"

I glance between him and Royce. Surely they've had more than enough time to figure out what the fuck we're going to do to get Aurora away from that conniving, selfish bitch.

"Xander's reaching out to a contact of his," Royce informs me as if that means anything at all. "For now, we play along with her game. Make her think I'm doing what she wants."

"Right, and what happens when she figures out you're not who you're pretending to be? There's only so long you can pretend to have some seedy connection with the black fucking market before it blows up in your face."

The pulsing of the blood vessels in his jaw is the only sign of Royce's irritation as he stares blankly at me. Waiting for me to cool my jets. Newsflash: I won't be calming down any time soon!

"She needs this to be a quick process. All I have to do is pretend to find her a buyer, get her to bring Aurora to a meeting with them, and then we take the kid."

Oh well, if that's all...

All I can do is blink stupidly at him because there are *so* many holes in that plan that I don't even know where to begin.

"Why does she need this to be a quick process?" I bite out instead.

Royce's lips purse. "My guess? Bertram's release."

"You think she's after money to start over with Bertram?" I ask, throwing out the first half-logical explanation that came to mind.

Royce shrugs. "Maybe."

"You think she and my dad are still a thing?" Grayson queries, lifting his head from his hands to look at Royce.

"That, or she's hoping they will be when he gets released, maybe. I dunno, I'm guessing, but what other reason could she have for choosing now?"

I absently nod my head in agreement. Truthfully, I don't give a single flying fuck about the why.

"Are they still married?" Royce asks Grayson.

"Haven't a fucking clue," he grunts. "I had assumed they weren't, though I actually don't know."

Stopping my pacing, I collapse into an empty chair. "Riley mentioned that they were divorced," I tell them, still not really caring. I want to get back to this sieve of a plan so we can brainstorm how to block some of the holes and not fuck it up.

"But does she actually know that, or is she just assuming, like I am?" Gray asks.

I give him an *I don't give a fuck* shrug. *Really, why does it matter when we have bigger things to worry about?* "You'd have to ask her."

"We're not," Royce states firmly, an edge to his voice that has me fully focusing back on the conversation.

"Why not?"

"She's probably as clueless as Gray. Moreso, you heard her that night. She was barely even around her mom after everything went down. She's not going to know anything more than we do."

There's something about the severity of his tone that has me narrowing my eyes on him. "Right, but we're going to tell her about her *mom* trying to sell her *daughter*... aren't we?"

He stares me down for so long that I already know the answer when he finally opens his mouth and states, "No."

"Royce," I growl in warning. "What the fuck do you mean *no*? We have to tell her! It's her daughter! She has a right to know!"

"So she can have more nightmares?" he counters. *Fuck.*

Dammit. I know he's right. The last thing I want to do is add to her already overloaded plate of worries. "What could she even do to help?" he continues to push. "You think her mom is going to just let her rock up and take Aurora away?" *Ehh, yes?* He must see the thought written across my face because he scoffs. "Don't be so naive, Logan. Lydia has custody of Aurora. Despite the shit she's currently doing, in the eyes of the law, she is more credible. Given Riley's documented history, she will have her word discredited at best and have her committed at worst."

My mouth opens and closes, nothing coming out. *Well, fuck. Is that possible? Maybe. Who the fuck knows. Is it a risk I'd be willing to take? Fuck no.*

"Maybe my lawyers could do something," I voice aloud. "I can call them later and find out."

Royce nods. "Do that, but I think we're out of time to do this the legal way. Shit like that takes time that we don't have. The only way I see it, is we have to play Lydia—make her think I am who she thinks I am."

"And you think Xander can help with that?" Grayson asks, the two of them filling me in on their pit stop at The Depot on their way home last night.

"I think he knows people who can."

"You better fucking be right," I half-growl, not the slightest bit happy about any of this. If it wouldn't get me arrested, I'd drive to that bitch's house now and just take Aurora myself. "So we play dress up, pretend to be some sick fucks who like to buy children, and get our girl's little girl back for good."

With the same daunting expression he wears in the ring, Royce nods. "That's exactly what we're going to do."

"Logan," Riley greets, a tentative smile slowly taking over her face and lighting her up from within. *God, she looks fucking stunning when she smiles.*

"Hey, Shortcake. Got you a coffee on my way over." I thrust out my hand, drinking in the flush that crawls over her skin every time I buy her one. It's adorable as shit. Makes me want to hand her the world on a platter and see how deep that blush goes.

"Thank you." Her voice is soft, and I hate how such a simple gesture means so much to her. Has no one ever taken care of her? It pisses me the fuck off how starved of love and affection she is.

However, I'm more than happy to drown her in mine.

Slinging my arm over her shoulder, I walk with her toward the library. She glances up at my wet hair before saying, "You left early this morning."

The pressure that's been residing in my chest since my conversation with the guys this morning cinches tighter. "Sorry, Shortcake. House meeting."

"Everything okay?" she asks, worried.

"Everything's fine." My smile is strained. I fucking hate lying to her. Especially about this, although I equally don't want to add to her stress, so she makes herself sick. I'm still haunted by the deadened look in her eyes when I found her in that shower. I refuse to let anything else drive her back to that state.

"How is Grayson doing?"

"He's processing."

She nods, chewing on her lower lip. "And the three of you... are you friends again?"

Blowing out a breath, I pull her to a stop and turn so we're facing each other. "Do you want us to be friends? Do you want Grayson in your life—in any capacity?"

Lips flattened, she doesn't immediately answer. "I don't want to come between the three of you, and I know I already have. With the truth aired out now, I think his hostility toward me might change... or maybe that's just wishful thinking." Her forehead wrinkles, eyes dropping to the ground, and I reach out, tugging her face up to mine.

"His head is a mess, but he says he believes you. He seems... repentant. He obviously needs to make his own amends, but I don't think he's a lost cause."

"Then you shouldn't give up on him. You and Royce mean a lot to him. With his dad being released soon, he will need you both now more than ever. I don't want him to go through all of this alone."

Tucking a stray strand of auburn hair behind her ear, I murmur, "So selfless. He doesn't deserve your concern."

"Maybe not, but what sort of world would we live in if we can't give people second chances and the opportunity to learn and grow?"

"Mmhmm. The real one, but I like your world better."

Her responding smile is bright and hopeful, and I fall headfirst into it.

"I don't know if Grayson and I can ever be friends or what... but I'm willing to put our past to bed and form an amicable alliance with him—for Aurora. She deserves to know her brother if that's something Grayson wants."

"I still find it insane that he's her brother."

She chuckles, and I take her hand, pulling her into the library.

"Yo, Logan! Over here!" Jonas, a freshman rookie on the team, calls out when he spots us crossing the library. I wave but don't head toward them.

"You can go sit with your team, Logan," Riley murmurs, keeping her voice respectfully low.

"And miss sitting with you? Not a chance, Shortcake."

She rolls her eyes but smiles. "Well, we can go sit with them —if you want. I mean, if you want me to sit with you. Maybe you don't want that. You know what, just ignore me. Let's go find—"

She's cut off as I change direction, my arm tightening around her shoulders as we head toward the two tables shoved together that my teammates are crowded around.

Seeing me approach, seats are shuffled over, creating a space for us.

"Guys, you remember Riley."

"The not-so-make-believe girlfriend," Gavin quips with a friendly grin. "Nice to see you again. I'm Gavin."

"I'm Jonas. I've seen you at some of our home games."

The guys go around the table, introducing themselves and making Riley feel right at home. I freaking love my teammates. We've always been a pretty tight group, which can be hard to do when people leave and new ones join every year. With the exception of a few dickheads, everyone gets along, though.

I lift my chin in greeting to Nico when he quietly introduces himself, offering no more than his name to Riley before he buries his nose back in his textbook. It's not out of rudeness, he's just the quiet type. Honestly, I'm shocked to see him here with the rest of the team. He's the *keep to himself* kinda guy. As a first-round draft pick for the Springview Timberwolves, he chose to get a degree before beginning his hockey career. Being only a junior, he's already the best damn goalie I've ever seen, and despite the fact I don't think I've heard him utter more than a handful of words, I like the guy. He reminds me of Royce—all dark and broody. He's got the same build and a fuckton of tattoos that he keeps hidden underneath all his goalie gear.

"So you're the reason Logan's stopped coming out with us," Jacob, another first-line forward teases, drawing my attention.

"Just cause I'd rather hang out with my girl than you all," I smirk, throwing an arm around Riley.

After peppering Riley with questions—where she's from, her degree, what the hell she's doing with me—*did I mention my teammates are assholes?*—we all settle down to get some work done.

"Ugh, I can't take in another word until I get some food in me," Gavin groans an hour later, sagging back in his seat. It's a miracle we managed more than fifteen minutes before one of us caved to hunger. We're all growing boys. We need our sustenance.

A murmur of agreement goes up around the table.

"You ready to grab some lunch?" I ask Riley.

She nods, and we pack away our things, following behind the guys as we leave the library. I tuck her under my arm as we walk through the quad, letting the team walk on ahead. Riley chuckles quietly as we watch Gavin get Jonas in a headlock, the rest of the team egging them on.

"I like them," Riley says quietly. "They seem like a good team."

"Yeah, they are."

Looking down at her, I find her already gazing up at me. "You shouldn't pull away from them because of me. They're your team, and you're their captain. You should make an effort to hang out with them."

Pressing a kiss to the crown of her head, I say, "I know. It's just so hard to peel myself away from you."

Her smile is endearing. "I'll be here when you get back."

My grin brightens. "You mean I can crawl into your bed afterward?"

"Mm, only if you promise to do that thing with your tongue."

"Baby, I'll do all the things with my tongue."

She bursts out laughing, and I wave goodbye to my team-mates when we enter the food court, spotting Royce sitting at our usual table. "Go sit with Royce. I'll grab food for you."

After telling me what she wants, I watch her sidle closer to the table before queuing up to get us food. With a tray in each hand—most of which contains food for me—I make a beeline for the table.

I lift my chin in a *hello* to Royce as I set a tray in front of Riley before claiming the seat next to her, not wanting to interrupt the two of them as Riley relays some theory she learned in her psychology class.

Shoveling a forkful of chicken and rice into my mouth, I can feel eyes on us, and I know more than a few people are wondering what the hell the deal is between the three of us. Pretty sure most of campus knows now that Riley and I are a thing. Except Royce's sudden reappearance back in the food court and the fact the three of us eat together every day, and how he brings her to school and drops her home as often as I do, has all the nosey assholes intrigued. Especially because Royce isn't a PDA person, so unlike me, he isn't all over Riley in public.

Thankfully, Riley seems to have stopped giving a crap about the whispers and curious eyes. Guess that's what happens when you have actual real-life problems to worry about.

"So you're saying, if I yawn in class, it's not because I'm bored, but because I'm trying to keep my brain alert?" I query, catching the tail end of what she is saying.

"Exactly."

"But what if I'm also bored."

Rolling her eyes, she snarks, "Then you're also bored."

"Does that mean I'm giving back to society if I yawn and then someone else yawns because I yawned? Because by that logic, I'm helping to keep their brain alert so they can take in more of the boring lecture."

Sighing, Riley picks a slice of pepper from her salad and flicks it at me, earning a rumbling laugh from Royce.

Her smile slips as a shadow falls over our table, and I glance up to find Grayson standing there, looking uneasy as his gaze bounces between the three of us.

For a moment, I think he's going to ask if he can sit, and I'm pretty sure Royce and I have already decided that it will be Riley's decision. So if she says no, we'll make sure Grayson doesn't push it.

However, because he's Grayson and he's an asshole, he simply drops his tray on the table and claims the open seat beside Royce, looking at each of our shocked faces with his typical arrogance.

Dickhead is going to get punched, if he's not careful.

Riley might want us to repair our friendship, and okay, yeah, I wanna do that too. I've hated being pissed at him. However, if he says a single thing out of line to Riley, I won't hesitate to punch him hard enough to choke on some teeth.

Dismissing Grayson, I drop my gaze to check on Riley. She's staring wide-eyed at him, her lips pressed into a flat line, but she doesn't object to his presence. Once she notices me looking, she gives me a subtle nod that she's okay.

An awkward silence reigns over the table as Riley and Grayson lock eyes. I swear, I don't dare breathe as I wait for whatever cutting remark he's going to deliver and the inevitable bruise I will have to leave on his face. But then he goes and blows my mind with a simple nod of his head—a silent peace offering. Riley reciprocates with a waned smile, and just like that, the bubble of tension pops.

I exhale, blowing out the tightness in my lungs before

saying, "Did you know you can give back to society simply by yawning?"

Riley groans, and Royce chucks a chip my way, which I catch in my mouth. *Mmm, yum.* And for a little while, all is right in the world.

RILEY

CHAPTER FORTY-SIX

"Grayson?" I question, staring stupefied at Royce across the table in the food court. "I don't know that that's a good idea."

"It's that, or you call in sick," he states, arms folded across his chest.

"Seriously? I'm not calling in sick because you can't babysit me tonight. That's ridiculous, Royce."

He arches an arrogant brow. "What's ridiculous is you thinking I'm going to let you set foot in that club with *him* there and not ensure there are eyes on you at all times. I'd rather it be me, but I can't get out of this meeting with Xander tonight. I'm sorry."

"Royce, you don't need to apologize. You've given up every weekend to be at the club." I can tell whatever this meeting is, its timing has seriously pissed him off, but it must be important; otherwise, I know he'd reschedule, despite my assurances. "I really don't think sending Grayson in your place is a wise idea, though. In case you hadn't noticed, we don't exactly talk to one another." He's sat with us at lunch most days—if he's not at the office—and I catch him watching me frequently, but we haven't spoken a word directly to each other since that day he showed up at my apartment. I'm trying to give him time to come to terms with everything... and admittedly, I haven't a clue what to say to him.

What do you say to the guy whose world you've obliterated, who also happens to be your daughter's half-brother, and the guy whose dick you keep finding yourself bouncing on?

It's a niche situation. Not one that most self-help books or the internet have an answer for.

"There's no one else, Babydoll. Logan has a game tonight and another tomorrow. Best I can do is get him to switch out with Grayson once he's done tonight."

"No, don't do that," I sigh, giving in to defeat. I can't have Logan coming to sit in the club until 2 am after playing all night and with another game tomorrow. He has to be on top form if he's going to be picked up by the Timberwolves. He's already given up one NHL spot for me, I won't let him fuck up his chances of getting another.

Royce's lips kick up in a smirk, knowing he's won this argument.

I glower at him but ultimately relent. "Fine, but I can't be held responsible for what I do to him if he pisses me off."

"I'm sure whatever you do, he had it coming."

I snort, shaking my head as Grayson comes striding toward us. My whole body still goes tense when I see him, preparing to do battle and not entirely accepting of this strange stalemate we've come to for now.

"Hey," he greets, setting his tray down on the table and sliding into the seat opposite mine.

"I've got that meeting with Xander tonight," Royce states, holding Grayson's gaze.

"Yes." Grayson looks at Royce expectantly, already sensing there's more than just that statement.

"And Riley has to work."

Grayson's brow arches in a *get to the point.*

"So, I need you to be at the club tonight to keep an eye on her."

Grayson's brows jump up his forehead and it would be almost comical if it didn't mean I had to spend all night with Grayson's eyes on me.

"You want me to sit at Lux all night and watch her dance?" he clarifies. "Why?"

"Her boss is a sleazebag. I don't trust him, and I don't want her left alone with him."

Grayson's gaze snaps to mine as if looking for confirmation.

"He gets off on perving on the girls, but I'll be fine for one night. You don't have to do it."

Royce makes a growl of disagreement, but I don't take my eyes off Grayson.

"I'll do it," he states, without giving it more than a second's thought.

Surprise flashes through me, but Royce merely nods before filling him in on Ben and telling him what to look out for.

"Ugh, sorry I'm late," Logan says near the end of our lunch hour. "Meeting with Coach ran long." He smacks a kiss on my lips before falling into the empty seat beside Grayson and stealing the leftover food on my tray.

"You ready for tonight?" I ask.

He nods, grinning viciously. "You know it, Shortcake. Coach just told me there will be a Timberwolves scout there."

"Uh, what are you doing here?" I ask as I step out of my apartment building that night to find Grayson waiting for me.

His brows scrunch in confusion. "I thought Royce drove you there and home?"

"He does. I just, uh... You don't have to."

He rolls his eyes as he pushes off the side of his fancy car. "You think Royce wouldn't knock me out with one punch if I let you walk by yourself in the dark?"

He definitely would. Still, I make no move toward his car, and noticing, he sighs. "We're going to the same place. Just get in the car, Riley." Pausing at his door, his eyes meet mine over the car. "Unless you're afraid to be alone with me in a confined space."

There's a haughty smirk playing on his lips that has me storming toward the car before I can talk some common sense into myself. As I slam the door closed, I swear I hear him chuckle.

Ugh, even when he doesn't hate me, he's still a fucking asshole.

He drops gracefully into the driver's seat, closing his door, and immediately, I feel like I'm suffocating. His cologne wraps around me, and his body is way too close. The proximity has mine responding and I become hyper-aware of every little movement I make.

As he pulls away from the curb and drives down the street, I cast furtive glances in his direction. This is awkward as fuck. Or perhaps it's just me. He seems perfectly comfortable.

He looks great, dressed in pants and a shirt that will fit in perfectly with the clientele at Lux. The scruff on his chin that had appeared in recent weeks is still there, giving him a ruggedness he didn't have before, although the bags beneath his eyes have lessened and he doesn't look so weighed down.

"I can hear your brain working all the way over here," he drawls, not once taking his gaze off the road. "Why don't you just ask me whatever you're thinking?"

"How are you doing?" I ask after licking my dry lips. "You seem... better."

He flicks his gaze my way momentarily, and I don't miss how his hand tightens around the steering wheel before he forces it to relax. "I am, in some ways. The not knowing for sure... it was driving me insane. There's still things I don't have answers to, and maybe I never will..." His mom. My heart clenches for him. "But I know now what type of man my father is. While it's still difficult to wrap my head around, knowing that gives me some peace of mind."

I fiddle with the hem of Logan's hoodie that I put on tonight to block out the chill in the air. "For what it's worth, I'm sorry he's not the dad you thought he was. I know what that feels like, and it sucks, so, yeah... "

The feel of his large hand on my knee stops me, and I blink down at where his heat seeps through my leggings and into my skin. His hand on my leg looks so out of place yet feels so right all at once.

He gives it a tight squeeze, and when I lift my head to look up at him, his features are twisted in pain. "I'm sorry you had to go through that. I'm sorry"—his voice breaks over the words— "You were alone. That you didn't feel you could come to me."

Tears burn the backs of my eyes, and I deliberately look away so he can't see how choked up I am. "I thought I was sparing you," I admit. "Although I think I only made things worse."

Grayson sighs, and his voice is rough when he speaks. "My father is the one who made everything worse. Not you. You were a fifteen-year-old girl trapped in a horrible situation."

"And you were a seventeen-year-old who didn't know to look out for anything wrong," I counter, sensing that he's beating himself up for missing the signs back then.

"Maybe," he says wearily. "I'll still forever regret not paying closer attention."

That's the thing about regrets. The *what-ifs* of choices made and paths untaken. They linger in the corridors of your mind, haunting with a poignant reminder of what could have been. Each regret a ghostly whisper keeping us awake at night. However, the bitterness of them comes from their permanence. Grayson and I can both wish we'd made different decisions, but that's all they'll ever be: hopeless wishes.

Perhaps if we'd done things differently, we wouldn't be where we are now. But it's equally possible it wouldn't have changed anything at all. We'd still be standing here awkwardly at this impasse, unsure how to venture forward with the past casting the way in shadow, tinting the colors with a muted hue of what could have been.

We're both silent as he pulls into the parking lot at Lux and turns off the engine. However, before I can unbuckle my seatbelt and get out, he reaches across the center console until his face is all I can see.

"Regardless of the past, I'm paying attention now. I forced myself to stay away from you, and look what happened. I've learned from that mistake. From now on, you, Riley, have *all* of my attention."

Well fuck, I don't know if that's good or bad.

Based on the blazing intensity in his eyes, I'm going to guess it's not exactly good. Yet, the clenching of my core says it's definitely not all bad.

"Don't be sick. Don't be sick. Don't be sick."

Glancing over my shoulder, I find Kelsey standing behind

me. We're all in line as we wait for our cue to head onto the stage for our first performance of the night.

"Still getting performance anxiety?" I ask her.

Wringing her hands, she lifts her head, looking at me with wide, owlish eyes. "Once I'm out there, I'm fine, but the entire day before my shift I'm a nervous wreck."

I nod, understanding. "I promise it gets easier. I used to be the same way." Although for entirely different reasons. "The more you do it, the easier it will get. Just make sure you're attending rehearsals and practicing in between shifts."

"I have been."

I smile reassuringly at her. "You're a natural out there. You don't have anything to worry about."

"Thank you, Riley. I really appreciate that."

The lights in the club go out, our signal to get into position, and I wish her good luck before we step onto the stage.

Strangely, I find myself more nervous than usual as I get into position, waiting for the lights to burst to life above me. I know it's got nothing to do with performance anxiety and everything to do with a certain someone sitting in the crowd watching me tonight.

It feels weird not having the weight of Royce's gaze brushing against my skin. I've gotten so used to the feel of it—of him—that I feel almost naked tonight knowing he's not here.

Still, when the lights come on and the music begins, my eyes lock with Grayson's across the room, and while it's different, that feeling of the world fading around me is the same.

Grayson's stare is just as powerful. Reeling me in as I sashay and sway on the stage, dipping and stretching in time to the music. His stare darkens with each arch of my spine and curve of my hip. Not once does he look away from me, and when I'm not on the stage, his attention is focused entirely on Ben.

"No Royce tonight?" Tara asks, catching me watching Grayson from the shadows at the edge of the room.

"He was busy."

"I'm guessing that's Grayson?"

I nod, turning to look at her when she says, "Huh."

"What?"

"Interesting how he's here when he supposedly hates you."

Looking back at Grayson, I tell her, "He knows everything."

"He believes you?"

"He does." I watch, intrigued, as Grayson gets up and goes over to the bar, ordering a drink before engaging Ben in conversation. I wish I could hear what they were saying.

"So he's here as part of an apology?" Tara asks, sounding confused.

"He's only here because Royce asked him to be. It's got nothing to do with me."

She huffs out a laugh that has me turning to arch a brow at her.

"Sure it doesn't," she says with a smirk. "'Cause any guy would give up his Friday night to babysit his friend's girlfriend."

Rolling my eyes, I tell her, "It isn't like that."

"Babe, the way he's been looking at you all night says otherwise. If you ask me, he kinda looks a lot like Royce when he looks at you like that."

Giving her a deadpan stare, I droll, "You should get your eyes checked. You're seeing things."

She laughs, pulling me away and bringing an end to our conversation as we prepare for our next performance.

By the time the club is closing, my skin is buzzing from the attention I've received from Grayson all night, and I'm about to throttle Tara. Of course, she had to make some remark or ridiculous gesture after every performance and refused to drop the topic no matter how much I begged.

Grayson catches my eye, and I hold up two fingers, telling him I'll be out in a few minutes. He nods before following the crowd outside, and I turn to get changed while Ben locks up.

"Gotta dash," Tara says, throwing on her clothes in a rush.

"Where are you off to in such a rush?" I ask curiously.

She gives me a sly smirk, and I roll my eyes. "Have you at least given the poor guy a heads up that you're a psycho?"

"Now, where would the fun in that be?" she teases, grabbing her bag. "I want all the deets tomorrow."

She points a finger at me and is already dashing out of the dressing rooms as I call, "There won't be any deets to tell!"

Sighing, I shake my head. The woman is incorrigible.

Spotting Kelsey sitting nearby as she wipes off her makeup, I point out, "You weren't sick."

She grins back at me. "I wasn't sick. Thank goodness. And now I feel on top of the world... is that crazy or what?" She laughs at herself, but I shake my head.

"Totally understandable. It's the adrenaline rush. I always leave here simultaneously buzzed and crashing. It's a weird mix."

She nods. "That's exactly how I feel. I thought maybe it would pass."

"Haha, maybe it does, but it hasn't for me yet."

We get chatting for a bit, and it's only when a couple of other dancers wave goodbye as they leave that I realize we're the last ones left.

Grabbing my hoodie, I carry it in my hand as I follow her out. "Do you need a ride anywhere?"

"Oh, no, that's okay. I'll order a cab."

"You don't—"

"Riley," Ben interrupts, my name a bark, yelled from the bowels of his office as we pass. "A word."

Kelsey's eyes widen as my body goes stock still, and I paint on a reassuring smile for her. "I'll see you next weekend."

"Y-yeah, okay." Her gaze darts to the ajar office door then back to mine, giving me a wan smile before slowly stepping back. When I give her an encouraging nod, she takes another step, and I stand there until she eventually disappears out of sight.

After she's gone, I take a moment to steady my breathing before slowly turning to face the doorway. Still, my feet remain rooted to the floor, and it takes another deep inhale for me to find the courage to step forward, wiping my palms on my leggings as I step inside and deliberately not shutting the door behind me.

Ben is sitting behind his desk, head bent over some paper-work, but when I clear my throat, he looks up, eyes raking over me with an emotion I can't identify before he slowly pushes to his feet, rounding the desk until he's standing in front of me.

"We need to discuss your attitude lately."

"My attitude?" I parrot, nerves slicking along my skin and up my spine.

"The way you spoke to me the other week is unacceptable. I am your boss. If I ask you to do something, you do it. You don't talk back to me or shirk your responsibilities. If I ask you to stay late, you stay late. If I ask you to keep your boyfriend out of here, you do it."

He's not here tonight, and yet, conveniently, tonight is when Ben chose to have this conversation.

"Now," he says, flattening his cheap suit. "I want you to apologize to me."

"Apologize?" I ask, dumbfounded.

His dark eyes flare at my defiance.

"I haven't done anything wrong. I've stayed late when asked, and as for my boyfriend... I told you you needed to have this conversation with him. I'm not the one asking him to sit through every shift. Whatever happened between you two is why he sits out there every night. If you don't want him to, then *you* need to sort that out with him."

His teeth grind, lips curling in a savage snarl as he glowers at me. In the space between blinks, he shoves at my shoulders, sending me backward into the wall with a thud.

"You don't get to act all high and mighty because you managed to enchant some guy with your pussy. This is still *my* club. You're on *my* time, which means you do as *I* say, or you can find yourself another job."

I'm so stunned that all I can do is stand there and listen to him spew his bullshit, only snapping out of it when he crowds me against the wall. His acrid breath slaps against my cheek and I turn my head to the side to avoid the stench.

Fingers dig into my cheek deep enough to leave crescent moon indents, and I cry out as my face is wrenched to his. "Don't you fucking look away from me," he hisses, spittle flying from his mouth and landing on my skin. "You're nothing but a slutty little whore, happy to sell your body every night on *my* stage. Yet you think you're too good for me?"

His laugh is unhinged, and I shove against him in a bid to get him to let go, to step back, to give me room to escape.

"I don't sell my body," I hiss, the words coming out garbled from his painful grip on my cheeks. "*You're* the one who took it upon himself to sell my body to whoever wanted to pay. You treat us like cattle. Selling us to the highest bidder all so you can line your own pockets."

"Shut up!" Using his grip on my face, he pulls me forward before smashing my head against the wall. Stars dance across my vision as pain ricochets around my skull, and I groan, my knees going weak.

I scream as he fists the back of my head, pulling on my hair as a burning sensation races along my scalp. I claw and shove at his hand as he drags me across the room before throwing me on top of his desk, knocking the air from my lungs.

"You're going to stay there and take what I give you. Maybe I can fuck that attitude out of you."

Despite the pounding in my head, I buck against the feel of his crotch against my ass and the hard press of his hand digging into my back.

"Stop it!" I yell, unable to believe this is happening as he gropes at my leggings. "Help! HELP!"

Holy fuck, how is this happening?

I'm spiraling. Losing any grounding I have as my breathing goes ragged and memories flood my brain, paralyzing me.

"Shut up, bitch," Ben snarls, grabbing the back of my head and pushing my face into his desk.

Tears stream from my eyes, my vision black as I attempt to fight him off. I hear the rip of my leggings but barely even register it as being real.

"I've been dying to sample this cunt since the day you walked in here," he growls. "Toity bitch thinking you're better than me. You're nothing but a cheap whore. You should be begging for my cock."

"No," I cry helplessly. "Please don't."

"Shut up!" he snarls, only making me cry harder as he fumbles with his pants.

From a far-off place, I hear banging, but I can't tell if it's real or in my head as I shut off my senses one by one until I'm back in the protective sphere in my mind. The one I haven't ventured into since the day Bertram was arrested. The one that was my sanctuary in the dead of night. That enabled me to walk away from that with my sanity somewhat intact.

I'm not so sure I'll be as lucky this time.

GRAYSON

CHAPTER FORTY-SEVEN

I drum my fingers against the steering wheel while waiting for Riley to come out. She indicated she'd only be a few minutes, and I check the clock for the tenth time, noting that it's already been fifteen minutes.

I've been scouring the faces of every girl as they left to see if one of them was her, but no one new has come out in a couple of minutes.

Royce told me not to leave her alone *at all*. He'll have my balls if something happens and I've been sitting in the fucking car. Starting to grow concerned, I climb out and stride toward the building where the last girl to emerge is waiting.

"Have you seen Riley?" I ask as a cab pulls into the lot and stops in front of her.

She looks up at me before glancing back toward the building. "Uh, yeah. Ben called her into his office as we were leaving."

My lips thin as everything within me goes on high alert.

"He sounded angry," she admits.

Fuck.

Without listening to another word, I turn away from her,

jogging up the side of the building where the girls all came from.

"Fuck," I hiss when I come to a steel door. It's one of those that can only be opened from the inside. All I can do is bang my fist against it. When no one comes to open it, I press my ear to the door, hoping I can hear something from inside, but all I get is silence.

"Hey!" I yell, banging on it harder. "Riley! Someone open the door!"

With each passing second, my heart rate skyrockets and my stomach twists with unease. Something isn't right here. Royce warned me about Ben, but I didn't think he'd actually try something. Not on my watch. *On the one fucking night Royce asks me to look after her.*

Hearing the sound of a car out in the lot, I run around to the front of the building in time for a girl I vaguely recognize from earlier to climb out. She jogs around the front of the door, muttering to herself, but stops when she sees me, gaze snapping to mine as it narrows.

"You're Grayson, right? What are you still doing here?"

Okay, she obviously knows me, so she must be friendly with Riley.

"Riley's still in there. I can't get in."

She must see the panic in my face as she doesn't question me as she gestures for me to follow her. "He probably asked her to stay late and help clean up," she explains as she inserts the key.

Except the faint cry I hear when she opens the door tells me he hasn't kept her late for work.

Practically shoving the girl aside, I race through the darkened club, following the sounds of distress as they grow louder. Reaching what appears to be an office, I come to a stop in the doorway, my stomach dropping at the sight before me.

"Oh my god." A gasp from behind has me realizing the girl followed me, but I'm too focused on the sight of Riley bent over the table in front of me, that slimy fucker on top of her as she whimpers helplessly.

I'm moving before I've even registered it, fisting the back of his shirt and pulling him off her as I wind my arm back and send it flying into his face. The momentum sends him spinning backward, and I follow as he crashes into the wall, pressing my hand against his chest and holding him there as I deliver punch after punch. I barely register the pain, my vision burned red as I decimate his face.

"Grayson. Grayson!" I don't know how long someone has been calling my name, but I'm breathing heavily, my hand and face splattered with blood, when I finally loosen my hold on the shitbag. He drops to the floor with a satisfying thud as I turn away.

"I need your help," the girl says, cradling a hysterical Riley. "She's having a panic attack. I can't get her to calm down."

The sick fuck is forgotten as I close the distance between us, cupping Riley's face in a firm grip. "Breathe with me, Riley," I say, struggling to keep my voice calm. "Breathe in. Breathe out." I take it slow, watching to see if she syncs her breaths with mine.

"It's not working," the girl pointlessly states.

"Fuck," I hiss, pulling Riley from her and dropping to the floor as I bundle her into my arms. I press her ear to my chest so she can hear the thudding of my heart as I focus on slowing it to an average pace and encourage her to breathe with me. "Breathe in. Breathe out," I repeat, stroking her hair with one hand and holding her tightly with the other.

"You're safe. I've got you. He can't hurt you. I won't ever let him hurt you again."

I repeat my mantra over and over, sending up a silent prayer when she stops hyperventilating. The rasps of her breathing are replaced with soft sobs that break my heart as I squeeze her tighter. "You're okay. I've got you. You're okay," I murmur softly.

"G-Grayson?" she eventually croaks.

"I'm here."

"Get me out of here, please."

"Anything, Tempest."

Holding her as gently as possible, I get to my feet, on a one-track mind, as I stride for the door. It's only when the girl calls out, "What do you want to do with him?" that I remember I left the shitstain unconscious on the floor.

Keeping Riley's face tucked against my shirt, I turn, noticing the savage look on the girl as she glares at Ben's mutilated face. "Leave him. Pretty sure Royce will want to pay him a visit once I fill him in."

She nods but makes no effort to leave. "I can't leave you here alone with him," I say, not truly caring, but I know I'd feel like shit if I left her here and something happened.

She scoffs, smirking at me. "That's disgustingly chivalrous of you, but you don't need to worry your pretty little head. Just get my girl out of here."

"Tara?" Riley hiccups, craning her neck.

The girl—Tara's—face softens as she smiles at Riley. "Hey, babe. When I told you I wanted the deets later, I was thinking more along the lines of you making out with your boy here."

Riley's laugh is more of a sniffle as she wipes at her nose. "What are you doing here?"

"Picked one hell of a night to leave my phone behind." Stepping closer, she runs her hand over the top of Riley's head. "You go home and let this one take care of you, yeah? He looks like he's going to hulk out if he doesn't get you out of here, and green is just such a vile color."

As Riley huffs out another watery laugh, I swear eternal

devotion to this woman who has managed to make her laugh twice in the last few minutes.

"I can't—"

Tara waves me off. "I called a friend. He'll be here in a few. We'll keep an eye on fuckface here until we hear from you about what you wanna do. Riley has my number and Royce probably has Rome's."

I hesitate for a moment longer, but she looks happy enough to be left alone, and it's not like Ben is in any fit state to do anything. Relenting, I walk out of the office with Riley in my arms.

As we reach the front of the building, the door is yanked open, and a wide-eyed Roman comes striding in, looking like he's about to rip someone limb from limb. We've never spoken much, but I recognize him from Royce's fight nights at The Depot. "You looking for Tara?" I ask when he spots us, his gaze dropping to where Riley is curled up in my arms. I instinctively pull her closer, on the verge of snapping at him to stop staring, when he nods, brows furrowed in confusion. "She's back there." I tilt my head down the hallway.

"Thanks," he grunts before striding past me, and feeling happier now that Tara won't be alone, I shove out the door and into the night.

I get Riley settled in the car, buckling her in before gently closing the door. She doesn't say anything, just stares blankly out the window. I hate how fucking fragile she looks. Not once since I spotted her in this club have I seen her looking so lost and breakable. It's disconcerting after all the shit we threw at her—*I* threw at her.

Walking around the hood, I pull my phone out and send a quick 911 message to the guys. Logan is probably asleep, but Royce is likely waiting up to talk about how his meeting with Xander went tonight.

Tucking the phone into my pocket, I slide in beside Riley, casting a quick look her way before starting the engine.

"Everything is going to be okay," I tell her as I pull out of the lot.

"Say it again," she rasps in a broken voice.

"Everything will be okay?"

She shakes her head. "What you said in there."

It takes me a second to figure out what she means before it clicks. "You're safe. I've got you. He can't hurt you now. I won't ever let him hurt you again."

With every sentence, she relaxes into the seat, and I repeat the mantra the entire way home.

"I can walk," she mumbles when I open her door outside the house and bundle her into my arms. *Yeah, if her legs are as weak as her voice, there's no way they'll carry her into the house.*

"Don't care," I grunt, using my hip to close the car door.

The lights are on inside, and as I approach the house, the front door opens, a rumpled Logan filling the doorway. "Short-cake," he rasps when he sees her, eyes rounding before he lifts them to mine. "What the hell happened?"

"Logan," Riley sobs, breaking down in a fresh wave of tears.

"Riley." Logan rushes forward, taking her from me. She clings desperately to his neck, crying harshly into his shoulder as he runs a hand up her back before striding into the living room and dropping onto the sofa.

I follow them inside, feeling like an outsider as I watch while Logan comforts her while she falls apart in his arms. "Shh, baby. You're okay," Logan soothes, his face fractured in pain as he listens to her broken sobs.

He looks at me over her head, questions brimming in his eyes, but before I can answer any of them, the front door flies open, and Royce barrels in. He doesn't even spare me a glance as he goes straight for Riley, crouching beside Logan and reaching out for her. Remaining in Logan's lap, she reaches out and pulls Royce to her, crying on him instead.

He holds her for a few minutes, whispering reassurances until he gently untangles her, settling her against Logan before he stalks toward me. "I fucking told you to watch her." The venom in his voice is poisonous. "What part of that did you not fucking understand, Van Doren?"

I'm shoved against the wall, and I reckon I'm seconds away from receiving a black eye when Riley hiccups, "It wasn't his fault!"

It's enough to stay Royce's hand as he twists to face her. Sniffing, Riley wipes at her red-rimmed eyes as she shifts on Logan's lap to face us—not that Logan lets her go far. "Ben waited until after the club had closed. He caught me on my way out... called me into his office and... a-and..."

Her whole body trembles as she struggles to force the words out, and wanting to take that pain from her, I blurt, "He had her bent over his desk when I got there. I was locked out...." I shift my focus to Riley. "I'm sorry—"

She shakes her head, wiping at her nose. "Not your fault."

"Where the fuck is he now?" Royce snarls.

"At the club. Tara and Roman are there, making sure he doesn't disappear."

Royce nods, turning to look at Logan. "Stay here with her."

I can tell from the tightness in Logan's jaw that he wants to come, but I'm not sure even the apocalypse could tear him from Riley right now.

Tightening his hold on her, he gives a sharp jerk of his head.

Royce remains frozen in the middle of the room before forcing himself to relax a little. With stiff movements, he crosses the space and bends down, bringing himself face-to-face with Riley. "Stay with Logan, sweetheart. I'll be back in a bit."

"Royce." There's a plea in her voice, but he merely kisses the top of her head before stepping away, and Logan distracts her as he strides out of the room.

I move to follow him, but when we're in the hall, he rounds on me. "I don't need your *help*."

With the muscle in my jaw ticking, I hiss, "I'm coming."

"You've done enough." He turns away, but I reach out and spin him back to face me. "I said I'm fucking coming. You didn't see..." I glance away, struggling to get a hold of my emotions. "I'm coming."

His astute gaze runs over me before he grunts a "fine." I follow him out to his truck, parked haphazardly on the road, and climb in.

"Tell me exactly what happened. Everything. Don't leave out a single detail," he orders, shifting the car into gear and pulling onto the road.

I do exactly that, explaining how I heard Riley scream and exactly how I found her when I got into that office, side-eyeing him as his fury reaches a boiling intensity, his hands clenching around the steering wheel and arms vibrating with rage as he flies through the streets of Halston.

We make it to Lux in record time, and despite me assuring him that Ben didn't cross *that* line with Riley—thank fuck!—he stomps inside like a grizzly bear coming out of hibernation, ready to devour the first thing he sees. He knows where he's going as he heads straight for Ben's office, and I follow.

Tara is sitting behind the desk when we get there, grinning with her feet kicked up on his desk as she plays with what looks like a letter opener. Roman is standing to the side, arms folded across his chest as he glares at her like she's a disobedient child.

Royce doesn't spare either of them a glance as he goes straight to Ben, who is still unconscious where I left him on the floor.

"He's been out the whole time," Tara states without any emotion.

"You two can go," Royce says, eyes cataloging the damage I did.

"No fair," Tara pouts. "Things were just getting interesting."

Roman sighs like he's used to her shenanigans. "Suits me." He darts a glance between Royce and Ben. "Call if you need help with that."

Royce's only response is a grunt as Roman manhandles Tara out of the office, and I hear her protesting all the way down the hall before the door slams shut behind them.

I walk over to stand beside Royce, the two of us looking down at Ben. I take some satisfaction in the fact his face is barely recognizable.

"Not a bad job," he states.

"Thanks."

"I would have done better."

I roll my eyes. "What's the plan?"

"This fucker's Halston days are done. Search his desk, see if you can find a home address or something."

Dismissing me, he bends down beside Ben's face, staring at it before he delivers a loud slap. Ben groans, but that's it. I move to rifle through the desk as Royce attempts to wake him.

"W-what..." Ben slurs.

"Welcome to your nightmare," Royce purrs in a tone that is pure steel wrapped in malevolent shadows.

My eardrums nearly burst as Royce drags the fucker to his feet, screaming. *Fuck, why didn't I punch him in the throat?*

Pinning him to the wall, Royce continues in that creepy-as-shit tone, "I warned you, Ben. I told you to stay away from my girl. But you just couldn't help yourself, could you?" Another scream as a loud snap echoes around the room, and I peer up, noticing one of Ben's fingers is now pointed the wrong way. *Sucks to be him.*

"Thought you were owed something because you're the boss in here, but you see, I told you before—the power you have here is imaginary. And now I'm going to take it all." Another crack followed by a pained whimper.

"See, I'm a possessive bastard. I don't like people touching what's mine. And I especially don't like when someone touches her against her will." This time, he snaps his entire wrist, and Ben howls in agony.

"When someone makes her cry." There's the distinctive snap of another bone breaking, and Royce loses himself to the violence as he systematically breaks every bone in both of Ben's hands.

When he steps back, Ben collapses to the floor, cradling his hands against his chest as he sobs. It's a disgusting sight. Pathetic. And so fucking satisfying.

Royce isn't done, though, and as he pushes Ben onto his back with the toe of his boot, I grab a letter off the desk and move to stand beside him.

"Let's see how fucking powerful you feel with busted balls and a crushed dick." Lifting his knee, Royce brings his foot down on Ben's crotch, and he wails like a dying cat. With a sick smile on his face, Royce does it over and over and over until Ben is on the verge of losing consciousness.

"Do you have that address?" he asks me, not even sounding out of breath.

"Yup." I hand him the letter with Ben's home address, and holding it in one hand, he leans down and fists the front of Ben's shirt, dragging him halfway off the ground.

"Now, given account of your... injuries... I'm going to give you forty-eight hours to get your sick, perverted ass out of this town, and if you don't, I'm going to find a new home for you six feet in the dirt with the worms and maggots."

Royce waves the letter in his face, ensuring he sees it. "I'm going to hold on to this, Ben Warden of 18 Creston Street. I'll be driving past in two days, and if there's any sign of you there, we'll be having another one of these little chats... and it won't be ending so well."

Royce drops him and straightens. He glares down at Ben with disgust. Delivering a final kick to his ribs, he turns his back to him, and I follow as we walk out of the club.

"You think he'll leave?" I ask when we're inside the truck.

"He'd be an idiot not to, but then again, he's proven so far he's not exactly smart."

Everything about Royce is brimming with barely contained rage. It fills the atmosphere, and I'm guessing the fact he's still worked up is why he hasn't made an effort to start the truck.

"How did tonight go?" I ask, hoping to distract him.

"Fine. Xander's *friend* is Dax," he tells me with a roll of his eyes. "If I'd known that, I could have gone straight to him."

"And Dax can help?" I press.

"He says he knows a computer guy who can create a profile and set everything up to look legit."

"Okay," I say, thinking. "So what now?"

"He's going to get this guy on it. Then I need to set up another meeting with Lydia so I can show her what I've got and discuss the next steps."

"And you're still convinced we shouldn't tell Riley?"

The un-enamored stare he gives me says everything.

"Yeah, okay," I agree.

After tonight, that would be the last thing she needs.

RILEY

CHAPTER FORTY-EIGHT

"*M*aybe I can fuck that attitude out of you."

"*Such a good girl for Daddy.*"

"*You're nothing but a cheap whore.*"

"*Daddy's good little girl.*"

I startle awake with a gasp, momentarily stunned as I blink at the dark ceiling above me.

I'm safe. I'm at the guys' house. I'm not alone.

He's not here. He can't hurt me.

I don't even know which *he* I'm referring to, but my mantra does its trick as I regulate my breathing, calming myself. The fact that I didn't wake Royce or Logan this time shows how exhausted they are. Which is understandable. This must be the fourth or fifth time since we climbed into bed several hours ago that I've woken. Every other time, one or both of them have awakened as well, but turning to look at each of them, they're thankfully still sound asleep.

Logan needs sleep after his game tonight, and especially with another one tomorrow. Technically, I guess today, since there are faint streaks of gray sunlight creeping around the edges of his curtains.

And Royce... Well, I don't know exactly what happened when he and Gray went back to Lux, but he came home with busted knuckles and a victorious gleam in his eye that I've never seen—not even when he obliterates his opponent in the ring. Either way, whatever he did, I'm sure he deserves his rest, too.

I, however, can't get back to sleep. I don't even want to. Every time I close my eyes, I feel his hands on my skin. The vile stench of his breath on my cheek. The arrogance of his words in my ear. I just... can't anymore. I can't lie here and know he's waiting for me.

I'm not sure what I need. I already tried washing him off me in a scalding shower. All I did was rub my skin raw until Logan took over, yet I swear I still feel him all over me. Inside me.

With a shiver, I wriggle out from between Royce and Logan. After my shower, Logan dressed me in a pair of his boxers and t-shirt, so I grab his hoodie from the back of a chair before I creep out of his room.

The house is silent as I head downstairs, deciding that caffeine is the only thing that will get me through this day. Caffeine and at least another three showers to slough off my skin.

Too lost in my head, I don't immediately notice that the kitchen is occupied.

"Riley."

I nearly jump out of my skin at his rough rasp, finding Grayson hunched over the kitchen island with a mug nestled between his hands. His dilated pupils and exhausted-looking eyes are on me, though.

"I, uh, didn't think anyone would be up." My eyes bounce back and forth between his. "Have you been to bed yet?"

He shakes his head. "Knew I wouldn't be able to sleep."

"Same."

At my admission, shadows creep across his face. I haven't seen him since he left with Royce last night, and honestly, my memory of him coming to my rescue is fuzzy. One minute, I was locking myself away in my inner sanctum, and the next, I heard his voice in my ear, bringing me back from the beyond with an alternate version of my mantra.

His eyes scan over me before returning to my face. "What can I do to help?"

My throat bobs at his question, and I wrap my arms around myself to stave off the chill at the reminder of last night. "You already did it," I say in a hoarse voice. "Y-you got to me in time. I owe you a thank—"

"Don't fucking thank me for that shit," Grayson barks loud enough that I flinch.

He catches it, his shoulder dropping as he exhales. "Fuck. I'm sorry. Just... don't thank me for not fucking being there."

"But you were there." I swallow roughly as the memories threaten to pull me under. "You were there when it mattered."

Grayson's entire body shudders at those words.

"I was still too fucking late." Coming around the island, he stands before me, looking at me with such a pleading expression. "Tell me what I can do to help."

The answer comes to me in a split second of insanity. "Touch me."

He flinches as though slapped, and, yeah, I imagine my request sounds ludicrous. Maybe I've finally snapped. Lost my marbles somewhere on the office floor of Lux.

Now that I've said it aloud though, I realize that's what I need. I need to not feel *his* hands all over me, and the only way to do that is to replace them with someone else's.

"What? No. I—Logan. You should ask Logan. He'd be gentle with you. Take care of you. He'd be able to stop. I—"

"I don't want Logan's gentle touch. Sweet and caring...

that's not what I need right now. I need someone to tear me apart. To rip me to shreds so I can put myself back together without the feel of him inside me." I sniffle, getting overwhelmed. *God, I just need him out of me.* "I can't ask Royce. Not with his past. It would be too much for him." I glance up at Grayson, begging. "Which leaves you."

He's frozen before me, face etched in agony.

"*Please,* Grayson." I don't give a shit if I'm begging. My sanity is unraveling, and if he turns me down, I'm certain I'll lose the last scraps of it that I'm clinging to. "I can feel him on me." I scratch at my skin beneath the hoodie. "He's all over me, and I don't know how to get him out." I hiccup over the words, scratching harder at my skin. The feeling is unbearable and growing worse by the second. "*Please.* I need to get him out, and I don't know any other way."

"Riley," he grits, restraint scraped raw. "I'm not capable of being gentle when it comes to you."

"I don't want gentle, Grayson. Bite me. Mark me. Fucking exorcise me. Just. Get. Him. Out! *Please,*" I tack on in a desperate whisper.

The plea has barely passed my lips before he pounces, his lips slamming against mine in a brutal kiss that knocks the air from my lungs and leaves me suspended.

His tongue forces its way past my lips, harsh and bruising, just like I wanted. Like I *need.*

"This what you wanted, Tempest?" Grayson growls against my lips. "For me to lay waste to this tempting body of yours. To irrevocably mark it as mine so no guy will even *think* about touching what belongs to me."

God, is that what I wanted? I don't even fucking know. I just know I need *more.*

"Answer me."

"Y-yes," I say breathlessly.

His responding growl vibrates through me before his hands land on my hips, and he pushes me backward. "Arms in the air."

I don't hesitate to lift my arms above my head and he pulls off my hoodie and t-shirt, leaving me standing in Logan's boxers in the middle of the kitchen.

"Hands on the countertop," he orders next, eyes flashing when I reach behind me to grab the edge of the counter. "You're going to do everything I say, aren't you, Tempest?" All I'm capable of is a nod. "This body is mine. Show me."

Stepping forward, he crowds me against the counter. His hand goes to fist the back of my head, except when I flinch at the pain and the reminder of last night, he smooths his palm over it before wrapping his hand around one side of my throat while his lips go straight to the other side as he sucks on the skin to the point of pain. I sigh in relief, even that little mark lessening some of the chaos inside me.

He moves to the juncture of my neck, this time sinking his teeth into my flesh, and I tremble.

"No man will ever again question who you belong to," he rasps, moving to scrape his teeth along my collarbone. "And neither will you. You can date and fuck those two upstairs, but you'll always be mine. You were mine *first*."

My breathing is erratic as he works his way down my body, marking my chest and breasts before dropping to his knees and biting his way along my stomach and over my hips.

With every mark he leaves, I feel as though the belt around my throat loosens. The tightness in my chest eases and my body feels less like *his* and more like mine.

"He doesn't get to claim any part of you," Grayson continues. "Not your body and definitely not your soul."

By the time he reaches the waistband of Logan's boxers, my thighs are clenched and I'm rocking into him with every press of his lips. Only, instead of going further, he sits back on his haunches and looks up at me.

"You want me to rip you apart, and I will, Tempest, but I have no fucking intention of leaving you to sift through the wreckage yourself. You'll fall apart on my tongue and I'll piece you together on my cock, do you hear me?"

I hesitate before nodding, and his pupils dilate as he stares up at me. "Your words, Tempest."

"Yes," I pant. I'm pretty sure I'd agree to anything he said if it meant getting his tongue and lips where I need him most.

His smirk is pure arrogance as he hooks his fingers beneath the waistband of the boxers and drags them down my legs until I can step out of them.

"Keep your hands on the counter," he orders in a thick voice before pushing my thighs apart and burying himself in my center.

"Oh god," I cry out, clenching my fingers around the countertop as he sinks his tongue inside me and hums against my sensitive flesh. He switches between tongue fucking me and brutalizing my clit until I'm a whimpering, trembling mess.

When my legs feel as though they're about to give out, he pulls them over his shoulders until I'm straddling his face, his hands squeezing my ass as he tugs me infinitely closer.

Suspended between him and the counter, my fingers dig into the worktop as I arch into every lick and suck until I'm coming apart on his tongue, just like he promised.

"Oh god. Oh god," I repeat my prayer on a mantra as my release blasts along my nerves, leaving me drained and sweaty.

Before I can even begin to come down, Grayson drops me to my feet, standing to wrap his hand around my neck and directing my attention to him. I blink up into his darkened eyes, lips and chin shining with my juices.

"When I'm making you feel so good, I *am* your God, and it's *my* name you'll scream when you're coming on my cock."

Using his hold on my throat, he maneuvers me to the kitchen island, spinning and shoving me down with a hand pressed to my back. I momentarily panic, memories of last night flashing through my mind as I push back against him. But Grayson's more assertive, and he forces me flat on the island counter, my ass in the air.

"Shhh," he soothes, running his hand gently down my spine when he notices my trembling.

"You want to be ripped apart, don't you, Tempest?"

"Y-yes." My voice shakes.

"Then trust me to do that."

His hands roam reverently over my back and down my ass before his fingers slide between my thighs. I gasp at the intrusion, but my anxiety is quickly replaced with pleasure as he massages my inner walls.

"The only ones who get to see you in this position are the ones in this house," he rumbles as he slowly fucks me with his fingers.

"Anyone else won't live to talk about it."

I moan at the level of possession in his voice. It definitely shouldn't be attractive but, holy fuck, it's hot as hell.

His fingers slide out, and I feel the press of his blunt head at my entrance. Once again, memories crash over me as I feel him behind me. So similar to last night.

Sensing that I'm no longer fully with him, Grayson bends over and sinks his teeth into my shoulder. The pain is sharp enough to bring me back to the present.

"The only people in this moment are you and me, Tempest. No one else."

I nod, my cheek rubbing against the granite. "No one else."

He slides his cock through my folds, testing. He must be

satisfied that I'm fully present because, in the next second, he's buried balls deep inside me as I cry out at the intrusion.

"Fuck," he rasps. "I won't ever get enough of this feeling. So fucking tight. The way you squeeze me, Tempest. Fucking perfect."

He presses a palm between my shoulder blades, keeping me in place as he grabs my hip and begins to move. His thrusts are brutal and savage. Exactly what I asked for. What I need. With every slam of his hips against mine, I feel him pushing Ben out from beneath my skin and replacing him with himself.

"Oh god," I garble, screaming when he delivers a hard slap to my ass.

"Try again, Tempest."

I blink, taking a second to scramble through my addled brain to understand what he means.

"Grayson," I pant, remembering.

"That's it. *I'm* the one making you feel so good. I'm the only one here. It's you and me, and *I'm* the one fucking this pretty little pussy of yours. *I'm* the one ripping you apart. You better fucking remember that."

"Grayson," I gasp, shaking like a leaf. "I'm going to come."

"Yes you are. You're going to come on my cock, Tempest. Right. Fucking. Now." He bites down on my shoulder, and I scream as I come, strangling him with my pussy.

Sagging against the island, I'm nothing more than a mess of limbs incapable of moving. He slides his hard length from me before gently turning me onto my back.

With his eyes on my heaving chest, he slides back inside.

"Tell me you're with me."

"I'm with you."

His stare drops lower, hovering over each mark he's left as he slowly fucks me.

His hands grasp my outer thighs before sliding until his

fingers brush over my scars. His gaze takes them in before wandering to where he's entering me.

"This pussy has been mine since you walked into my house at the age of fifteen." His hands glide over my hips and up my sides. "This body is mine." His stare flicks to mine, eyes blown wide and giving away just how feral he is behind his carefully controlled movements. "I'm a possessive fuck. It's one thing to share you with my two best friends, but I refuse to share you with anyone else. Even the figment of a memory."

Reaching over to the knife block, he slides one out, and my breathing hitches as he brings it to my skin, the flat side cold against my heated skin.

"If he's beneath your skin, then I want him out," he growls. There's a menace to his tone—an unhinging that would scare most people, but not me. I've seen too much of human nature's dark side to fear Grayson's demons.

And considering my damage is just as depraved as his, I arch my spine, forcing the tip of the blade into my skin as I moan, "Yes."

There's a prick of pain, followed by the high of slicing skin, only better because I'm not alone in a bathroom, bleeding out my agony. This might be a bloodletting, but instead of pouring out my pain... I'm opening myself up to possibility. I'm banishing the demons that have haunted my mind for so many years and making room for the prospect of hope and love and a future that I've never truly allowed myself to dream of.

"Again," I rasp, groaning when Grayson cuts another slice as he bottoms out inside me. The pleasure is indescribable. Fucking and cutting rolled into one and delivering a double whammy. It's a high I could chase for the rest of my life.

"Yes," I hiss as another drag of the blade splits my skin, and my head falls back against the island as I close my eyes.

When Grayson dips forward, running his tongue along the

nick, I moan, sliding my hand into his hair and holding him to me as he licks and sucks. His lips are stained red when he pulls away, and leaning up, I capture them with mine, tasting the mix of copper and unbridled desire on his tongue.

That kiss is his undoing. The last restraints on his control shatter, and the knife clatters to the floor as he slides a hand to the back of my head and drags me to the edge of the counter so he can fuck me the way he wants to.

We come together in a collision of crazed need and unfiltered desire. Each thrust of our hips is frantic. I claw at him with frenzied movements and he attacks my mouth with a frenetic need that sends me spiraling.

"Come for me right now, Tempest."

"Come with me," I gasp, barely getting the words out as he fucks me relentlessly.

"I will. There's only you and me, and I want to wring every ounce of pleasure from your body before I mark it as mine."

The level of his possession is my ruination, and I come whimpering his name. On his next thrust, he buries himself deep inside me, holding me to him as he groans into my hair.

For long seconds, we stay like that. Hearts clashing beneath our ribs.

When he finally slides out, I collapse against the island in exhaustion. My eyes close as the sweat on my skin goes cold, and I can smell the copper in the air.

"I need a shower," I pant.

"No." His responding growl has me cracking open an eye. Finding him kneeling between my spread thighs, staring hungrily at my aching core, I lean up on my elbows.

"What do you mean *no?* I need to shower, Grayson. I'm covered in sweat and blood and *your* cum."

His eyes flash to mine. "Exactly. You're covered in *me.*"

"I'm too tired to deal with you," I mutter, collapsing back on the countertop. However, he doesn't give me a second of peace, and a moment later, I feel his fingers pushing their way inside me.

"What are you doing?" I whine, too sensitive for him to do anything else.

"Making sure I stay inside you." He massages my inner walls, rubbing his cum into the very lining of my pussy.

"You're insane," I grumble, too tired to fully comprehend the extent of his possessiveness.

I leave him to it as exhaustion washes over me, threatening to pull me under. When he's done, he puts my boxers back on before cleaning the cuts on my chest and torso. When he's satisfied, he helps me into my t-shirt and hoodie. Then he carries my half-asleep ass into the living room and settles me on the sofa.

On the verge of succumbing to sleep, I'm barely aware of the brush of his fingers as he pushes my hair out of my face and murmurs, "You should have gone to Logan. Now that you've given me this, I won't stop until I have all of you."

CHAPTER FORTY-NINE

"What the hell did you do to her?" Logan's hiss wakes me from the dead of sleep, but I keep my eyes closed as I listen. "She looks like she was mauled by a wild animal."

Grayson doesn't verbally respond, but when Logan says, "Don't look so fucking smug," I can only imagine his expression.

"You better not have hurt her," he continues.

"I didn't do anything she didn't beg me for," Grayson drawls.

"Do you *want* me to beat the shit out of you?" Logan growls. "I might not be able to do it as thoroughly as Royce. However, I can still beat you fucking senseless."

"You're foaming at the mouth like a rabid dog," Grayson retorts, likely only infuriating Logan more.

I'm about to open my eyes and intervene when Logan hisses so venomously that for a second I question if it's even him speaking, "Have you forgotten that she was fucking *attacked* yesterday?"

"I can assure you, Logan, I won't forget yesterday for the

rest of my fucking life," Grayson retorts just as viciously, and I have no doubt if my lower half wasn't spread across his knees he would have Logan in a chokehold. "I was the one that had to see that shit. That had to bring her back from the fucking brink. I'll be old and gray with an addled brain just like Gran, and the look in her eyes will still fucking haunt me."

The agony behind his words makes it difficult to breathe, and unable to listen to another word, I stretch, acting as though I've just woken up. My entire body aches in the most delicious of ways as I work the muscles.

"Hey, Shortcake," Logan says, his tone a direct contrast to the one he just used on Grayson as he crouches by my head, where I'm sprawled out on the couch. "How are you feeling?"

"Better."

I miss Grayson's reaction, but Logan must have seen it as he snaps his head in his direction, pointing a finger at him. "You shut up before I staple your mouth shut."

Turning back to me, his anger is instantly replaced with concern as he strokes a hand down my hair. "Royce went to get food. Do you think you can eat?"

I nod as I push myself upright. "Food sounds good."

With gentle touches, Logan helps me to my feet. "What's wrong?" he asks, panicked when I wince.

"Nothing," I assure him, straightening. "I'm fine."

"You made a face."

When I don't immediately answer, Grayson jumps on the opportunity. "Her cunt's sore from the fucking I gave it this morning."

Fuck me. Remind me again why I thought dating more than one guy was a wise idea? The irony is I'm not even dating Grayson. Nor do I even know if I want to.

"You little shit—" I plant a hand on Logan's chest as I look at Grayson's smug face over my shoulder.

"That is entirely enough out of you. Thanks for the help earlier, but if you're just going to piss off my boyfriend, then you can eat your food in your room."

The arrogant smile drops from his face as his eyes darken in warning. "Sounds like someone needs another reminder of who exactly they belong to."

Spine straightening, I twist fully to face him, feeling Logan's steadiness at my back as I drive a finger into Grayson's chest.

"First and foremost, I belong to myself. If there is anyone else I belong to, it is Royce and Logan since I'm dating *both* of them. You, Grayson Van Doren, own *no part of me.*"

Okay, so he absolutely owned my pussy this morning, but that is not the point I'm trying to make right now.

Logan chuckles behind me, the vibrations reverberating through my back as he places a hand on my hip and squeezes.

I don't intend for my words to be meant as a challenge, but based on how Grayson's eyes flare with a promise and his lips curl upward, that's precisely how he interprets them.

He chuckles this dark, masculine thing that slinks over my skin like melted chocolate. "I own *all* of you, Riley James. You just don't know it yet."

I hear the rumble of Royce's truck as he pulls up outside.

"Now come on," Grayson says. "You need to refuel after this morning... Unless you need me to prove my point in front of *both* of your boyfriends."

Reaching up, he gives the hand I still have pointed at his chest a squeeze before pushing it aside and walking past Logan and me into the kitchen.

I groan as Logan turns me in his embrace, eyes searching mine as he cups my cheek. "How are you feeling today?" he asks, expression pained.

I give him a wane smile. "Better," I assure him, surprised to find that it's the truth.

His tongue darts out to lick his lips, and he nods, looking unsure before he blurts, "I didn't want to ask you yesterday, but did he..." His face goes taut, anguish and fury battling for dominance, and I reach up to cup his face in my palms.

"No," I assure him. "No. Grayson got there before..."

His shoulders are stiff as he nods, wrapping his arms around me and burying his face in the crook of my neck.

We pull apart as Royce walks in. His eyes run over me, before shifting to Logan, and he asks, "What happened now?"

The distress is gone from Logan's features as he places his hand in mine, entwining our fingers as he smirks at Royce. "Just our girl schooling Grayson and him giving her hell back."

"So a typical day with the two of them, then," Royce states, unsurprised. He holds up the takeaway bag with the delicious smell of bacon wafting from it. "Breakfast."

"I should head home soon," I say once I've devoured my breakfast of bacon, pancakes, and syrup. Fucking delicious and exactly what I needed. Between that and the sex with Grayson, plus the fact Logan keeps one hand constantly on me and Royce's burning stare that never leaves me the entire time through our meal, I'm feeling a hell of a lot more like myself than I expected to after last night.

"No." I'm not the least bit shocked that that one-word response comes from Grayson. He's gotten very demanding since yesterday.

I arch a brow in his direction. "Last I checked, you didn't have a say in what I do."

"You don't need to go home," he argues.

"Despite your best efforts, I don't live here, which means none of my things are here. So, yeah. I do need to go home."

"Ben left town this morning," Royce segues, and I swivel my head toward him.

"How do you know that?"

Grayson chuckles. "Didn't even wait the full forty-eight hours you gave him."

Royce flashes a savage smile that's all teeth. "So he had one working brain cell after all." Turning to me, he says. "I drove past his house. Looked like a bomb had gone off in it. Must have grabbed whatever he could and took off."

"So he's just gone?" I question.

"Yup. And he knows if he ever shows his face here again, it'll be the last thing he ever does." I shiver at the malice in Royce's tone, believing he means every word.

"What about Lux?" I ask.

"Who gives a fuck?" Grayson asks, a bite to his tone.

"Since it's my place of work, *I* give a fuck. And so will the other girls who rely on it to pay their bills."

Grayson scoffs indignantly. "You're not going back there."

"Excuse me." I glare at the asshole across the table. *God, how did I forget how infuriating he is?!*

"I don't think now is the time for this conversation," Logan interjects, attempting to smooth over the situation.

"You can bet your stubborn fucking ass I'll be going back there, Grayson. It's my *job*."

"You don't need it," he argues, getting worked up. "We have money."

I blanche and Logan groans, knowing exactly what hole Grayson is digging for himself.

"I am not a charity case," I hiss. "I don't want your pity handouts."

"With Aurora being a Van Doren, she's entitled to her share of the family fortune. You can have some of that."

My teeth grind, and I swear, Grayson is lucky there is a table between us or else I'd wrap my hands around his neck and strangle him. "Aurora is a *James*, and any money she may be entitled to from your family is hers. Not mine."

I can see I'm really starting to irritate him as his jaw ticks and he glowers at me. Gone is the heat and possession from this morning, and now he looks like he wants to murder me as badly as I want to murder him.

"Why are you so fucking stubborn?!" he snarls.

"Why are you such a raging asshole?" I counter.

"Alright," Royce barks authoritatively. "That's enough of that. There'll be plenty of time to discuss Lux. You're obviously not going in tonight"—he cuts a glare my way, but no, I had no intention of working tonight, if the club is even open—"which means we're all free to attend Logan's game... assuming you want to go, James."

I cast a glance Logan's way, catching him watching me with excited anticipation. The thought of spending the rest of the day in his clothes, holed up on the sofa, does sound amazing. However, how can I pass up the opportunity to watch him play? Especially when he looks like it would make his entire weekend if I was there.

"Of course, I'll be there." I smile sweetly at him, and he grins broadly. "I never even asked how your game went last night. Did the Timberwolves' scout show up?"

Logan scoffs. "Do you even have to ask, Shortcake? Obviously, we kicked ass, and yup, the scout was there. Just gotta cross my fingers now and wait and see."

"There's no way you didn't impress him," I say, reaching over to squeeze his hand. It mustn't be enough contact for him, though, as he hauls me onto his lap. The tension in the kitchen suddenly dissipating as Logan regales us with the highlights of last night's game.

It feels weird to be at one of Logan's games with Grayson. The last time we sat in these seats, I was here against my will. And look how far we've all come... Well, maybe not Grayson and me, but hey, he's not looking at me like he hates me, so that's a win.

The two of them have stood like bodyguards on either side of me since we got out of the car, ensuring no one got within touching distance of me. Admittedly, I appreciate it. I was more nervous than I expected when we got here, and I saw the crowds, but if it looked like someone was going to knock into me, one of them would shove them aside.

We stopped to grab our usual overload of snacks on our way in, and I've been munching on popcorn as the lights dim, signaling the start of the game. Except, it's not the usual pre-game music that comes on. Instead, some techno version of *I Will Survive* plays over the speakers and I turn to Royce in confusion.

"What's going on?"

He shrugs, seeming just as baffled.

Leaning forward in my seat, I look toward the tunnel where the Huskies usually emerge in time for the entire team to spill onto the ice. I gape in amazement as the whole team breaks into some sort of flash mob. Except it's unorganized chaos.

A couple of guys are re-enacting a popular TikTok dance, while another is doing the running man on the opposite side of the rink.

"What is happening?" I laugh, not daring to even blink as I watch the mess unfold before me with the biggest grin on my face. I'm on the edge of my seat, eyes bouncing between each of the players.

The song cuts to *Apologize* by Timbaland ft One Republic, and the guys all couple up, spinning one another on the ice.

Grayson points toward where one of the players is down on his knees, pretending to beg for the other's forgiveness.

As the chorus hits, Logan comes skating over, a mischievous grin on his face and adoration swimming in his eyes.

"Of course," Royce drawls, understanding dawning. Still, there's a small smile playing on his lips as Logan smacks his hand against the plexiglass. I can't stop smiling as I do one better and press a kiss to my fingers before bringing them to my side of the glass.

He sinks his teeth into his lower lip, and I melt to putty right there and then in a stadium full of people for this incredible man who always manages to put a smile on my face on my darkest days.

The song switches to *Unholy* by Sam Smith and Kim Petras, and the guys drop to the floor, doing those groin stretches that have women everywhere drooling.

"Don't look, baby!" Logan yells, flattening himself against the plexiglass. I giggle hilariously as Royce shakes his head, and Grayson rolls his eyes, laughing.

Grenade by Bruno Mars comes next, and Logan skates away as he and the team form a group in the middle of the ice. They begin to move one by one, small at first, but as the song reaches a crescendo, they spread out over the ice. As they dance to the music, Logan is right in front of me, and I can't look away from him.

The entire stadium is on its feet, cheering them on without any understanding of what is happening. Their moves are all uncoordinated, and it's obvious this was thrown together at the last minute, but I love every second of it. The fact he was able to rope the entire team into this... it's... there are no words.

The song jumps to *Real Love* by Martin Garrix and Lloyiso and Logan skates over as a stadium attendant appears and unlocks the door at the end of our row.

Logan steps through as the crowd around us goes crazy. "Pretty sure he's here for you, Babydoll," Royce says when I don't move. Slowly, I get to my feet and shimmy to where Logan is waiting at the end of the row with an outstretched hand.

With his skates on, he towers over me and I have to crane my neck to look up into his face.

"Trust me?" he asks with a hint of vulnerability.

"Always."

His expression softens, and he gets me to stand one foot on each of his skates as he steps onto the ice. I cling to him. I'm sure this is not at all allowed, but it doesn't look like Logan cares, so I don't either.

"You did all of this for me?" I ask, hands around his neck as the stadium passes in a blur and I stare into his eyes.

"Don't you know by now I'd do anything to make you smile?"

"I'm starting to catch on."

He twirls me around the ice, and it's impossible to believe that I was at my lowest last night when I feel so light and happy at this moment. It's truly a miracle that Logan can bring out the best of me in the hardest of times.

"I would do anything for you, Riley," he says reverently. "If I could take away your pain, I would. Since I can't, I'll settle for ensuring you remember that there may be dark days, but they don't define you. And even when the night seems unending, I'll be here, holding a lantern of hope and reminding you that dawn is patiently waiting on the horizon."

Tears track down my cheeks as I stare into his eyes. With one hand wrapped tightly around my waist, he lifts his other to cup my face, brushing my tears aside as the lyrics *I'm only human, but I feel like this could be some real, real love* drapes over us.

Lyrics have never felt more fitting.

The way he looks at me. It steals the air from my lungs. The lines on his forehead soften and a subtle smile plays on his lips as he stares at me with such passion. Such adoration.

"I am so crazily in love with you," he rasps, voice thick with emotion. "With your strength. Your resilience. Your softness and your fire. There isn't a thing about you, Riley James, that I don't love. I know you're not there yet. That I haven't earned that, yet I can't hide how deep I am in this anymore."

My voice is choked, as more tears race down my cheeks as I cup his face. "How could I not love you, Logan? How could I not love someone who makes it his mission in life to make me smile? It hurt so bad before because I was already halfway in love with you."

His throat bobs at the reminder. "Never again," he vows. "You are and will always be my first priority. Nothing in the world matters as much as you do."

"I know." My smile is shaky but firm as I close the distance and press my lips to his for the entire stadium to see.

"I love you," I whisper when we pull apart.

There's an extra shine to his smile. A warmth in the creases of his face. "I love you more, Shortcake."

RILEY

CHAPTER FIFTY

"I'm not having this argument with you again." I sigh in exasperation.

"I'm not saying you can't go home," Grayson argues. "I'm saying you can't go home *yet*."

I throw my hands up in frustration. "What's the difference?" Folding my arms across my chest, I tap my foot impatiently as I stare Grayson down in his hallway. Royce is leaning against the doorframe, watching, and Logan has made himself at home on the stairs with a bag of freaking popcorn.

It's Sunday afternoon, and I've spent all weekend with the three of them hovering over me. I'm pretty sure they're waiting for me to have a psychotic break and snap. Except I'm not. I'm fine... Well, as fine as one can be when they can't sleep because every time they close their eyes they have nightmares.

I'm... surviving.

It's not like there's anything else for it.

I don't have the luxury of crumbling.

"What's the difference between going home now and going home later?" I argue.

"The difference is I'll have security in place later," Grayson states so casually that it takes a moment for the words to register.

"Security? *What* security?"

"The best security money can buy that I can get away with putting in a building I don't own—a problem I'll have to rectify if you're planning on living there much longer."

My mouth opens and closes. *Geez, there's so much to unpack there.*

"I think you broke her," Logan whispers without actually lowering his voice.

It startles me out of my inner thoughts. "What do you mean *security*?"

I can already picture my building crawling with men in suits, scaring the other residents and eventually getting me evicted.

"Cameras covering every inch of the building and in your apartment. Really, the *lack* of security at that place should be criminal," he utters in derision.

"You put cameras in my apartment?" I shriek in outrage. "Without asking me or getting my consent?"

"Ohhh, you're in trouble now," Logan says, seeming far too much like he's enjoying himself.

Dismissing both of them, I focus on Royce—the voice of reason.

"Sorry, Babydoll," he says casually. "In this instance, I agree with Gray."

I roll my eyes. How could I have expected anything different from Mr. Protective? "Of course you do."

"So what, you can all perv on me any time of the day or night?"

"I hadn't thought of that, but now that you mention it..." Grayson smirks and I swear, I'm this close to throwing my phone at his face.

"All of you are being ridiculous."

"Hey!" Logan protests with a pout.

I point a finger at him. "Don't *hey* me. I haven't heard you disagreeing with them."

His nose scrunches. "I'm not going to disagree with protecting you."

"I don't need protection in my own apartment," I argue, though I can tell it's a lost cause.

Setting the popcorn aside, Logan gets to his feet and comes to stand in front of me. His touches are so gentle as he cups my face. "We just need to know you're safe. This is more about us than you. It'll give us peace of mind, so we're not constantly blowing up your phone." He glances over his shoulder. "And prevent Grayson from getting it in his head to kidnap you again."

The asshole snorts but doesn't dispute Logan's words, so I feel the need to lean around his large frame to glare at Grayson. "Don't even think about it," I hiss.

"No promises, Tempest."

"I hate him," I mutter so only Logan can hear.

He chuckles. "So, Shortcake, will you appease the overbearing needs of three protective assholes?" He gives me those puppy dog eyes, and how the hell can I resist?

"I hate you too," I pout.

He only grins. "No, you don't. You love me."

I huff out a breath even as my lips stretch into a smile. "I take it back."

"Nu-uh. No takesie backsies."

The moment is interrupted by the ringing of my phone, and lifting it, my face lights up when I see it's a FaceTime. "It's Aurora."

"I wanna say hi," Logan says, moving to stand beside me as I answer the call and Aurora's face fills the screen."

"Mommy!"

"Hey, baby!"

"Hi, Aurora." Logan waves at the screen.

"Baby, you remember Logan from last week?"

Aurora's face scrunches up. "Yes. His favorite color is wrong."

It's a struggle to bite back my laugh, and I can tell Logan is the same. "You know, I've been doing some soul-searching, and I think you're right. Pink really is the best color."

"Obviously," my three-year-old says with all the attitude of a teenager.

This time, I can't hold back my snort.

"Tell me all about your week," I ask her.

"Come on," Royce says quietly, shoving Logan out of the camera's view. "Let them have some time."

He drags Logan away as I move into the living room and settle on the sofa. Aurora regales me with everything she's been up to this week.

After a few minutes, I peek up and notice Grayson standing in the doorway, his eyes intent on my phone screen with a rare sheen to them.

Catching me looking, his gaze shifts to me, and I only hesitate for a second before waving him closer.

"Sweetheart, I want to introduce you to someone."

Grayson warily comes to sit beside me, and I shuffle closer so I can get him in the camera. "This is Grayson. My... friend."

"Hi, Aurora." His voice is tentative, filled with enough emotion to make me want to cry.

"Hi," Aurora responds nervously.

"Grayson was just telling me the other day how much he wants to throw a princess tea party," I say to her, watching as her eyes instantly light up with interest. "Only he's never done

one before. So I was thinking we could show him how it's done some time."

Aurora's head bobs up and down enthusiastically.

"I can wear my tiara!"

"You can! And put on your princess dress."

Aurora's eyes go round. "We can all wear princess dresses."

"What a great idea." I barely get the words out through my fit of laughter. "I think Grayson would look so pretty in a princess dress, don't you?"

"Everybody looks good in a princess dress," my little girl states in a *duh* tone.

And now I have visions of all three men dressed in princess dresses, and I can't decide if it's hilarious or the cutest thing ever.

"You are so right," I agree.

Grayson is a silent spectator as Aurora and I chat until I hear my mom's voice in the background, and Aurora says she has to go.

"Bye, baby. I love you."

"I love you, Mommy. To the moon and back."

"To the moon and back."

"Bye Gayson."

"Bye," Grayson croaks before the phone screen goes black.

I lower the phone to my lap, shifting so I can see his face.

"She's..." He swallows, seemingly stuck for words.

"She is," I agree.

His gaze slowly lifts to mine, shining with emotion I've never seen him express. "I... thank you."

"She's your family," I say easily. "No matter what happens with you and me, the two of you will always have that." I tilt my head to the side. "I think you could both really benefit from a relationship."

His tongue runs along his lip as he swallows. "You want me to have a relationship with her?"

"If that's what you want. But you have to want it, Grayson. If you're unsure, I need to know because once you're in, there's no backing out. You can't just disappear on her. I know she's the result of a lot of pain and anguish, but she's an innocent victim in all of this. She doesn't deserve your anger or mood swings. She deserves the Grayson I remember."

He looks physically pained and emotionally wrought as he sits silently, thinking.

"You don't need to decide right now," I say, giving him the out, because he *does* need to be confident about his decision and I know this has all been a lot to process.

"No." My chest slices open, thinking he is saying no to having a relationship with her because, *damn*, I really wanted them to have that. "I don't need time. I want whatever you're willing to give me with her. I want to know her. I want to be there for her." His gaze bores into mine with such all-consuming intensity. "For both of you."

***

That night, I'm curled up in my bed, reading a book. Grayson finally gave me permission to come home—*cue eye roll*. While I enjoyed my weekend with the guys, there's something to be said about being in your own space.

Although I admit that I'm anxious about sleeping alone. And a little bit regretting turning down Logan's and Royce's offers to stay with me. Even if a part of me demands that I learn to deal with this on my own. There's bound to be a night when neither of them can stay, and I need to learn to deal with the demons by myself. I've done it before, I can do it again.

As I turn the page, I glance up, pausing when I notice a

green light on the newly installed camera. Of course, I came home to find one installed in my bedroom. I guess I should be grateful the bathroom was camera-free. I still believe the entire thing is overkill, but ripping them out will only result in new ones being installed tomorrow.

Somehow, I just know it's Grayson watching. I stare into the camera for a minute, but when the light doesn't turn off, I give it the middle finger before returning to my reading.

An hour later, when I turn out the light and climb beneath the covers, the light is still on, and despite myself, I find some comfort in knowing one of them is watching over me while I sleep.

When I wake in the morning, Royce is curled around me and the light on the camera is switched off. And I didn't have a single nightmare.

RILEY

CHAPTER FIFTY-ONE

"Girl, it is so good to see you!" Tara says when we arrive at The Depot on Thursday night. She pulls me in for a fierce hug. "How are you?" She searches my face, but my smile is genuine. "I'm okay."

I truly am. The guys—all three of them—have been by my side all week, ensuring no other students get too close, and if I haven't fallen asleep with either Royce or Logan, then I wake up to one of them having snuck into my apartment in the middle of the night. And every night, I fall asleep to the green light on my bedroom security camera.

It's... weird. And yet, it's working. I've barely had any nightmares, and despite it being less than a week, I feel relatively okay. That's not to say I'll always be okay. I know how these things go, but for right now, I'm feeling more myself than I could have expected.

She glances at the three tall shadows at my back before returning her attention to me. "Are these three assholes taking care of you? Need me to beat some chivalry into them? I'll do it. I'll even take on Ruthless."

Royce chuckles while Grayson scoffs. "We've met once. You don't even know me."

Tara pierces Grayson with her sharp stare. "I know everything I need to know about you, *Grayson Van Doren*. You treat my girl with anything less than the love and respect she deserves, and no one will ever find your body again."

Grayson's wide eyes bounce back and forth between us, trying to determine if Tara's pulling his leg or not. I'm about ninety percent certain she's being serious.

"With a love declaration like that, I'm thinking I might have to leave them for you," I tease.

"Pssh," Tara says, draping her arm over my shoulder and navigating me toward the bar. Of course, my three ever-present shadows follow. "We would be so hot as a couple. Everyone would be mesmerized. We'd blow guys' minds everywhere."

"Yeah, pretty sure that's not what they'd be blowing," one of the guys retorts, and Tara and I share a look before we both crack up laughing.

"My favorite girl," Xander calls with a smile when we rock up at the bar.

I hear a growl from behind before Grayson snaps, "She's not *your girl*."

Huffing out a breath, I toss him an exasperated look over my shoulder. "For the hundredth time, I'm *not yours* either."

Fucking caveman needs to get his tendencies under control. The other day, he nearly ripped the head off a junior in the food court because he was staring at me. Poor guy was just staring off into space, and Grayson had him nearly pissing his pants as he tried to explain himself.

Grayson's eyes narrow on mine, but I dismiss him as I turn back to Xander.

"As your only sister, *I'm* supposed to be your favorite girl."

Tara pretends to huff as Xander hands out beers to each of us, except Royce, who is here to fight tonight.

Xander gives his sister an *are you crazy* look. "By definition, as my sister, you're destined to be my least favorite person *ever*."

Tara gapes at him. "How dare you! Take that back!" Twisting the top off her beer, she tosses it at him.

"See, maybe if you didn't do vicious stuff like that, you *would* be my favorite person."

"Whatever," Tara mumbles with an eye roll. "I'd rather throw shit at you, anyway."

"Has anyone ever told you what a delightful personality you have?" Xander snarks, and damn, get me popcorn and a seat cause I could watch this sibling show all day.

"The voices in my head tell me every day," Tara taunts with a smirk.

"Tara," Xander growls in mock exasperation as he pinches the bridge of his nose. "You're not supposed to tell people about the voices in your head. It's bad for business, and being that we're related, everyone thinks if you're crazy, I'm crazy. Definitely not the impression I like to leave girls with."

"Better than the impression of your micro dick." She smirks viciously.

"Aaand we're done with that," Logan interjects. "I don't *ever* need to hear about Xander's micro dick."

"I don't have a micro dick," Xander hisses in frustration.

"Bro, no judgment here," Logan says, holding up his hands.

"I hate you," Xander growls at Tara as she air kisses him.

"Guess what," she says, practically vibrating as she turns to me. "You are looking at the brand-spanking new manager of Lux."

"No shit, seriously?" I gasp, grinning madly at her. "That's amazing, Tara!"

She shrugs casually. "I mean, the boss was desperate. Apparently, he's in the process of selling the place and couldn't afford to shut it down. Since I've been working there the longest, he offered me the position."

"That's so great!"

"Yup. So just let me know when you want to be scheduled in."

"She doesn't," Grayson growls at the same time I say, "I can do this weekend."

He turns to glare at me at the same time I twist to scowl at him.

"No, you can't," he argues.

"For the last time, you get no say in what I do with my life." I turn pleading eyes on Royce, who claps a hand on Grayson's shoulder.

"She's capable of making her own decisions. It's not like one of us won't be there to watch her every move."

"Kinky," Tara murmurs, smirking into her beer.

"Put me down for tomorrow night," I tell her decisively. "Rip off the Band-Aid."

"Okay. Tomorrow night," Tara agrees, while Grayson grumbles under his breath and we all ignore him.

Xander's attention shifts to Royce, saying, "Can I talk to you out back when you get a moment?"

"Sure. I'll be there in a sec."

Xander nods before heading down the bar to fill drink orders.

"What's that about?" I ask Royce quietly.

"Just sorting out match schedules. Nothing to worry about." He presses a quick kiss to my lips. "I'll be back in a sec. Stay here with Logan and Grayson, okay?"

I nod, watching as he disappears into the crowd.

"So tell me how delicious four-way sex is," Tara says, not

bothering to lower her voice. Logan chuckles before having the good grace to engage Grayson in conversation far enough away for us to have some privacy.

"There is no *four of us*," I argue. "There definitely isn't any four-way sex." She pouts like a disappointed child. "I'm only dating Logan and Royce," I remind her. She knows this because I already told her. Crazy bitch just won't believe me.

"Uh-huh."

See!

"And yet you're staring at Grayson's ass."

"I am *not* staring at his ass! I'm staring at *him*. If you're looking at his ass, then that's on you."

"He does have a fine ass, though."

Dammit, now I *am* looking at his ass. It does look pretty damn good in those jeans.

"I prefer my guys more rough around the edges, yet there's no denying that's one nice ass," Tara continues, causing me to sigh as I glare at her.

"Are you done yet?"

She throws her head back, laughing. "Are you? Don't think I missed that eye drop. You totally checked out his ass."

Grinning, I playfully shove her shoulder. "Well, you hyped it up so much, I couldn't *not* look."

"Uh-huh, whatever helps you sleep at night... Although maybe cuddling up to Grayson's ass would help with that."

"Shut up!" I half squeal as I slap a hand against her forearm, causing her to burst into hysterical laughter so loud that it draws Grayson's attention our way. His eyes narrow, brows furrowing as he watches the two of us, and like the mature adult I am, I stick my tongue out at him.

He huffs before snapping his gaze away.

"Girl, you are so fucked."

"Huh?"

Still laughing, she points between me and Grayson. "*That.*"

"What?"

She merely shakes her head, leaving me confused about what she's talking about. Maybe she knocked back a few shots before I arrived, 'cause she's not making any sense.

"Ehh, okay, while you figure out how to explain yourself, I gotta go pee."

"Sure thing. I'll be here when you get back."

I barely make it three steps through the crowd before a large palm wraps around my arm, yanking me to a stop.

"Where are you going?" Grayson's gravelly voice rumbles through my ear, and wide-eyed, I twist to face him before my gaze slowly drops to where he's still holding me.

His drops too, but instead of letting me go, he shuffles closer.

"To the bathroom," I say, sounding more breathless than is natural.

With a nod, he gestures onward. "Lead the way."

"You're *not* coming with me."

The asshole only arches a single eyebrow. "I'm in charge of babysitting you."

Spine snapping upright, I fold my arms over my chest. "So is Logan, yet I don't see him trying to follow me into the women's bathroom."

Grayson's eyes narrow in irritation. "Royce literally threatened to drag us into the ring against him if we let you out of our sight tonight."

"That sounds like a you problem."

When his hold only tightens, and he looks about two seconds away from ripping my head off, I heave out a frustrated sigh. "It's the bathroom. It's right there." We're basically standing right at the door. "I'll be two minutes, and if I'm not back, you can come storming in like a hero to the rescue."

Grayson scowls, but thankfully doesn't argue.

Pulling from his hold, I spin in my heels and march away before he can argue, although I still feel his eyes drilling into my back until I slip through the doorway into the back hallway.

Pushing into the bathroom, I quickly relieve myself, taking a moment to breathe in the quiet, away from the noise, bustle, and heat of the main bar.

When I step into the deserted hallway, I hear hushed voices coming from behind a door slightly further down. I pause, recognition sliding through me.

There's another murmur, words I can't hear, though I recognize that voice as Royce's. Moving as quietly as possible, I inch closer.

"You're sure this profile will be enough to fool her?"

"I'm going to pretend you didn't just insult me." The voice sounds gravelly, as though it's coming through speakers. Perhaps from a phone? I try to peer through the crack in the door, but it's too narrow to make anything out.

"Blue is the best," another voice states, this one coming from a person standing inside the room.

"Alright," Royce reluctantly relents. "Did you find anything else on her? Has she been in touch with anyone else?"

"Nope. She's clean as a whistle otherwise, and she seems to believe you are who you're claiming to be."

What the hell? Who is this *she,* and who the hell is Royce claiming to be? A sick sense of unease settles in my stomach and I slowly back away from the door, convinced I don't want to hear anything else.

Before I can turn and flee, the voice I faintly recognize from within the room says, "Let's see if I can still beat you in the ring."

My mind spins with possibilities as I numbly make my way out to the main bar.

What the hell could Royce be caught up in? A profile for who and who is *her*?

My stomach twists as I push through the crowd. I spot Tara chatting away to Logan at the bar and make a beeline for them when hands clamp down on my shoulders.

"What's wrong?" Grayson barks.

"N-nothing."

"You're pale."

"I'm sweaty. It's warm in here," I snap back, deflecting as I try to summon a smile that will hopefully placate him. Instead, it only seems to make his frown deepen. *Note to self: start practicing my resting Royce face in front of the mirror.*

"You're lying."

I sigh, pulling myself from Grayson's grip. "Prove it."

His lips flatten in disapproval, but whatever. If Royce is involved in something, he likely knows what it is. He might even be a part of it.

Turning my back on him, I stride over to Tara and Logan, accepting a fresh beer and sipping on it while Tara fills the silence and Grayson looms beside me like a pesky, unwanted pet who can't take a hint.

I absently nod and hum along to whatever Tara is saying, like the shitty friend I am, as my mind spins.

That is until she starts freaking out beside me. "Oh shit. Oh fuck. Oh shitty fuck fuck."

"Huh? What's wrong?" My head snaps up, and I follow her shocked stare across the room to where Royce and... "Is that Dax?" It was dark in the club that night and he was dressed *very* differently, but there's no mistaking the tall, broad man adorned head to toe in tattoos as he steps into the ring alongside Royce.

They shake hands, grinning maniacally at one another.

When Tara emits a croak that sounds as though she's dying, I tear my gaze from the ring in front of us to look at her. Her face is pale as she stares back at me with wide eyes.

"I thought you said he never comes here?" I ask.

"He doesn't. I mean, maybe on the odd occasion, but his fights are usually broadcast. If he does so, I always know not to be here."

My brows lower. Is it a coincidence that his fight tonight wasn't made public, and he's also the voice I vaguely recognized from the room alongside Royce's? What super-secret, hushed-whispers-behind-closed-doors business do he and Royce have together?

Tara's head swivels back to the ring and I follow. The bell goes, and the two men launch themselves at one another.

I watch with sick fascination as they attack each other like wild beasts. They hold nothing back. Dax is the picture of raw power, his imposing stature speaking of years of intense training. From what Tara has told me, he is in the professional circuit. He literally makes a living beating the crap out of other people. As he drives his fist into Royce's side, a tinge of worry for him enters my bloodstream.

Royce's moves are fluid, his intense, focused gaze never wavering from Dax despite the bloodthirsty screams from the crowd, baying for blood—but whose, I'm not sure.

The tension in the room is palpable as they engage in a fierce, almost choreographed dance of combat. Every move is met with a calculated response, and neither man gives an inch. My eyes dart back and forth, following every move with bated breath. There is no clear winner. Both men are evenly matched, and I know the outcome will be impossible to predict.

It's a blunt reminder that Royce could easily have killed Ben that night.

In my periphery, I am aware of money exchanging hands and bets being placed. I wonder who on, especially watching the two of them go at it, I wouldn't know who to bet against. Dax is more practiced, his precision uncanny. On the other hand, Royce has a determination about him. His anger and resolve drive every punch and kick, whereas Dax is almost treating this as a game, with a small smirk plastered to his lips.

The tension in the air is palpable as the battle between them reaches its climax. My eardrums threaten to burst from the crowd's screaming. I'm faintly aware of Logan shouting words of encouragement from somewhere beside me, yet all of it comes to me as if underwater, my focus so intent on Royce that I'm not even sure I'm blinking.

Both men's bodies glisten with sweat, their breaths heavy and labored. Blood drips from a gash to Royce's head, and Dax's nose looks like it might be broken. Both of them wear battle scars as they grin at one another as though this is all in good fun.

In a flash of luck, Royce finds an opening, delivering a precise and powerful blow to Dax's instep. He stumbles back. Royce goes in for the kill, a bloody-toothed smile on his face as he presses his advantage, delivering a series of rapid, punishing blows.

Dax falls to the mat, tapping out as screams threaten to shatter the bottles of alcohol lined up behind the bar.

Unlike in his previous fights, Royce doesn't continue to beat on him until he's a bloody, unconscious pulp. This time, he's not too lost to the beast to see the man beneath him. Instead, as the crowd erupts, Royce reaches out a hand and helps Dax to his feet.

"I've gotta go," Tara says, her voice unusually small as she pushes her still-full beer into my hand. I notice hers are shaking, and the color hasn't returned to her face.

"Are you okay?" She gives me a quick nod, her gaze constantly flicking back toward Dax as though expecting him to suddenly move and pop up before her. "Do you need me to come with you?"

Another shake of her head. "No. I'm fine. I just can't—" She waves in Dax's general direction as he puts on a show, bowing to the crowd like he was the winner. "Go check on your man. I'll be fine." Her smile is tight, and I worry on my bottom lip as she all but runs for the exit.

When I tear my eyes from her retreating form to look at the ring, I notice Dax's focus pinned on her with the same steely intensity he wore in the ring as she disappears into the night.

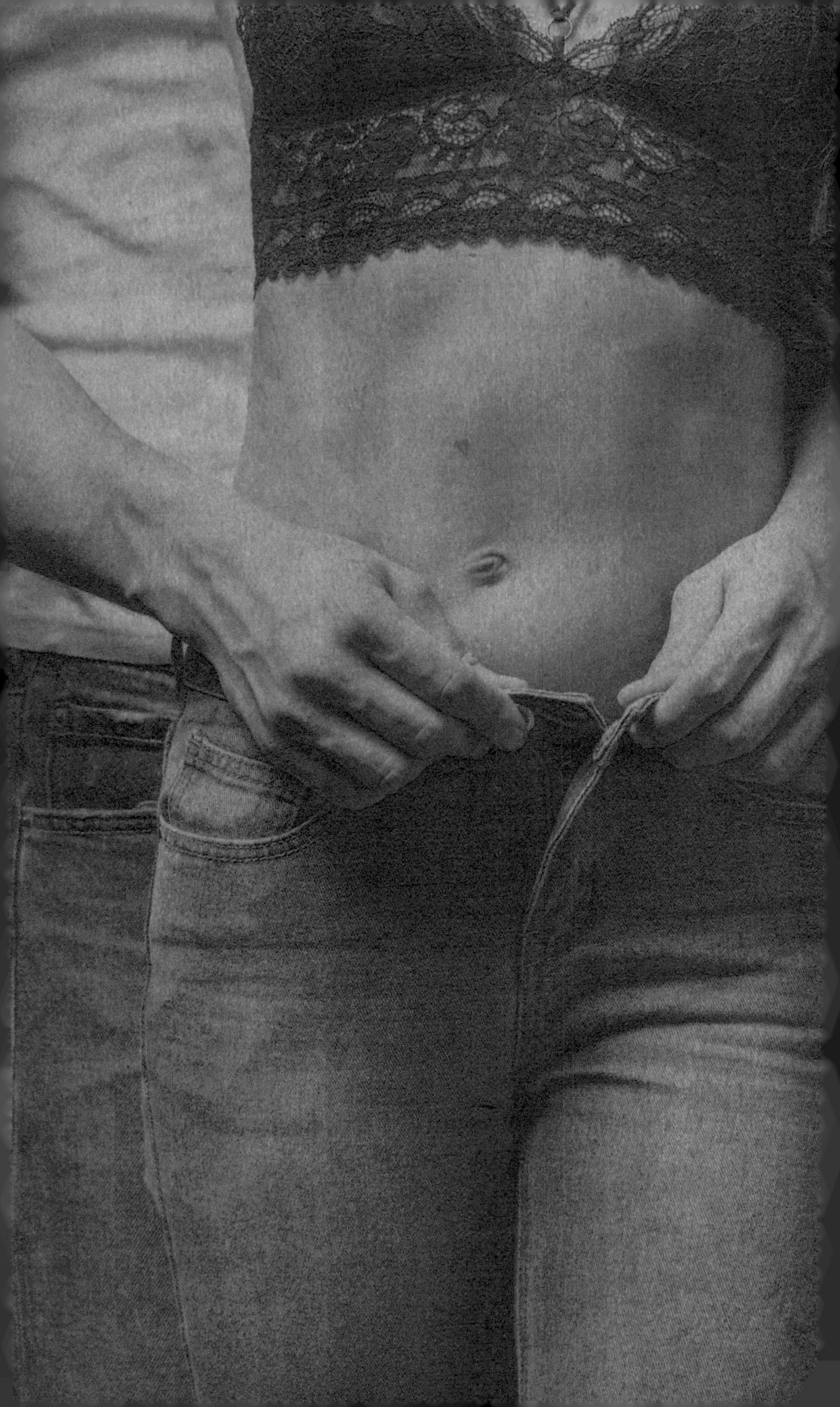

RILEY

CHAPTER FIFTY-TWO

"I didn't know Royce and Dax knew each other," I say casually to Logan, feeling him out as we walk to campus the next morning. I'd planned to ask Royce about it last night, but he said he had to stay behind at The Depot after. That, and for the first night since Ben's attack, he didn't sneak into my bed after I fell asleep.

"Royce and Dax are... competitors. Opponents. Strange friends that beat on each other every time they're in a room together," he responds easily.

"Guess that explains why I overheard them talking with Xander when I went to the bathroom."

Logan goes stiff, deliberately not looking at me for a long moment before slowly saying with forced casualness, "They were probably just catching up before the fight. Did you hear what they were saying?"

I shake my head. "I couldn't make it out."

His shoulders drop in what looks a lot like relief. "You're not missing much. Just their god-awful smack talk. Trust me. Royce probably told Dax he'd seen more fight in a dead fish. Dax would have responded with something equally weak as you fight like a grandma with two left feet, and Royce probably pushed him over the edge by saying something stupid like *you're about as intimidating as a fluffy bunny*. Then I imagine Dax stormed off in a huff 'cause the guy's ego is as fragile as a China cup."

"So nothing else is going on?" I hedge.

"Why would something be going on?" he asks rigidly.

I shrug a shoulder. Honestly, I'm not sure, and if I tell Logan I'm feeling paranoid since Royce didn't crawl into my bed for one night, he'll think I'm insane. Which, clearly, I am. This is why I didn't want to let either of them get too close, why I didn't want to become too dependent on them. Because then, when they pull back or let me down, I'm left second-guessing myself and missing what I had.

"I guess it wouldn't," I eventually mutter aloud. Side-eyeing him, I tack on, "However, if it was, you'd tell me, right?"

He seems to suck in a breath and hold it for a moment too long before he gives a sharp jerk of his head. "Of course, I would." Wrapping an arm around my waist, he tucks me in against him. "Everything is fine. Everything is going to *be* fine. You just focus on going back to Lux tonight. Are you sure you're ready for that?"

I keep my eyes on him for a moment longer before taking his change of subject for what it is. "I can't let my fear control me. Besides, it's not like Ben will be there. Tara is in charge now. Things will be different, and she won't let anything happen."

"Even if it does, Royce or Grayson will be there."

Ugh, please let it be Royce. He's the more reasonable out of the two... and crazily, the less volatile. Grayson is liable to rip me off the stage if someone so much as looks at me wrong. He has become entirely insufferable since Ben's attack. How he can one-eighty so quickly is beyond me. Somewhere between accepting my truth and finding out about Aurora and Ben's attack, he has gone from hating me to thinking he owns me.

And it is driving me insane. Royce is possessive with how he stares at me, and Logan with his public claimings, but Grayson is on an entirely different level.

The insanity of it all is that I'm not even his. Nor do I have any plans to change that. I'm glad he wants to have a relationship with Aurora and no longer hates me. I may even like how overprotective he is—not that I would ever tell him that. It reminds me of how I imagined he would be if I was his when I was fifteen.

The problem is, I'm not fifteen. I'm not that naive little girl anymore. I've been looking out for myself for a long time now, and I don't need him to bulldoze his way into my life and start running it for me.

If he keeps on like this, we're going to come to blows... and we all know how it ends when that happens.

Spoiler alert: Me dripping with his cum.

"Have you heard anything from the Timberwolves' scouts?" I ask, changing the topic.

"Nah, nothing yet. It's early days, though."

"What if they don't take you on?" I ask, chewing on my lip.

Logan shrugs. "Then they don't take me on."

"How can you be so calm about it all? I mean, what if you turned down the Penguins and now you don't get an NHL contract at all?"

"I'm sure my agent will be able to get me something, but as long as I have you, whatever happens, it'll be fine."

I sigh, shaking my head. I hate how I'm the reason he might never play professional hockey. "You shouldn't have to give up your dreams," I tell him.

Pulling me closer, he looks down at me with a smile that's all sunshine and rainbows. "Who said anything about me giving up my dreams? I'm holding the most precious dream of all."

———

"Grayson will have to go with you to Lux tonight," Royce says that afternoon. We're sitting in his truck outside my building. Logan had a team meeting before tonight's game, so Royce brought me home after class, saying we needed to talk. "I'm sorry."

"Oh." *Fuck.*

I know it's stupid, but disappointment stabs through me. It was only last weekend that I was telling him he didn't need to apologize for not being able to babysit me for one shift, and now alarm bells are going off because he's skipping again.

"Did something come up?"

Rubbing at the back of his neck, he glances away. "Yeah. There's something I need to deal with."

Vague.

"You can talk to me, you know."

His smile is fleeting, not reaching his eyes. "I know, Baby-doll. It's nothing you need to worry about." He reaches across the truck to stroke his thumb over my cheek. "How are your nightmares?"

"They're better. I've only had a couple this week."

This time, his smile is more genuine. "Good. That's good. I'm glad."

"Do you want to come up? We can chill for a while before I need to get ready."

"Sounds perfect, James."

He follows me up to my apartment, and while I grab my book from my bedside table, he retrieves a sketchbook and pencil he keeps here, and we settle on the sofa. I read while he draws, and it feels so natural and so us that it extinguishes all my fears.

However, as the sun goes down, he starts spending more and more time texting someone on his phone. The way he keeps constantly frowning, it's clear something is bothering him. Something he doesn't feel comfortable talking to me about.

I shouldn't push, but after showing him that I knew about the accusation in his past and didn't believe it or care, I thought he'd be able to trust me.

"I know you said I don't need to worry," I begin, sitting upright on the sofa when he sighs at his phone for the third time in the past half hour. "But something is clearly wrong."

"It's nothing I can't handle."

My brows scrunch. "That doesn't mean you should handle it on your own. It's okay to lean on me, Royce."

"Ry," he says softly, tucking a strand of hair behind my ear. "You've had so much to deal with recently. I don't want to add to your load. My problems are my problems."

"So if I told you that my problems were my problem and that I didn't want to worry you with them, you'd just leave it be?" I argue with an arched brow.

He chuckles, the first genuine smile gracing his gorgeous face. "You've got me there. I promise I've got this handled, though. There's some shit going on, but it'll all be resolved in a couple of days."

"Do you not trust me?"

"Ry," he rasps, voice rough as he hauls me onto his lap so I'm straddling him. My hands come to rest on his pecs, and I feel the steady thud of his heart beneath my palm. "There is no one I trust more. I trust you with my life. I know you're tough, but you've been put through so much recently." Cupping the back of my neck, he pulls my face to his and presses his fore-head against mine. "I can't stand seeing you wake up every night with nightmares and that fear in your eyes when someone other than us gets too close. The last thing I'm going to do is add to your burdens. Trust me to handle this."

I swallow roughly. "Okay."

Tilting his head up, he captures my lips, and I fall into his kiss as I cling to him. His tongue runs along my lips, and I happily open for him, needing to feel him everywhere. To reassure myself that he's here and everything will be okay.

He grows hard beneath me and I grind down on his crotch, making him groan.

"Riley," he growls, hands squeezing my hips as he tries to push me back.

"Please," I plead, chasing his lips. "I need to know you're here with me."

"Fuck, baby." His voice scrapes along my skin like gravel as he tightens his hold. "I'm here with you. There's nowhere I'd rather be. Nowhere else I'm ever going to be other than right here with you."

I whimper as I mold myself to him, sealing his lips with mine and ravaging him with my tongue.

"Show me," I beg. "I want to be your filthy girl."

"Babydoll. You're always my filthy girl. Always such a greedy slut for me." His hands slide to my ass, grinding me more firmly against him. "Are you wet for me?"

I can't tear my lips from his as I nod.

"Show me. Stick your fingers in your panties and show me."

God, that's so hot.

I scramble to undo the button of my jeans before shoving my hand in my panties, coating my fingers in my excitement. They glisten as I lift them to show him, my core clenching at the way his pupils dilate, and his expression grows ravenous as he wraps his hand around my wrist and brings my fingers to his lips before sucking them into his mouth.

He hums around my fingers, sucking every last drop from them before releasing me with a wet pop. "Delicious. Always so ready for me."

"Yes. Please."

His hand lands on the base of my throat before slowly sliding up. "What does my little whore need?"

"You," I rasp, my pulse beating a war cry at the promise in his eyes.

"Mm. Need you to be more specific, Babydoll."

"You inside me."

"What part of me inside you? My fingers. My tongue. My cock."

Eh, all of the above, please.

"Your cock."

His smirk is all sinful wickedness. "If you want me to split you apart with my cock then you better get those jeans off, James."

On legs like jelly, I jump to my feet, yanking off my jeans and panties in one go while he pulls out his dick. God, it's so thick and veiny, pulsing in his hand and leaking with precum.

"See what you do to me, James?" he rumbles as he fists himself. "You get me so unbelievably hard. I could spend the rest of my life buried inside you, and it still wouldn't be enough."

I whimper, unable to blink as I stare down at him.

"Come here and take what's yours, Ry."

Climbing back on top of him, I hover over him and reach between my legs to line him up with my entrance before slowly lowering myself onto his hard length.

He hisses while I groan, my eyes rolling back in my head at the intrusion. The way his piercing scrapes along my walls. It's like nothing I've felt before and I can't get enough of it.

We're chest to chest, both of us heaving as he sinks deep

inside me. Sliding one hand to the back of my head, he rests his forehead against mine as we both bask in this moment. "I'm yours, Riley. You own every piece of my black soul. Don't ever doubt that."

His piercing eyes burn with such passion that there's no disputing the sincerity of his words, and with a hand on my hip, he lifts me before slamming up into me, and I gasp before groaning. Falling forward, I kiss him with everything I have as our bodies meld into one. And when we come together, it's like our souls unite and fortify in a way that can never be untangled.

Before he leaves that night, he steals a too-quick kiss from my lips, but by the time I can draw back, he grasps my chin, holding me in place as his eyes scour my face. "I'm with you," he reiterates. "I'm always with you. Be careful tonight. Stay near Grayson and try not to kill one another. I love you."

He says those three words with such casualness that by the time they register, he's already gone, leaving me gaping at the door as my heart jumps out of my chest and melts into a puddle on my kitchen floor.

Oh my god, Royce King just told me he loves me!

"You can do this," I tell myself as I stand outside Lux, staring up at the pink neon sign. "He's not here. No one is going to hurt you."

Grayson growls from beside me, ruining the whole *pretending he's not here* thing I had going. "Not unless they have a death wish. I still don't understand why you're doing this."

"You don't need to understand," I drawl, not looking at him. "In fact, you don't even need to be here. Feel free to leave."

He scoffs. "Yeah, that's not happening, Tempest."

Okay, now I do spin around to glare at him. "You can also stop calling me that."

His smirk is filled with haughty arrogance that is somehow both enticing and infuriating. *God, I hate him.*

I go back to ignoring him as I wipe my sweaty palms on my jeans, the erratic beating of my heart and the knot in my stomach making me feel physically sick. Then, I take one final, bolstering breath before stepping toward the door.

Saliva coats my mouth as I step inside, glancing around the darkened club. It's already bustling with customers, a performance underway, and bartenders mixing drinks behind the bar.

"Riley," Tara calls when she sees me. It's weird to see her dressed as management instead of as a dancer, but she has managed to find the line between professional yet sexy with the skirt and top she's wearing tonight. "It's good to see you." She hugs me, and it chases away some of the demons at my heels. "Are you sure you're up for this?"

I nod, refusing to back down. She searches my face, yet must see my determination as she doesn't try to talk me out of it. "Okay, well, get ready. If it's too much at any point or you feel you're done for the night, just say."

"Thanks, Tara. You're a good boss."

"Oh my god, don't call me that. That sounds weird." She bursts out laughing before shifting her attention to Grayson. "I'm guessing you're the babysitter tonight. Well, you can sit your grumpy ass right over there"—she points to Royce's usual table—"and no interfering or starting anything with my customers."

Grayson merely grunts something that doesn't entirely sound like an agreement, before someone calls Tara's name and she excuses herself.

Casting a glance at Grayson over my shoulder, I head

toward the dressing rooms, but when I enter the back hallway, I realize Grayson is still following me.

"What are you doing?" I ask, frowning at him.

He scoffs. "If you think I'm letting you out of my sight, you're sorely mistaken."

"You can't come into the *ladies* dressing rooms."

"No, but I can wait outside."

I blink at him before deciding the argument isn't worth the oxygen. Instead, I turn my back on him and storm down the hallway. It's only when I close in on the office that my steps falter, and memories of Ben's acrid breath on my skin, his fingers digging into my cheeks, rush to the forefront of my mind.

A tidal wave of fear threatens to engulf me as my breaths come in shallow pants.

Only a large, warm, familiar palm on my back breaks through the memories, shattering them one by one as Grayson steps up behind me. He turns me so he's holding my head to his chest, my ear over his heart as I use it to steady me while he whispers words I can't make out.

Even after I've calmed down, he doesn't immediately let me go. Running his hand over my hair, he promises, "Nothing will happen," with a certainty and vehemence that I know not to doubt. "You've got this," he murmurs. "Hold your head high and go out there and prove to yourself that that worthless piece of shit doesn't define you. That he holds zero fucking power over you. That Riley James is un-fucking-shakeable."

Perhaps it's the fact that Grayson Van Doren is providing me with the strength and courage I'm sorely lacking, or the fact that he believes I'm unshakeable. Hell, it could just be that he didn't throw me over his shoulder and carry me out of here. Whatever the reason, I find comfort in his words, and there's a protective shield wrapped around me as I push my shoulders back and lift my head to meet his steely gaze.

He nods, seeing it, before nudging me past the office and into the dressing room. And throughout the rest of the night, when I'm on the stage, and I feel that shield weakening, I catch his gaze, then what I see staring back at me... tempers me.

RILEY

CHAPTER FIFTY-THREE

"What are you doing here?" I blurt, spotting Grayson leaning against the side of his slick black sports car on Tuesday morning. I didn't think Logan had hockey practice this morning, and usually, when he does, Royce picks me up.

Grayson... Grayson doesn't pick me up. Not ever. He sits with us at lunch, but unless we're all going to The Depot—something the guys all did together before I came along—or when he's on babysitting duty at Lux—like last Friday—he's blissfully absent from my life.

I like it that way.

Grayson has this way of stealing all of my attention and I don't like it. I don't like how, with each passing day, I catch glimpses of the boy I used to know. It makes it difficult to remember that only six weeks ago he was holding me against my will inside his house.

Pushing off the side of his car, his eyes drop, taking in the boots, black tights, and knee-length skirt I'm wearing before raking over my puffy winter jacket and finally coming to rest on my face. "Taking you to school."

He gestures toward the car as though it should be obvious, but it's really not.

I don't move from the doorway. "Why?"

He huffs out a breath as though I'm being deliberately obtuse. "Royce and Logan are busy today."

My brows furrow because neither of them mentioned that to me. Although, I've barely spoken to Royce. He hasn't crawled into my bed in the middle of the night all week and I hate how much I miss it. How much I miss him. I'm clinging to his *I love you* like it's a lifeline that will bring him back to me because I have no idea what's going on, and it's worrying me. Whenever I've tried asking Logan about it, he assures me he's just busy and everything is fine, before promptly changing the subject or distracting me.

"Busy with what? What the hell is going on? Because despite Logan's assurances, I know *something* is going on."

He averts his gaze, lips pursed. "We'll explain everything later."

My eyebrows hit my hairline. I was expecting more evasive bullshit. And while that's still technically what he's doing, he's now officially set a deadline. "Tonight?" I clarify.

He nods, lips still pressed into a thin line and expression unreadable.

I lick my lips nervously. "Is, uh, everything okay?"

My voice wobbles and he picks up on it, gaze snapping to mine and latching on. I'm not sure I'm breathing. Seconds. Minutes. Hours. I'm not sure how long we stay locked like that before something in his expression gives. A softness creeping in at the edges. "Yeah. Everything's going to be fine. Great, hopefully."

I don't understand, but I nod anyway.

Hitching a thumb over his shoulder, he points at his car. "School?"

"Oh. I can walk."

He closes his eyes as though praying for patience. It mustn't work, though, as he barks, "Get in the car, Riley. Now," before pinning me with a stare that promises punishment if I defy him.

Trapped inside the small confines of his car, I'm cocooned in the smell of his aftershave—something decadent and oaky. It smells good. *Really* good, and I scowl out the window because it's not helping me keep a level head when I'm around him.

The journey to campus is quiet, but not awkwardly so.

"Thanks, uh, for the ride," I mumble when we reach campus, not entirely sure how to navigate this new dynamic. It's one thing when we're all together, and the guys are a buffer between us, and our back and forth is mostly snarky. Another is when we're at Lux, and there's no talking at all. But this feels entirely too intimate and... boyfriendy.

Assuming this is where we part ways, I give him a stiff smile as I get out of the car and head toward my first class. Except, my brand new shadow continues to follow me as I traverse the campus paths.

"What are you doing?" I bark, whirling on him when I've had enough of feeling his eyes on me, his presence at my back.

"I'm supposed to walk you to class."

I huff out an aggravated breath, because it's sweet when Logan does it but overbearing when Grayson stalks behind me like I'm an errant child incapable of making it there on her own.

"I'm a big girl, Grayson. I can get to class all by myself."

His lips flatten and my eyes narrow on him, trying to get a read on what he's thinking. Does he actually *want* to walk me to class? He is not the type to follow Royce and Logan's orders, especially when they aren't around to ensure he follows through. Could his need to stay close have anything to do with whatever is going on with them?

"What's going on?" I demand, crossing my arms over my chest and taking a stand in the middle of campus.

"Nothing," Grayson is quick to answer.

"Then stop stalking me! You think I don't know that you're the one logging into my cameras in the middle of the night to watch me sleep?"

There is absolutely no repentance in his smirk. "I did like the show you and Royce put on for me the other day."

My mouth drops in shock. "You were watching that?" I hiss, outraged.

Leaning in, he purrs in a voice as smooth as silk, "I didn't just watch it, Tempest."

This fucking asshole. Now I'm picturing him jerking himself off while he watched us.

The flush that hits my cheeks is the response he was looking for. "So pretty when you blush for me. I wonder what other parts of you I can turn red."

"No." I pin him with a glare as I take a step back. "You and I are not doing... that again. It was a one-time thing."

He has the audacity to laugh. "And what about all the other times?"

"*You* instigated those."

"Like you didn't enjoy them."

My glower is molten. "I mean it, Grayson. It's not happening again. I have two boyfriends for that."

"And yet it's me you came to that morning."

"You know why," I hiss.

Closing the distance I just put between us, he keeps his voice low as he says, "I do. And that's why I know it wasn't a one-time thing. You won't stay away. You *can't*."

My teeth grind as I glare at him.

"I hate you."

Again, that arrogant chuckle. Grasping my cheeks in his

hand, he stares at me with a scorching intensity that incinerates me. "You hate to love me, Tempest. And that's okay 'cause I hate to love you too. Now do as you're told and get to class."

Spinning me, he smacks me on the ass, the momentum sending me stumbling forward.

I practically run away from him, the sound of his laughter echoing in my ear.

Hate to love me, my ass. There is no love about it. Nope, none at all.

"There you are."

I groan as Grayson pops his head inside the empty classroom I was hiding in.

"What are you doing here? How did you even find me?"

The fucker just grins as he walks in, closing the door behind him and holding up a food court takeaway bag. "You missed lunch."

"I'm not hungry," I grumble. I'm not about to admit that I didn't want to sit at our regular table, just the two of us. Easier to avoid him... Or so I thought.

"Tough shit," he barks, any sense of smugness dropping as he sets the bag on the desk I'm working at, along with a set of plastic cutlery. "You have to eat." When I roll my eyes, he simply growls, "Riley," in warning, and with no intention of this being the hill I die on, I cave and grab the bag, finding fries inside and grabbing a handful before stuffing them in my mouth.

"Happy?" I garble around the mouthful.

"Not until you finish all of it."

Ugh, whatever. I am hungry so it's no hardship to eat it all before balling the bag up and dropping it into the trash can.

"Thank you. You can go now."

"Such a charmer," Grayson retorts, showing no signs of leaving as he gets comfortable in a chair at the desk beside mine.

"I mean it, Grayson. I'm not doing this with you."

"Doing what? I thought we were studying."

"Not together, we're not. We are not friends, Grayson. We don't even like each other. You feel bad because of our past, and you think you need to have some sort of a relationship with me in order to have one with Aurora—which isn't true."

Grayson's features have tightened into a familiar hard mask. "Tell me more about how I feel, Riley."

"How about you tell me how you feel," I counter. "'Cause if you think I'm buying this whole, *I'm fine* act, you're wrong. A lot of shit has gone down the past week, and it's been a good distraction, but that's all it's been. Eventually, you're going to have to face your dad. Face who he is. What he's done."

His bark is caustic. "You think I don't fucking realize that? My dad is getting released in sixty-eight days, and you're not the only one who has to come to terms with that."

"So talk to me about it," I snap. "We're in this together."

Shaking his head, he pushes to his feet, hands planted on the desk as he leans over it. "So what?" he snarls. "You can fix me? Newsflash, Riley, I'm not fixable. And frankly, the notion of you being the one to do it is laughable." His laugh scrapes along my skin, harsh and bitter. "I kidnapped you. Chained you to a stripper pole in my house. Made you dance for us and ordered you to give Royce a blowjob. Yet you're offering to *fix* me? I hurt you! Be angry, for fuck's sake!"

As if his words light a spark, something inside me snaps. I don't need to take this shit—take any more of *his* shit. I thought we could have an adult conversation about this, but silly me. I knew the Grayson I was catching glimpses of—the one who looked at me with awe after our phone call with Aurora. The one who helped me through a panic attack *twice*—wasn't here to stay permanently because I recognize the Grayson in front of me as the self-sabotaging version I was tormented by over winter break.

"There she is," he purrs, a smug smirk on his disgustingly handsome face.

"Fuck you, Grayson," I snarl before marching toward my table, starting to throw my things into my bag.

"That's it, Riley. Walk away."

I freeze, hands fisting before I whirl to face him, a murderous expression on my face.

"Let's get one thing straight," I hiss. "I'm not walking away. You're the one pushing me." My head cocks, and there is a mocking edge to my tone as I say, "Poor little Grayson with his confusing feelings that are too big for him to control. It's far easier to hate on me than confront how you're feeling, right, Grayson?"

His body is strung tight before he leaps out from behind the desk. He's before me in the blink of an eye, hand fisting the front of my sweater as he drags me into his chest. "You have no idea *what* I'm feeling," he growls before spinning me around and shoving me down on the desk. My hands come up, bracing myself before my face can collide with the wood.

I feel his solid presence at my back, his warm breath dancing along the skin behind my ear before he whispers, "You wanna know how I'm *feeling*, Riley?" I shiver against his warning, his body pressing down on mine. "I'm so fucking angry. Disorientated. I'm a lost fucking mess, and I don't know how to control any of it. I don't *want* to control it. I'm fucking drowning in it all, and if I don't let it out, I think it's going to suffocate me."

His hand slides into my hair, tangling the strands around his fingers before he fists them and tugs. My head is wrenched back, causing my back to arch. My chest presses into the table, and my ass... my ass slides along the hard bulge in Grayson's pants. His nose skims up the column of my neck, eliciting goosebumps in its wake. "The only time any of it stops is when you're quivering beneath me."

"So let it out," I rasp, mentally noting that this moment right here is where I lost whatever sanity I had.

He goes rigid behind me, nothing but the steady rise and fall of his chest and the warm puff of his breath on my skin.

I wait, my pulse pounding in my ears, and I can feel the irregular stutters of his breathing against the side of my neck. I'm expecting him to rip my clothes from me, which is his usual MO when we're both angry and pressed together, but he surprises me when his hand lowers to the waistband of my skirt and stops.

"I don't know any other way to make it stop." His voice breaks over the words, fracturing my heart in the process, and I give him the consent he seems to be waiting for.

Pushing my hips back, I rub my ass over the hard length in his pants. "Make it stop."

It's an order... but it's also a plea. Because of that standstill he's referring to, I feel it, too, when we're together. It's why I went to him the morning after Ben's attack.

Shoving his hand beneath the waistband, he slips beneath my tights and into my panties. His fingers instantly find me soaking wet, and the groan that comes from the back of his throat has my knees growing weak.

Nothing except our breathing infiltrates the air as his fingers slip inside, and I go slack as pleasure rolls through me.

"Why did you have to come back and stir up all these feelings? Make me crave you," Grayson rasps, voice somehow sounding both angry and awed as he slowly pumps his fingers into me. "I can't get enough, and yet I know I should stop."

I'm incapable of voicing any sort of response as he continues pushing me to the brink with each rub of his thumb over my clit and the scissor of his fingers.

"I'm toxic, and your presence is gasoline to my flames. Even now. Even knowing... I see you and all my carefully constructed walls crumble."

It says a lot about my mental state that I take his words as a compliment and not the warning he intends.

His need for me, his desperation, gets me all hot and bothered, despite my complex feelings regarding this man. Which is why, when he buries his face in my hair and growls for me to come, I obey.

Breathing heavily, I can feel Grayson at my back, his ragged breath in my ear as I collapse against the table. I'm still catching my breath when he murmurs, so low I barely hear it, "I wish I could be the man you want me to be, but I'm not him anymore."

It's the dejection in his tone. The utter hopelessness that has a tear leaking from the corner of my eye. I remain where I am so he won't see it. Knowing he doesn't want nor would he appreciate my pity. Not that these are pity tears, but they'd make him just as uncomfortable.

What they are are tears of loss. For the kid I once knew. The man he could have been—*should* have been. If not for me. If not for his father. I'm not giving up hope that there isn't still some version of that man hidden deep inside him, but I also now realize just how challenging it will be to find and coax him out.

Gathering myself, I press back against him and he moves away, letting me up. Turning, I look up at his haggard expression. "Feel better?"

Exhaling, he nods.

"Good." Taking a step forward, I shove at his shoulders with as much strength as I can muster. The unexpected move catches him by surprise and he stumbles back a step, eyes going wide as he stares at me in shock. "Since we're *expressing* our emotions today, I need to unleash a few."

Stepping into him, I shove him again, allowing all the anger I felt when I woke up in that house, chained to his stupid fucking stripper pole, to rise to the surface. The fear when he grabbed my throat and squeezed. The hostility when he chased me through the field. The hopelessness when he held a knife to me.

Everything I haven't allowed myself to feel because it has been one hit after another since the semester started, but now I realize there can be no way forward unless we go back.

I know he sees the swell of emotions taking over, but he doesn't tell me to stop as I continue pushing him backward until he falls into a chair.

"You kidnapped me," I seethe. "Chained me up. Nearly ruined my relationship with Logan. Tore away my personal safety and tried to humiliate me." My body vibrates with all the anger I've buried deep since Royce took me home that day. "And you never even fucking apologized."

"I didn't."

His voice is so calm—too calm. It throws me off, and I stare down at him in confusion. He's not angry at my outburst, but he doesn't sound remorseful either.

It only serves to spike my anger to new levels, and in a moment of insanity, I whirl around to grab the unused plastic knife from my table. I jab the plastic tip into his neck, hand trembling as angry tears sting my eyes. "You *used me*. You took all of your hatred out on me without giving a damn about what I wanted." The tears overflow, and at this point, I'm no longer sure if they're angry tears or repressed emotional ones. "You held me hostage. Nicked my skin. You didn't listen when I told you to stop."

There. The first flash of remorse. Grayson's eyes drop, and

his Adam's apple bobs when he swallows. I jab the knife deeper into his skin, surprised it doesn't snap under the pressure I'm exerting.

Lifting his head, Grayson's stare expresses a grim acceptance as he says, "Let it out." Going still, I stare down at him, convinced I'm misunderstanding. He can't mean...

He pulls me down so I'm straddling him. "You're right. I did all those things, so do the same to me. Use me. Let it all out. Make it stop." One side of his lips quirks. "You know you want to. You want to hurt me the way I hurt you. I know you feel it, too."

"Feel what?" I rasp, my hand shaking so badly around the knife that it must be hurting him.

"How the whole world stops for a brief moment when we're together."

I suck in a gasp, my chest heaving as I skim his steady gaze.

My mind snaps. That's the only obvious conclusion I can draw as both of my hands go to his belt, unbuckling it before ripping open his jeans and palming his burning hot erection before pulling it from his boxers.

I pause, staring down at my skirt and leggings with no idea how to proceed, but then Grayson's hands move to the outside of my thighs, lifting the skirt until it's bunched around my hips, and his fingers disappear between my thighs. A moment later, there's a ripping noise, and my gaze flicks to his.

Even as his eyes burn with desire, he lets go of me, his hands dropping to his sides in a silent display that this is my show. *I'm* the one in charge. Holding his stare, I don't give myself a chance to overthink it as I reach down and push my panties to the side before lowering myself onto him.

He grunts, his body stiffening as I steadily take him inside of me until my hips meet his, and I feel deliciously full. I remain there, unmoving, as I catch my breath.

"Fuck, Tempest," Grayson groans, voice strained.

It snaps me out of my reverie, my eyes clashing with his and flaring with memories. My teeth grind as I snatch the knife I'd dropped onto his lap and hold it to his neck, pushing it against his skin as I lift myself off him before slamming back down.

We both moan, and he hisses another curse. I can feel his legs trembling with the urge to buck his hips, but he remains unmoving as he lets me have my way with him. "This means nothing," I hiss at him, throwing his words from that night in his face. "A hole to be filled. A warm body to come in."

A groan that sounds like half pleasure, half pain bubbles out of him, his pupil-blown stare fixed on me as I do exactly what he said and *use* him.

A few more thrusts and a sheen of sweat gathers along his temples.

"I'm not going to stop until you submit to me," I spit at him.

"Riley," he rasps, head falling back as his hips shift ever so slightly before he manages to stop the action.

"Repent, Grayson." I jam the knife so hard into his neck that he winces but doesn't pull away. He takes every rock of my hips. Every stab of my knife. Every slap of my words.

"Repent!"

He flinches, a red bead gathering on his neck before it spills over, carving a crimson path down his throat before disappearing beneath his jacket.

"Fuck, Riley," he hisses, but I can't tell if it's from pleasure or pain. "I'm sorry. I'm so fucking sorry. I should never have done that to you. It was fucked up. *I'm* fucked up." He somehow manages to laugh, a cold and demented noise that sounds all wrong. "I'm clearly my father's son."

I stall on top of him, staring at him with wide eyes as his admission sinks in.

"Move!" he bites out. "Use me. I deserve this. *You* deserve it."

Without giving it much thought, I begin to move again, teeth clenched as I choose to ignore his confession for now. "You're right," I admit slowly. "I do deserve this. I deserve to come and feel that moment of world-stopping bliss, and you deserve to be deprived of it."

He groans, understanding that I'm ordering him not to come, and we fall silent as I take my pleasure until my walls clench around him. He curses under his breath as I fist the front of his jacket and sink into that moment where the world stops turning and my problems stop existing, and there's nothing except warm skin and hard breaths and pleasure.

Falling forward, I rest my forehead against his shoulder. "I regret many things, but this won't be one of them," I say breathlessly.

"Good," he croaks. "You should never regret claiming back pieces of your dignity. Especially when those pieces were stolen in the first place."

We remain there, in that moment, his hard cock still inside me and my face pressed against his jacket until the cold seeps in, forcing us apart.

When I pull back, I catch sight of the trickle of blood running down his neck. Perhaps I should feel bad, but all I feel is vindicated. He's left plenty of marks on me. About time I returned the favor.

Dragging my stare to his face, I find him watching me. "This changes nothing," I tell him. "I'm still not yours."

"I know what this was. And you're right, it changes nothing, because you, Riley James, have always been mine. One day soon, you're going to realize that."

Before I can stop him, he smacks a quick kiss on my lips before easing me off him, and I'm too wrung out and stunned to correct him as we both fix ourselves. However, before we leave the room, Grayson catches a hold of my arm and brings me to a stop. I turn, staring up into his face, wrought with indecision.

He licks his lips, hesitating before confessing, "My Gran has Alzheimer's disease. She's been saying all these things recently."

My eyes search his face, seeing this for what it is. "About your mom?"

He nods. "And about you. She—She was the one responsible for my dad's arrest. I didn't know if anything she was saying was true, but I found this box in her closet at the nursing home... It contained papers proving Dad had embezzled from the company. When she heard he'd been arrested, she gave the police the evidence they needed to charge him with something."

Tears sting the backs of my eyes as I press my lips together. He goes quiet, his head hanging, so I can't see his face, but I sense there's more. "What else was in the box, Gray?"

Slowly, he lifts his face to mine, and the desolation there slices me open. "There were pictures of my mom. Her journal. He—he abused her. Terrorized her. If Gran is correct—and she has been about everything else—he might have killed her."

"Grayson." His name is etched in pain. "I'm sorry."

He merely nods.

"So before that day... I knew. I knew before you told me. I believed you."

"Ah, so that's why you didn't choke me out," I tease, attempting to bring some levity to the conversation and take away some of the devastation hanging over him like a raincloud.

"I should have listened earlier."

I give a one-shoulder shrug. "It is what it is. Regrets won't do either of us any good. You believe me now, and that's what matters."

———

My last class of the day finished several hours ago, and I've been avoiding facing Grayson after our... whatever the fuck you could call that... earlier by plowing through all my assignments for the semester in the library.

It's not that I don't want to go home—because I do. I need a shower. And a nap. Maybe a large glass of wine.

It's the text on my phone that has me superglued to my seat, refusing to leave the pretend safety of the library.

GRAYSON

Don't even think of leaving this campus without me.

I don't think I can look at him. Not after what we did—what *I* did—earlier. What the hell was I thinking? That was... insane. Crazy. What normal person would role-reversal reenact such a moment from their life?

Why the hell do I always lose my ever-loving mind in Grayson's presence?

I don't think I'll be able to look him in the eye and not feel guilt or shame... except it's neither of those emotions I'm feeling right now. If anything, I feel justified. Powerful, even. Like I clawed back some of the pieces Grayson unrightfully stole.

So maybe I'm avoiding him because I feel bad that I don't feel bad about what I did. *Gah, talk about complicated!*

Instead of wasting more time thinking about Grayson, I focus back on my psychology assignment.

I had half a mind to walk home as soon as I was done for the day, but I knew he'd show up at my door, angry and probably ready to fuck my brains out again, and as much as my girly bits would be down for that, my brain is putting her foot down. One confrontation with Grayson is enough for one day.

Which is why I'm currently sitting in the library, stewing instead of working. Because I'm not ready to face him yet. Honestly, I'm surprised he didn't demand I meet him ages ago. All classes are done for the day and my stomach has been rumbling in a not-so-quiet demand to be fed for nearly an hour now.

I force myself to focus on my assignment for another forty minutes before I can no longer ignore the hunger pangs and reluctantly grab my phone and text Grayson.

ME

I'm ready to go home now.

A reply comes through instantly.

GRAYSON

Then pack up your things and meet me at the door.

My head whips up, scanning the tables until I spot him sitting at one on the far side of the room. *What the hell? Has he been here this whole time?* Not letting myself dwell on what it might mean if he has, I stuff my books into my bag and meet him at the exit.

Without exchanging a word, I follow him to the student parking lot and into his car, ignoring how my body melts into the leather when he puts on the heated seats.

The car rumbles to life with a soft purr before he eases it out of the space and through the school gates onto the road.

"Grayson," I groan wearily when he misses the turn for my apartment. "Where are we going?"

"Ours."

It appears he has been reduced to one-word sentences now.

With a sigh, I roll my head to the side. "Why?"

His gaze drops to his phone in the holder in the center console and I notice it lighting up with a message. "The guys should be back shortly."

My eyes narrow on him as I straighten in my seat. "What's going on? Why won't anyone tell me?"

"We will."

That's all he says, and by the way he astutely avoids eye contact, I know he's not going to say anything more. With a shake of my head, I return to staring out the window until we park outside the townhouse he shares with Royce and Logan.

"I'm going to take a shower," I tell him as soon as we walk inside, not stopping or looking at him before I begin climbing the stairs, intent on showering and changing into something of Logan's before hiding out in his room until he gets home.

"I'll make dinner," Grayson says behind me, the statement so mundane that it stops me in my tracks. I gaze down at him through the balustrades, but he's not looking at me as he sheds his coat and kicks off his shoes before striding down the hall to the kitchen.

When he's out of sight, I shake my head and head up the stairs to shower.

Half an hour later, I'm lounging on Logan's bed in a pair of his athletic shorts and a hoodie of Royce's that I stole from his room. I've been scrolling through my phone, blatantly ignoring the now furious growls of my stomach, but it's nearly ten at night, and my stomach is done being ignored.

"Fine," I snap, throwing my legs over the side of the bed. "I hear you. You're hungry. I guess I'll subject myself to Grayson's delightful personality so you can be fed." Perhaps he'll have taken his dinner to his room.

In my socks, I pad down the stairs, quiet as a mouse as I strain my ears, listening for any sounds that would tell me where Grayson is in the house. He has a nasty habit of creeping up on me, and I'm not in the mood.

"I was beginning to think you were too chickenshit to join me," he drawls when I step into the kitchen, finding the asshole himself sitting at the circular kitchen table with a bowl of pasta in front of him. Another bowl sits in front of the chair opposite, and I toss a glare his way before striding over and pulling out the seat.

We eat in silence, the clinking of cutlery against porcelain sounding loud in the otherwise quiet room. With every chew, my eyes rake over the tight lines on Grayson's face. The tension from earlier still lingers in the air between us, but it's quietened to a low simmer.

Too lost in his thoughts, Grayson seems unaware of my blatant perusal. It's been years since I've had the opportunity to openly stare at him like this. I used to do it across the dinner table when we were teenagers, not that he ever noticed, too engrossed in conversation with his father or sneaking peeks at his phone beneath the table.

Occasionally, he'd catch me looking and wink, unaware of the visceral reaction such a simple action had on me.

My gaze catches on his eyes, once filled with warmth and a mischievous spark, are now clouded with a storm of emotions. *I'm a lost fucking mess, and I don't know how to control any of it.* I believe it. I think Grayson has been angry for so long that it's become all he knows. Letting go of those bottled-up emotions scares him, because without them, who is he? What more terrifying feelings lie buried beneath?

He clings to his anger like a toddler to his pacifier. It's a comfort. It's what he knows. And facing the unknown without it... well, that's just too daunting to contemplate.

His phone lights up on the table, and his brow creases as he glares at the screen before returning to his food. It lights up again, those creases only deepening. It sends a flutter of unease swooping through my stomach.

"When will Logan and Royce be home?"

His eyes flash to mine before returning to his phone. "Soon."

"Where are they?"

"Out."

I grind my teeth. "Out where?"

"They'll explain when they get home."

I strangle my sigh in the back of my throat, changing tactics. "Why do you look so worried?"

When his gaze rises to meet mine this time, it pauses on my face, some of those creases smoothing out. "I'm not. Everything is fine."

I slam my fork down on the table. "I am so sick of hearing those words. I'm not a child to be coddled. I've survived twenty years on this earth just fine—most of them spent looking after myself and the last four looking after another person. I did not need or ask for three domineering assholes to step in and take charge and keep me in the dark like I'm incapable of handling the grittier aspects of life."

"Are you done with your temper tantrum?" he drawls, and my gaze drops to the small nick on his throat as I momentarily consider stabbing him with my fork.

"You're hot when you're contemplating homicide."

It's such a Logan thing to say that it snaps me out of my violent thoughts, my eyes snapping to his. "Tell me what's going on. I can handle it."

"I know you can." He says it so casually that my head rears back, and I blink at him, his words taking a second to process. "You're more capable than I give you credit for."

"Then why will none of you tell me what is going on? Is it about Bertram?" My voice grows shaky. "H-has he been released?"

Grayson's voice softens. "No. Not yet."

"Ben, then?" I surmise, wracking my brain for anything else it could be.

"No."

"Then what?" I demand, getting to my feet so I'm peering down at him. "Because I'm not an idiot. Royce has been absent all week, and Logan has been doing his hardest to distract me from noticing. Now they're both missing, and you've had this worried look on your face every time your phone has buzzed today. Something is going on, and if you don't tell me what it is, I will assume the worst."

Sighing, he leans back in his chair, eyes scouring my face with a weary expression. I wait with bated breath as he gathers his thoughts, and no matter how bad I think the situation is, it is nothing compared to what spills from his lips.

"Your mom is trying to sell Aurora. Royce found out and interceded. He's been working with Dax and Xander for weeks, pretending to be a middleman who can negotiate a sale for her.

Tonight, Royce and Logan are meeting your mom to complete the deal. If all goes well, they'll come home with Aurora and she'll be all yours."

I fall into my chair under the weight of his confession.

If all goes well, they'll come home with Aurora.

But what if everything doesn't go according to plan?

What if...

My hand covers my mouth as bile burns up the back of my throat.

Before I can utter a single word, there's the sound of a key in the front door, and I'm out of my seat and running before Grayson can hold me back.

ROYCE

CHAPTER FIFTY-FOUR

My phone buzzes with a new message, and I barely glance at it before stating, "Got a location."

"Good. We all know what we're doing?" Dax asks, staring at me first as he waits for confirmation before turning his intense stare on Logan.

For once, Logan's expression is deadly serious as he nods, cracking his knuckles as though we're about to dive into a brawl and not meet a five-foot-three woman who wouldn't risk breaking a nail to take us on. I know he's found the last couple of weeks hard. Lying to Riley, it's not something he likes doing. Especially the last few days.

I couldn't believe it when he told me she overheard me talking to Dax last week. And even though he assured me she had heard nothing, I could tell in recent days that she was suspicious of something.

Fuck. The worry in her eyes when she looks at me these days. It fucking slays. Despite telling her I love her, I can tell she thinks I'm pulling away. I've tried to put her mind at ease, but it's hard when my words say one thing and my actions say another to her.

I just need this night over with so we can go home with Aurora, and for the first time in a long time, everything can be right in her world.

I've spent the last four days working closely with Dax and his men to make tonight happen. To give us the highest chance of success. Failure is not an option—not when so much is on the line.

Dax and I have met a handful of times at The Depot. In all instances, it has resulted in making the other bleed, and usually, him besting me in the ring. He's the only fucker who has ever been able to, but he does it with such charm that it makes it impossible to hate him for it.

Even when he lost to me last week, he took it with such ease, like it meant nothing. I guess for him, it didn't. It was for fun, unlike his regular fights on the circuit.

Something I have come to realize this week, though... Dax is not purely a fighter on the circuit. There's no fucking way he could be and have the contacts and manpower he has. He knew exactly who to call about putting together a fake profile for Aurora that I was able to show Lydia at my meeting with her last Friday—proof that I was able to deliver what she wanted— along with generating activity from bot accounts. The guy, Blue, was even able to hide her Craigslist post so whoever it was intended for couldn't see it, only showing up if Lydia were to sign in. He was also able to hack into her phone and track her whereabouts and who she communicates with. From there, we were ultimately able to determine that she's not doing business with anyone else that we need to be worried about.

Tonight, he has an entire team of men ready to go. Logan, Dax, and I will be going to the meeting spot, but his team will be spread out nearby, ready and waiting should shit go sideways.

I had initially planned to go with Dax and one of his men,

but Logan point-blank refused to be left behind. Even when I pointed out that we'd be leaving Riley alone with Grayson all day, he still refused to budge. Said she'd forgive him when she found out what we'd done. I'm sure he's right, I was just surprised.

In fact, I think Logan might be as in love with that little girl as he is with her mother.

Which is deeply, *deeply* in love.

Not that I can blame him. The time apart from Riley to arrange all of this has been torture in itself. Not that lying to her and acting as if everything is fine—which has been Logan's job —would be any easier.

I don't want her to worry, but fuck, now that we're here... if we fail...

"You still sure you wanna do this your way?" Dax asks me, pulling me from my spiraling thoughts.

"Yes. Unless she screws us over or we don't get Aurora, then Lydia leaves alive."

It's an argument we've gone back and forth on. Dax is pro-killing the bitch who thinks it's acceptable to sell a little girl to sick men on the internet—a stance I agree entirely with. Fuck, I want to kill this bitch more than anyone... except, perhaps Logan, who has never looked more bloodthirsty in his life.

However, we discussed it, and despite Logan and I both agreeing that Riley would probably be okay with her mom's demise given the circumstances, we don't want to traumatize Aurora any more than necessary.

Dax nods, accepting my final word on the matter. "Then let's go get this little girl."

All of us have been camped out at The Depot most of the day, fine-tuning plans that we cemented days ago, and we're all ready to move. To get this over with.

I've been communicating with Lydia via text and phone

calls for the last few days, keeping her apprised of the fake bids that have come in, and given that she wants a quick turnaround, we agreed that the auction on Aurora—hold while I barf—would end at six p.m. tonight with the transaction occurring ASAP afterward. Lucky for us, tonight's top bidder lives right here in Halston. *What a coincidence, eh?*

We pile into Dax's blacked-out SUV and begin the tense and silent journey to Springview.

"Take the next left," I instruct Dax when we're thirty minutes away from the location Lydia sent, following the directions on my phone. The closer we get, the more nervous I become. I can sense Logan feels the same way. The tension in the car has grown thicker with each passing mile.

Away from the freeway, the roads become darker and more remote as we head further out into the country until only the high beams and stars overhead guide our way along the winding tree-lined roads.

"Should be just up ahead," I mutter, eyes flicking between the blue dot on my screen and the road in front of us. A minute later, we pass a worn sign stating Blackwater Basin is two miles ahead.

Wheels crunch over gravel as we pull onto a lane, rolling slowly along it until we're forced to a stop at a pair of gates with a *no-trespassing* sign hanging haphazardly across them.

"Thank goodness I brought these," Dax sighs, grabbing bolt cutters from the glovebox before jumping out of the car.

"This the place?" Logan asks, voice hushed as he leans between the two front seats to peer out the windshield.

"Yup."

"Doesn't look as though she's here yet."

"She will be," I state confidently. Lydia wants her money and to be rid of this kid for whatever reason. She'll come.

"She better be," Logan alters, an edge of menace in his voice that has me turning in my seat to look at him. In the dark, his face is cloaked in shadow, but I can see the hard lines and his jaw pulsing as he glowers out the window. He's a man on a mission tonight. Ready to shed blood if it means getting Aurora to safety.

"We're not leaving without her," I assure him, my voice mimicking the violence written into his tense posture.

His response is a sharp nod. An agreement. A promise.

Dax slinks back through the darkness to the car, the gates now unlocked and opened wide enough to fit the car through. We bump down the gravel road for another few minutes before it opens onto the reservoir's edge. Adjusting the car to face the way we came, Dax puts it in park, leaving the headlights on.

I peer out the window at our remote location. Blackwater Basin is where people come to walk and breathe in the fresh air during the day, but at this time of night in the dead of winter, it's eerily still. Or perhaps it only feels that way because I swear none of us is breathing inside the car.

"She's late," Dax grumbles, apparently not liking being kept waiting. I glance at the illuminated dashboard clock, noticing that he's right. It's precisely 8 o'clock, the time we agreed to meet.

"She'll be here," I reiterate, glancing his way before returning my focus to the track road we appeared from.

The seconds tick by, and I glance his way, unable to take the silence any longer. "When are you heading back?"

"Soon as we're done here. My next fight is in two days."

"Well, I appreciate you coming out to help. We owe you one."

"Don't sweat it."

One side of my lips quirks up. "I was hoping you'd hang around long enough for me to kick your ass again."

He snorts. "You got lucky. Don't let it go to your head, *Ruthless.*"

I huff under my breath at his mocking tone.

Flicking his gaze to Logan through the rearview mirror, he asks, "Have you given my offer any consideration?"

"Not really," I admit with a grimace.

"What offer?" Logan butts in, shoving his head back between the seats to stare at me.

"I offered Royce a spot on the circuit as one of my fighters," Dax states with zero apology.

"Dude!" Logan's eyes go wide. "That's awesome! Are you gonna take it?"

"I dunno." I swipe a hand through my hair, giving myself time to think. It's a great offer, and with football off the table, I'd probably have jumped at the opportunity a couple of months ago, but I'm not the same lost, angry guy I was then. Now, I have more to think about than just myself. And the truth is, I don't want to leave Riley.

That sort of lifestyle... I'd be traveling all the time for competitions, while Riley will be here for the next three years. She'll already have to deal with Logan flying all the time for games, even if he does manage to get a spot with the Timber-wolves next year. I don't want her to be alone if I'm always away.

Lord knows she can't be left with Grayson. I don't trust him not to blow everything up if he's left alone with her for more than a day or two. Or for her to kill him. The two of them are dynamite together, and while it can be entertaining to watch at times, it's too explosive for them to be left to their own devices.

Hell, if they made it through today without some sort of catastrophe, it would be a miracle.

Plus, now we're bringing Aurora home, and I want time to

settle into this new dynamic, to see where it goes, and to discuss it with Riley before making any decisions.

Logan smirks, knowing damn well my hesitation.

"It's cool." Dax waves a lazy hand. "The offer stands. There's no rush. You'll wanna graduate, anyway. I'm thinking I might be around a bit more anyway, so you can just let me know what you decide in the summer."

"You're gonna hang around Halston?"

"I'll be in Springview, mostly. Wanna keep an eye on *Rogue*, but I have some unfinished business in Halston, too."

We chat for a bit longer, and as the clock rolls into a quarter past the hour, Logan growls, "Where the hell is she?"

"Maybe you should try ringing her," Dax suggests.

I'm already pulling my phone from my pocket and navigating to her number before pressing call.

The sound of her phone ringing echoes in the cab as we wait anxiously.

"What the fuck, why isn't she answering?" Logan asks, a tinge of panic in his voice.

Hanging up, I redial, refusing to give in to the fear starting to seep in.

It rings out again.

"Shit." The phone creaks from clenching it so hard. "What do we do?" I ask Dax.

He taps his finger against the steering wheel, staring out into the darkness as he thinks.

"Let's sit tight for a bit longer. She might be driving." Pulling out his phone, he says, "I'll check in with my guys, see if anyone has spotted her," as he fires off a message.

A moment later, his phone pings and his expression flattens. "No sign of her."

"Fuck," I snarl, slamming my hand down on the dashboard.

"I don't understand, what happened? I thought she was on board?"

"She was," I argue, frustrated. "Or, fuck, I thought she was. That's what she led me to believe."

"So why wouldn't she come, then?"

I shake my head, not having a fucking answer.

Shit. This can't be happening. There is no fucking way we can go home to Riley without Aurora. Just the thought of it has my stomach nearly emptying.

Not knowing what else to do, I call the bitch again.

It rings and rings and just as I'm about to hang up, she answers.

"Ruthless."

"*Lydia,*" I hiss, putting the phone on loudspeaker. It takes every fucking bit of my restraint to keep my voice somewhat civil. "We had a deal."

She sighs, not sounding the least bit chastened.

"I know. I'm sorry. I got a better offer that I just couldn't turn down. I'm sure you understand. It's just business."

Just business. We'll see if she still thinks that when she's suffocating to death at my hands.

"I don't understand. I told you the highest bid amount." I can feel Logan hanging on to every word as he glares at the phone with the same murderous intentions flitting through my mind.

"He approached me separately. Must have seen your ad or something. When I got your bid tonight, I reached out to him, and he offered more."

My teeth grind as I try to process all of that. Who the fuck is this *he?* And how the hell did he find out about Aurora 'cause it sure as fuck wasn't from the fake ad that no one other than us ever laid eyes on.

"How much did he offer?" I ask instead. "Perhaps my buyer would be willing to pay more."

"It was exorbitantly more than your highest bid," she states dryly.

Fuck. Of course, it was because we fucking lowballed her, not realizing there was another buyer in the mix and assuming as long as it was a decent sum, she'd take it.

I look at Dax, unsure what to do. It'll seem suspicious if our highest bidder suddenly agrees to pay so much more, but fuck, I'm desperate. I don't give a shit if it drains all of our accounts. Grayson, Logan, and I agreed we'd pay whatever it took to make this happen. Didn't give a shit if it bled us dry.

"At least let me ask him," I say, trying not to sound desperate.

"No need. The transaction has been made."

The what?!

"You've handed the package over?" *God, if my voice isn't strangled as I spit those words out.*

"It's all done. I'm sorry for wasting your time. You can pick up your payment at any time—monetary or otherwise..."

I wrack my brain for something I can ask. Something that would give me a clue. Anything... but no matter what I ask, it will only put her on high alert.

Hands shaking with fury and failure, I hang up the phone, dropping it before I drive my fists into the dashboard, over and over. Plastic cracks beneath me, and I'm aware of Logan shouting somewhere nearby, but all I can think about is how we let her down. Let *them* down. Riley will never forgive us. We were this close to saving her daughter, and now...

Now, we have no idea where Aurora is or who has her.

GRAYSON

EPILOGUE

K*nock. Knock.*

I groan as I wrench my glued eyelids apart. My eyes feel gritty as I blink into the early morning light through the living room window. *Fuck,* I couldn't have been asleep for more than a couple of hours.

It was a rough fucking night.

The worst of my entire life.

Sitting upright, I glance over at Riley, where she finally passed out from exhaustion between Royce and Logan. Even now, her face is swollen and blotchy from her tears. *God, that noise.* If heartbreak had a sound, it was Riley last night when Logan and Royce came home without Aurora.

I've never seen a person break like that. Shatter so thoroughly. So completely that no traces of the broken pieces remain.

She cried so hard that she made herself sick, and there wasn't a goddamn thing any of us could do except hold her while she crumbled.

I don't know what we're going to do now.

How we get Aurora back.

Royce and Logan were defeated when they got home last night, but we can't just give up. Riley won't give up, so neither will I. She's out there somewhere, and I will do whatever it takes to get her back. To ensure her safety.

I don't need to have ever met Aurora to know she's family. My half-sister. Riley's daughter. She's blood, but she's also more than that. She's everything to the woman who is my obsession, which means no one is safe from my wrath.

Getting to my feet, I stretch out the kinks from having slept on the sofa instead of a bed, but we all wanted to be close to Riley last night, and she was too fragile to move.

The doorbell rings, and I glower in the direction of the door before snapping my attention to Riley, breathing out a breath when she doesn't wake.

Logan does though, eyes red-rimmed and glare severe. "Whoever the fuck that is, get rid of them."

"On it."

Exiting the living room, I pull the door shut behind me before opening the front door. A man stands on my front stoop, his back to me, so all I can see is his expensive-looking black suit and freshly polished dress shoes. Except, I recognize the set of those shoulders and pepper-colored hair.

Sure enough, the man turns around to face me, a wide smile stretching across his face, and everything inside me constricts.

"Son." His gaze runs over me before returning to my face. "Good to see you."

"Dad," I croak, glancing up and down the otherwise empty street. "What are you doing here? You're not meant to get out for another two months."

He waves a dismissive hand. "Nothing a few greased hands couldn't expedite."

Head spinning, I consciously pull the door closed as far as I can, preventing him from seeing inside the house. He notices the move, his eyes flashing with displeasure.

"I just got released from prison, Grayson. The least you could do is invite me inside. It's time the entire family was back together."

ACKNOWLEDGMENTS

Every now and again, a character pops into your head, and you just resonate with them. This book was that for me. I connected with not just Riley but Logan, Royce, and Grayson. Their pain and heartache. Their hope and how they strived for a better future for themselves. These characters sucked me in and wouldn't let me go until their story was out in the world for you all to read. I hope these characters have ingrained themselves in your DNA as deeply as they are in mine.

Certainly, this book would be nowhere near as good as it is without the help of my amazing team. Nikki who is always ready to listen to my rants and suggest ideas when I get stuck (which is a lot). Thank you so much for being on this crazy journey with me.

Another thanks to my alpha and beta readers for trudging through the mess that was my first draft and still loving it.

A massive thank you to my editor and friend, Angie for handling the dumpster fire I gave her initially and helping me build this book into what it ultimately turned out to be.

A special mention to Caitlin too for everything she did to make this book and these characters story perfect!

I also have to thank my tiktok and street teams, and those who signed up for the blog tour with Peachy Keen to help promote and spread the word about this series. I appreciate all your hard work promoting every week.

I need to thank my husband who is always my rock and support.

Lastly, thank you to all of you, the readers, for picking up this book and reading it. Without you none of this would be possible!! If you loved this book, please help me spread the word by leaving a quick review.

ALSO BY R.A. SMYTH

Crescentwood Series

A dark, high school bully reverse harem with a stalker and gang element.

Pacific Prep Series

A dark, academy bully reverse harem with a taboo relationship.

Black Creek Series

A rival gang-mafia reverse harem with a vigilante FMC. Contains MM.

The Ruthless Boys of Ridgeway

A college, friends-enemies-lovers, second chance reverse harem with a stalker and secret society elements.

Halston U

A college, hockey, stepbrother, enemies-to-lovers reverse harem with a revenge plot.

ABOUT THE AUTHOR

R.A. Smyth is best known for writing contemporary dark romance filled with unexpected twists, mystery, and plenty of steam. Rachel lives in the UK with her husband and two golden retrievers, and when she's not busy thinking up crazy cliffhangers to drive her readers insane, she enjoys inflicting the same torture on herself by reading incomplete series.

She has always been an avid reader, starting from the Harry Potter books as a kid. It's an interest that has grown into an obsession over the years and becoming an author has been a secret lifelong dream of hers.

www.ingramcontent.com/pod-product-compliance
Lightning Source LLC
Chambersburg PA
CBHW050943210726
48287CB00004B/1107